DEA CROSSING

A John Decker Novel

ANTHONY M.STRONG

⬜W⬜S WEST
STREET

ALSO BY ANTHONY M. STRONG

THE JOHN DECKER SUPERNATURAL THRILLER SERIES

Soul Catcher (prequel) • What Vengeance Comes • Cold Sanctuary
Crimson Deep • Grendel's Labyrinth • Whitechapel Rising
Black Tide • Ghost Canyon • Cryptic Quest • Last Resort
Dark Force • A Ghost of Christmas Past • Deadly Crossing
Final Destiny

THE CUSP FILES

Deadly Truth

THE REMNANTS SERIES

The Remnants of Yesterday • The Silence of Tomorrow

STANDALONE BOOKS

The Haunting of Willow House • Crow Song

AS A.M. STRONG WITH SONYA SARGENT

Patterson Blake FBI Mystery Series

DEADLY
CROSSING

West Street Publishing

Copyright © 2022 by Anthony M. Strong
All rights reserved.

Cover art and interior design by Bad Dog Media, LLC.

ISBN: 978-1-942207-40-5

To Sonya

DEADLY
CROSSING

ONE

THE SECOND PROPHET, Hesire, and his three acolytes hurried through the vast temple complex of Karnak, on the east bank of the Nile in the capital city of Thebes, under the cover of a hot and moonless night. They passed silently beside the Temple of Amun and the breathtaking Great Hypostyle Hall, the centerpiece of the Precinct of Amun-Re. But they did not stop to marvel at its majesty, for this was not their destination.

In a secluded corner of the site, almost forgotten and overshadowed by the larger temples, stood a building of less prominence. A shrine dedicated to Sekhmet, a bloodthirsty goddess known by many terrifying epithets, including the Mistress of Dread, the Mauler, and the Lady of Slaughter.

It was to this smaller temple that Hesire and his men now journeyed. Between them, held by her arms and exhausted from her struggles to escape, was a young woman who would have fought back with renewed vigor had she known the grisly fate that awaited her within its walls. She wore a white robe.

1

Her dark and lustrous hair was braided so that it fell down her back in a tight weave. Earlier, she had been bathed and anointed with Kyphi, a perfume of saffron, cinnamon, myrrh, and honey, meant to honor the gods.

As they approached the Temple entrance, Hesire spoke in a low voice. "I alone shall venture inside with the offering. The rest of you must wait out here and guard the door."

"Yes Hem-netjer," the men replied in unison, referring to the Second Prophet by his priestly title, servant of the god.

Hesire took the woman by the arm and steered her toward the temple entrance. His companions took up positions, one on each side, while the third pulled the temple doors closed after the Second Prophet and his captive ventured within.

It was cool inside the temple, almost cold. The air carried a sweet odor of incense. Torches lit the outer chamber; their orange flames creating shadows that danced and flickered across the sandstone walls and floor. The room was empty save for an oblong slab of red granite that stood in the center. Its sides were covered in symbols—hieroglyphics that gave praise to the ancient deity who dwelt within this space. The top was smooth and featureless, polished to a glasslike sheen. A pair of shackles hung down at each end.

Hesire thrust the woman toward the altar and tugged at the straps of her robe, removing it, and leaving her exposed. The ceremonial garment would be needed again, and she had no more earthly need for vanity.

"Climb up onto the altar and lay on your back," he instructed her.

The young woman shook her head. She glanced back toward the doors, perhaps gauging her chances of escape, but there was nowhere to go. The Temple was sealed, and those doors would not open again until the Second Prophet was ready to leave, which he would do alone.

"Climb up onto the altar or it will be the worse for you," Hesire growled.

The young woman hesitated, then stepped forward and sat upon the cold smooth stone surface. She swung her legs up then took one last pleading look at the Second Prophet.

"Lie flat," he instructed her. "Look up to the heavens and pray that Sekhmet will receive your soul."

The woman lowered herself down, pale smooth skin glowing under the light of the torches. Hesire told her to raise her arms above her head. He took the shackles that hung from the altar and secured her wrists, then went to the other end and did the same with her ankles. Now she could not move. Her chest rose and fell in quivering breaths. She closed her eyes and her lips moved silently, but Hesire could not tell if she was praying for mercy or just overcome by terror. Either way, her life would soon be at an end.

From deeper within the temple, entering through a tall doorway flanked by granite obelisks, a figure clad in flowing ceremonial robes appeared.

Hesire dropped to his knees and bent his head low. This was Amenmosep, the high priest and a god in his own right. He looked young, thirty years of age at most, but he had been around much longer. At least if the rumors were true. Some said he was alive when Narmer, the first of the pharaohs, sat on the throne of Egypt almost two thousand years before. Others said he was older even than that, predating the Egyptian civilization itself. But no one really knew.

Amenmosep approached the altar. Around his neck he wore a chain upon which hung a stone amulet. A flat disk carved with symbols that no Egyptian could read even if they got close enough, which was unlikely. The amulet hung on a silver chain. Likewise, the rings on the high priest's fingers were crafted from silver. There was no gold allowed in this temple, nor anywhere near Amenmosep.

Now Hesire looked up.

The high priest stood at the altar, observing his offering in the same way a cat might study a helpless mouse.

"Please, spare me, I beg of you," she wailed, straining against the shackles, her back arching as she struggled to escape his gaze.

"Hush." Amenmosep laid a hand on the woman's stomach.

Hesire couldn't tell if it was meant to be calming, but she seemed visibly relaxed, at least until the high priest reached into his robes and withdrew an iron bladed dagger with an ornate silver hilt. Her eyes widened, and she cried out, the sound quickly silenced as Amenmosep drew the knife across her throat in a fluid movement that sent blood spilling from the hapless young woman onto the table below.

Her eyes fluttered. Her mouth opened and closed. She tugged at her restraints.

Amenmosep bent low and placed the amulet upon her neck, holding it there a moment as the girl's blood flowed over it. Then he raised the amulet and pressed it against his mouth, sucking and licking. And in that moment, Hesire swore he saw a trail of energy leap from the dying woman and encircle the high priest.

Amenmosep let the amulet drop back to his chest. He turned and started back toward the inner temple even as the fading woman's energy kept flowing into him.

Hesire waited for the high priest to retreat so he could rise and let his acolytes inside to clean up. But now he heard a commotion outside the temple. There was shouting and the brief sound of blade striking blade, before an eerie silence fell upon the scene.

Amenmosep turned. His gaze snapped toward the temple doors.

They flew open and crashed back on their hinges.

Men spilled into the room. The pharaoh's elite guard. They carried spears, the tips of which glinted yellow in the weak torchlight. Corselets of intricately weaved mail fashioned from the same metal hung from their shoulders. Hesire guessed that it was gold. Heavy, but necessary for what they had come to do. Capture the god priest and put an end to him once and for all.

Amenmosep didn't retreat. He stood defiant and let out a bellow of anger. "Get out of my temple!"

But his words fell on deaf ears. The soldiers surged forward while behind them came more men carrying what looked like an enormous net fashioned of pure gold.

Hesire stood to defend his high priest. Beyond the temple doors, he saw the bloodied remains of his acolytes lying in the dust. He stepped forward and removed a dagger from his belt. A small weapon against such heavy odds, but he carried nothing else.

"Out of my way, blasphemer," one of the guards muttered, giving Hesire a hard shove backward. The Second Prophet stumbled and almost fell but regained his feet and lunged toward the soldier. But before he could plunge his dagger into the man's heart, a burning pain exploded in Hesire's chest. He looked down to find the shaft of a spear embedded deep within him. The soldier on the other end gave it a tug and pulled the weapon free.

The attacking horde surged around him as if he were a rock in the river.

Hesire clutched at his wound as the last beats of his heart ticked away the seconds to eternity. He turned toward Amenmosep, who now looked more like a cornered animal than a god. The priest snarled and fought, but his enemies were too many. They encircled him and caught the priest in their golden net, then surged forward.

As the man he served was dragged to the floor and

subdued, Hesire sank to his knees and uttered a prayer to Sekhmet that she would receive his soul in the afterlife. Then the darkness closed in, but not before Hesire saw a new figure stride into the temple, surrounded by a contingent of royal guards. It was the Pharaoh himself, come to make sure the millennia-long reign of Sekhmet's high priest was finally over.

TWO

VALLEY OF THE KINGS, EGYPT-JUNE 1911

DR. ALEX HAWTHORNE of the British Museum stood in the doorway of his tent in the shadow of a limestone cliff that towered a thousand feet toward a cobalt sky. He watched as a clutch of white-robed workers dug in the soft scree and sand of the valley near the cliff floor and carted away the debris in wheelbarrows.

Further away, sitting on the horizon, was the pyramid-shaped peak known as El Qurn, or The Horn. As the highest point in the Theban Hills, it dominated the landscape and provided a clue regarding why the ancient people that populated these lands had chosen this valley when they abandoned the Giza Plateau near modern-day Cairo in favor of rock-hewn burials. To them, El Qurn was a sacred place, inhabited by the gods who looked down on the valley and protected it.

"Breathtaking, isn't it?" said a female voice from his rear.

Hawthorne turned toward his wife and smiled. "It's magnificent."

"And to think, you would have preferred I stay behind in our sweltering rooms in Luxor, contenting myself with reading and sewing while you have all the fun." Rosalind Hawthorne put an arm around her husband's waist and peered toward the distant peak.

"I'd hardly call it fun. All these months swatting away mosquitos and scrabbling in the dust, digging for a tomb that probably isn't here. Maybe Theo is right. There are no discoveries left to be made in the Valley of the Kings." Theodore Davis was an American lawyer who had secured the concession to dig in the valley and controlled all excavations therein. It was only thanks to an agreement he had struck with the British Museum that Hawthorne was even here.

"Theo has spent too long baking under the sun. He's not thinking straight," Rosalind said. "Would you rather be back in London sitting in your stuffy office while others take all the glory?"

"You know I wouldn't." Hawthorne swatted at a bug that buzzed around his head. "But we've been digging here each summer for two years and have yet to find anything of significance. There's only so long the museum will continue to fund my expeditions if we don't make it worth their while."

"Egyptology is a game of patience. You know that."

"You're right, of course." Hawthorne turned to step back into the tent. He never got that far.

From behind him, where the workers were digging at the base of the cliff, there was a loud crash followed by excited voices.

Hawthorne turned back to see a cloud of dust billowing up from a yawning chasm around which several workers had gathered, shouting and motioning with their arms.

His dig foreman, Mahmoud, was already sprinting toward him, his face plastered with dust.

"Doctor Hawthorne, come quickly. The ground collapsed. Zahur fell into the hole."

Hawthorne exchanged a worried look with Rosalind, then turned back to his foreman. "Is he hurt?"

"Don't know." Mahmoud gestured for the pair to follow him back to the worksite. "Too much debris."

"Show me." Hawthorne took off after his foreman and followed him to the hole with Rosalind at his heel. He pushed through the throng of workers who stood leaning on shovels and staring down into the chasm.

The hole was at least ten feet wide and fifteen deep. The billowing dust had settled to reveal vertical walls and strangely symmetrical edges. Sand and rock littered the floor of the hole. There was no sign of Zahur. A tingle of excitement mixed with concern for his lost worker edged up Hawthorne's spine.

He turned to one of the Egyptian workers. "Fetch me a ladder and some lamps. Quickly now."

"You're not going down there, are you?" Rosalind asked. "It's not safe."

"It's as safe as it's ever going to get," Hawthorne replied. "And besides, Zahur is down there somewhere. He could be hurt."

"And you think there might be something worth exploring," Rosalind said with a hard edge to her voice.

"Let's hope," Hawthorne replied, looking down into the hole. After two years with little more than a few pot shards and a small statue to show for his efforts, he was due some luck. This might be it.

The men were back with three lanterns and a wooden ladder lashed together with rope. They heaved the ladder down over the edge until it stood on the bottom with only two rungs above the lip.

"Mahmoud, follow me down," Hawthorne said before stepping onto the ladder and testing to make sure it would hold his weight. Satisfied, he took a lamp from one of the workers and started climbing down.

When he reached the bottom, he looked back up to see his foreman clambering down behind. He waited for him before turning to the debris-strewn floor of the hole and lighting the lamp.

There was no sign of Zahur.

"He's not here," Mahmoud said, surprised.

"Maybe he's in there." Hawthorne raised his lamp and shone it toward an oblong opening in the cliff face. The light penetrated only a short way before succumbing to the inky blackness beyond.

"A tunnel," breathed Mahmoud. "Do you think it's—"

"A tomb?" Hawthorne could not keep a tremble from his voice. "There's only one way to find out."

Mahmoud turned and barked orders up to the men staring into the hole. Three of them scrambled down the ladder with shovels and picks. Together, they moved toward the tunnel, but before they could step inside, a shape loomed out of the darkness.

"Zahur," Mahmoud exclaimed, running forward and greeting the man as he exited the tunnel. "Are you hurt?"

"No. Not hurt." Zahur shook his head and brushed sand from his white robe. He looked at Hawthorne. "You must come with me. There is a door."

"Show me." Hawthorne all but hustled the man back into the tunnel and followed him for thirty feet until it dead-ended.

"Here. This is the door. I could not see, but I felt it with my hands," Zahur said. "There is a seal."

Hawthorne lifted his lantern, and the door came into view. It was actually two doors with copper handles bound by rope and a clay seal. They shone in the lantern's glow, a lustrous deep yellow. Lines of ancient hieroglyphics covered every inch from top to bottom.

Hawthorne touched the doors with the palm of his hand. "Cold to the touch. Feels like gold."

Mahmoud raised an eyebrow. "Gilding on an outer chamber door? Surely not."

"See for yourself."

Mahmoud placed his hand against the door and ran his palm across the surface, tracing the hieroglyphics. "This is most irregular."

Hawthorne bent down and studied the rope securing the doors. "The necropolis seal is intact. Grave robbers didn't find it, which means no one has entered this tomb since it was closed."

"No one has ever found an intact tomb in the Valley of the Kings," said Mahmoud excitedly.

"Until now." Hawthorne turned his attention to the hieroglyphics. He was searching for a particular symbol. A vertical oval with a tangential line would confirm this as the tomb of a pharaoh. Incredibly, he found it. "A cartouche."

"Let me see it." Mahmoud leaned close, squinting to see by the light of the lantern, then uttered a single word. "Amenmosep."

"Are you sure you read it right?" Hawthorne frowned. "There is no pharaoh named Amenmosep."

"Maybe he was not a pharaoh."

"Which means he might have been a high priest," said a female voice.

"You shouldn't be down here," Hawthorne said, looking over his shoulder toward Rosalind, who now stood in the tunnel with a cluster of workers at her back. "It's not safe."

"Don't be silly. I'm not standing up there all on my own while you make the discovery of a lifetime." Rosalind pushed forward to get a better look at the door. "Whoever this Amenmosep was, he must have been awfully important."

"He considered himself a god," Mahmoud said, still

studying the door. "It is written here. He claimed to be over a thousand years old at his death."

"The man had a talent for self-aggrandizing," said Hawthorne.

"There's more." Mahmoud looked up at his employer. "A curse."

"Ooh. Do tell." Rosalind clapped her hands together with glee.

"It is not to be taken lightly." Mahmoud narrowed his eyes. "Such words carry great weight."

"They're still just words," Hawthorne said, bending to study the column of hieroglyphs containing the curse.

"What does it say?" Rosalind asked, unperturbed by the foreman's warning.

Hawthorne held the lantern closer to the door. "Whoever may disturb the slumber of Amenmosep shall forfeit their existence that he may walk again among the living to wreak eternal carnage." He lowered the lantern. "A wee bit dramatic."

"And rather ominous." Rosalind's breath caught in her throat. "Maybe we should leave him be."

"Or maybe we should see what treasures lie beyond these doors," Hawthorne said, reaching out and gripping the rope and seal with both hands. "And curse be damned."

THREE

JOHN DECKER MOVED along the street under cover of darkness and watched the solitary figure ahead of him turn left through a brick archway into a narrow alley running between a shaving parlor and a tobacconist in London's East End.

He picked up the pace and hurried toward the archway. On the opposite side of the road was a pub. The Horse and Plow. Pale yellow light spilled from its windows and splashed across the cobblestone road. A huddle of working-class men in thick winter coats stood outside under a flickering streetlamp holding mugs of frothy beer. They paid Decker no heed as he reached the alley and peered cautiously around the corner to make sure he wouldn't be spotted before stepping between the buildings and following the man he had been tailing for the last thirty minutes.

Except his quarry was nowhere in sight.

The alley was empty.

Had the man spotted him and sped up his pace?

Decker cursed under his breath and sprinted to the other

end of the alley where it spilled onto a residential street of squalid terraced houses. He looked both ways. Nothing. Even though the road was too long for the man to have reached either end, even at a run, he was gone. Decker wondered if he had ducked out of sight into one of the houses. But that was unlikely. The man lived nowhere near this area of the city and probably knew no one who did. London's East End was mired in poverty and overcrowding. It was a slum filled with some of the poorest inhabitants of the city. Not the kind of place his target would normally frequent, Decker knew.

So where had he gone?

Decker turned back into the alley and retraced his steps. If the man had not reached the other end, then he must have vanished somewhere within. It didn't take long to find out where he might have gone.

Halfway along, in the darkest section of the alley, was an iron door recessed into the brickwork. If he hadn't known it was there, the door would have been easy to miss.

When Decker tried the handle, it opened inward to reveal a short corridor running behind the shaving parlor. At the end was a set of stairs that led to the rooms above.

Decker stepped inside, closed the door, and hurried along the corridor. He mounted the stairs and found himself in an open area covering most of the building's footprint. The room was dark, lit only by the glow of a streetlamp cast through a row of dirty windows that overlooked the road outside, but Decker could see enough to make out sewing machines and wooden racks containing bolts of fabric. This was a sweatshop. A factory that churned out cheap clothing to sell in the city's markets.

At the far end of the room were four doors with frosted glass panels that probably led to offices. Three of them were dark, but one was not. Pale light flickered behind the glass. And now Decker heard the low murmur of voices.

This was where the man had gone. Decker was sure of it.

He approached the door, weaving around a row of carts that contained stacks of shirts and pants all neatly folded and ready to go.

The voices were louder now.

Decker stood to the right of the door, making sure he could not be seen through the glass panel, and listened.

"You're sure the Order have not discovered us?" Asked a gruff voice.

"Sure as I can be." This must be the man Decker was following.

A third voice piped up. "Good. In less than a week, I'll have the girl out of the country."

The man Decker had been following spoke again. "And the other cargo?"

"All in hand. It will be in my possession by the time I sail. You have my word."

"What about the Cabal?"

"If we're lucky, they won't be aware of our plans until we are out of their reach."

"Let's hope so, for all our sakes. the Order of St. George is one thing, but the Cabal . . . Let's just say I'd rather not go up against them unprepared," Decker's quarry said.

"I'd rather not go up against them at all." This was the gruff voice again. "But we might not have a choice. They surely know about the cargo and its arrival in the city. They're probably planning to steal it themselves."

"Which is why we must get there first and move it safely out of their reach."

"Agreed."

"Is everyone aware of what they must do?" Asked the gruff voice.

There was a murmur of agreement.

"Excellent. Mr. Garrett, keep monitoring the Order. They

might not be as dangerous as the Cabal, but they can still cause problems."

"Understood."

"Now, gentlemen, we should go our separate ways. You have your tasks. Do not fail."

The voices fell silent. A moment later, Decker sensed movement on the other side of the door. He shrank back into the shadows between two racks heavy with fabric.

Three figures stepped out. Decker recognized the first as Daniel Garrett, the man he had been trailing. The second to appear was unknown to him. But he knew the third all too well, at least by sight, because that face had haunted his dreams for almost five months. He was tall and sanguine, wearing black from head to toe. Decker had first noticed him in the sleepy village of Mavendale, sitting at a table in the corner of the pub. It was only a brief encounter, but Decker was sure this man had abducted Mina and spirited her away. And now they planned to move her. Frustratingly, they had not said where to, which meant a more direct approach would be needed to glean that information.

The three men headed away toward the stairs at the other end of the room and soon disappeared. Decker stayed where he was for a few minutes longer, making sure it was safe to move, and he would not be spotted. Then he slipped from his hiding place and followed in the footsteps of Garrett and his companions back down to the alley.

By the time he exited the building, the three men were nowhere in sight. They had scattered and slipped away into the darkness like rats. That was fine. Decker had what he needed. He turned the collar of his woolen peacoat up against the chill wind that whipped between the buildings and headed back in the direction from which he'd come, more hopeful of finding Mina than he had been in many months.

FOUR

THE MAN in the Black Suit hurried away from his clandestine meeting without so much as a backward glance toward his companions, who had gone in the other direction and quickly split up, eager not to be observed together. He reached the end of the alley and turned onto the residential street beyond where a motor car with an open front cab sat idling at the curb. A new Renault Type AG built in France the year before. He climbed into the rear enclosed cabin and settled back on the red leather bench seat.

The automobile pulled away from the curb and slipped through the streets, its headlamps casting two pale shafts of light onto the road ahead. If anyone were to see this vehicle, they would wonder who it contained, and how they could afford such a swanky ride, especially in one of the poorest areas of London where most people still traveled by horse and carriage, or more likely on foot.

As the car made its way through the city, the Man in the Black Suit turned and peered through the oblong rear window. He was on edge tonight. The Cabal was closing in. He could sense them drawing near.

Which was why he was alarmed to see a second set of headlights piercing the darkness behind their own vehicle. Motorcars were scarce in the city, especially at such a late hour. The Man in the Black Suit leaned forward and slipped the front window open. He addressed the driver in a voice barely loud enough to be heard over the automobile's engine.

"We have company."

The driver nodded and pressed down on the accelerator, nudging the car faster. The vehicle behind them kept pace as they turned onto Cannon Street. Up ahead, St. Paul's Cathedral loomed out of the darkness. The driver slowed and swung the wheel, throwing the car into a steep right-hand turn onto Bread Street, which ran one block adjacent to the cathedral.

The Man in the Black Suit twisted to peer back through the rear window, expecting the vehicle behind them to turn and follow. But instead, it continued along Cannon Street without slowing. They weren't being followed by the Cabal. It was merely a pantechnicon—one of the new motorized delivery vans that were revolutionizing transportation and replacing their horse-drawn counterparts. It had probably come from the docks in the Borough of Southwark across the river. Where it was going, the Man in the Black Suit had no clue, nor did he care. It was good enough that they weren't being followed.

He leaned forward again and instructed the driver to continue on to their destination, then settled back and closed his eyes, satisfied that they were safe, at least for now. There would be much to do in the next few days, and opportunities for rest would be few and far between. At least until London and its associated dangers were far behind them. Soon they would be in New York, hidden from both the Cabal and the Order of St. George. Then the real work could begin.

FIVE

IT WAS ALMOST midnight by the time Decker made it out of the East End and flagged down a hackney carriage near Tower Bridge, close to the underground headquarters of the Order of St. George, which would be empty at this time of night except for a small contingent of men who guarded the facility around the clock. But he didn't instruct the cab driver to take him home. Instead, he gave the man a different address in the suburbs.

They crossed the bridge and rode through the city for thirty minutes before pulling up at a grand home sitting among lavish gardens. Decker paid and climbed out, then instructed the driver to wait for him with the promise that he would be well compensated for doing so.

At some point along the way, it had begun to rain. A steady drizzle misted the air and seeped through the folds of Decker's coat. He hunched against the rain and hurried up the path to the home's front door, glancing backward to make sure that the cab was still there before knocking twice.

A minute later, the door opened to reveal Thomas Finch

wearing a heavy velvet robe tied with a sash. If it surprised him to see Decker on the doorstep, he didn't show it.

"I'm sorry to disturb you at such a late hour," Decker said. "But I have information that cannot wait until morning."

"You had better come in." Finch motioned and stepped aside.

Decker stepped into the house and removed his coat, hanging it on a rack near the door. The sound of footsteps on the second-floor landing drew his attention. He looked up to see Finch's wife, Lily, standing at the railing with a concerned look on her face.

Finch looked up at her. "Go back to bed, darling. There's nothing to worry about. I should join you again soon."

Lily hesitated for a moment, then nodded and retreated back toward the bedroom.

Finch raised a hand and motioned for Decker to follow him. "Come, we shall talk in the study."

Decker followed the ex-Grenadier guardsman and now leader of the Order past the stairs and through a set of double doors into a comfortable room with bookshelves on every wall laden with leather-bound volumes. An ornate desk stood in the center, with a wingback leather chair on each side.

He waited for Finch to close the doors and take a seat behind the desk before settling into the chair opposite. "I was right. There is a mole within the Order of St. George. A traitor."

"And you know who this person might be?" Finch leaned forward in his chair and observed Decker with narrowed eyes.

"I do." For the past four months, The Order had made it their priority to locate Mina, who had been taken against her will at the end of a grueling case in the small village of Mavendale. It was not clear who had taken her or why, and The Order was no closer to locating her now than they had been at the outset. Until tonight. Decker had become convinced that there must be a traitor within their organization. Someone who had helped orchestrate Mina's abduction. To that end, he had spent much of his time pursuing this mystery person believing it to be their best chance of gleaning the information necessary to recover her. He had observed the behavior of several operatives who possessed the means and opportunity to mount such a betrayal, and tonight his diligence had paid off. "I followed one of our operatives to a clandestine meeting this evening. He met with the man who abducted Mina and another gentleman that I didn't recognize. They discussed moving her, although to where they did not say."

"And the name of this operative?"

"It's Daniel Garrett."

Finch raised an eyebrow in surprise. "Garrett? He's been with us for nigh on a decade. One of our best men. Are you absolutely sure?"

"A hundred percent." Decker hated delivering bad news. He knew how close Finch was to the operatives under his command. Finch had handpicked most of them himself from the ranks of either the Grenadier Guard or other elite military regiments and counted many of them as friends. "He has been tasked with monitoring The Order while this group carries out their plans."

"A group that remains nameless to us," Finch said. "We don't even know their motivations."

"I know one thing. This isn't just about Mina. These people are looking to get their hands on something else. They intend to take both Mina and this stolen object, whatever it might be, out of the country. Judging by the conversation, they must have booked passage on a ship of some sort to achieve that goal."

"Then we must find out how and when they plan to sail."

"We had better do so quickly. I got the impression that their departure is imminent," Decker replied. "And there's something else. They aren't just worried about us. Their primary concern appears to be a rival faction called the Cabal."

"I'm not familiar with any such group."

"Neither am I." Decker rubbed his neck to relieve a tight knot of tension. "But we need to find out. I have a bad feeling about this whole situation."

"Agreed." Finch stifled a yawn. "Do you think Garrett knows we are on to him?"

"Not likely. He wouldn't have led me across town to that meeting if he suspected."

"Very good." Finch nodded. "Under normal circumstances, I would suggest keeping him in the dark and observing him in the hopes that he will lead us to Mina, but we don't have the luxury of time if what you say is true."

"Which is why I came here tonight instead of waiting until the morning."

"You did the right thing. I'll have Garrett pulled from duty first thing tomorrow. We'll get the truth out of him one way or another."

"Exactly how do you intend to do that?" Finch's comment made Decker uneasy. If Garrett wouldn't talk willingly, and Decker suspected he wouldn't, the easiest way to loosen his tongue was also the most repugnant.

"Don't worry. We won't resort to torture," Finch said, reading Decker's expression. "Frankly, I'm disappointed that you would think such a thing of us."

"If history has proven anything, it is that morals are often forsaken in the interests of expediency," Decker replied.

"You needn't worry. My morals are still intact. There are other ways to make a man talk. Garrett will tell us what we want to know."

"I hope so, for Mina's sake."

"And in the meantime, we should be on the lookout for any unusual activity that might provide a clue regarding the other item this group plans to acquire and spirit out of the country."

"I agree," said Decker, breathing a sigh of relief.

From somewhere deep within the house, a clock struck one. Its melancholy peal echoed on the still air inside the house.

Finch looked up. "Lily will be wondering where I have gotten to. If you don't mind, I'm going back to my bed."

Decker nodded.

"Did you tell your cab to wait?"

"Yes."

"Let's hope he did so." Finch stood and walked Decker out of the study.

"Agreed," Decker replied, opening the front door. If the cab driver had gotten bored and taken off, it would be a long walk back to the suite of rooms Decker currently occupied near Hyde Park. He was relieved to see it still sitting there.

"You did good work tonight, John," Finch said, slapping Decker on the back. "Now go home and get some rest. I have a feeling tomorrow will be a long day."

Decker didn't reply. He merely nodded at Finch and made his way down the path toward the waiting cab. He climbed in and glanced toward the house, but Finch had already closed the door and turned off the lights.

Decker told the driver where to take him and settled back while the empty streets rolled by. Mina was out there somewhere in the dark and brooding city, and perhaps they had taken the first step to get her back. But even as he entertained that thought, Decker could not shake a sense of foreboding that lingered even as he climbed into bed and fell into a restless sleep.

SIX

IN A WINDOWLESS ROOM far beneath the streets of London, within a facility that had previously served as one of the first tube stations in the city, John Decker sat opposite the man he had followed the previous evening to a secret meeting at the back of a second-floor sweatshop in one of the seediest areas of the metropolis.

On the other side of a wooden table, with his hands secured behind his back by a pair of heavy brass handcuffs that also looped around the spindles of his chair, Daniel Garrett glared at Decker with the defiance of a man who didn't yet know that he was backed into a corner with no means of escape.

It was nine a.m.

Garrett had been apprehended less than fifteen minutes before as he entered the facility by way of a birdcage elevator secreted within the walls of a solicitor's office that had once been a genuine business but now served only as a cover for the Order of St. George.

Decker had entered the room five minutes ago along with Thomas Finch, who now leaned against the wall with his arms folded and spent that time quietly observing the man who had

24

betrayed Mina and the Order, summing him up and hoping that this extended silence would unnerve his adversary. It was a trick Decker had used in interrogations while serving as a homicide cop in New York back in his own time. It had worked on more than one occasion. But if Garrett was worried, he kept it well hidden.

Now Decker cleared his throat and spoke up. "You met with two men last night above a shaving parlor in the East End."

"I don't know what you're talking about." Garrett met Decker's gaze with cool indifference. "You must have me mixed up with someone else."

"I don't," Decker said. "You left the rooms that you rent in a lodging house on Hackney Road around ten. I followed you to the meeting. You talked with two other men for approximately fifteen minutes, and then the three of you went your separate ways."

"All right. Fine. I met with a couple of gentlemen in the East End last night. So what?" Garrett licked his lips. "It was a private matter. Nothing that need concern the Order."

"You're lying."

"This is ridiculous." Garrett's gaze shifted over Decker's shoulder to Finch, who was still leaning against the wall. "Thomas. We've known each other for over a decade. You're the one that brought me into the Order. We've stood side-by-side and faced down all manner of creatures and demons. Did we not deal with the Monster of Glamis together? Did I not save your life on that occasion? Do you really think I would betray you?"

"The events at Glamis Castle took place many years ago, my friend," Finch replied. "People can change."

"They can, but I have not."

"Hey. Talk to me, not him," Decker said, slamming a fist on the table. "Tell me about that meeting last night."

"There's nothing to tell. As I said, it was a personal matter."

"One of your companions talked about moving a girl. Getting her out of the country. The girl he was referring to is Mina, correct?"

Garrett shrugged. "I don't recall any such conversation."

"And what about the cargo you intend to move with her?"

"You must have been listening to someone else's conversation." Garrett cocked his head to one side. "Are you sure it was me that you followed? The streets are very dark at that time of night. Especially in the East End."

Decker ignored the deflection. "Tell me about the Cabal. Who are they?"

"I have no idea, but they don't sound friendly."

"On that, we agree," Decker said. "Let's go back to the beginning. It was you that betrayed Mina."

"I didn't do anything to Mina. In fact, I was here in this very facility when she was taken."

"You might not have been physically involved, but you provided the information necessary to abduct her. You told the man who took Mina where to find her and how to subdue her."

"You have an active imagination, Mr. Decker. You should write fiction." Garrett tugged at the handcuffs restraining him. "I should very much like it if you removed these now. You can also consider this my resignation from the Order of St. George."

"We're way ahead of you." Decker leaned forward with his arms on the table. "You haven't been employed by the Order of St. George since you walked into this room. And as for taking off the handcuffs . . . Well, that isn't going to happen. Not unless you start talking."

"Then we appear to be at an impasse because I have nothing to say." Garrett swallowed, his Adam's apple bobbing up and down. "But you might want to consider this. The people I met with yesterday evening have great concern for my safety. If they don't hear from me within the next day they might become concerned enough to do something rash."

"I thought your meeting last night was nothing more than a personal matter," Decker said.

"I think we've moved past that ruse," Garrett replied. "Thomas doesn't appear inclined to release me regardless of my protestations, and you clearly overheard our conversation, which leads me to the inevitable conclusion that I'm not going to talk my way out of this by playing dumb."

"A wise assumption." Decker leaned forward. "I'm going to make this easy and get right to the point. Tell me where Mina is, give us the information we need to get her back, and you can go on your way. Whatever else you are planning is not our concern."

"How stupid do you think I am?" Now it was Garrett's turn to lean forward, at least until his restraints stopped him. "You won't release me if I tell you where Mina is. And honestly, why would I? We both know she's not like you and me."

"She's a founding member of the Order," Finch said, taking a step toward the table.

"And she's a vampire." Garrett tugged at his restraints. The chair skidded out from under him. "A member of the Cabal, even if you've all convinced yourselves that she isn't. She was never on our side. She's a scourge."

"That's not true." Finch was at Decker's side now. He glared at Garrett. "You know nothing about Mina or her past. She isn't like the others."

"We know that already. That's why we took her. She's something special. Like nothing we've ever encountered before. A foot in the world of the living, a foot in the world of the dead. And the secrets that run through her veins will bring down the Cabal and all the vampires everywhere in the world. You mark my words."

"She's not your enemy."

"She's not our friend either. Either way, it doesn't matter. She's the key to defeating all of them."

"What happened to you?" Finch sounded genuinely hurt. "What changed?"

"What do you think?" Garrett tugged at his restraints again. Anger flashed in his eyes. "All this time, you were led by her. The very thing the Order of St. George was set up to fight. How could I not turn against you?"

"She helped us defeat Jack the Ripper. Without her, he would still be out there." Finch paced to the door.

Decker remained silent. The circle of time that led to this confrontation was baffling to him. If it wasn't for Mina's encounter with Abraham Turner in the twenty-first century, she would still be a normal young woman free of the curse that had been thrust upon her. And now, all this time in the past, she was paying the price for a sequence of events that looped back upon itself in ways he could barely even fathom. The reality was that her actions had stopped Abraham Turner from continuing his reign of terror in the future, but in the process, she had set in motion a timeline that led to the founding of the Order of St. George, which later became CUSP, and all that followed. They were all here at this moment in time because of her. Likewise, she was in her current predicament because of events that would not happen for over a hundred years. It made his head hurt just to think about it.

Apparently, Finch felt the same way. He sighed and rubbed his forehead. "This is pointless. We're getting nowhere." He motioned to Decker, jerking his head toward the door. "Let's take a break."

Decker looked up and nodded. "I agree."

SEVEN

IN THE CORRIDOR, Decker turned to Finch. "What do you think he meant about Mina having the ability to bring down the Cabal?"

"I wish I knew." There was a pained expression on Finch's face. "If we can't get him to talk, all is lost."

"How much do you know about Mina's past?" Decker asked. "Or rather, her future."

"We've already gone over this," Finch said. "I know that Abraham Turner escapes his prison in the cellar of a house in Hayes Mews over a hundred years from now and that you and Mina destroy him for good. I know that we can't interfere with that timeline much as I want to. I also know that the culmination of that encounter with Abraham Turner creates the Mina that founded the Order of St. George along with myself. She's a time traveler. Mina shared that with me. She's also a hybrid. Part human, and part vampire, thanks to that encounter with Abraham Turner."

"I'm not sure that vampire is the right word," Decker said. "At least, not in the traditional sense. These creatures drink blood and derive life from it for sure, but only whatever life span was left in their victim before they die. They steal the unused years of those they murder, adding them to their own life expectancy. In that sense, they are more like a parasite."

"Parasite. That's a good word for the creatures." Finch frowned. "You think these monsters are what Garrett refers to as the Cabal?"

"I think it's highly likely." Decker had always assumed that Abraham Turner was not the only one of his kind. That much was obvious. But he had hoped they were a rare breed. An anomaly. Now he was forced to think otherwise. The group that Garrett had aligned himself with was hell-bent on bringing down what they perceived as a vampire scourge, and Mina was smack in the middle of their plan. That was why they had taken her. As Garrett said, she had a foot in both worlds. She wasn't vampire or human, but a combination of both. Her encounter with Abraham Turner had left Mina in the unfortunate position of being neither one thing nor the other. It was a psychological tug-of-war that played out within her daily, Decker knew. It only made sense that what Garrett called the Cabal were, in reality, creatures like Abraham Turner that had been living among mankind for centuries, maybe even millennia, and feasting off their misery.

"None of this does us any good in getting Mina back," Finch said. "Under other circumstances, I might be just as willing as Garrett and his cronies to wipe these creatures from the face of the earth, but not at the expense of Mina. We cannot allow them to put her in the middle of this."

"I agree. Who knows what they plan to do with her." Decker rubbed his chin. "The problem is, Garrett won't talk. He's not going to give us her location just because we ask him nicely."

"Then we have to stop being nice."

"We've already gone over this," Decker warned. "We can't become the bad guys just to get the answers we need."

"Don't worry. We aren't going to abandon our morals." Finch pushed his hands into his pockets. "There are ways we can apply pressure to Garrett. Everyone has a weakness. The trick is finding it."

"And his threat that something may happen to Mina if we don't allow him to check in with whoever he's working with?"

"I'll wager it's nothing but a ploy. Garrett has been working against the Order from the inside for a lot longer than just the last few days. He wouldn't risk regular contact with whoever his true allegiance lies with."

"Which is why it took so long to discover him," Decker said. "Until that meeting last night, he was keeping his head down."

"Exactly. Garrett can't risk detection. He'll only contact the people who have Mina if there is a good reason to do so. Other than that, he'll want to blend in and remain unnoticed."

"At least until they have Mina out of the country and beyond our reach."

"Which doesn't give us much time," Finch said. "We'll keep working on Garrett, but in the meantime I'll start checking passenger manifests for all the ships departing in the next week. Maybe we'll get lucky."

"I wouldn't hold your breath," Decker replied. "They won't book passage for Mina using her real name. We don't even know if they intend to use a commercial ocean liner or where they are taking her."

"That is true," Finch said. "But doing something is better than doing nothing."

"If I had paid more attention back in Mavendale, this wouldn't be happening," Decker said. He looked down at the floor.

"You can't blame yourself." Finch put a reassuring hand on Decker's shoulder.

"Mina is my responsibility. Everything that happened to her is because of me."

"That's nonsense, and Mina will tell you so herself when we get her back." Finch stepped toward the door, beyond which Garrett waited. "Let's have another crack at it, shall we?"

EIGHT

AT SEVEN O'CLOCK THAT NIGHT, John Decker emerged from the secret headquarters of the Order of St. George and stepped out of the fake solicitor's office into the frigid evening air. He made his way toward the river. Ahead of him was Tower Bridge, already an icon of old London in his own time but completed less than two decades ago in this one. In front of it, sitting like a dark sentinel on the shoreline, was the Tower of London.

He paused and looked up at the old building. In centuries past, it had housed more than its share of traitors. Now the only traitor that mattered was sitting in a cell deep beneath the city streets. As expected, Garrett had refused to talk despite hours of interrogation. A discrete search of his rooms organized by Thomas Finch proved just as fruitless. Garrett and his cronies had covered their tracks well and made sure not to leave lying around anything that would incriminate them or otherwise hinder their plans. Which meant that Decker's only hope was convincing Garrett to spill the beans. And quickly because he could feel the clock ticking. Mina would soon be moved out of the country, and they might lose her forever. That was not an acceptable outcome.

"Penny for your thoughts?" Said a female voice to Decker's rear.

He turned to find Eunice Gladstone, the secretary and discreet gatekeeper who guarded the entrance to the Order's underground facility, standing on the pavement behind him wearing a thick wool coat. A pink handbag dangled from one arm. Her hair was pulled back into a tight bun.

"I'm not sure my thoughts are worth a penny tonight," Decker replied.

Eunice approached the low stone wall that separated the grounds of The Tower from the city at large. She leaned on it and squinted up at the building silhouetted against the starless night sky. "You know, back in the day, they had ways to make a traitor talk. All manner of fiendish devices designed to loosen the lips. Sometimes, when I walk past here late at night or early in the morning, I swear I can still hear the faint echoes of the prisoners' desperate screams reverberating through the years."

"Your point is?"

"Thomas Finch will get the information you need. You mark my words. He won't give up."

"Is this your way of telling me I shouldn't pry too deeply into his methods?" Decker wondered if Finch meant it when he promised not to torture Garrett.

"No. I'm just trying to lighten your mood." Eunice rubbed her hands together to warm them up. She glanced down the street. "Walk me to my bus?"

"With pleasure." Decker motioned for Eunice to lead the way and then walked alongside her. "How long have you been working for the Order?"

"Long enough," Eunice replied without elaborating further.

"Do you like your job?"

"I sleep well at night knowing that I play a small part in

keeping the country safe from threats no other organization is qualified to deal with."

"That's not the same thing," Decker said.

"Yes. I like my job." Eunice slowed and turned to Decker. "Are you probing to see if I, too, might be a traitor, Mr. Decker?"

"I'm just making polite conversation," Decker said as they continued on toward the bus stop.

"You're not a very good liar." Eunice smiled. "But it's alright. One can never be too careful. Although I have to say, I had *my own suspicions about you* at first."

"Really?"

"Absolutely. Showing up out of the blue with no background and looking exactly like a sketch Mina made decades ago. You have to admit, it is rather unusual."

"And now?"

"I think you're something of an enigma. Maybe one day you'll tell me your secrets, Mr. Decker, of which I'm sure there are plenty."

"Maybe." Decker smiled.

"But not today," Eunice said as they reached the bus stop. "I have a bus to catch, and you a traitor to deal with."

NINE

THOMAS FINCH SAT in his office deep beneath the streets of London with his eyes closed and classical music—Beethoven's Sonata Pathétique, which was his favorite—playing lightly in the background thanks to the Victrola phonograph he had purchased and installed the year before.

It was nine o'clock at night, and the facility was mostly empty. Finch would not normally be here so late, but he was waiting for a specialist he had contacted earlier in the day when it became clear that Daniel Garrett was not going to talk. At least not willingly.

If John Decker had known what Finch planned, he might have objected, which was why the American had been kept in the dark. They did not have time for niceties. The information inside Garrett's head must be extracted quickly if they were to save Mina.

Finch took some small measure of comfort in the fact that he was technically keeping his promise not to torture his former operative. There would be no pain inflicted upon the man tonight. This was not necessarily because Finch objected to such measures when the need arose, but more because intense

36

physical suffering was a poor way to obtain information. Those on the receiving end of torture were likely to say anything just to make the pain stop. That made the intelligence they provided unreliable.

Two light knocks came from the other side of Finch's door.

"Come." He opened his eyes as the door opened.

Harry Chambers, a burly giant of a man recruited from the King's Fusiliers, stood on the other side.

"Doctor Van Beek is here to see you," he said. "I showed him into the library."

"Very good." Finch pushed his chair back and stood. He went to the phonograph and lifted the needle gently from the rotating disk beneath and set it back upon its cradle before turning and exiting the office.

Doctor Van Beek was sitting in a plush leather chair with his hands neatly in his lap when Finch entered the library.

"I do hope you were not greatly inconvenienced by my urgent summons today," Finch said, approaching the doctor. "But I had no other recourse."

"Not at all," the doctor replied, standing up and shaking Finch's hand. "You pay me a healthy retainer to be available for situations such as this."

Finch withdrew his hand and flexed it. The doctor's grip was like a vice. "If you will follow me, I'll take you to the patient."

Finch watched the doctor retrieve a brown leather Gladstone bag from the floor next to his chair before stepping back into the corridor.

They made their way through the facility with Finch in the lead and Harry Chambers at the rear, following behind the doctor. They soon left the comfortable opulence of the upper chambers and descended a set of concrete steps that led to a dank and gloomy sub-level.

From somewhere off in the shadows, Finch could hear water

dripping. The corridors here were lit at intervals by filament lamps that had been put in the year before when the entire facility was wired for electric lighting. Finch was proud of this achievement. Even Westminster Abbey did not have permanent electric lighting yet, having been installed the prior year for King George V's coronation, but then promptly removed again. Now, though, Finch thought that the yellow glowing bulbs gave the sub-level an eerie feeling.

He shook off the sudden frisson of unease and stopped at a metal door flanked by two more ex-soldiers.

Daniel Garrett was already there when they stepped inside, strapped to a chair in the middle of the room that was, in turn, bolted to the floor with heavy metal brackets. He was shirtless, a thin sheen of sweat glistening on his skin despite the chill that laced the air.

He stared forward with unblinking eyes, face unreadable, and didn't react when the three men approached him.

Doctor Van Beek set his bag down on the floor and unlatched it. "I have to warn you, gentlemen. This procedure is highly experimental, and we don't fully understand the side effects."

"But it won't kill him, right?" Finch asked.

"Goodness, no." Van Beek rummaged in the bag and came up with a large and wicked-looking syringe. "This drug is used regularly in hospitals as an anesthetic to relieve the pain of women giving birth without rendering them totally unconscious. They call it twilight sleep."

"What exactly is the drug in that syringe?"

"Scopolamine mixed with morphine. At high doses, it induces an almost trancelike state that leaves the subject susceptible to hypnotic suggestion. The patient's ability to lie is greatly reduced, and they will often tell the truth under questioning without consciously realizing that they are doing so."

"If the drug is used on pregnant women, why are you concerned with the side effects?" asked Harry Chambers.

"It's not the drug itself that worries me," Van Beek replied. "It's the dosage. In order to elicit the desired results, we have to administer a massive dose. Much more than would normally be given to a woman during childbirth. One of the side effects is amnesia. The patient won't remember anything they said or did while under the influence of the narcotic. But there could be other effects that we just don't understand yet, including long-term ones."

"It's only one dose. I'm sure he'll be fine," Finch said, ignoring the small voice inside his head that told him he was, technically, if not directly, breaking the spirit of his promise to John Decker.

"Very well." Van Beek applied pressure to the plunger at the end of the syringe to clear the needle of air. A small arc of liquid shot out and landed on the floor.

Now Garrett reacted. He tugged at his restraints and fixed Finch with a glowering stare. "You can't do this to me. It's not right."

"I'm sorry, my dear chap, but we have no choice." Finch didn't bother to point out the irony of Garrett's statement. He was mad that they were going to drug him, while at the same time, he saw nothing wrong with playing a hand in the abduction and imprisonment of Mina. Finch motioned to Van Beek. "Let's get this over with."

Van Beek nodded and leaned close to Garrett, who twisted and bucked in the chair even as the doctor slid the syringe into his arm and depressed the plunger.

For a long minute, nothing happened. Garrett continued to thrash and fight against his restraints. But then his movements slowed, and his head dropped to his chest. He gave a small sigh, followed by a low snicker.

"Mr. Garrett?" Finch kneeled on one knee in front of the restrained man so that they were on the same level.

Garrett remained silent; his head bent low.

Finch looked up at the doctor. "Can he hear me?"

"He can hear you."

"Mr. Garrett, I am going to ask you some questions," said Finch. "And I would like you to answer me truthfully. Do you understand?"

Garrett smacked his lips together and ran his tongue along them with a wet slurping sound. He lifted his head and nodded, the movement slow and exaggerated. "Yes, I understand."

"Wonderful." Finch couldn't help but smile. A whole day spent interrogating this man had been for naught, and now, with a simple prick of the needle, Garrett's deepest secrets would be laid bare. It almost felt too easy . . . Almost.

TEN

A LITTLE AFTER nine o'clock at night, while Thomas Finch was interviewing a heavily drugged man in a secret facility near the Tower of London, Professor Alex Hawthorne was locked in an examination of his own, albeit with a much less chatty subject, three miles away in a back room at the British Museum.

The mummy of Amenmosep, removed from its tomb in the Valley of the Kings the year before, now lay exposed on a table in front of him. Hawthorne was still no closer to knowing who the mummified man had been in life than he was on the day they broke through the inner doors of the burial chamber to discover a room packed so tightly with golden objects that they could barely move within its confines. Even the body had been draped with gold chains and trinkets inside a stone sarcophagus with three coffins nested, one within the other like Russian dolls. Incredibly, each of the coffins was made of the same glittering yellow metal. It had taken a sturdy pulley and rope system and six months of backbreaking labor to raise each of the heavy lids, set them aside, and expose what lay beneath.

Now, after a further three months of wrangling with the

Egyptian Board of Antiquities, the mysterious Amenmosep, who was not mentioned in any of ancient Egypt's official records, was finally at the museum and ready to be studied along with a small but fascinating selection of the funerary objects found within the tomb. The rest of the objects retrieved from the burial site, which had been formally dubbed KV59, were now in a storage facility at the Cairo Museum.

The discovery, which should have made headlines around the world for the wealth of gold found within the burial chamber, was instead a closely guarded secret. The Egyptian authorities feared it would unleash a wave of modern tomb robbers into the valley looking for treasure, and since no one knew who the mysterious occupant of KV59 actually was or even if he was of royal lineage, it had been decided to keep the discovery secret until the British Museum unveiled an exhibit centered around the tomb later in the year.

Hawthorne wasn't sure he agreed with the decision, but it was not up to him. Not that it mattered, because he would still be the first to examine this mummy and learn its secrets. And the first of those had presented itself just a few minutes ago when Hawthorne noticed an irregular lump beneath the bindings wrapping the body.

Under normal circumstances, he would have waited until the next day to probe the unusual protrusion when his assistant and the rest of the curatorial department staff were present. But after waiting so long even to get the mummy into the country, his excitement got the better of him.

Hawthorne stepped away from the table and made his way through the empty receiving and restoration lab in search of an implement with which to probe the bindings and reveal the object beneath.

As he passed the open lab door, Hawthorne cast a furtive glance into the gloomy corridor beyond. He always found the museum unnerving at this time of night when he was alone within its cavernous walls, and this was no exception. Once the doors closed for the day and the curious public was ushered back out onto the streets, the dead, albeit in glass display cases and storage containers, outnumbered the living by at least ten to one. The Egyptian wing alone contained over a hundred mummies. The largest such collection outside of Cairo. This building was, he thought to himself, basically nothing more than an impressive and publicly accessible crypt.

Hawthorne made his way to a wooden chest sitting against the far wall and opened the top drawer. Inside were an assortment of tools and instruments laid out neatly on a velvet liner. He found what he was looking for, a pair of metal instruments with L-shaped hooks at one end that would not have been out of place in a medical facility.

Returning to the ancient corpse, he slid the hooked end of one tool under the folds of the mummy's wrappings above the protrusion and gently pried it back. The fabric was old and brittle, as was the ancient resin applied to the topmost layers of wrappings to seal them from moisture. The wrappings gave with little resistance. Hawthorne moved slowly, careful to keep the damage caused by his probing to a minimum. A small plume of centuries-old dust puffed up as he worked the bindings aside, using the second tool to pull away successive layers.

And then he saw it, poking out from between the folds of ancient linen.

A glint of gold.

Hawthorne's heartbeat quickened. It was not unusual to find small trinkets and amulets wrapped within the bindings of an Egyptian mummy, but this was much bigger than anything he'd ever encountered before. This was no jade bead or tiny carved statuette that laid so flat within the cocoon of fabric as to be practically undetectable. It was a tablet of pure gold, at least four inches by six and a quarter of an inch deep, judging by the impression it left on the bandages. It lay on the mummy's chest like a breastplate. Hawthorne abandoned his tools and plucked the edge of the oblong tablet, moving it slowly back and forth to work it free from the folds within which it had been imprisoned for millennia.

At first, the bindings refused to release their treasure, but then, all at once, the tablet came loose, and Hawthorne got his first look at the strange object and the hieroglyphics that covered its surface both front and back.

With shaking hands, Hawthorne cradled the tablet and placed it on the table, eager to decipher the message written upon it. He turned and picked up a hand-held magnifying glass from a second smaller table to his rear and hunched down over the object. But before he could start to read, a noise in the corridor outside the workroom drew his attention.

Footsteps.

Hawthorne cursed and set the magnifying glass aside. The museum employed guards who patrolled the halls and galleries at night to make sure nothing was amiss, but they rarely ventured into the workrooms and chambers in the private recesses of the building and out of public view.

"Who's there?" Hawthorne called out, not bothering to hide his irritation. "I say, who's there?"

His question went unanswered, but he didn't have to wait long before a pair of shadows fell across the open doorway to herald the arrival of his unwanted visitors.

Hawthorne stepped away from the table, expecting some stray guard far off his route around the public galleries or lost museum assistant to reveal themselves. Instead, three stocky men in flat caps and overalls appeared in the doorway. Men who clearly did not work for the museum. And in their hands, they carried pistols.

ELEVEN

DECKER WAS RESTLESS.

After a light dinner consumed at the kitchen table in his suite of rooms on the second floor of a Georgian building near Hyde Park, he retired to the formal sitting room and settled into a comfortable chair in front of the fire, where he stared, morose and sullen, into the leaping flames.

It had been six months since he first arrived in the past, and Decker was no closer to getting home now than he was then. Half a year separated from Nancy, and the only person he could talk to about his predicament had herself been missing most of that time. In his bleakest moments, Decker wondered if he would ever see Nancy again. This thought had haunted him across the months as he acclimatized to life in an era so different from his own that, at times, he despaired of ever getting used to it.

It wasn't even that he was in another country. It was more that the comforts he took for granted in the twenty-first century were not available at the start of the twentieth. Automobiles were a rarity, although he knew they would someday soon become commonplace. Telephones were a luxury that allowed only limited communication and could not connect internationally. Electricity was a commodity enjoyed mostly by the rich. There was no internet. No television or even radio. Worst of all was the pollution, which he had always considered more of a twenty-first-century problem, but which plagued the city in ways he could not have imagined. More than once, he awoke on a cold winter's morning to find a thick blanket of smog covering the streets. The result of coal being burned for warmth in homes and factory chimneys that churned out noxious emissions, the thick and choking London fog made it hard to breathe and brought tears to the eyes.

But all of that paled compared to his grief over losing Nancy, possibly forever. During the long nights spent huddled in his quarters, Decker had wracked his brain for a solution to his predicament. After all, he and Mina, along with Colum, Rory, and Adam Hunt, had found a way to escape the Bermuda triangle after becoming stranded on a Bahamian island not long after the close of World War II. He had no idea if the others had made it home after taking to the air and flying through an electrical storm in a commandeered Lockheed Electra, but he clung to the belief that they had. Because to think otherwise would mean that he and Mina were truly adrift in time. And there was circumstantial evidence that at least some of his group had made it back to their own time in the form of a wrecked 1940s-era Electra buried in the tropical jungle on CUSP's island retreat of Singer Cay. The plane might simply have crashed because the pilot lost control, not an uncommon occurrence back then, or it could have gone down because Colum, who was piloting their plane, got thrown forward in time by the triangle, which meant there was no one left in the cockpit to fly it.

Decker chose to believe the latter.

Which was why he hadn't completely given up hope.

But to return home, Decker needed to find a portal through

which to travel. And luckily, he knew of one point in time where he could find one. Celine Rothman would marry Howard Rothman III in a lavish beachfront ceremony at his opulent resort on Singer Cay later that year. Having done so, she would make her way to the penthouse suite to change out of her wedding dress and never be seen again. At least until she showed up over a century later at Decker's own wedding after falling through a rift in time. If Decker could somehow make his way there and be in that room when the storm clouds gathered and the lightning cracked, he might be able to follow her through. But it was a long shot and could strand him even further in the past, or worse, kill him. Not to mention the difficulty of pulling off such an accomplishment in the first place.

And then there was Mina. Decker had no intention of leaving her in the past. If he couldn't rescue her and take her with him, then he would remain here until such a time as he could.

Decker closed his eyes and pictured Nancy. He wondered what she was doing at that moment, even though he knew that it was pointless. She wasn't doing anything because she hadn't even been born yet and the future had not technically happened. Except that it had, and it would. He could almost hear Rory lecturing them about time being an illusion. That it didn't really exist and was merely the brain's way of dealing with an eternal universe. Yet that was no comfort. Real or not, a gulf of years separated the two of them. Was she going to spend the rest of her life mourning his loss, or would he find his way back to her before she even knew he was gone?

Such was the vagary of time travel. He could spend months or even years in the past but arrive back in the present moments after he left. Assuming, of course, that he had the means to do so.

But even though Decker's absence might be no more than a

few minutes, days, or weeks, from Nancy's point of view, every minute he spent separated from her irreversibly aged him. What good would it do to find his way back home if it meant spending decades in the past? She would still be young, and he would be old. The life they might have shared would be wiped out. This thought worried him almost as much as never getting home at all.

Decker took a deep breath and pushed the maudlin thoughts from his mind. To save the future, he must concentrate on the present. And the first order of business was recovering Mina from the clutches of whoever had taken her. After that, he would find a way to get them home or die trying. It was the best he could do under the circumstances. He only hoped it was enough.

TWELVE

PROFESSOR ALEX HAWTHORNE FROZE. He stared at the trio of men standing in the doorway with a mixture of shock and terror. He'd never had a gun pointed at him before, let alone three of them all at once.

"Who are you, and what do you want?" he asked in a timid voice that did little to hide his state of mind.

The tallest of the three men stepped into the room, his eyes alighting on the mummy. "Do as we say, and you won't get hurt."

"How did you get in here?" he asked, even though the answer would not alter his predicament.

"Never you mind that." The tall man, who was obviously in charge, nodded toward the mummy. "Is that Amenmosep?"

Hawthorne was momentarily taken aback. While the mummy laid out on the table in front of him carried significant archaeological value, it paled in comparison to the monetary value of the golden items still packed in crates piled around the walls of the room. "You're here for the mummy?"

"Answer my question. Is that Amenmosep?"

Hawthorne nodded. He could see no point in lying about it

and putting his life at risk for the sake of a desiccated old corpse wrapped in decaying linens.

The man crossed to the mummy, motioning for his companions to follow. He stared down at it with a strange expression on his face that looked almost like revulsion to Hawthorne. When he saw the disturbed bandages and golden tablet resting on the table next to the mummy, his eyes narrowed, and he turned to the archaeologist. "What is this? Where did it come from?"

"I found it," Hawthorne replied in a croaky voice. "Inside the wrappings. I was about to read the inscription when you arrived."

"You removed this from the mummy?" The man's eyes now widened in alarm.

"Yes." Hawthorne wondered if this was what the men had come for rather than the mummy, but then dismissed the idea. He had only discovered the tablet a few minutes prior to their entry, which meant they couldn't have known of its existence.

The man soon affirmed his deduction. "Put it back where you found it. Quickly."

Hawthorne hesitated a moment, then picked up one of the curved instruments he had used to part in the bandages. He pulled back the upper layer, then picked up the tablet with his free hand. It was heavy, and he almost dropped it because he was shaking so much but managed to control his fear long enough to slip the gold tablet back under the mummy's wrappings, pushing it far enough inside to make sure the tablet did not work its way loose and fall back out.

"Good." The man appeared to relax visibly. He let out a long breath before continuing. "There was an object recovered with the mummy. A round amulet made of stone."

"There were lots of objects found in the tomb, many of which are still in Egypt," Hawthorne replied, surprised at his own small yet sudden defiance. He was aware of the amulet to which they referred because it was one of the few funerary items in the tomb that was not made of gold. They had discovered it inside a canopic jar that should have contained the internal organs of the tomb's occupant.

"The Cairo Museum does not have this particular object. We know it was shipped here to London." The man leveled his gun at Hawthorne. "I would suggest that you cooperate and answer my question. It is not worth dying over something of so little value."

Hawthorne swallowed, his eyes roaming to a dark oak plan chest against the far wall, upon which set an assortment of smaller items from the tomb already removed from their crates. A gilt statuette of Osiris, god of the underworld. A solid gold hair comb, its tines still as bright as the day it was made. A polished gold disk with a sculpted handle in the shape of a papyrus stem that would have been used as a mirror. And sitting among these objects, the canopic jar with the stone amulet on its silver chain still inside.

The tall man read Hawthorne's expression. He motioned to his closest companion, who moved swiftly across the room and plucked the canopic jar from its resting place. He opened the lid and looked inside, then nodded.

"You have been most helpful," the tall man said to Hawthorne, taking the canopic jar in one hand while keeping the gun trained on the archaeologist with the other.

His companions dragged an oblong crate filled with straw across the floor from the far end of the room. The same crate that had held Amenmosep on his long journey from a dusty tomb to the vast halls of, arguably, the greatest museum in the world and certainly the biggest.

They dropped it next to the table and positioned themselves at each end of the mummy, lifting the fragile corpse and carefully depositing it back inside the box before dropping the lid in place.

The tall man watched them work with a glint of satisfaction in his eye. When they were done, he smiled. "Get the crate down to the loading docks. Hurry! The museum guards change shift at midnight."

The men, neither of whom had spoken since they entered the room, kneeled and gripped each end of the crate. They lifted with obvious effort and started toward the door, with one man forced to walk backward. They had almost made it out of the room when the lead man's leg caught the corner of another crate, and he stumbled and let go of the precious cargo, his end of which dropped to the floor with a thud.

"No," Hawthorne cried out of instinct, imagining the damage inflicted upon the crate's frail contents. He rushed forward and tried to step around the tall man who still held the canopic jar, but found his path blocked and the gun pressed into his abdomen.

He realized, too late, that his sudden movement had been interpreted as resistance. He lowered his arms to swat the gun away just as a sharp crack filled the room.

Hawthorne clutched at his stomach and staggered back. He looked down in shock to see blood seeping through his fingers. Overcome, he sank to the floor next to the table that had recently held the culmination of his life's work.

"Help me," he pleaded, looking up at the three men in terror. But no help was forthcoming.

The tall man observed him for a moment, his face a picture of astonishment. Then he turned to his companions and barked a terse order. "Pick up the crate. We need to get out of here. Now."

THIRTEEN

THE THREE MEN hurried through the corridors of the museum's private collections area, where thousands of items not on public view were catalogued and stored. Some of these, like the recently arrived artifacts from tomb KV59, would be used in future special exhibits. Others, those deemed too sensitive, fragile, or dull for public consumption, would never see the light of day. John McCann cared for none of them save those he was currently ushering toward the loading bays at the back of the building. The crate containing Amenmosep, and the canopic jar within which the high priest's amulet had resided for millennia.

"You shot that man," said one of his companions, struggling to keep up the pace with his end of the heavy crate.

"It was unavoidable," McCann replied. "I thought he was trying to stop us."

"Do you think he's going to die?" The man asked. His name was Simon, and he was the youngest of the trio, only recently recruited to the cause.

"I don't know. Maybe." McCann didn't want to think about

that. It hadn't been his intention to hurt anyone. In fact, he'd made that promise to the guard who let them into the building and looked the other way in exchange for the equivalent of half a year's pay. Right now, however, he was more concerned that one of the guards he hadn't bribed would investigate the gunshot, than his broken promise to a man who had abdicated his duties and morals for a sum of cash that would probably end up in the pocket of a backstreet bookie—a man who ran an illegal gambling operation—before the month was out. That was why they had chosen this particular guard. If the guard's employers at the museum had known about his weakness for betting on everything from the horses to illegal bare-knuckle fights in the back alleys of the city's worst slums, they might have thought twice about employing him. But their oversight had provided a perfect opportunity that McCann and his colleagues were more than willing to exploit.

"It must be almost midnight," said the third man, glancing around nervously. "The guards will be changing shift soon."

"I'm aware of that," McCann replied. They were almost at the loading bays now, where the museum received artifacts shipped from around the world. As they crossed through a large warehouse space stacked with crates shipped from around the world and yet to be unpacked and transferred to their respective departments, McCann saw the guard hovering near a pair of large wooden bay doors, one of which stood open just wide enough to allow them through.

"You took yer time," the guard said as they approached.

"We're here now, aren't we?" McCann replied, not bothering to mention the archaeologist who was bleeding out with a bullet in his gut at that very moment. The last thing he wanted was to offend what little integrity the man had left and have to dispose of him, too.

"You'd better get that loaded up right quick and make

yourselves scarce," the guard said, nodding toward the crate. "You don't have much time."

McCann glanced beyond the man toward a waiting horse and cart that stood in the courtyard behind the museum. "You needn't worry about us. We'll be gone before you know it."

"Suits me. I'm itching to be done with this sordid business. Now give me the rest of my money."

McCann told his accomplices to load the crate onto the cart and waited for them to step through the open door before turning back to the guard. He rummaged in his pocket and pulled out a small wad of pound notes. He had paid the man half the money upfront when they met in a nearby pub the previous evening but withheld the rest to ensure the guard's compliance. Now he handed over the remainder of the bribe. "You don't need to count it. The money's all there."

"I trust that it is." The guard stuffed the cash into a pocket inside his jacket. "But just so we're straight, I know what you look like. If you've swindled me, my next stop will be a police sketch artist."

"There's no swindle." McCann's hand moved to the gun that was now concealed in his trouser pocket. When the guard found out about the archaeologist, he might decide to pay the local constabulary a visit, anyway. But murdering the man would only give the authorities more excuse to search for them, and besides, McCann could not abide needless killing. If the guard caused problems later, well . . . they knew where he lived.

"I'll be on my way then," the guard mumbled, perhaps sensing that it would push his luck to linger. He tipped his hat at McCann and retreated, soon disappearing into the darkness between the stacked crates.

McCann slipped through the partially opened door, looking left and right to make sure they were not being observed. His companions hefted the crate up into the back of the open cart and lifted the tailgate. One man mounted the cart and climbed into the front, taking the reins, but Simon hesitated.

"Did you tell the guard about the archaeologist?" he asked, approaching McCann and stopping him before he could climb up into the cart.

"Don't worry about it." McCann tried to sidestep his colleague.

"I am worried about it. I didn't sign up for murder."

"Neither did any of us. It was an accident. Get out of my way." McCann shoved Simon to the side and deposited the canopic jar into the cart.

As he went to scramble up after it, Simon grabbed his arm. "We can't leave him to die."

"We have no choice. You know how important our work is. Nothing can get in the way of that." McCann turned and grabbed Simon by the lapel of his jacket. "Now get in the damned cart."

"No." Simon twisted free. "I'm going to help him. I won't be a party to killing an innocent man."

"Don't be stupid," McCann growled. But it was too late. Simon was already sprinting back toward the doors. He slid between them and disappeared into the darkness beyond, his footfalls getting fainter as he went.

The other man looked down at McCann from the front of the cart. "You want me to go after him, boss?"

"No. There isn't time."

"What if he gets caught?"

"He won't talk. He knows better." McCann cursed and climbed into the cart. "Besides, he doesn't know about the girl or what our plans are for her."

"He knows about the mummy and where we're taking it. We can't leave him behind."

"We don't have a choice," McCann said, hoping that he was

right about the young man not talking because someone was coming now. He could hear their cart and the clack of the horse's hooves in the alleyway behind the museum. Probably the fresh guards arriving for the midnight shift change. "Let's get out of here."

FOURTEEN

NO SOONER HAD John McCann and his remaining associate fled the courtyard at the back of the British Museum, heading west toward the swanky residential districts of Fitzrovia and Marylebone with their illicit cargo, than another horse-drawn vehicle appeared through the alley and into the courtyard from the opposite direction. This one was sleek and black, pulled by two horses of the same deep coal coloring. But these were not museum guards arriving for the midnight to eight a.m. shift. Instead, two tall and regal-looking gentlemen, each of whom would have topped McCann by a good four inches, stepped out of the carriage once it had come to a halt. They wore double-breasted dress coats over fancy waistcoats and white linen shirts. A silver fob watch hung from the pocket of each.

They paused on the cobblestones, looking around, then proceeded wordlessly through the back of the museum via the same doors that McCann had recently fled through, and into the building beyond.

The two men moved quickly, crossing the storage area stacked with crates, and navigated the corridors that crisscrossed the private areas of the museum with a singular purpose.

They reached a set of steps and started up. Ahead of them were the workrooms and offices occupied by the curatorial staff for each of the museum's departments.

They had barely made it halfway up when a voice spoke from their rear.

"Oi. Who the devil are you two, and what are you doing here?"

The men stopped on the stairs and turned to see a guard standing at the bottom, staring up at them.

"I asked you a question," the guard said in a thick cockney accent. "What are you two buggers up to?"

The men exchanged a silent glance.

"All right, let's 'ave you back down 'ere." The guard's hand rested on a short nightstick hanging from his belt, colloquially known as a truncheon. It was his only weapon.

Without hesitation, the two men complied, descending the steps and approaching the guard, who raised a hand to stop them as they drew near.

"That's quite close enough."

Around the guard's neck hung a tin whistle on a chain, used to summon the other museum guards in an emergency. The man's hand moved up to his chest and clutched the whistle. His other hand rested on the truncheon, sliding it half free of his belt.

The two men didn't give pause. They parted, one moving to each side of the guard in a lightning-fast pincer movement. A knife flashed in the hand of one, the blade long and sharp. The guard had enough time to register the threat and let out a startled yelp before he felt the bite of steel against his throat.

He stumbled, clutching at the wound as blood slicked his shirt. His mouth opened and closed but no sound came out.

Then, suddenly overcome by his mortal affliction, he sank to his knees and gasped for breath.

One of the pair kneeled beside him and reached for his pocket watch, which he opened to reveal not a timepiece within, but a stone amulet etched with strange symbols. Then he descended upon the man and suckled at his neck, tongue probing the wound, even as the guard's life ebbed away.

Less than a minute later, their grisly task completed, the two men continued on their journey toward the curatorial wing, ignoring the thick wad of pound notes that had spilled from the dead guard's jacket pocket and onto the floor. Money he would never get to spend.

FIFTEEN

SIMON FITZPATRICK HURRIED BACK through the museum toward the room where the archaeologist was even now bleeding out. He knew he shouldn't have left his companions behind in the courtyard. Knew that he would most likely get caught and might even be blamed for the assault, but he wasn't willing to let an innocent man die for a cause he knew nothing about. That was not what he stood for.

When they had first entered the museum, McCann had guided them straight to the department responsible for Egyptian antiquities with unerring accuracy despite the maze of corridors that made up the private areas of the venerable institution. Now, trying to retrace his steps with only a vague memory of their previous route, Simon was not sure he was even in the correct wing. The museum was vast, and beyond the public galleries, everything looked the same. But he couldn't go back now. He was committed to saving the life of this man, and he suspected that his bridges were burned with McCann and the people that he worked for.

He stopped to get his bearings at a point where two corridors branched and felt a flicker of relief. He recognized this place. Or at least, he thought he did. They had passed through here with their crate on the way out of the building. He was sure of it. As if to prove his suspicion, Simon noticed a thin blade of straw that must have fallen through the slats in the crate as they were carrying it. It lay in the right-hand corridor, turned as if pointing the way for him.

Simon took off with renewed vigor and soon came upon the room where the archaeologist still sat slumped on the floor, his back against the table where Amenmosep's mummy had, until recently, laid.

The man was in a dire state. The bullet had been fired point-blank into his gut, and Simon knew even as he stepped into the room that it would be impossible to save him. The archaeologist's eyes were already glazing over, and his breathing was shallow. A pool of crimson blood circled him like an abominable lake. Mistake or not, Simon was now a party to murder.

He sank down next to the stricken man hoping he could render some small measure of aid, but even as he did so, he knew it was pointless. Perhaps if he were a doctor, and this was a medical facility, there might be a way to reverse the steady trickle of life that drained out of the archaeologist, but neither of those things was true.

Simon leaned close to the man and uttered a heartfelt apology. He would have said that his death would not be in vain, that it would save the lives of countless other people in the future, but that would be a hollow promise that Simon was not even sure to be true. And it would make no difference to the man's final moments.

Resigned to the futility of his efforts, Simon stood and stepped away from the dying man. He looked around the room, his eyes alighting on a desk near the far wall and a silvery black and white framed photograph of a finely featured woman posing with the great pyramid of Giza sitting in the background. The archaeologist's wife, perhaps? Simon felt a tinge of remorse. He pulled his eyes from the image and focused on his immediate predicament.

He could do nothing to reverse the unfortunate events that had unfolded here and must now save himself. McCann had been right. This was a fool's errand. If he was lucky, he could slip back through the building undetected and escape without anyone ever knowing that he was ever there.

Simon took one last look around the room and turned toward the door. And then he saw them. Two figures dressed like society gentlemen. They stood in the doorway and looked back at him with an equal measure of surprise.

For a moment, no one spoke.

Then one of the gentlemen stepped into the room, moving with a serpentine grace that made Simon shudder. He looked around and scowled.

"Where is Amenmosep?" he asked, stepping close enough to Simon that he could smell the rot on the man's breath.

Simon didn't answer. He didn't know who these people were, and he had no intention of giving up his colleagues so easily.

"Tell me," the man said, his mouth curling into a snarl. "Or it will be the worse for you."

Simon's breath caught in his throat. "I don't know," he said, which was not strictly true.

"Very well," said the man, gripping Simon by the lapels of his jacket and pulling him close. "It matters little to me how we do this."

Simon was overcome by a sudden sense of his own mortality. He tried to pull away from the stranger, only to find the man's grip was stronger than he imagined. And then he saw the knife. It was a stiletto with a double-edged blade and a groove running down the middle to channel the blood of its victim.

Simon's eyes flew wide.

The well-heeled stranger appeared not to notice as he lifted the knife and drew it across Simon's throat with a deft flick of the wrist. The man behind him took a step forward as if drawn by the sight of blood.

"Have no fear," said the man, drawing Simon close even as his life force spilled from the ragged wound. "You shall live forever, in a sense."

If Simon had not been preoccupied with his own imminent death, he would have wondered at the strangeness of the man's words, but it was all he could do to focus on the world that was quickly fading around him. And then he had the strangest sensation that he wasn't dying at all, but instead being absorbed into a greater whole. Becoming one with . . . he didn't know what. At least until his consciousness faded entirely and blinked out. But not before a single word echoed through his dying mind. A word that betrayed the secret he had been sworn to keep and would now divulge.

Titanic.

SIXTEEN

WHEN JOHN DECKER arrived at the underground headquarters of the Order of St. George at nine in the morning, he found Thomas Finch waiting in the small but sumptuous office assigned to him in the days following Mina's disappearance.

Since that time, Decker had filled one wall with every scrap of evidence he could muster regarding her abduction, all centered on a map of the city upon which he had marked and then crossed off likely locations where she might be held.

Finch stood in front of the impromptu evidence board, perusing Decker's collection of leads, which included newspaper articles about human trafficking inside the city and reports of strange deaths that matched the modus operandi of Jack the Ripper. This was not because Decker believed that Abraham Turner was once again roaming the streets—he knew exactly where the vampiric creature currently resided—but because he didn't believe that Turner was the only such creature out there.

When Decker entered the office, Finch turned to him. "Ah, good. You're here."

"As are you," Decker said, wondering why Finch was standing in his workspace. "I expected you to be interrogating Garrett already."

"There's no need." Finch stepped toward the door. "Please, accompany me to my office. We have much to discuss."

"Or we could just talk here," Decker replied, eager to hear what Finch had to say.

"My office is more comfortably appointed. I merely came here to await your arrival. It was quicker than sending someone to fetch you after the fact."

"In that case, lead on," said Decker, bemused. He followed Finch out into the corridor, and they walked silently through the facility, moving at a brisk pace.

When they arrived at their destination, Finch took a seat behind his desk and waited while Decker settled into a seat on the other side. He remained silent for a moment as if gathering his thoughts, then cleared his throat and spoke. "Mr. Garrett came around to our way of thinking and decided to cooperate late last night. He told us everything he knows."

"Really?" Decker was suspicious. "Just like that?"

Finch nodded. "I can be very persuasive."

"Do I want to know?"

"Relax. We didn't hurt a hair on his traitorous head. Garrett is perfectly fine. He's languishing in a cell on the lower level as we speak."

"Then what are we waiting for? If we know where Mina is being held, we should be on our way to rescue her right now instead of wasting time here."

"Therein lies the problem. We don't know where she is because Garrett doesn't know where she is." Finch grimaced. "The people who took Mina have a doctrine of doling out only the information an operative will need to perform their assigned tasks."

"Compartmentalization." Decker swore under his breath.

Mina's abductors were more organized than he had hoped they would be.

"Huh?" Finch looked confused.

"Never mind. Just a fancy word for the same thing you just said." Decker sighed. "Did you get any useful information out of him?"

"We did, indeed. We might not know where Mina is at this present moment, but we know where she will be a little more than twenty-four hours from now."

"Where?" Decker leaned forward.

"All in good time," Finch said. "We gleaned another piece of information from Garrett relating to the mysterious cargo he discussed at his clandestine meeting two evenings ago and it is most curious."

"Go on." Decker was more interested in learning about Mina, but he knew Finch would not be dissuaded from discussing this other matter first.

"Have you seen the front page of the Times this morning?"

"No." Decker shook his head.

Finch reached into a desk drawer and withdrew a folded newspaper. He tossed it across the desk toward Decker, who picked it up and studied it.

A bold headline in large lettering was splashed across the top half of the front page.

Two men killed in robbery at British Museum.

A smaller subhead underneath, read:

Ancient Egyptian mummy stolen by brazen crooks.

"The cargo is a stolen Egyptian mummy?"

"Yes." Finch nodded. "A man named Amenmosep. There isn't much information about him in the historical record save for the writings inside the tomb within which he was discovered. The ancient Egyptians considered him some sort of god who was said to have been alive since the first of the pharaohs. Thousands of years."

A horrible thought raced through Decker's mind. He had worked a murder case during his time as a homicide detective in New York that also involved a stolen Egyptian artifact. In that instance, it had been a dangerous group known as the Cult of Anubis looking to resurrect their long dead god. They had needed a host body for that god to inhabit. They had lured Decker and a female Egyptologist he was working with to an abandoned factory in order to obtain that host. Had Mina been abducted for a similar reason? He hoped not. "What else do we know about this Amenmosep?"

"That's where it gets strange. According to Garrett, the mummy was stolen because the group he works for believe it to be the same type of creature as Abraham Turner, only a much older specimen. Maybe even the first of its kind."

"You've got to be kidding me." Decker had been worried the Cult of Anubis was operating here in early twentieth-century London, but now he realized it was something much worse. It also confirmed his suspicion that Turner had not been the only one of his kind. "They don't know what they're dealing with. Even if that creature has been buried for thousands of years, it could still be alive."

"I'd say it's a distinct possibility. The tomb was packed full of gold, which is not an unusual occurrence for an Egyptian burial site, but in this case, I believe it was put there because of the metal's distinct properties in subduing creatures such as Abraham Turner. There was even a warning etched into the tomb's door. A curse, if you will, warning that death would come to anyone who awakened Amenmosep."

"Great." Decker groaned. "What possible use could Garrett and his co-conspirators have for Mina and this creature? Garrett isn't a vampire, and I'll wager the same about the rest of his group."

"No. They aren't creatures like Turner. In fact, quite the opposite. They are looking for a way to wipe out such monsters. They have been tracking them for centuries, passing the knowledge down through their ranks. Now they have what they believe to be one of the oldest and purest specimens on earth and a hybrid creature. Part human, part vampire."

"Mina."

"Precisely. She's like nothing they have ever seen before, and they hope she might hold the key to destroying creatures like Abraham Turner forever. Which is why they are moving both her and the mummy out of the country as quickly as they can. Specifically, they are taking her to the United States on a liner that leaves Southampton at noon tomorrow. They have booked passage under false identities."

"Great," said Decker. "All we have to do is show up at that ship and make sure they don't board."

"It's not as easy as that. Like I said, they are traveling under assumed names and will surely keep Mina out of sight as much as possible. And they will be hard to spot given the sizeable crowds that will surely be on the dock and the number of passengers boarding the ship."

"Then we ask the cruise line to detain them when they board," Decker said.

"That was my first thought, but for all we know, they have a crewmember in their employ who will sound a warning. We can't risk tipping them off, or they might not even show up. Then we may lose Mina forever."

"Well, we can't just let them get on that ship and sail away with Mina," Decker said.

"Indeed, we cannot. Which is why you and I will also be on the ship. Once underway, we will locate Mina and retrieve her. To that end, I have secured us first-class accommodations. Expensive, but necessary if we are to move freely throughout the vessel."

"You said the vessel is heading to New York?" Decker asked. For the first time since arriving in the past, he felt a glimmer of hope. If all went to plan, he and Mina would be one step closer to getting home. They would be in America. And with enough time to reach Singer Cay before Celine Rothman had her encounter with the Bermuda triangle and ended up at Decker's wedding in the twenty-first century. Maybe fate was finally smiling upon him.

"Yes. We will dock in New York on the morning of April seventeen, which will give us almost a week to find Mina and rescue her."

"That shouldn't be a problem," Decker said. Garrett had apparently divulged the names under which Mina and her captors would be traveling. It would be a simple task to find out which cabin they occupied from the vessel's head steward.

"I hope you're right. Because once our problem is resolved, we will be in for an interesting ride. Mina's captors didn't just choose any old ship to traverse the Atlantic. They booked passage on the fastest and grandest vessel in the White Star fleet. And on her maiden voyage, at that."

Decker's chest tightened. He wasn't sure he wanted an answer to his next question, but he had to ask. "What's the name of this ship?"

Finch leaned back in his chair and folded his arms. "R.M.S. Titanic."

SEVENTEEN

DECKER WAS silent for a moment as he digested this information. Then he shook his head. "We can't get on the ship. We have to find Mina before she boards."

"That will not be easy," Finch replied. "Garrett doesn't know her present location, only that she will be on board the Titanic under the assumed name of Eleanor Swan along with a man who will be posing as her husband, and their valet, who in reality will probably be tasked with guarding Mina during the voyage."

"You have to trust me. We cannot board that ship."

"What do you know that I do not?" Finch leaned forward. "And I would remind you that Mina has already shared many aspects of the future with me, which I have sworn never to divulge to another living soul or attempt to alter."

"I can't say, but you must listen." Decker had no intention of telling Finch that in less than a week, the Titanic would be on the bottom of the ocean along with many of its crew and passengers. When they were still on Singer Cay in the 1940s, Rory had hypothesized that the universe dealt with changes to the past by creating an alternate future in order to avoid a paradox. He couldn't risk Finch trying to prevent the sinking while he and Mina were still stranded in 1912 because that might jeopardize their return home in ways he could not anticipate.

"If you're worried about changing the past and ending up stranded in an alternate reality, you do not need to worry," Finch said as if reading his mind. "Mina is from the future, and she altered the past by being here and aiding in the capture of Abraham Turner. She also helped found the Order of St. George."

Decker had considered this and dismissed it. "Mina did nothing that hadn't already been done. the Order of St. George is part of history in my reality and will eventually become the organization I work for in the future. I can't say for sure that Mina was involved in establishing the Order, but it would make sense. Mina was always destined to travel back in time and do the things she has done, so her presence here, and by extension, my presence, will not result in a paradox that requires reality to split. I cannot say the same for my own actions going forward. I'm sorry, but I can't take you into my confidence regarding future events surrounding the Titanic. We simply cannot get on that ship."

"I contend we must." Finch drew in a long breath. "Answer me one question if you are willing. Does anything dreadful befall the Titanic in the first twenty-four hours of her voyage?"

Decker shook his head. He couldn't remember the exact date the Titanic sank, but he knew it was several days into the journey when the vessel was two-thirds of the way across the Atlantic. He felt it was safe to affirm that nothing bad happened to the liner so soon after she sailed.

Finch appeared to relax. "In that case, I propose a compromise. The ship will make two stops in its first twenty-four hours. It will sail from Southampton across the channel to Cherbourg in France. After that, it will steam overnight and pick up more passengers in Queenstown, Ireland. There will be an opportunity to disembark the vessel at that point. If we can find Mina within the first twenty-four hours of the voyage, we can escape the ship prior to whatever ill fate you see in store."

Decker did not like the plan. There were too many things that could go wrong, not the least of which was failing to rescue Mina in time to get off the ship in Ireland. He also didn't like the fact that Finch appeared determined to accompany him on board. He couldn't let the man risk his life in that manner. But he also realized that if they didn't locate Mina prior to sailing, it was the best chance that they had. "I'll agree to your compromise on two conditions," he said at length.

"Name them."

"The first is that we keep trying to locate Mina with whatever time we have left before they take her onboard that ship."

Finch nodded. "That is a given. I have no intention of sitting back and waiting. But you must understand that our chances of success are slim given that we have no more clue to her whereabouts now than we did before we apprehended Daniel Garrett. What is your second condition?"

"That if it becomes necessary to rescue her on board, you do not accompany me. I should go alone."

Finch looked pained. "I cannot agree to your second stipulation."

"I don't see why not." Decker was surprised. "As sole head of the Order in Mina's absence, you are needed here. There's no reason for you to become involved in this undertaking any more than you have become personally involved in any others since my arrival in London and for many years before that, I suspect."

"There are things you do not know," Finch said. "Which is why I must insist upon accompanying you. It is the only course of action I can take and arguing further on the matter is pointless."

"Then tell me," Decker said, meeting Finch's steely gaze with his own. "Make me understand because even though I can't divulge what the future holds for the Titanic, I assure you it's the last place you'll want to be."

"I appreciate your effort to shield me from whatever fate may have in store, but I need to be on the vessel, no matter what the consequences. I am not willing to budge on that point." Finch fell silent as if an internal debate were raging within him. Finally, he spoke again. "But I understand how hard it is to argue a point on trust alone, even though that is precisely what you're asking of me regarding your knowledge of the future. Therefore, I will take you into my confidence, but only under the strict proviso that you never breathe a word of it to anyone outside of this room. Do I have your word?"

"You do," said Decker. "My lips are sealed."

"Very well. Mina is not just a coworker to me." He reached into his pocket and removed a small silver locket which he opened. Inside was a small tintype photograph of Mina, probably taken a decade or more before judging by the browning around the photo's edges. He stared at it for a long moment, then closed the locket and returned it to his pocket before turning his attention back to Decker. "She has been, and always will be, so much more. That is the reason why I must accompany you on board the Titanic. Mina is the mother of my child."

EIGHTEEN

DECKER LOOKED at Thomas Finch in stunned silence. "When you say that Mina is the mother of your child, are you referring to your daughter, Daisy?"

"Yes." Finch's gaze drifted to a photograph of his daughter inside a gilt frame that sat on his desk.

Decker had seen a similar photograph many months before when Finch provided him with a hot meal and a bed at his home in the days after he arrived in London. The seventeen-year-old Daisy leaned more toward her father's features and shared none with Finch's current wife, Lily, who Decker had assumed to be the teenager's mother. Now that he looked more closely at the photograph sitting on the desk, he saw not just a likeness to Finch but also Mina. Her face was the same oval shape, and her eyes shined with the same brilliance. "Does she know?"

Finch shook his head. "Lily and I have raised her as our own. It is a secret that weighs heavily upon me, but Mina insisted it must be so."

"I see." Decker was shocked. He knew Mina had spent twenty years in the past by the time he arrived in 1911, but until now, the full implications of that had not sunk in. In the blink of an eye, between the Lockheed Electra flying through that storm in 1942 and his unexpected arrival in 1911 London, Mina had lived decades of her life trapped and alone in the past. He wondered what circumstances had led to Finch and Mina having a child and why she would subsequently abandon that child to his care and stand by as he married another woman.

Finch observed Decker with an expression that bordered on pained. "I'm sure you have a lot of questions, but I hope you will forgive me for not elaborating further upon the situation. I promised Mina many years ago never to divulge the secret of our child or why we are no longer together with another living soul. But I will say that it was not my choice to walk away from her or to hide the true identity of our daughter."

"It's okay," Decker said. "What happened between you and Mina is your business and yours alone."

"I'm glad that you see it that way," Finch said. "Maybe one day Mina will see fit to take you into her confidence, but until that time comes, it is not my place to betray her wishes."

"I understand." Decker's eyes alighted once more on the photograph of Mina and Finch's daughter. "I suppose that continuing my efforts to talk you out of accompanying me aboard the Titanic would be pointless?"

"It would, so you might as well save your breath."

"That's what I thought." Decker stood up. "If there is nothing else to discuss, I'll take my leave. Perhaps I'll have another chat with Mr. Garrett and see if there's anything that he neglected to tell you even if it is only the name of one of his other associates. I would rather find Mina quickly and avoid getting on the Titanic altogether."

"I assure you we extracted all the relevant information from him," Finch said, looking up at Decker from his seat behind the desk. "We were thorough. But feel free to confirm that for yourself, although I'm sure he is back to his sullen, unhelpful self by now."

"If you have any other ideas for getting Mina back before tomorrow, I'm all ears," Decker said.

"I do not," Finch replied. "Much to my dismay."

"That's what I thought." Decker walked to the door and stepped back into the corridor beyond. He closed the door behind him and returned to his own office, where he sat and glumly looked up at the investigation board that covered one wall.

Over the past four months, he had developed and discarded countless leads, talked to every shady character he could find that the Order had ever encountered, and searched the darkest corners of the city without success. Theorizing that the Man in the Black Suit must have received inside help in abducting Mina, he had investigated and discounted almost every member of the Order of St. George until only a few suspects remained. And it paid off, thanks to Finch's ability to make Garrett talk. Even if they didn't know where Mina was being held, they knew where she would be the following day.

The longer he thought about it, the more Decker was convinced that he had no choice but to board the Titanic and search for her there. Finch had used some means of coercion on Garrett, and he didn't want to dwell too much on what that might have been. Decker suspected that even if there was more information locked inside the man's head, he would not part with it willingly, which meant it was pointless to interrogate him further.

But there was another matter to which Decker must now turn his attention. Stopping Thomas Finch from boarding the ship. Regardless of what Finch said or his personal relationship with Mina, Decker could not allow him to risk a watery grave in the mid-Atlantic. the Order of St. George needed a leader, and Decker was not sure that he and Mina would escape with their lives if he could not locate her in time to disembark in Ireland. Which meant that one way or another, he must make sure that Finch did not get on board. The question was, how?

He also had the robbery at the British Museum to consider. The people Garrett worked for were not just transporting Mina to America. They were taking a stolen mummy they believed to be one of the oldest and most powerful vampires ever to walk the earth. That theft had already cost two men their lives, and if the slumbering Amenmosep was awakened, it would cost many more. Decker had seen the carnage left behind by Abraham Turner, and this creature was older and considerably more dangerous. Decker's only consolation was that Amenmosep would likely go down with the ship and be lost in the depths forever. At least, he hoped so . . .

NINETEEN

AT FOUR IN THE AFTERNOON, Mina sat in the window and looked out upon the manicured lawns and meticulously maintained terraces that surrounded her prison, as she often did when left to her own devices. The room in which she was confined, and had been for the past four months, was amply appointed with a large fourposter bed, a chaise lounge, a table with a single chair for taking her meals, and bookcases along one wall that contained every imaginable type of fiction including many of the classics. There was also a phonograph with a selection of recordings to keep her entertained. But despite the apparent luxury of her surroundings, this was a prison, nonetheless.

Mina did not know where she was being held, only that it was a country house somewhere in the home counties surrounding London. Maybe Buckinghamshire or Surrey. She had been unconscious when she arrived here thanks to the drugs administered by her captor, a man of unusual complexion in a jet-black suit who had ambushed her after she answered the door of her room above the pub in Mavendale.

But he wasn't the only person who occupied the country estate. There were others, although how many, she did not know. She often spied horse-drawn carriages and less frequently, motorcars, coming and going along the driveway barely visible at the periphery of her vision from the vantage point of the window, which was fitted with thin iron bars on the outside to prevent any thought of an easy escape.

She did know that there were at least three other occupants of the grand house besides the Man in the Black Suit. She also knew that beyond this room, horrors awaited. Most mornings at nine o'clock, she was handcuffed and taken from her room by two men wearing white tunics of the sort often seen in hospitals and led down the back staircase to a cellar that must once have held wine but had now been converted into what could only be described as a chamber of horrors.

Here, the handcuffs were removed, and she was told to strip. After that, she was subjected to all manner of tests, many of which were painful, degrading, or oftentimes both. These humiliating ordeals were presided over by a small man who wore a white tunic much like her escorts, except there was a stethoscope around his neck, which appeared to be more for show than anything else. He was bald, with deep-set eyes behind horn-rimmed spectacles that gave him the appearance of a mole. The procedures were often presided over by the Man in the Black Suit, who hovered wordlessly at the edge of the room.

She dreaded the trips down to the cellar and looked forward to the rare days when they did not occur. But at least she was still alive.

More than once, while confined in the cellar laboratory, she had heard screams from somewhere deeper in the building. They echoed off the concrete walls and sent a shiver up her spine. Especially since many times, they were abruptly cut off. She didn't know the identities of the unfortunates who cried out so, but she guessed they were undergoing ordeals much worse than her own. They also appeared to be dispensable because she had never actually seen another captive and was sure no other prisoners were held in any of the upstairs bedrooms.

That was what gave her hope of living long enough to escape her prison. She was more important alive than dead. And although she was not privy to the Man in the Black Suit's ultimate goal, she suspected her kidnapping had something to do with the unique nature of her existence. She was human, yet half monster, thanks to her encounter with Abraham Turner. She was a chimera. Neither one thing nor the other. Assuming that her captors did not kill her, either on purpose or by accident, she would probably survive a thousand years or more thanks to the life force she had absorbed from her creator when he met his end at the hands of John Decker. Given the opportunity, she would certainly outlive those who currently held her captive. But that was of little comfort at the moment.

Mina rose from the window and made her way to the chaise lounge. She settled upon it and picked up a book she had been reading more to distract herself from the horrors of this place than anything else when she heard the grating of a key being turned in an old lock.

She looked up in time to see the bedroom door open.

The Man in the Black Suit stood in the doorway.

In all the time she had been held captive, he had never visited her in these chambers. The only occasions she had encountered him, except for their first fateful meeting back in Mavendale, was in the cellar laboratory, and not once had he spoken to her directly.

Now he cleared his throat and addressed her. "We shall be leaving this place shortly. We have a long journey ahead of us. I expect you to behave yourself, or there will be dire consequences."

Mina said nothing in reply.

Her captor stepped into the room, followed by the two men in white tunics. One of them pushed a wheelchair. The other approached Mina with a syringe in his hand.

She recoiled, scooting back on the chaise lounge to evade him. This new development felt dangerous. She had no idea where they wished to take her, but she had no desire to go. Whatever unpleasantness had occurred in the basement of this house, she was sure that worse awaited her at the other end of whatever journey the Man in the Black Suit wished to take her on.

"Please, my dear, don't make a scene." The Man in the Black Suit spoke in a voice that might have been soothing under different circumstances, but in this situation, it just sounded menacing. "It will do you no good. You only delay the inevitable."

Mina had no intention of going easily. She leaped to her feet and made a dash for the open bedroom door, trying to dodge the two men who now advanced upon her. But it was no use. They were expecting such a move and easily cornered her. One man snaked an arm around her waist and reeled her in while the other advanced with the needle.

She squirmed and fought but lacked the strength to break free, thanks to the drugs regularly administered during her basement sessions that were meant to keep her docile.

The man with the needle grabbed her wrist and pulled it painfully toward him, then sank the needle deep into the muscle of her upper arm with his other hand.

Mina felt the contents of the syringe shoot into her bloodstream, bursting through her veins like liquid fire. She let out a frantic howl and tried one last time to escape, but it was no use. Everything was becoming fuzzy. Out of focus. The last thing she registered before she lost consciousness was The Man in the Black Suit observing her with a wan smile as the two men in white tunics lowered her into the wheelchair.

He folded his arms and nodded.

"Excellent," he said. "Take her directly to my carriage. I shall follow shortly."

And then Mina's world faded to black.

TWENTY

AT A LITTLE BEFORE nine in the evening, John Decker left his suite of rooms near Hyde Park, descended to ground level, and stepped out into the dark street beyond. It wasn't raining for once, which appeared to be unusual for the city, and the sky was clear. He hurried the short distance from Hyde Park Corner to the Sloane Square underground station and caught the District Railway, taking it eight stops and disembarking at the Mark Lane Station near Tower Bridge.

He exited the station and made his way straight to another underground station, except this one was no longer in use and had been converted into the subterranean headquarters of the Order of St. George.

The Solicitor's office that served as a cover for the entrance to the facility was closed since it was after normal business hours, but Decker let himself in through the back entrance with a key Thomas Finch had provided to him several months earlier.

A guard sat on a wooden chair in the corridor beyond the door. He looked up at Decker's entry and then, recognizing him, nodded a silent greeting before turning his attention back to the newspaper spread on his lap.

Decker hurried past the guard to the birdcage elevator that would take him down into the underground labyrinth below, relieved that he had not been challenged regarding his presence there at so late an hour. He had only visited the facility this late on one other occasion and had been in the presence of Thomas Finch. This time he was neither with Finch nor on official business. He was here because it was the only place he could think of to obtain what he needed in order to prevent Finch from boarding the Titanic the next day.

Decker waited for the elevator to descend and then hurried through the darkened corridors and tunnels until he came to a nondescript door with the word infirmary stenciled in red lettering on white paint. If an operative was injured in the field, this was where they would be treated because visiting one of the city's many hospitals might arouse suspicion regarding the source of the wound and the Order's clandestine activities.

Tonight, the infirmary was empty, much to Decker's relief. He crossed through the outer ward, passed the treatment room, and entered the pharmacy.

Here, metal medicine cabinets with glass doors lined the walls. Inside each was a vast assortment of tinctures and drugs, arranged depending upon their use. Decker was searching for one drug in particular, which he knew was always stocked thanks to its anesthetic capabilities.

After a brief search, he found what he was looking for. A large glass jar containing a colorless and dense liquid. The label read trichloromethane, but Decker knew it by its more common name. Chloroform. He opened the cabinet and removed the jar, then transferred it to a metal worktable sitting in the middle of the room. He wouldn't need this amount of the drug, and certainly didn't want the guard to see him carrying it out, so Decker found a smaller empty vial and transferred some of the liquid from the larger container using a funnel before returning the jar to the medicine cabinet.

Making sure that everything was just as he left it, Decker pocketed the vial and hurried back through the infirmary and into the corridor beyond. It was possible that someone would notice his theft, but he thought it unlikely. Besides, it didn't matter. By the time anyone went to use the jar of chloroform again, Decker would already be on the Titanic, and Thomas Finch would be all too aware of his deceit. But it was a necessary subterfuge, given how the great ocean liner's story would end. Decker simply could not allow Finch to board that ship and, likewise, could not tell him the reason why.

He only hoped that his plan would work. Finch was stopping by Decker's suite of rooms early the next morning, and from there, they would travel to Waterloo Station and catch the 9:45 a.m. first-class boat train to Southampton docks. At least, that was how it was meant to happen. If successful, Decker would be the only one on that train. But first, he must exit the building without arousing suspicion.

After riding the birdcage elevator back up to the surface, Decker found the guard still sitting in the same place, reading the sports section. The FA cup semifinals had recently concluded, and the man was engrossed in an article debating who had the better chance of winning the final and taking the trophy.

This time, when Decker approached, he looked up and engaged in conversation.

"Whada ya think," he said in a thick brogue that Decker found hard to understand. "West Brom or Barnsley?"

Decker had no opinion. He barely understood the game of soccer, and what little he did comprehend had come from talk he'd overheard in various pubs. But the guard wanted an answer, and Decker did not wish to linger, so he shrugged and said, "Barnsley, for sure."

The guard grinned. "You're a good man."

Decker nodded and moved past him, opened the door, and stepped back out into the rear courtyard behind the building. The vial of chloroform weighed heavily in his pocket. The door closed behind him. Decker breathed a sigh of relief and wasted no time in putting some distance between himself and the guard.

Fifteen minutes later, he was back on the District Railway and heading home.

TWENTY-ONE

THE MAN in the Black Suit sat in the back of the Renault motorcar and watched the countryside slip past under a clear and moonlit sky. It was late in the evening, and they were finally approaching Southampton after a long three-hour drive that had taken them around London, passing close to Windsor and its famous castle before heading south through Basingstoke and Winchester.

Within the vehicle's rear cabin were two other passengers. James Clay, a beefy man who had spent a decade in the Somerset Light Infantry and fought in the Second Boer War, was making the trans-Atlantic trip under the guise of The Man in the Black Suit's personal valet. But in reality, he was there to keep an eye on the third occupant of the vehicle, a young woman who was slumped unconscious on the bench seat opposite the two men.

Under different circumstances, The Man in the Black Suit would have taken the first-class boat train from Waterloo Station the next morning rather than incur the expense of a long trip in the Renault and accommodations in Southampton, but he did not wish to draw attention to their sleeping charge and preferred to stay out of public view unless absolutely necessary.

There was another reason for his desire to keep a low profile. The museum robbery. It had not gone as planned, and now one of his operatives was dead, along with a museum curator. The Man in the Black Suit glanced down at a newspaper on the seat next to him, and the front-page story that told him all he needed to know. The curator had been an accident, shot during the robbery. But his operative, Simon, had died after someone slit his throat and left him to bleed out. The police were baffled by the gruesome differences between the killings, but the Man in the Black Suit knew exactly who had murdered his operative and why, because he recognized the method of killing. The Cabal must have shown up intending to steal the mummy, but arriving too late, had stumbled across Simon trying to save the curator. They slit his throat and took his life force. It was the only scenario that made sense. No one else would be roaming the museum looking to cut throats.

"You alright, boss?" Clay asked, observing him from the other seat.

"Just concerned." The Man in the Black Suit picked up the newspaper. "If the vampires killed Simon, they might know about Titanic. They could follow us aboard. Amenmosep must not fall into their hands."

"We've taken precautions. Everything will be alright."

"I hope you're correct." The Man in the Black Suit put the paper down again and looked out of the window.

Ahead of them was a large four-story red brick building with white painted corner blocks and tall arched windows on the ground floor, all sitting under a two-story mansard roof that elevated the total height to six. This was the South Western Hotel, a favorite destination of well-heeled passengers staying overnight prior to their trans-Atlantic crossings because of its convenient location on the docks opposite Berth 44, which right now held the pride of the White Star Line, the R.M.S. Titanic, awaiting her departure at noon the next day.

When the automobile pulled up outside of the hotel, two porters in dark red uniforms and caps stenciled with the hotel's name in gold rushed to meet them.

The driver stepped down from his open-air front cabin and proceeded to unload baggage, which one of the porters ferried quickly into the hotel lobby on a cart. Next came a wheelchair, which the driver positioned next to the curb.

Clay opened the vehicle's rear door before hoisting the unconscious Mina off the bench seat and lifting her down and into the waiting wheelchair. He draped a thick blanket over her so that only Mina's head was showing. When the remaining porter stepped forward to help Clay with the wheelchair, he brushed the man off.

"I'll handle the young lady," Clay said brusquely.

"Of course, sir," replied the porter, looking taken aback.

"She's not been well, and my employer would prefer that I alone tend to her," Clay said when he saw the expression on the man's face, resorting to their cover story about Mina's current condition. The last thing he wanted to do was leave a stubborn memory in the porter's head should anyone ask questions later.

The Man in the Black Suit stepped down from the automobile and placed a hand on Mina's shoulder. "My wife is very frail," he said, addressing the porter. "I do hope you understand."

The porter nodded. "Very good, sir."

The Man in the Black Suit reached into his coat pocket and withdrew a black leather wallet. He extracted a crisp pound note, which he handed to the porter. He kept another in reserve for the second porter, who was waiting in the lobby with their luggage. "This is for your discretion."

"Thank you kindly, sir," the porter said, his eyes growing

wide. And with good reason, since he earned less than three pounds a week.

"You're welcome," said The Man in the Black Suit. The tip was, he knew, enough to ensure the man's silence in the short term while not being large enough to become memorable in its own right later. "And now, I would very much like to get settled in."

"Of course, sir." The porter walked ahead of Clay, who was pushing the wheelchair, and The Man in the Black Suit. He held the door open and then directed them to the registration desk. Behind them, in the street, the Renault was already sliding away from the curb, its driver heading back to the country house outside of London.

The Man in the Black Suit approached the registration desk and greeted the desk clerk. Ten minutes later, the trio were heading upward in an elevator to the fourth floor and soon arrived at a two-bedroom suite with a striking view over Southampton docks, including the moored R.M.S. Titanic and the River Test, whose terminus flowed into The Solent and English Channel beyond.

Clay took Mina directly to one of the bedrooms and lifted her gently from the wheelchair. After undressing her, he pulled back the covers and laid her in the bed before returning to the suite's comfortable living room.

"We'll need to administer another shot soon or risk her regaining consciousness," he said to his employer, who was standing by the window gazing out at the mighty ocean liner that would soon carry them across the Atlantic to New York and safety.

"Our baggage should be here shortly," said The Man in the Black Suit.

As if on cue, there was a light rap on the door of their suite. Clay answered to find the porter who had taken their bags when the car pulled up.

Clay motioned for the man to bring the bags in, watched him remove them from the luggage cart, then handed him a pound note. This elicited the same amount of gratitude displayed by the other porter, even after The Man in the Black Suit asked for a similar amount of discretion on his part.

The porter retreated, pulling the suite door closed behind him.

Clay picked up the smallest bag and put it on the table. He unzipped it and rummaged for a few moments before coming out with a compact medical kit in a leather pouch. He removed a syringe, filled it from a small glass bottle that contained a colorless liquid, and made his way into the bedroom where Mina slumbered. As The Man in the Black Suit looked on from the doorway, Clay lifted her arm, laid atop the sheets, and slid the needle into her upper arm.

Mina didn't stir.

He depressed the plunger, then removed the needle as gently as he had inserted it and made his way back into the lounge area.

"The doctor said we should administer a shot every twelve hours to keep her sedated," Clay said, referring to Herman Reiner, the small bald man with horn-rimmed glasses who had overseen Mina's care since she had arrived at the house on the outskirts of London. Although care, Clay thought, was perhaps not the right word. He had no interest in Mina's well-being, only in unlocking the secrets held by her unique physiology.

"I would have preferred he was here in person to tend to his ward." The Man in the Black Suit took a seat on the plush Queen Anne-style sofa. "But it cannot be helped."

"Indeed." Clay shuddered. He was glad the weasel-faced little man was not joining them on the Titanic. Reiner would follow later on a different ship after he had tied up the loose ends of his lengthy experiments in England. After that, Mina's well-being would be the furthest thing from the doctor's mind.

In fact, the gloves would come off. Anything that had happened to the young woman so far would be but a prelude to the horrors that awaited her in the United States when Reiner's experiments entered their second phase. He cast a glance back through the door into the bedroom, looking at the sleeping woman, and strangely, felt a glimmer of compassion. One way or another, she would soon be dead.

TWENTY-TWO

AT EIGHT-THIRTY ON the morning of April twelfth, Decker paced nervously back and forth in his second floor sitting room. He went to the window and looked down on the street below in time to see the black motorcar that Finch often used to get around the city, sweep up to the curb and stop. The rear door opened, and Thomas Finch stepped out, then made his way toward the building.

Decker let out a deep sigh. He was about to do something that, under other circumstances, he would find abhorrent, but in this case was necessary given the deadly events that awaited the ship upon which they were about to sail. The plan was to disembark in Queenstown, which would provide a full twenty-four hours with which to locate Mina and liberate her, but that outcome could not be guaranteed.

Decker went into the kitchen, where the chloroform sat in a vial next to a folded washcloth on the countertop. He unscrewed the vial and poured half the contents onto the cloth before re-securing the vial.

A sweet odor filled the air. Faint but recognizable if Finch had ever been around chloroform before. Decker would have to move quickly once his boss entered the apartment, or else he might find himself sidelined and thrown into a cell next to Daniel Garrett while Finch proceeded aboard the ocean liner alone.

Decker folded the washcloth in half to prevent the drug from evaporating before he had a chance to use it and returned to the sitting room, running through what would come next in his mind. He could not allow himself even a moment of hesitation.

There was a knock at the door.

Decker slipped the folded washcloth into his pocket and proceeded to the entryway, where a rattan suitcase of a suitable size to carry waited near the front door. Decker had packed this the evening before, and it was the only luggage he was going to take on the journey.

He reached for the front door handle, then hesitated, briefly wondering if he should just take Finch into his confidence and tell him about the ship. But even as he entertained the thought, he knew it would do no good. Regardless of the Titanic's fate, Finch would insist upon accompanying Decker. He reached down and slipped a hand into his pocket, gripping the washcloth, then unlatched the door with the other and opened it.

"I was beginning to think you'd left me behind," Finch joked, cutting a little too close to the truth for Decker's liking.

"I was in the little boy's room," Decker said.

"Huh?" Finch looked confused.

"Never mind."

"Sometimes it's like you speak a foreign language."

"I could say the same about you," replied Decker, remembering some of the strange period turns of phrase that had left him stumped over the past four months.

"Whatever. You ready to go?" Finch asked, glancing down at the suitcase.

"Not quite." Decker motioned for Finch to enter. "I want to show you something first."

"Really?" Finch raised an eyebrow.

"Yes. It's about Mina," Decker lied. "I really think you should see this before we leave. It's in the sitting room."

His boss lingered a moment in the doorway, and for a second, Decker thought Finch had seen through his plan, but then he stepped into the entrance hall and walked past Decker toward the sitting room. "Let's make this quick."

"You can count on it," Decker said, falling in behind Finch. He slipped the washcloth from his pocket and unfolded it. Then, in a fluid movement, he caught up with Finch and snaked an arm over his shoulder, clamping the washcloth against the other man's face.

Finch stiffened and tried to turn around with a startled grunt, but Decker wrapped his other arm around Finch's waist and held him close while he kept the chloroform-soaked washcloth pressed against Finch's nose and mouth.

The seconds ticked by as Finch struggled against the sudden attack. He brought his elbow back and rammed it hard into Decker's gut, but somehow Decker held on even as Finch brought his elbow back a second time, but now there was no power to the blow, and his legs buckled under him.

Decker held the washcloth against Finch's face for a few moments longer, relieved that the chloroform had done its job. For a while there, he thought it wasn't going to work, and he would have to explain himself to the enraged Finch before he ended up jobless and homeless. He hoped Finch would forgive him when he knew the truth, but that would probably happen anyway when and if he returned to London.

Finch was out cold now. A dead weight.

Decker dragged him into the bedroom and laid him on the bed after removing Finch's heavy coat. Then he made sure to position Finch on his side with one arm at a right angle, and a leg bent back to stop him from accidentally rolling into another position.

When he was satisfied Finch was safe, Decker turned his attention to the coat and rummaged through the pockets until he found what he was looking for. Two postcard-sized first-class boarding cards for the Titanic. He couldn't help but linger a moment to inspect them. The White Star Line's name was printed in black ink across the top. On the left was their swallow-tailed burgee, a red flag billowing with a single white star on it. There was a warning, also in red regarding the conditions of transportation, followed by the details of which steamship the ticket was for, where it was sailing from, and the date. Written in neat handwriting atop one ticket was Decker's name, while on the other was Finch's. On the back were their cabin details and number, boarding instructions, and their names, typed in blue ink this time.

Decker pocketed both tickets, then retreated toward the bedroom door before stopping. There was one more thing that might come in useful. He went back to the unconscious Finch and slipped a hand into his jacket pocket, hoping the object he sought was still there. It was. Decker withdrew the silver locket containing the photograph of Mina, then he crossed the room, stepped out, and closed the bedroom door. He secured it with a barrel bolt he'd fitted the previous evening. The chloroform wouldn't last very long. Unlike in the movies and on TV back in his own time, the drug wore off quickly and was of no use in keeping a person unconscious for extended periods. Finch would be up and around before Decker even made it to Southampton, but the bolted door should hold him for a while, and he certainly wouldn't make it in time to catch the train and, likewise, the R.M.S. Titanic.

Decker discarded the washcloth and returned to the sitting room. He picked up an envelope addressed to Finch containing a note he had written earlier. It was only a partial explanation and still did not give a warning of the tragedy that was going to occur several days hence. But it was the best Decker could do under the circumstances, and he didn't want to leave with no explanation at all. He returned to the bedroom and slipped the note under the door.

That only left one task.

Finch's vehicle was still waiting at the curb, expecting both men to appear at any moment so that it could take them to the train station. If he didn't get rid of the chauffeur, his efforts would be for nothing.

Decker hurried back through the apartment, picking up his suitcase and jacket as he went. He stepped out into the corridor and pulled the door closed, then took the stairs down to the ground floor. He left the suitcase out of sight inside the building's lobby and approached the black motorcar.

"There's been a change of plan," Decker said to the chauffeur, who was sitting up front with one arm leaning out of the open window and a cigarette between his fingers. "After discussing with Mr. Finch, we have decided this motorcar is too conspicuous. The people who took Mina will no doubt be looking for us at the train station and also the docks in an attempt to stop us from following them and retrieving her. We need to appear less obvious. You are to return to headquarters. Mr. Finch and I will take a cab to the train station."

The driver flicked a short finger of ash from the end of his cigarette and observed Decker. "Mr. Finch mentioned nothing of this to me on the way here."

"That's because we only just discussed it." Decker wondered if the chauffeur was going to be the downfall of his plan. "He asked me to relay the message while he answers the call of nature. He might be a while. Of course, I can disturb him to come down and tell you this himself, if you prefer?"

The chauffeur looked unsure. But Decker guessed he wouldn't want to look as if he was questioning Finch's orders or choice of messenger, especially since Decker had been given carte blanche at the Order of St. George to aid in his efforts to locate and rescue Mina. As such, Decker held almost as much sway as Finch.

The chauffeur finally came to a decision. "I have to get his bag from the boot."

"I can do that," said Decker helpfully. He went to the back of the motorcar and opened the trunk, which was a literal trunk sitting above the rear bumper. He removed Finch's suitcase, which, unlike his own, was constructed of soft tan leather, then returned to the front of the vehicle. "All good."

The chauffeur flicked more ash from his cigarette, then drew his arm back inside the car and put the vehicle in gear with a metallic grind. He inched forward, turning the wheel to pull out onto the road, then peered sideways through his open window and called back as the vehicle picked up speed. "Good luck to you both. Bring Miss Parkinson back to us safe n' sound."

"That's the plan," Decker called after him. Then he turned and hurried back into the building with Finch's suitcase, which he swapped for his own, then reemerged and went in search of a cab to take him to Waterloo Station and the boat train.

TWENTY-THREE

THE FIRST-CLASS BOAT train from London took two hours to reach Southampton. Another train carrying second- and third-class passengers had already left earlier that morning and those were already boarding, and in the case of third-class, being fumigated first, which Decker found bizarre.

During the journey from London to the coast, Decker sat quietly near the back of a carriage more luxurious than any train he had ever rode before and listened to the steady clack of wheels on rails. Steam from the locomotive engine up front was visible through the window as it billowed above the carriage. They wound out of the city and through countryside dotted with small towns and villages full of cottages with thatched roofs that looked like something out of a vintage Christmas card. It was surreal and breathtaking, and his thoughts turned to Nancy despite his best efforts not to dwell on his predicament. She would love this nostalgic trip through the English countryside, and he could almost picture the glee on her face as she craned her neck to take in every small detail.

But Nancy was not here. She was thousands of miles and a gulf of years away from him, and now he was about to board an ocean liner that might seal his fate before he ever had a chance to get back to her.

Decker swallowed a heavy lump in his throat and focused on the present. There were dangers beyond the ultimate fate of the ship he was about to step aboard. By now, Thomas Finch must have woken up and might even have busted his way out of the bedroom Decker had locked him in. He would also have read the note Decker had slipped under the door crack. Not that it mattered. By the time Finch made it back to the Order of St. George, it would be too late, even if he jumped in his motor car and told the chauffeur to drive to Southampton as if his life depended on it. Decker also had Finch's ticket for the ship tucked along with his own in his coat pocket.

But there were other dangers, like the people who had abducted Mina. While Decker had used them as an excuse to dismiss Finch's chauffeur earlier that morning, he knew they would be watching for any sign of trouble. Garrett had insinuated that his lack of communication would alert them to the Order's knowledge of their plans, and while Finch theorized that this would not be the case—that he wouldn't risk contacting his colleagues unless absolutely necessary for fear of discovery—it was not a given. For all Decker knew, Garrett had a prearranged check-in that would send Mina's captors scurrying back into the woodwork if it were missed. Or worse, they would go on the offensive and actively try to stop Decker from following them. He would have to be careful.

Decker's rumination was interrupted by a sharp whistle as the train pulled onto the docks and came to a stop. He looked out of the window to see an incredible sight. A huge expanse of black-painted steel plates held together by thousands of rivets towered above him and fell away to the left and right. Above this was a white-painted band, and higher still, rows of decks. Somewhere above this, Decker knew, were four huge funnels sitting atop the vessel.

ANTHONY M. STRONG

Decker drew in a sharp breath, overcome at the spectacle of being in the shadow of the largest man-made object in the world. A ship so famous, or maybe infamous, that over a century after it sank, almost everyone in the world knew its name.

He was still staring up at the ship, awestruck, when a conductor came down the aisle and interrupted his wonderment.

"Alright there, sir?"

Decker tore his eyes away from the ocean liner. "Sorry?"

"Time to get off, sir," he said, then nodded toward the ship. "You'll be wanting to board, I'll wager, rather than sit on this here train, otherwise you'll end up back in London."

"Right." Decker realized that most of the other passengers had already left the train and were making their way across the docks. He stood and grabbed his suitcase, then slid past the conductor, made his way to the front of the carriage, and stepped down onto the platform. Then he pulled his coat tight to keep out the chill and followed the rest of the first-class passengers toward the covered gangplank.

This was it. The point of no return. He had twenty-four hours to find Mina and disembark with her at Queenstown, otherwise he might never leave the ship at all.

TWENTY-FOUR

THE MAN in the Black Suit stepped onto the first-class gangplank with James Clay following to his rear and pushing the unconscious Mina in the wheelchair. Beneath them was a drop of at least fifty feet to the dock where crowds of onlookers had gathered to watch the great ship depart. Further away, toward the ship's aft section, he saw the second- and third-class gangplank and, beyond this, a towering crane sitting on the dock. Another smaller crane, this one on Titanic, was lifting a pallet of cargo, primarily wooden crates held in place by sturdy netting, to deposit into one of the vessel's six holds. He wondered if his own cargo was on that pallet—the recently stolen mummy of Amenmosep, who had lain in a deathly slumber for millennia. Soon, maybe he would be roused, but not yet.

The Man in the Black Suit's hand rose to a chain around his neck, where a stone amulet nestled under his shirt. This was the other item stolen during that robbery, which had resulted in the deaths of a professor who worked for the museum and one of his own men. The museum employee's death had been an unfortunate mistake. The other had been killed in a gruesome fashion, his neck opened up by a knife, and his blood drained. This was the work of the Cabal. The Man in the Black Suit shuddered. The quicker they were on their way and out of the Cabal's reach, the better.

"Good morning, sirs," said a steward as they stepped off the gangplank and onto the ship's promenade deck. "May I inspect your tickets?"

"Certainly." The Man in the Black Suit reached into his pocket and produced three tickets which he handed to the steward.

"Would you like me to fetch a porter to assist you with the young lady?" asked the steward, glancing at Mina in the wheelchair.

"No, that will be quite alright." The Man in the Black Suit shook his head. "My valet is more than capable."

"Very good, sir." The steward bowed his head. His gaze drifted back to Mina. "Will you require any special consideration?"

"Again, no. My wife will be fine so long as we are not disturbed. She will spend the trip resting in our suite."

"I understand." The steward studied their tickets and then handed them back. "You have adjoining rooms on C deck. The room numbers are on the back of your tickets. C16 and 20. Follow the promenade deck until you come to the first-class entrance. You'll find a staircase there, behind which are three elevators. Please proceed down to C deck and follow the corridor directly in front of you to the left. Your staterooms will be on the port side. A porter will deliver your luggage shortly."

"Thank you," replied The Man in the Black Suit, pocketing the tickets and motioning for Clay to follow him with Mina.

It didn't take long to find their accommodations. They rode down the elevators and followed the corridor, joining the excited throng of first-class passengers eagerly exploring the ship.

The cabins were accessed by a narrow passage perpendicular to the main corridor with a porthole at the far end. The door was on the right and led into a room that contained one regular bed and two bunk beds. Beyond this, accessed via a connecting door, was a second similarly appointed stateroom with its own corridor access allowing the rooms to be sold as separate accommodations if a suite was not required. On the right was a bathroom with a water closet and private bathing facilities, a luxury on any oceangoing liner.

They could have purchased cheaper accommodations in first-class, but The Man in the Black Suit had no intention of letting their captive leave the suite and, as such, required private facilities.

Clay wasted no time lifting Mina from the wheelchair and laying the still-unconscious woman on the bed in the second room.

He turned and checked the door leading into the corridor to ensure it was locked.

"We'll need to give her another injection," said The Man in the Black Suit, watching Clay work. "I don't want her waking up until we've left port."

"I'll take care of it now," Clay replied. He opened his bag and removed a syringe and the vial of sedative.

"While you're doing that, I'm going to take a look on deck and make sure we weren't followed," said the man in black as Clay prepared the syringe. He turned and left the cabin, closing the door behind him, and retraced his steps along the corridor to the first-class entrance, then up to the promenade deck. It was almost noon, and the liner would be sailing soon. Other passengers lined the railings, looking down on the crowd gathered to watch the great ship depart.

The Man in the Black Suit made his way along the Promenade, keeping his eye open for anyone showing him undue attention. He didn't think the Cabal knew of their plans,

ANTHONY M. STRONG

but he was a cautious man and wasn't willing to put his faith in the hands of assumption.

When he reached the end of the promenade, noticing nothing out of the ordinary, he crossed to the ship's port side. There were fewer people here, and he paused at the railing to look out over the channel toward the other piers where smaller liners were docked, including the steamers New York and Oceanic. He would have preferred to book passage on one of those vessels rather than the floating palace he was now aboard, but their coal bunkers were empty, and their trans-Atlantic crossings canceled. A coal strike that had ended only days ago after five weeks had prompted the White Star Line to transfer all available fuel from its smaller vessels to the Titanic rather than delay her departure. She was the largest vessel in the world—a wonder of modern technology—and as such, her maiden voyage would be remembered through the ages. The White Star Line could not allow anything to interfere with that.

The Man in the Black Suit cast one more glance over the River Test, and the English Channel beyond, before stepping back inside and making his way down to C deck and his suite. When he entered, Clay had finished administering the sedative to Mina and was busy unpacking their travel bags. The Man in the Black Suit retreated to the other stateroom, sat on his bed, and wearily closed his eyes. They had a long journey ahead of them, but soon they would be at sea, where their enemies could not touch them. And that was good enough for now.

TWENTY-FIVE

JAMES FULLER WATCHED a pallet of crates being lowered through a hatch into the Titanic's forward hold. They had already unloaded six such pallets, heaving the wooden boxes aside and stacking them in their assigned places, with the heaviest on the bottom to make sure their weight was evenly dispersed in the hold. There were other items, too. A luxury Renault motor car. Cases of wine. Books. Soap and cosmetics. There were even several crates of rare orchids bound for flower sellers in New York. Bags of mail and packages making the transatlantic crossing occupied a smaller hold aft of the one Fuller now worked in.

Next to him, Frank Maloney, one of five other dockers currently working the forward hold, scratched his head and grumbled. "It's a never-ending chore loading this ship. If we were working the Oceanic, we would have been done by now."

"Quit your complaining," Fuller said as the pallet settled onto the deck. "We're being paid, aren't we? The longer it takes, the more pennies will be in your pocket come tonight."

"Doesn't help my back when I can't stand up tomorrow,"

Maloney said in his thick Irish brogue. "Should have given this up years ago."

"And do what?" Fuller started pulling the netting from the cargo. "It's either dock work or signing on as a crewman, and we'd probably end up on the black gang."

"Maybe this gig ain't so bad after all," Maloney conceded. The black gang had one of the hardest jobs on the Titanic, shoveling coal into the huge furnaces that drove the turbines. The work was hot, dirty, and exhausting. It also meant long hours locked in the ship's belly . . . And all for half the pay a deck steward would earn. "And we get to go home tonight, too."

"Not until we get this cargo stowed, we don't." Fuller enjoyed working the docks. He knew men who had taken jobs as firemen or stokers on the grand liners and was all too aware of the grueling work schedule and dangerous conditions aboard the ships. No thanks. That was not for him. Load the cargo and get the hell out. By the time Titanic started its journey across the English Channel to Cherbourg, Fuller would be in the King's Head downing a few pints of ale along with Maloney and most of the other dock workers.

He motioned for Maloney to take the other side of the crate, and together, they heaved it across the hold and stacked it next to a similar pile of wooden boxes before returning and grabbing another crate.

This one was lighter.

"Put it up here," Fuller said, motioning to the taller stack of crates behind the one they had previously moved.

"You sure about that?" Maloney didn't look convinced. "Looks awful high."

"Just get it up there." Fuller gripped his side of the crate and lifted.

Maloney set his feet and grunted, pushing the crate above his head and trying to slide it sideways onto the stack. But whatever was inside the crate had not been packed tightly enough. It shifted, altering the center of gravity and causing Maloney to stumble. He cursed and tried to catch himself, but the crate slipped from his hands.

"Watch yourself there," Fuller cried, alarmed, as the crate ripped from his hands and swung down in an arc toward him.

He jumped backward out of the way in the nick of time.

The crate slid off the stack and smacked into the floor, balancing on end for a moment before crashing sideways and landing hard on the deck.

A couple of the other dockworkers glanced around and then turned their attention back to their own work. If something had gotten broken, they wanted nothing to do with it.

"Shite." Maloney looked on in horror. "I sure hope that whatever is inside there wasn't fragile."

"Too late now." Fuller looked down at the crate with folded arms. "What in tarnation were you thinking?"

"Wasn't my fault," Maloney protested. "Whoever packed that crate did a piss-poor job of it. I'm lucky I didn't break my wrist."

"Well, no use crying over spilled milk, as my old grandma used to say." Fuller stepped toward the crate. "Let's put this where it belongs before the foreman comes around and sees it. I don't fancy getting my pay docked over something that will just end up in some rich guy's mansion."

"Sounds good to me." Maloney stooped to pick up the crate, then groaned. "Aw, hell."

"What is it now?"

"The side of the crate is busted out on this end. We try to lift it up onto that stack, it will probably fall apart."

"Then we don't put it up there," Fuller said, pointing toward the crate they had previously moved. "Just put it on top of this one. That should be good enough."

"If we'd done that in the first place, this wouldn't have happened."

"You're the one that dropped it, not me." Fuller gripped the end of the crate and waited for Maloney to take his end. Together they lifted it, careful not to do any further damage.

When they were done, Fuller stepped back, rubbed his hands on his pants, and studied the damage. One end of the crate was smashed open. Part of a plank had broken off, leaving a gaping hole near the corner. It didn't look repairable. Fuller could not see the cargo inside and didn't know if it was damaged, but he didn't care. "Anyone asks, it was like that when we took it off the pallet."

"Amen to that." Maloney brushed off his hands and turned toward the other crates still waiting to be moved. "Let's get the job done. I want off this ship."

Fuller didn't reply. He was already thinking about the pub and how good it would be to sink his first pint of ale and quench his thirst. He might even buy Maloney a mug of beer. If he didn't drop anything else and break it, that was.

TWENTY-SIX

JOHN DECKER STOOD in front of the grand staircase and looked up in awe. He could hardly believe where he was. He thought he would be prepared for this moment, but he was wrong. It was so much more than he ever could have imagined, even though he knew the ultimate fate of the vessel he had just boarded.

Once, when he was still living in New York, Decker had attended a Titanic exhibit that was touring the country. He stared at the artifacts in their glass cases and wondered about the lives of those who had once owned them. Had they drowned in the frigid waters of the North Atlantic? Were they lucky enough to board one of the lifeboats? The exhibition had been both fascinating and poignant. It had stayed with him long after. But never in his wildest dreams had he imagined that he would be on that very ship as it prepared to leave Southampton for the journey it would never complete. It was incredible but also terrifying.

"Excuse me, sir. Did you need help?"

Decker turned to see a steward hovering behind him with a quizzical look on his face. "No, thank you. Just taking it all in."

"It is rather nice, don't you think?" said the steward, without a hint of understatement.

"I do," Decker replied. The grand staircase, spanning six decks, was the jewel in the crown of Titanic's first-class section. Above him, topping the staircase, was a wrought iron and glass dome with a glittering chandelier that sparkled with thousands of cut-glass jewels. The woodwork was exquisite, with sweeping balustrades and intricately carved panels that Decker thought would have been more at home in a royal palace than an ocean liner.

"Have you found your cabin yet, sir?" asked the steward, still eager to be helpful.

"No, I haven't," Decker replied. "But I'm sure I can find it without much trouble."

"If you show me your boarding pass, I can give you directions," said the steward.

Decker reached into his pocket and took out the boarding pass, which he handed to the steward. Thomas Finch's boarding pass was folded and tucked into his other pocket, so he did not confuse the two. His thoughts turned briefly to Finch. Had he escaped the bedroom and made it back to the Order of St. George's headquarters? Was he even now racing toward Southampton in a frantic effort to catch up with Decker? If he was, then his efforts would fail. It was a two-hour train ride to the coast and longer by car.

The steward examined his boarding pass. "Your cabin is A 32. Just keep going past the grand staircase. You can't miss it."

"Thank you, I will do that." Decker took the ticket back and returned it to his pocket.

"Very good, sir. If you need anything at any time, day or night, just call for one of the first-class stewards."

By the time I need something, assuming I'm still on the ship by then, the stewards will have better things to do, Decker thought ruefully. He nodded and said thank you, then continued past the grand staircase with his suitcase in hand. As he went, Decker couldn't help wondering if the man who had just helped him would still be alive in a week. He suspected that thought would cross his mind often during his time on the ship and resolved not to dwell on it.

Decker made his way down the first-class corridor, following a gaggle of excited passengers who could hardly believe their luck at being on the maiden voyage of such a luxurious vessel.

The steward was correct. His cabin was easy to find. Decker let himself in and closed the door, then put his suitcase on the floor. He took a moment to study his surroundings. Finch had purchased two cabins, one beside the other. Upon boarding, Decker had possessed the forethought to collect the keys for both, figuring that it might be useful to have access to a second room that was not in his own name. If he found Mina, she would need somewhere to sleep. Both cabins had a fold-down upper bunk above the bed to allow a second person to occupy the room if it was necessary. The plan had been for Finch and Decker to share a cabin once they rescued Mina and let her take the other one. With Finch out of the picture, there was no reason for that plan to change.

Decker lifted his suitcase onto the bed and opened it. He rummaged around in the clothing and soon found what he was looking for. A Webley and Scott model 1906 pistol. He slipped the gun into his belt and covered it with his shirt, then turned toward the cabin door to go up on deck. The Titanic would depart soon, and Decker did not wish to miss the view of Southampton as they pulled away from the dock.

As if to prove him right, a rumble from below shuddered under his feet. The Titanic's engines were coming to life and powering her huge turbines. Soon they would be underway.

Decker took one last look around the cabin, then stepped into the corridor and hurried back toward the promenade and history.

TWENTY-SEVEN

IT TOOK ALMOST two hours for Titanic to clear the dock and point her bow toward the English Channel, mostly thanks to a near collision as they left port. The SS City of New York, moored next to another White Star liner, the RMS Oceanic, drifted dangerously close to the Titanic after her hawsers snapped thanks to the swell created by the larger ship.

Decker watched the commotion from the first-class promenade deck as a pair of tugboats desperately tried to intercept the wayward New York and avoid a collision that would delay the Titanic's maiden voyage. Had their efforts failed, Decker mused, the mighty ocean liner might have been spared a cold dark grave at the bottom of the Atlantic, but that was not what happened, and even though he held his breath and hoped history would change, Decker knew it was pointless.

The New York was brought under control, and the Titanic slipped into the English Channel and set a course for Cherbourg to pick up more passengers. After that, the ship would sail overnight to Queenstown in Ireland and was scheduled to arrive around noon the next day. That left Decker with less than twenty-four hours to find Mina and disembark or risk freezing to death in the North Atlantic, along with two-thirds of the passengers surrounding him.

There was no time to waste.

Decker stepped away from the railing, pushed through the excited crowd on deck, and then made his way back inside.

He slipped a hand into his pocket and removed a piece of paper on which he had written the information provided by Garrett during the dubious interrogation Finch had carried out a couple of evenings before.

Her captor had booked passage for himself and Mina under false identities. The same went for the man traveling as their valet, who Decker suspected was actually there to help guard Mina.

The one piece of information Decker did not have was their cabin assignments. Without that, it would be almost impossible to locate them since it was unlikely her captors would allow Mina on deck, and Decker didn't know what the men accompanying her looked like. He suspected the Man in the Black Suit would be one of them, but even that was no help. There were too many passengers on board, and the chances of locating him in a public area were slim, especially since her captors would, no doubt, keep their heads down.

Decker's only chance of quickly locating Mina was to find out which cabin she was in. There were too many variables to have a plan beyond that. He didn't know if the man posing as her husband and his valet were the only people traveling with Mina. He also didn't know if they had weapons or what precautions they had taken to ensure their safety.

Decker's hand went to the gun hidden under his shirt. He was armed, which would at least level the playing field. Or so he hoped. Beyond that, he would have to play it by ear until he had more information.

Up ahead was the grand staircase. First-class passengers

milled around, giving their luxurious surroundings barely a second glance. Decker spotted a bedroom steward heading toward the first-class cabins carrying a pile of folded towels.

He approached the man and intercepted him. "Good afternoon. I'm searching for a friend who's traveling in first-class. Would you be able to tell me their cabin number? They don't know I'm aboard, and I would like to surprise them."

The steward shook his head. "I'm sorry, sir, but I can't give out information regarding other passengers. If you tell me their names, I can pass a message along for you."

"I would prefer to surprise them with my presence," Decker said. "We haven't seen each other for a very long time. Are you sure there's nothing you can do?"

"I'm afraid not, sir. The privacy of our first-class guests is of the utmost importance."

"I see." Decker had hoped that locating Mina would be a straightforward process since he knew the false names she and her captor were traveling under. "Is there another person I can speak to? Someone with more authority."

The steward hesitated, torn between passing the buck to his boss and offending a first-class passenger.

Decker reached into his pocket and pulled out a pound note which he offered to the steward. "I understand it might get me no further to speak with your superior, but I would appreciate your help in this matter."

The steward looked at the pound note, then took it. "You want to speak with the purser. He's your best bet, although the rules are very clear, so I wouldn't get your hopes up."

"Thank you," said Decker. "Where can I find the purser?"

"Take the grand staircase down to C deck. He will be in his office on the first-class landing."

"Wonderful." Decker thanked the steward again and headed for the stairs. He went down two decks and soon found the purser's office right where the steward said it would be.

The door was standing open. A thin man wearing black trousers, a white shirt, and a bow tie was sitting at a desk, flicking through what looked like a passenger manifest.

When Decker knocked, he looked up.

"Can I help you?"

"I hope so." Decker explained the situation just as he had to the steward.

The purser pushed his paperwork aside and looked up at Decker. "I regret that I cannot divulge that information. I hope you understand."

Decker tried again, elaborating on his story. "I was hoping you could make an exception under the circumstances. My friend and I have not seen each other for almost a decade, and there will be no opportunity to catch up with him and his wife in New York. We were only booked on the same ocean liner by pure luck, and I don't want to waste it."

The purser was having none of it. "I understand your situation, sir, but the rules are very specific. If you would like me to relay a message to your friend, I can have him meet you in the restaurant or perhaps in the first-class smoking room."

"That's quite alright," this was the exact solution the steward had offered. They were clearly following a rigid rulebook. "Perhaps I shall run into my friend on deck during the crossing and surprise him there."

"Perhaps." The purser cleared his throat. "Is there anything else I can help you with, sir?"

"Nothing."

"Very good, sir." The purser turned his attention back to his paperwork.

Decker lingered a moment in the doorway, then retreated. He would get nowhere by applying more pressure on the purser or his staff. He would have to find the cabin within which Mina was being held by other means. Now all he needed was to figure out how.

TWENTY-EIGHT

THE MAN in the Black Suit stood at the porthole in his suite and looked out at the frothy ocean beyond. He could not shake a feeling of unease that had come upon him the previous evening in the hotel. It had all been too easy. Despite telling himself that the Cabal could not possibly know their plans, his mind kept returning to Simon Fitzpatrick, the operative killed during the theft at the museum.

It should never have happened. The team he had sent to secure the mummy had gotten away with Amenmosep and the amulet as planned, even if an unfortunate incident had left a museum employee dying from a gunshot wound to the abdomen.

But instead of climbing aboard the carriage with his colleagues, Simon had grown a conscience and ran back inside. And for what? To aid a man who could not be saved. And not only because the archeologist's injury was fatal, but because the Cabal would have finished him off just like they killed Simon.

Not that The Man in the Black Suit felt bad about the death of his young operative. Simon had sealed his own fate by the actions he took. It was more that he didn't know how much the

Cabal now knew. While they were not vampires in the true sense of the word, they did have the ability to steal the remaining years of life from those they killed and add them to their own, and so much more. In absorbing the life force of those they murdered, the monsters who made up the Cabal also took their memories and knowledge. Whether this mental transfer was complete, or just random snatches of disjointed information, The Man in the Black Suit did not know, but it worried him. Simon had been kept in the dark regarding knowledge outside the purview of his duties. He did not know about Mina, or why she was being transported to America, for instance. But he was aware of the ultimate destination of Amenmosep, and therein lay the problem.

The journey from London, and their brief time on the ship so far, had been uneventful. But if the Cabal knew where they were taking Amenmosep, one of the oldest and most powerful of their kind, that would not be the case for long. The Cabal had already tried to take Amenmosep from the museum. Having failed in that endeavor, they would stop at nothing to retrieve him now and restore the ancient monster to life, which would be an easy enough task. The only thing stopping the mummy from regaining consciousness after his long slumber was the gold tablet placed within his wrappings. The ancient Egyptians had known the power of gold, and maybe that was why they prized it so much. As an element created in the heart of stars, it was as close to solidified sunlight as could be found. While regular daylight only caused a measure of discomfort in these horrid creatures, the concentrated power of pure gold—assuming you had enough of it and could get close enough—stopped them in their tracks and induced a sort of coma. It was the closest thing to death for members of the Cabal, and still it was not enough. Remove the gold, and the vampire sprang right back to life.

If only stakes and garlic worked like they did in literature, thought the Man in the Black Suit with a measure of sadness, then the battle would be easier to win. Maybe his own wife, taken so many years ago by one of these creatures, would still be alive. But instead, Olivia lay in a cold dark grave with her throat cut while the unholy creature that killed her lived on thanks to the unused years of her life. That was how he had come to join the organization known as The Watchers. A group who had been observing the Cabal and looking for ways to defeat them since the fifteenth century at least. In the deepest pit of his grief, while he still believed Olivia had been murdered by a human monster, they approached him and opened his eyes to the truth. They had invited him to join them. Now, all these years later, he held high office within the organization and would probably be its leader one day soon. This had provided him with a unique opportunity to pursue his own solution to the Cabal thanks to a spy buried deep inside the Order of St. George, whose approach to threats such as the Cabal was less inspired. Instead of looking for a permanent solution to their scourge, the Order merely subdued them and left the problem for future generations.

That was what had happened with Jack the Ripper, otherwise known as Abraham Turner. This particularly vile creature had been known to The Watchers for decades before Thomas Finch and Mina—a woman who had come out of nowhere and had no past—dealt with him after founding the Order of St. George at the behest of her majesty, Queen Victoria, herself.

The Man in the Black Suit had decided that they needed a man on the inside, a mole of sorts, to observe and report back on this fledgling organization. And it had been easy enough to orchestrate. This prudence had paid off. The man chosen for the job, Daniel Garrett, had been easy to turn and was more than willing to repeat the whispers within the organization about Mina. Whispers that she never aged and had somehow crossed paths with Abraham Turner over a century in the future, where they had engaged in a final battle that left her changed forever. She was neither woman nor monster, but both at the same time. And in this, The Man in the Black Suit saw an opportunity.

Then came the discovery in Egypt. A tomb in the Valley of the Kings that contained an occupant hitherto unknown to history. But he was known to the Cabal. At least through legend and lore.

So here they were, sailing to the New World on the most luxurious liner in the world. And waiting at the end of their journey was an answer gleaned from the combined secrets of their precious cargo. At least, that was what The Man in the Black Suit hoped, because then he would finally get his revenge on the monsters that had robbed him of his beloved Olivia. All he needed to do was get Mina and the slumbering creature in the hold across the ocean in safety and deliver them to Herman Reiner at their advanced facility hidden within acres of woodland in Upstate New York far from prying eyes.

"Sir?" Clay approached from the bedroom where Mina was resting in a drug-induced sleep.

"Yes?" The Man in the Black Suit turned to his underling, drawn from his dark musings.

"Are you alright?" Clay asked with furrowed brows.

"Why do you ask?"

"You've been so quiet since we lifted anchor. Unusually so."

"I'm tired. That's all." The Man in the Black Suit hoped the small lie would satisfy his companion.

"I can prepare your bunk if you would like to rest?"

"That won't be necessary." The Man in the Black Suit stepped away from the porthole. He forced a smile, which seemed to satisfy Clay, because he turned and retreated back into the room that contained Mina. But he still could not shake the feeling of unease that had stalked him since the previous day. Was the Cabal onboard the ship even now, searching for

Amenmosep, and by extension, those that dared to spirit him away? There was no way to know. All he could do was pray they weren't, and in his experience, praying rarely worked.

The Man in the Black Suit raised a hand and touched the amulet nestled under his shirt. the Cabal would come for it if they had followed him onto the ship, he was sure. Because without it, the mummified creature in the hold was powerless to regain his strength and longevity, even if the Cabal freed him. Which meant that the amulet must be kept far from those who were searching for it. Not an easy task. The Man in the Black Suit sighed and turned back to the porthole. It was going to be a long and worrisome crossing.

TWENTY-NINE

JOHN DECKER SAT in his cabin and stared at the slip of paper containing everything he knew about Mina and her captors. Three names were written on the sheet. Eleanor Swan, Charles Swan, and Stanley Burrows. These were pseudonyms of course, but that didn't matter, since those names would be the ones listed on the passenger manifest. The same manifest he had seen the purser leafing through in his office. All Decker needed was to get into that office and look at it, and then he would know where Mina was even if he didn't yet have a plan to liberate her. The question was, how to do it?

The purser had been less than helpful, and Decker didn't believe he would become any less so. But there was only one such purser aboard, at least according to the information in his cabin. The man was not only in charge of the victualing department, mostly stewards, that handled the accommodation needs of the first-class passengers, but also served as a point of contact for passengers who wished to send messages to shore via the Marconi radio or purchase tickets for the Turkish baths, squash courts, and other amenities aboard the liner. He could not staff the office twenty-four hours a day, which meant there might be an opportunity to access that manifest.

It would mean breaking into the office, though. Something he could not do while passengers and crew were milling around since the office was located next to the C deck grand staircase—one of the most trafficked locations on the ship since it provided access to first-class suites and staterooms on five decks plus restaurants, lounges, smoke room, reading room, and even a fitness center. Complicating matters was the vessel's imminent arrival in Cherbourg to collect more passengers. They were scheduled to arrive in France around six in the evening, and had Decker been able to swiftly locate and extract Mina, he would have disembarked there, but he had never thought this to be a real possibility. Queenstown on Ireland's southern coast would be his next chance to escape the doomed ship, and he had every intention of meeting that deadline. That gave him nineteen hours to complete the task he had come here to do.

For now, though, Decker was at a loose end. He decided to take a stroll and explore the ship. After all, how many times did one find themselves living such a well-known moment in history?

He picked up the gun, was about to slip it into his belt, but then thought better of it. Walking around armed was a bad idea if he didn't need to be. All it would take was for a passenger or crewmember to spot the weapon and the gun might get confiscated. Worse, he could end up in the brig, or whatever passed for such a thing on this ship. That would effectively end his quest before it began. Instead, he picked up the gun and hid it under the mattress of his bed, then left the room.

Decker descended to C deck first and approached the purser's office. He wanted to scope it out and see how easy it would be to access later. As expected, the office was closed overnight. A sign posted next to the door notified passengers that it was open from 9 A.M. to 9 P.M. The purser was still there, hunched over a stack of paperwork. He was, no doubt, preparing for the next influx of passengers when the ship stopped at Cherbourg. Decker lingered a moment, giving the flimsy looking lock on the door a surreptitious glance, then retreated before the purser noticed his interest. The last thing he wanted was anyone noticing his interest and remembering it if his late-night intrusion into the purser's office came to light, which he hoped it would not.

He returned to A deck and stepped through a revolving door into a corridor that led to the reading and writing room, and the first-class lounge beyond. He poked his head into the reading room, which looked more like a fancy parlor in a country house than a public seating area on an ocean liner. It was spacious and lavish, with a large common area and a smaller alcove divided by a porticoed doorway. Circular leaded windows that looked out onto the promenade deck admitted shafts of light that brightened the room. Silk-upholstered couches and reading chairs were interspersed among fluted columns. Miniature palm trees in pots stood in the corners, bringing a botanical feel to the room.

A steward with a white cloth draped over his arm approached Decker. "Would you like me to show you to a seat, sir?"

"No, thank you." Decker shook his head. He continued on to the first-class lounge where men and women in formal dress were gathered, talking among themselves. He wondered how many of these people were millionaires and decided that probably most of them were. After taking a minute to soak in the luxury, he made his way through the lounge, nodding at the occasional passenger who turned his way with a curious stare. Then Decker found himself in another corridor with a revolving door.

Up ahead was another staircase and the smoking room. Beyond this, according to a sign on the wall, was the verandah and palm court, whatever that was. Decker had no interest in the clogged atmosphere of the smoking room, where affluent men gathered to talk business and engage in one-upmanship. He turned around and made his way back through the first-class lounge, passed by the grand staircase, and returned to his room.

He was tired. The late-night trip to procure the chloroform he had used to subdue Thomas Finch, combined with a night of restless slumber, followed by the two-hour train journey to Southampton and time spent boarding the Titanic, had left him drained. Decker went to the narrow bed against the wall opposite a porthole beyond which he could see only a thin sliver of watery horizon. He lay down, pulled the covers up, and closed his eyes. The slight rock of the ship was comforting as the huge vessel continued its journey across the English Channel toward Cherbourg. Soon Decker fell into a fitful slumber, and waiting there, as often happened in his dreams, was Nancy. Which meant that for now, at least, he was contented.

THIRTY

AT SEVEN-THIRTY IN THE EVENING, Billy Rankin made his way out of the linen store closet on C deck and hurried past the maids' and valets' saloon toward the first-class suites forward of the grand staircase. As a bedroom steward, it was his job to make sure the wealthy travelers occupying the opulent accommodations on this deck received all the attention they expected. At least when it came to the three suites he was responsible for. These accommodations were some of the most expensive on the ship. Only a handful of larger accommodations on B deck, including the sprawling two-bedroom suites occupied by the likes of Bruce Ismay and wealthy Pennsylvania banker Thomas Cardeza, were more expensive. Those accommodations fit for kings, or in this case, millionaire businessmen, even came with their own private promenades and sitting rooms.

At the grand staircase, Rankin paused, juggling the pile of linens to remove a folded sheet of paper from his pocket. This was a list, printed in small type, of the cabins assigned to each first-class party. He had already circled the three cabins he was responsible for and now referenced the sheet of paper to make sure he was heading in the right direction. All three cabins had already been prepared in Southampton prior to the first passengers setting foot on the ship, but no sooner had they gotten underway than a mishap had occurred in cabin C 61. The lady occupying it, an older woman traveling with her industrialist husband, had spilled a small measure of red wine on the bed linens after they departed Southampton. It was his job to switch out those soiled linens for fresh ones, which he proceeded to do as soon as he got his bearings. Rankin had never worked on a ship as large as the Titanic before and had boarded only the previous day, which gave him little time to familiarize himself with the vessel's layout and the location of the accommodations he would be responsible for.

After changing out the bedsheets, Rankin gathered up the dirty linens and stepped back into the corridor after accepting a suitable tip for his efforts. Stewards on transatlantic liners were notoriously underpaid and made most of their money from gratuities. Rankin was no different.

He made his way back toward the linen store, smiling and nodding at passengers as he went. He didn't notice the two well-dressed men who followed from a discrete distance. Men who had been observing Rankin ever since he stopped to check the passenger list that was now back in his pocket. He reached the linen store and opened the door with his elbow, then stepped inside and bundled the soiled linens into a large canvas basket on wheels. Early the next morning, while the well-heeled passengers on C deck were still snuggly in their beds, another steward would take the dirty bedding to the drying room, where it would be stored at a controlled temperature to avoid mildew growth until they docked in New York. There were no laundry facilities on the ship. Not for passengers and certainly not for items such as bed linens, which were stocked in sufficient quantities to avoid such needs.

Rankin hummed a tune to himself and turned to leave the

storage room. It was only then that he noticed the two men who had been following him. They had slipped into the room behind him and quietly closed the door. Now they stood blocking his exit.

"I'm sorry, gentlemen, but this area is out of bounds to passengers," Rankin said, not so much alarmed as confused. The two men were dressed in morning suits with light-colored waistcoats and ascot ties. Both wore top hats. They certainly had no business in the linen store, but perhaps they required assistance, and Rankin was not about to spoil the opportunity for a fat tip. "Is there something I can help you with?"

"You most certainly can," said the taller of the two gentlemen, who possessed the pallid skin of one who shunned the outdoors. He took a step forward while his companion remained near the door with a hand resting on the handle. "We require information regarding the whereabouts of a certain party traveling aboard this vessel."

"I'm afraid I can't help you with that," Rankin said, swallowing hard. He sensed the threat posed by the two men who had appeared behind him and were now blocking his exit. They looked like typical first-class passengers with their fancy suits and polished shoes, but beneath the refinement, Rankin could tell they were nothing of the sort. They were dangerous. He took a step forward and tried to maneuver past them to the door. "You might want to speak with the purser. He'll be more able to help you."

"We're speaking to you," replied the gentleman, placing a hand on Rankin's chest and pushing him backward.

The other man was still standing near the door, and now Rankin realized that he wasn't merely resting his hand on the handle, but he was holding the door closed to prevent entry from the outside. He fought back a wave of panic.

"You need to step outside right now, both of you," Rankin said with all the authority he could muster.

"I don't think so." The tall man pushed Rankin against the bulkhead, then slipped a hand into the steward's pocket and removed his passenger list.

"Now listen up. You give me that back right now, or I'll have you removed from the ship," Rankin said, his voice cracking. He pushed back against his captor but found him to be surprisingly strong.

"I think perhaps we should remove *you* from the ship," the gentleman replied, passing the list to his companion before reaching into his jacket pocket and removing a deadly-looking thin-bladed knife that glinted under the light bulb attached to the ceiling inside a wire cage.

Rankin's eyes flew wide. He made another attempt to escape, but his attacker anticipated his struggle.

"I'll make your death easy," the tall man said in an almost serpentine voice. Then he slammed Rankin's head back into the bulkhead so hard that the steward was momentarily stunned even as he opened his mouth to scream for help.

The knife flashed.

Rankin felt a touch of steel against the side of his neck. Just enough to nick the artery and send blood spilling onto his white steward's jacket and the shirt beneath.

The tall man's companion stepped away from the door and took the knife, leaving the man free to remove another object from around his neck. A strange-looking stone disc with symbols etched into it, which he pressed against the small wound inflicted by his knife. He lifted the amulet to his mouth and licked it, his tongue sliding across the pitted stone surface and lapping up the blood.

Rankin regained his wits. He twisted sideways to break free of the tall man's grip and opened his mouth to shout for help, even as slick hot blood continued to pump from the wound on his neck. But before he could draw enough breath to cry out, the second man gripped him by the hair and yanked his head forward. In a movement so fast that Rankin barely comprehended it, the man pressed the knife against the back of the steward's exposed neck at the base of the skull and rammed it upward into his brain stem, severing it instantly. The last image of Rankin's life, before his consciousness snapped off like a switch, was the tall man leaning close and pressing his lips against the wound on Rankin's neck, suckling at the blood that flowed there.

———

No sooner had Rankin's life flickered out than the tall man pulled his lips away from the unfortunate steward's neck. He looked at his companion, who was wiping blood from the knife with a discarded pillowcase he had taken from the laundry cart. "Help me lift him into the hamper."

"He'll be missed," said the other man even as he helped dump the steward into the large laundry basket and throw more laundry on top to conceal him. "This was risky."

"But necessary to secure the information we needed. We'll come back later and dispose of the body. We can wheel it up on deck in the hamper later tonight when the ship is quiet and push it overboard into the Channel. If anyone comes looking for this man, they'll think he jumped ship in Cherbourg or Queenstown."

"And what if the body is discovered in the meantime?"

"It won't be," said the tall man, projecting a confidence he wasn't entirely sure of. "We've barely gotten underway. It's unlikely anyone else will come in here for fresh linens before morning. And even if they do, they won't rummage through the dirty ones and find the body."

"You can't be sure of that."

"No, I can't. But even if someone finds this man, they won't be able to tie his death back to us." The tall man took the knife back from his companion and returned it to his inside jacket pocket, then turned toward the linen store door. "Come along. Tonight, we will reclaim Amenmosep's amulet, and then he will walk among the living once more. In the meantime, let's retire to the smoking room for a brandy. I believe we deserve it."

THIRTY-ONE

MINA OPENED her eyes and was immediately overcome by an overwhelming sense of disorientation. She blinked to clear her vision and tried to think through the drug-induced haze that still clouded her mind. The last thing she remembered was the Man in the Black Suit showing up in the room she had been locked in for the past four months. With him came two underlings in white tunics who had injected her with what she assumed must have been a powerful sedative. She had a vague memory of being transferred to a wheelchair as the Man in the Black Suit looked on, and then nothing until now.

But where was she?

The small space she now occupied was swaying gently, and she could hear the faint rumble of engines mixed with lapping water. Above her was a porthole. She was aboard a ship. An ocean liner by the looks of the cabin. She was also lying on a bed with one wrist handcuffed to the headboard. A second empty bed occupied the far wall. There were two doors, one at the foot of her bed and the other on the wall opposite. One or both of them probably led into a corridor, but since she was shackled, that did her no good.

"Hello?" she called out in a rasping voice. She tugged at her restraints, but even though her strength had increased since the fateful encounter with Abraham Turner that left her changed, she could not break free. She was hungry, dehydrated, and dizzy from the drugs administered by her captors. "Is anyone there?"

She heard footsteps from somewhere beyond the cabin before the door on the far wall opened. A burly man that she didn't recognize fixed her with a narrow-eyed gaze.

"What's all the commotion in here?" he asked.

"Where am I?" Mina responded.

"You're where we want you to be. Beyond that, it's our business." The man leaned against the doorway with folded arms. "Now, keep the noise down, or it will be the worse for you."

"It's all right, Mr. Clay. She'll behave herself," said a voice from the man's rear. Mina recognized it as the person who had kept her confined for the last four months. The Man in the Black Suit. He stepped into view and looked at her. "You must be hungry, my dear."

Mina didn't reply despite the pangs that gnawed in her belly.

The Man in the Black Suit smiled. "You don't need to reply. I shall have a steward fetch you something to eat from the restaurant. I made special arrangements prior to boarding given your . . . supposed ill health. Do you have any requests?"

Again, Mina didn't reply.

The Man in the Black Suit nodded. "In that case, I shall make my best guess." He turned and left, closing the cabin door behind him.

The man named Clay sat down in a chair next to the door. He watched her with an unwavering gaze.

Twenty minutes passed in uncomfortable silence before The Man in the Black Suit reappeared carrying a tray upon which

ANTHONY M. STRONG

was a chicken sandwich cut into four neat triangles and sitting on a bed of lettuce with cherry tomatoes encircling it. A knife and fork sat next to the plate, presumably to eat the salad. A small ceramic cup of salad dressing completed the tray.

"I opted for a mundane menu item since you were loath to give me guidance. I assume this will suffice since you have eaten many such sandwiches during your stay with us." He waited for Mina to swing her legs off the bed and sit up before placing the tray next to her. Then he turned to his companion. "I would be most grateful if you would watch our guest for the rest of the evening. I shall be in the smoking room where a rather lively game of cards is taking place."

"No trouble," said Clay.

The Man in the Black Suit turned and left without another word. A moment later, Mina heard a second door open and close. She was now alone with her guard, who she might easily have overpowered if she were in full form and not handcuffed to the bed. But given her current situation, she felt it more prudent to wait and bide her time, especially since she didn't yet know where she was or if anyone else on the ship would be sympathetic to her plight. She pulled the tray close with her free hand and picked up a quarter of the sandwich, which she ate with gusto.

Clay stood up and went to the adjacent cabin before reappearing with a newspaper. He settled back into the chair and started to read.

Mina continued eating and finished the remaining sandwich in short order. Then she turned her attention to the salad. It was only when she speared a lettuce leaf with her fork and picked it up that she saw the monogram on the plate for the first time—a red flag with a single white star above the shipping line's name—and her blood ran cold because there was only one White Star Line vessel she was familiar with that sailed in April 1912.

136

She turned away from the plate and addressed the man sitting opposite her in his chair. "What ship are we on?"

Clay lowered his newspaper. "What is it to you?"

"Tell me," Mina said, her voice rising in alarm. "Please. It's important."

"Ship's name is Titanic. It's her maiden voyage. You're lucky to be traveling in such luxury. You should thank us."

Mina's breath caught in her throat. She was overcome by a surge of panic that momentarily eclipsed better judgment regarding revealing the future. "We must get off this ship, or we'll die."

"Is that right?" Her captor smirked.

"Yes. It's going to sink, and more than half the passengers and crew will die. You have to believe me."

"Nice try, but we're aboard the one ship on the planet that won't ever go down. She's unsinkable, in case you haven't heard. A marvel of modern engineering, they say."

"This ship *will* sink, and if you don't listen to me, they'll be plucking your frozen corpse out of the ocean a few days from now." Mina pushed the tray away. She had lost her appetite because it wasn't just her captors who would go down with the Titanic. Mina would, too, because she was handcuffed to a bed and could not escape. And there would be no timely rescue because in the four months she had been imprisoned, there had been no sign of Decker or the Order of St. George. No one knew where she was, and that terrified her.

Clay shook his head and returned to the newspaper with a bemused smirk. "You're going to have to do better than that if you want me to undo those handcuffs."

"It's true. I swear."

"Yeah. Well, I don't see no crystal ball anywhere in this cabin, so how about you shut the hell up and let me read?" Clay glanced back up at her. "Unless you'd like me to get my needle and send you back to sleep, that is."

That was the last thing Mina wanted. She shook her head and looked down.

"That's what I thought." Clay lifted the paper again. "Now, be a good girl and keep quiet."

THIRTY-TWO

DECKER SLEPT until nine in the evening. When he awoke, the ship had left Cherbourg and turned its bow toward Queenstown in Ireland, three hundred and seven miles distant. He rose and changed clothes, then left the cabin in search of food. He had intended to eat in the dining saloon, the cost of which was included in his ticket, but he had slept too late, and it was now closed. The only option left to him was the à la cart restaurant on B deck, and it was to this that Decker went.

When he stepped inside, its elegance immediately struck Decker. The walls were lined with French walnut paneling. Mirrors set into the paneling imitated windows to make the room feel less enclosed. The ceilings were decorated with flower and ribbon carvings that extended to the columns interspersed throughout the room. A large buffet table occupied one wall, atop which sat a feast of items like caviar, fresh lobster, and quail eggs among its more unique delights. A three-piece orchestra on a raised dais played classical music while white-shirted waiters bustled among the eager dinner guests already seated.

Decker allowed himself to be led to a table and placed his

order. Since he had a large amount of cash at his disposal thanks to Thomas Finch and the Order of St. George, and because he intended this to be his only night aboard the famous liner, Decker ordered a filet mignon, which he ate with gusto. He did not order any alcohol because he wanted to keep a clear head.

After he finished eating, Decker stood up and threw his napkin down on the table, then surreptitiously palmed a silver salad knife, which he tucked up into his sleeve. That done, he turned and left the restaurant, then wandered back through the ship and up to the promenade deck. He stepped outside into the chilly evening air and stood at the railing, staring out over the dark ocean sitting beneath a starless sky. Somewhere off in the distance, lights twinkled. He wondered if it was another ship or some faraway settlement on England's southern coast. Eventually, the lights faded, leaving only a sheet of blackness with no visible horizon and the sound of water lapping against the hull far below him.

It was almost eleven o'clock. When he had first stepped outside, there were still people strolling about and taking in the evening air, but now the promenade deck had emptied, and Decker found himself alone. That was good. It meant people were retiring to their cabins and staterooms for the night. He lingered another few minutes even though the temperature dropped to near freezing, then turned and stepped back inside.

The first-class landing and grand staircase were empty, too. The only soul Decker saw was a lone steward who rushed from the direction of the first-class lounge and headed for the accommodations in the forward section of the ship. He disappeared without a second glance.

Decker went to the grand staircase and started down. The ship felt different at night. Earlier, it had been a bustling hive of activity, with crew and passengers milling in all directions. There was laughter and excited chatter. Now the magnificent vessel was silent save for the faint rumble of engines that emanated from the bowels of the ship. He didn't encounter anyone as he descended the stairs, and a strange feeling that he was the only person left on the gigantic ship overcame him.

Decker shook the feeling off. He was on C deck now with the purser's office to his left. Since this entire section of the ship was mostly given over to first-class accommodation with only the second-class promenade encircling the second-class lounge and library toward the rear of the ship, it was unlikely he would encounter any other passengers at this late hour.

He approached the purser's office, which was locked and dark, just as he expected. A sign hanging in the window told him that the purser would return at nine a.m. the following morning.

Decker paused and glanced around, making sure that he was still alone. He took out the knife that he had removed from the à la carte restaurant earlier and slipped it into the keyhole. He applied pressure back and forth, shifting the knife to strike and lift the lever inside the lock. Soon he heard a gratifying click. But he wasn't in yet.

Decker withdrew the knife and checked to make sure he was still unobserved. Satisfied he was still alone, he pushed the knife blade between the door and the striker plate on the jamb. He wiggled it deeper until he found the bolt and leveraged it backward out of the jamb, then turned the knob with his other hand.

The door opened.

Decker breathed a sigh of relief and slipped inside, then pushed the door almost closed, making sure that the lock did not catch again because, unlike doors in the twenty-first century, this one had a keyhole on both sides, allowing it to be locked from inside the office with a key. If it closed on him and he was unsuccessful in picking the lock a second time, which was a possibility, Decker would be trapped inside the office until the purser showed up the next morning.

The office was dark, and Decker didn't dare turn the lights on. He went to the desk, but the passenger manifest was gone. Had the purser taken it with him when he retired for the night? Decker searched the area around the desk but came up empty. He opened the desk drawers and rifled through them, careful not to disturb anything and betray his presence when the purser returned in the morning.

Still nothing.

If he couldn't find that manifest, his hopes of quickly rescuing Mina would be dashed.

Then he noticed a slim drawer above the desk's seat well. He slid it open, and there was the manifest.

Decker pulled it out and sat down, then leafed through it until he found what he needed. Eleanor Swan, Charles Swan, and their supposed valet, Stanley Burrows, occupied a suite of cabins on the same deck as the purser's office. C16 and C20. Decker removed from his jacket pocket the sheet of paper containing the pseudonyms Garrett had provided during questioning and wrote the cabin numbers down. He returned the manifest and closed the drawer, then stood up and pushed the chair back against the desk just as he had found it.

He glanced around to make sure everything was in order, then stepped toward the door. But as he went to open it, voices reached his ears.

Decker froze.

They were getting closer, and judging from the conversation, they were not passengers. Was the purser returning to the office with one of his stewards? If so, they would notice his intrusion immediately since the office door now stood ajar. Yet still, he was loath to push it closed, partly because he did not wish to get trapped, but also because it would do no good. There was nowhere for Decker to hide in the small room. All he could do was wait and hope.

THIRTY-THREE

FIRST-CLASS BEDROOM steward Arthur Phillips hurried through the corridors toward the service stairs that led down to the crew quarters on E deck. This was where he would find the baggage steward, the one man on the ship who could give him permission to access cargo hold number three, located deep beneath the passenger decks near the boiler rooms.

He hated to disturb his superior at such a late hour, but when a first-class passenger asked that their belongings be fetched from below—in this instance, a suitcase that had been erroneously placed in the hold by a bellboy who misunderstood its owner's instructions upon boarding—there was no other course of action but to fetch the item. And Phillips was happy to do so even though it meant a long trek into the lowest regions of the ship and then a climb back up carrying the suitcase, which would undoubtedly be heavy, because the task would earn him a handsome gratuity, and Phillips needed every penny he could get in order to support his growing family back in Southampton.

Phillips reached the service stairs and started down. The crew quarters were located on the port side of E deck, while the starboard side comprised second and third-class cabins and even a few first-class accommodations. The baggage steward was one of twelve men who slept in the superior steward's dormitory near the aft of the vessel. It was a cramped space but nowhere near as crowded as his own accommodation, which was only a little bigger but housed more than twice that many men. Not that he would get a chance to lay his head down anytime soon. Still, the quicker he retrieved the luggage, the sooner he would be able to retire for the night. It would undoubtedly be his last task of the day.

The question was, how long would it take him to locate the item once he gained access to the hold? The luggage master kept a list that noted the placement of larger cargo items, but they would stow smaller objects, such as the suitcase, on secure racks with only the hold number provided on a claim slip given to the owner.

Phillips hurried his step and practically raced along the corridor to the dormitory. The door would be unlocked because stewards came and went at all times of day and night, depending on their duties, but he knocked anyway out of courtesy.

The man who answered was bleary-eyed and had no doubt been asleep. He wore a pair of cream-colored Long Johns, as did most crewmembers when they slept because the crew accommodations were not heated, unlike the first-class passenger cabins Phillips tended to.

"What do you want?" asked the man in a gruff voice. He was obviously annoyed at having been awoken. Most of the stewards on board started their shift early in the morning and worked long into the night, so any chance for rest was jumped upon.

"I need to see Mr. Bessant," replied Phillips, referencing the baggage steward by name.

The man grumbled and shook his head, then called over his

shoulder. "Edward. There's a bedroom steward here to see you."

A second man appeared, also wearing nighttime attire. This was Edward Bessant, and he looked about as pleased as his colleague, who was already climbing back into a bunk to the right of the door.

"What is it, man?" Bessant asked. "I have to be on duty at six a.m. to prepare for our arrival in Queenstown, so this had better be good."

Phillips swallowed hard and explained the situation.

Bessant looked perplexed. "You woke me up just to ask if you could go down to the hold?"

"Yes." Phillips nodded. "I assumed it was necessary to inform you of items removed from the hold. That was the rule on the last ship I worked on."

"Good grief, man. You could have just retrieved the bag and told me about it tomorrow. Not that you even needed to do that. If a passenger wants their belongings, just go fetch them. That's what you're paid to do."

"I apologize." Phillips realized he had made an error in judgment. He had also wasted time in visiting the baggage steward when he could have already been on his way down to find the suitcase. "It won't happen again."

"See that it doesn't." The baggage steward yawned and started to close the door. "Now, be off with you. And use some common-sense next time."

"Yes, sir. I will," stammered Phillips, but his superior had already closed the door, leaving him alone in the corridor.

THIRTY-FOUR

DECKER STOOD to the side of the purser's office door, out of sight, and held his breath. The voices sounded like they were right outside, but so far, no one had entered. He risked a quick glance through the door's inset window out onto the C deck landing and saw a pair of stewards standing five feet away, deep in conversation.

One man held a silver tray, upon which were a pair of empty plates and dirty cutlery. The remains of a room service request. The other man carried nothing. They continued their conversation and ignored the purser's office and the door that stood ajar. But all it would take was for one of them to glance sideways, and Decker would be discovered. He reached out and gripped the doorknob, easing the door further closed as much as he dared.

After a few minutes, the men finished their tête-à-tête, and the steward with the silver tray turned and started down the grand staircase to the deck below. The other steward straightened his jacket and entered the corridor on the other side of the landing, leading toward the second-class promenade.

Decker's shoulders slumped in relief. He waited a short while to make sure that neither steward was coming back and then inched the door open and slipped back out onto the landing. He pushed the door closed and used the knife to reengage the lock's bolt, repeating the process he had used earlier to gain access to the office. The purser would now be none the wiser regarding his intrusion.

The two cabins that Mina and her captors occupied were on the same deck as the office and only a short walk away, but Decker resisted the urge to go in that direction. He knew nothing about the men who were holding her and how prepared they were to defend themselves. They were surely armed. Decker had brought a gun aboard, and it was likely that Mina's captors would have done the same thing, which was why he decided to retrieve the Webley and Scott pistol from his cabin first.

Beyond this, he had no plan except to familiarize himself with the location where Mina was being kept.

He briefly considered involving the ship's crew and telling them she was being held against her will, but there was no guarantee anyone would listen to him, and even if they did, he would be putting all their lives in danger. Better to assess the situation and then decide.

Decker arrived back at his cabin and stepped inside. He went to the bed and removed the gun from under his mattress where he had hidden it earlier. Even though he knew it was loaded, he double-checked before pushing the weapon into the waistband of his trousers and letting his jacket fall over it. Then he left the cabin again and headed toward the grand staircase and C deck two floors below.

THIRTY-FIVE

CLAY HAD FINISHED READING his newspaper an hour ago and now sat quietly with his arms folded and waited for his employer to return from the smoking room. Mina had lapsed into a brooding silence ever since her ridiculous attempt to convince him the ship was going to sink in a bid to escape.

That wasn't going to happen.

Clay might not be the smartest person aboard the Titanic, but he was sure of one thing. The ship would bring them safely to New York and then Mina would discover that her troubles had only just begun. Whatever horrors she had endured in the basement of the country house outside London would pale in comparison to the procedures Doctor Reiner intended to perform in the States. Clay wasn't exactly sure what those procedures would entail, and he didn't want to because Reiner was a vicious and sadistic man who reveled in the suffering of others even as he proclaimed that his work was for the greater good.

Which it was, although that was purely circumstantial, Clay thought. Reiner would have happily carried out his experiments no matter the cause he worked for or their validity.

The newspaper was still in his lap. Clay set it aside and stood up. Mina was lying on the bed facing the other way, seemingly ignorant of his movement. But he didn't trust her. She was cunning even if the crazy claim she had made about the ship said otherwise. He went to the bed and checked that her handcuffs were still secure, then stepped out of the cabin and into the private bathroom shared with the other cabin they had booked. His bladder was full, and there was nowhere his captive could go in the few minutes that she was out of his sight.

He lifted the seat and did his business, grateful that their suite contained private facilities because most did not, even in first-class. This one even had its own bath, which meant they did not need to use the public bathing facilities aboard the ship. His employer had spent a considerable amount of money ensuring their privacy, and Clay intended to enjoy every minute of it. Even the bathroom.

He flushed and returned to Mina's cabin, whistling a little tune under his breath, and re-took his seat. With any luck, his boss would return from the smoking room soon, and then they would all retire for the night, with Clay sleeping on the second bed in the same room as Mina to keep an eye on her. That she might cause trouble while he was sleeping did not worry Clay. His years in the military had taught him to sleep with one eye open as the expression went. He would awake at the slightest sound, alert and ready for trouble. His hand found its way down to his belt and the Model 1911 Colt semi-automatic he kept there. It was a new weapon that Clay had only acquired the previous month, but he already liked it better than the Webley Mk IV service revolver he had carried previously.

He felt safer with the gun by his side, even though he doubted he would need it during the crossing. After all, part vampiric creature or not, Mina was just a slip of a girl. He had faced much worse in the Boer War and the years that followed, working for whoever was willing to pay him the most. Clay was nothing if not an opportunist, which was why he enjoyed working for The Man in the Black Suit. It was easy work and much less dangerous than fighting a war, even if his employer characterized their vendetta against the vampires as such.

And the perks were good, too.

The Army had made him sleep in the hold of a troopship along with hundreds of other men. There was nowhere soft to lay, it was constantly damp, and the smell of body odor and stale urine was unbearable. Now he got to relax on a luxury liner and eat fancy food as they steamed toward a place that offered myriad opportunities for a man such as him. Clay had landed on his feet, and he knew it.

He watched Mina. She hadn't moved and still lay with her back to him. The tray containing the remnants of her mostly eaten meal sat atop a dresser near the bed. Somehow a fly had found its way into the cabin and was circling the scraps of food on the plate in lazy circles. Clay wrinkled his nose. He hated bugs. They were dirty, and they spread disease. He picked up the tray and stepped out of the cabin into the adjacent one where his employer would sleep. He went to the door and opened it, then put the tray out in the corridor where a steward would notice it, no doubt, and take it away.

He closed the door and padded back toward Mina's cabin, stopping along the way to rummage in his travel bag, which he had stashed in the outer cabin's wardrobe earlier that day. He had brought along a couple of books to read on the journey, and he now located one before closing the bag and continuing on. But he had barely made it across the cabin when there was a soft knock. He turned, irritated. Had a steward come along already and discovered the tray? Was the man looking for a tip in order to remove it?

Clay put the book down and went to the door, then pulled it open ready to give the unfortunate steward a piece of his mind. But it wasn't a steward that waited on the other side. In fact, it wasn't a member of the ship's crew at all.

THIRTY-SIX

ARTHUR PHILLIPS MADE his way through the ship, hurrying through the passenger accommodations, and stepped outside onto the deck. He descended a set of steps, then crossed over the open area where the cranes that loaded cargo into the hold stood like a pair of silent guardians, their boom arms locked in position, hooks lashed to prevent them swinging in the brisk and frigid wind that sliced across the bow. He came to the other side and hurried back inside, relieved to be out of the weather.

He was now in the crew section, where the crew galleys and mess area were located, along with a small hospital—that was in reality just two cramped rooms with a bed in each—and a carpenter's store. He proceeded to the lamp store, and retrieved an oil lantern, then checked the fuel and wick to make sure it was in prime operating condition, because it would be beyond dark where he was going.

Leaving the store, he made his way along a short corridor toward the front of the ship. To his left was a narrow doorway. This led down into the blackest regions of the Titanic, first as a flight of stairs to the deck below, then a pair of twin spiral staircases that wound their way down through several more decks to the bottom of the vessel inside a claustrophobic oblong shaft with access to crew areas on each deck. Near the bottom, above the fireman's access tunnel that cut through Titanic's belly under the huge boilers and engines that powered the ship, was his destination.

There were six holds on the Titanic, three forward and three aft. The one he wanted was enclosed between watertight bulkheads B and C.

Phillips reached the cargo hold landing and came to a stop. The only illumination now came from his lantern. He turned up the wick to increase the light and approached a metal door set into the shaft's outer wall. Beyond this was the cargo hold.

The door was held closed by a heavy latch system, which he now disengaged. He opened the door and stepped into the hold, then closed and secured the door behind him, which was standard procedure.

That done, he stopped to get his bearings. The cargo hold was one of the biggest on the ship and fell away in all directions. He swept his lantern around, looking for the racks that contained smaller items stowed by the passengers, but saw nothing. Under his breath, he mumbled a curse. He had hoped this would be an easy fetch, but now it looked like he would have to explore the entire hold to find the suitcase. He started toward the closest bulkhead, passing by stacks of crates piled one atop the other. As he stepped between them, the light from the lantern illuminated the narrow passageway and something else.

A glint of metal flashed off to the steward's right.

He turned toward it and saw a crate with one corner busted open. Straw poked out from the jagged hole. The dockworkers must have damaged the crate when loading it, which was typical. They were a careless bunch hired straight out of the pubs around Southampton and paid by the day. Some rich toff in one of the sprawling suites above would be mad as hell when the ship docked in New York.

He shrugged and lifted the lantern to light his way forward. Damaged cargo was not his concern. But then the flash came again. Phillips turned his attention to the crate and held the lantern closer to the hole. Whatever was inside appeared to be wrapped in linen or maybe bandages. The object that caught the lantern's glow was tucked inside the cloth wrappings. He could see the corner of it poking out from under the cloth.

Phillips reached his free hand inside the crate, pushing aside the straw used as a packing material. His fingers touched the wrapped object, and he recoiled because it felt like . . . a man's arm. He fought back a wave of panic. Was there really a dead body inside this crate? A corpse wrapped up in bandages.

He almost turned and ran, deciding that whatever had caught his attention was not worth the trouble. But he could still see the object sitting there just out of reach, and for all the world, it looked like gold.

Phillips took a deep breath and quelled his nerves, then pushed his arm back into the hole and felt around, ignoring the brittle cloth under his fingers and the bumps of what he swore were desiccated ribs.

"Come on, man. Get yourself together," he said to the empty cargo hold, his voice echoing back to him off the steel walls.

With his arm in the hole, he couldn't see what he was doing, but soon his fingers brushed against cold, hard metal. He closed his hand and eased the object free, grimacing. A moment later, he withdrew his arm and looked down to see what he had found.

The object was heavy. A flat tablet of yellow metal stamped with weird writing that he couldn't read. Pictures of birds, strange scrolling lines, and half-moon shapes. They were etched into the smooth surface in rows. But it wasn't the symbols on the tablet that made his eyes grow wide with wonder. It was what the object was made of. His initial hunch had been correct. This was a bar of solid gold and must be worth a small fortune.

He wondered why such a valuable item would be stashed in a straw-filled crate along with what he was now sure was a corpse. He almost put the tablet back, but he didn't. The man who had sent him down here to fetch a suitcase would probably give him a tip that amounted to a couple of shillings at most. A paltry amount compared to how much the gold block was worth. He could sell it in New York and support his family for a year. Maybe even longer than that.

And as for the passenger who owned this piece of cargo, they would assume the tablet had been lost when the crate had busted open during loading. The White Star Line would compensate them for the damage, and all would be well. Besides, anyone who could afford first-class passage on such an elegant liner—because Phillips knew it wasn't some poor steerage passenger who had brought such a large crate aboard —could afford to lose a small golden trinket such as this. But to Phillips, the money would mean salvation.

His wife was pregnant for the third time, and they could barely feed the mouths already occupying their small cottage on the outskirts of town. There would be plenty of time in New York to hawk this item to some backstreet pawnbroker, and no one would be any the wiser. By the time he was back in England, the money would be untraceable, even assuming anyone bothered to ask how he could come by such an amount.

With his spirits raised and a smile on his lips, Phillips slipped the gold tablet into the inside pocket of his jacket and continued. A minute later, he stumbled upon the rack that contained the suitcase, further convincing Phillips that it was his lucky day. Now he wouldn't have to search the rest of the hold.

It was sitting on a top shelf with the baggage tag visible and the cabin number printed on it. He set the lantern on the floor and then raised himself on tiptoe to reach for the luggage.

At that moment, a splintering crash echoed from the direction in which he had just come.

Phillips gave a surprised squeal and whirled around, peering into the gloom for the source of the noise. Had another crewmember come down here and accidentally knocked something over? It didn't seem likely. But it was also not likely that a piece of cargo would have fallen on its own. He wondered if it was the crate within which he had found the gold tablet. Had he somehow disturbed it when he retrieved the treasure? That was impossible. It was sitting lower to the ground than most other crates, and he had only reached inside. He hadn't moved it.

Still, it was quiet again now. If some poorly placed cargo had tumbled to the ground, it was not his concern.

Phillips gave the darkness beyond the lantern one more look, then started to turn back toward the suitcase high on the shelf. Then he heard a footstep, followed by another. And after that, a low snuffling noise that made the steward's blood freeze in his veins.

THIRTY-SEVEN

DECKER MADE his way down to C deck without a clear plan. He knew Mina was being guarded by two men and which cabins they occupied, but beyond that, little else. Were more people associated with the Man in the Black Suit aboard the ship? It was likely that Garrett had told Thomas Finch all he knew, but that didn't mean he knew everything. Proof of this was evident in the fact that Garrett was aware of the pseudonyms Mina's captors would be traveling under, but not where Mina was being held prior to boarding the ship. Whatever group had snatched Mina was, apparently, just as secretive as the Order.

Which left Decker with a problem.

If he barged into that room, he would no doubt meet stiff opposition from those within. Even if he could subdue them, it didn't prevent the possibility that Decker would still find himself outmatched and outnumbered by people Garrett had not mentioned. Yet Decker did not have the luxury of time. In less than twelve hours, the Titanic would arrive in Queenstown, which would be his last opportunity to disembark before the gigantic liner set its sights on New York. A trip it would never complete. That meant Decker had no choice but to liberate Mina quickly, which also meant he must take a significant risk.

When he weighed up the odds, Decker decided he had no choice but to gain entry to the cabin where Mina was being held and deal with whatever unforeseen circumstances presented themselves.

But first, he wanted to scope out the location of the cabins occupied by the supposed Mr. and Mrs. Swan and their valet.

Decker descended the grand staircase to C deck and then headed for the port side first-class corridor forward of the landing. It was eerily quiet, with no sign of other passengers or crew. He walked at a leisurely pace, as if he hadn't a care in the world, while his hand rested close to the gun concealed under his jacket. The cabins he was looking for were up ahead on the left. Decker counted down the cabin numbers and slowed as he approached them.

His plan had been to saunter past, at least on his first pass. He wasn't sure what this would gain him other than familiarizing himself with their location, but Decker had learned that patience was always better than haste.

The suite of cabins occupied by Mina and her captors had two entrances. The door to cabin C 20 was down a short access corridor with a porthole at its end. C 16 would be in another corridor tangential to the one he was now traversing but further along. This corridor also had access to a third cabin that could be booked to create a three-room suite. Garrett hadn't said if the people who took Mina had also booked that cabin, but he suspected as much. After all, they wouldn't want a stranger in such close proximity who might hear Mina if she cried for help. He didn't know which of the cabins Mina occupied but decided it didn't matter. He would check each one in turn before planning his next move.

Decker reached the access corridor for cabin C 20 and turned left, intending to scope it out quietly. If anyone saw him, which was unlikely, he would simply pretend to be lost. But when he drew close, Decker noticed something odd about the cabin door.

It was not completely closed.

The door stood an inch ajar, which would probably have gone unnoticed by all but the most observant passerby, of which there would be few in this lightly trafficked accessway, especially at this time of night.

But it set Decker's internal alarm bells ringing.

Kidnappers rarely left doors unlocked, let alone unlatched. He stopped and listened but heard no sound from within the cabin. Decker reached under his jacket and slipped out the pistol, which he held in the low ready position as he had been taught during his NYPD days as a homicide detective, and nudged the door open wider with the toe of his shoe.

If he expected any response, there was none.

Decker waited a moment to ensure no one would come charging from within the cabin, then stepped across the threshold.

He soon discovered why there had been no resistance to his entry. A man was sprawled on the floor between the cabin's beds. He lay face up in a widening pool of his own blood, which flowed from a gash that had opened his neck under the jawline. At first, Decker thought he was dead, but then the man let out a barely perceptible moan.

Decker glanced around quickly to make sure the attacker was not still present, but apart from the wounded man, the room was otherwise empty. He kneeled down. The man was trying to say something. His lips were moving, but he was too weak.

Decker leaned forward and placed an ear close to the man's mouth.

The dying man coughed, then spoke in a barely audible rasping voice. "Vampires. Two of them. Both ma . . ." Another coughing fit wracked his body. He drew in a gasping breath. "Both male. They . . ."

Another cough.

The man's eyes grew wide, as if he knew what lay in store for him, then he let out a last rattling breath, and his face slackened. The man was dead.

Decker climbed quickly to his feet. His thoughts turned to Mina, and an icy dread enveloped him. Had she also fallen victim to the same murderer as the man in this cabin?

Scared of the answer but needing to know, he crossed quickly to a door that led into a short inner hallway connecting the cabins. Decker was relieved to find it empty. Then his gaze alighted on a pair of wrought-iron handcuffs that lay discarded on the bed. Next to these was a key, no doubt liberated from the gentleman in the other cabin. This must be where they had been holding Mina. Her handcuffs had been removed, which meant she was probably still alive. That was better than the alternative. But where was the third occupant of the cabin? Taken along with Mina?

Decker slipped the gun back into his belt and returned to the first cabin. He kneeled next to the dead man again, careful to avoid the crimson halo of blood, intending to searching him for clues. But before he could do so, there was a sound at his rear.

Footsteps.

Decker turned, whipping the pistol back out, to find himself looking down the barrel of a gun.

THIRTY-EIGHT

PHILLIPS SWIVELED AROUND, prickles of fear running up his spine, just in time to see a shape emerge from the darkness. A lumbering twisted form that looked almost like a man. Except its skin was leathery and dry, and it loped forward with its back hunched and arms dangling. Pieces of dirty cloth hung from its frame as if it had clawed its way out of the bandages that wrapped it. But it was the face that scared Phillips the most. It had the countenance of a corpse with dull, dead eyes and a slack jaw filled with jagged teeth.

Phillips stumbled backward until his back bumped the rack, then he turned and ran. In his haste to escape, he tripped and inadvertently kicked the lantern, which tipped over and extinguished with a tinkle of broken glass.

Darkness rushed in around him.

Phillips fled into the dimly lit hold as fast as he dared. He bumped into a stack of crates, sending the top one tumbling to the deck, but he didn't care. He could hear the creature behind him, and it was getting closer.

He stumbled forward, eyes darting to the left and right as his vision grew accustomed to the gloom. Phillips was utterly turned around. He had no clue how to reach the spiral staircase leading to the upper decks and safety. He tried to retrace his steps but found himself hopelessly lost amid a maze of barrels, crates, and shipping boxes.

Behind him, somewhere off in the darkness, he could hear the creature shuffling along. Phillips stifled a whimper and kept going. He ducked left between another pile of crates, then right and left again in an attempt to lose the impossible creature that was now stalking him. He risked a glance over his shoulder and, in doing so, smacked his leg into a box with the words 'French wine' stenciled on the top. He pitched forward and hit the deck. The wind burst from his lungs. Red hot stabs of agony flared up his leg and his wrist twisted underneath him as he landed. For a moment, he thought it might be broken, but then the pain ebbed, and he could think clearly again. All he wanted to do was lay there until his battered body didn't hurt anymore, but there was no time to nurse his wounds. He scrambled back to his feet and staggered forward, praying he would find a way out.

Then, up ahead, a shape loomed. He recognized it as a motorcar. One of the expensive toys the millionaire industrialists liked to drive around the city as if they were better than everyone else. But now it represented something else—a place to hide.

Phillips pushed himself to move faster and reached the vehicle. It was a large automobile with an open front cab, white tires, and sweeping lines. Two large headlights sat at the front, looking like a pair of bug eyes. A badge on the front identified the car as a Renault town car.

This was the closest he'd ever been to such a fine vehicle, and under different circumstances, he would have stood and marveled at it, but now he raced to the enclosed rear cabin and tugged on the door handle. Mercifully, it opened, and he tumbled inside, closing it again as quietly as possible.

He lay in the well beneath the seat and held his breath. How far behind him had the creature been when he climbed into the car? Had it seen him crawl inside? Phillips didn't know. But hiding here was better than running around blindly in the cargo hold, looking for a spiral staircase he might never find in the darkness.

Something hard and uncomfortable was digging into his rib cage. He realized it was the gold tablet he had found in the busted crate. He slipped it from his pocket and laid it on the floor in the seat well. The creature that now stalked him had been in that crate along with the strange tablet, swathed in cloth bindings. He was sure of it.

An image sprang into his mind. There was only one type of corpse he knew that was wrapped in cloth—an Egyptian mummy. But ancient dead guys from sand-filled tombs didn't come back to life, and they certainly didn't chase people through the hold of a modern ocean liner. Yet the evidence of his own eyes did not lie. Somehow, even though it made no sense in a rational world, a monster had broken out of that crate and was now hunting him. The question was, how long would it keep looking?

He glanced at his wristwatch but could not see the dial in the car's pitch-black interior. It felt like he had been hiding here for a while—at least fifteen minutes. Maybe the creature had given up. He shifted position and sat up, maneuvering himself onto the red leather bench seat and peering cautiously out the side window.

He saw nothing but darkness and the vague outlines of stacked cargo before his breath fogged the window, and he was forced to swat the condensation away. When he did, his heart almost slammed out of his chest.

The creature hadn't given up. It was slinking toward the car down a narrow alley between two towering stacks of crates and moving his head from side to side in a slow sweeping motion.

Phillips sucked in a startled breath and dropped back onto the seat, scooting as low as he could. Maybe it would continue right past the motorcar without even giving it a second glance. After all, if this creature really were an ancient Egyptian mummy come to life, it would have no idea what an automobile was or that someone could climb inside. But even as he convinced himself that his hiding place was safe, a shadow fell across the car's interior.

The creature paused, its silhouetted form visible beyond the window.

Phillips didn't dare move. He bit his lip to stop the whimper of fear that bubbled up. Then he heard a scratch of nails on metal, and the car's passenger side door handle slowly lowered.

The door swung open.

Phillips willed himself to escape. The driver's side door was right there. All he had to do was scramble out and run. Except his legs would not work. He was frozen by fear.

A bulbous, leathery head with scraps of hair still clinging to the scalp pushed its way past the door. Pale milky eyes swiveled in his direction. The creature inched forward into the enclosed cabin.

Now Phillips found the will to move. He screamed and scooted toward the opposite door even as the creature lunged forward with its own rasping cry of glee. It landed atop him like some macabre lover and gripped his jacket with bony hands, pushing him back down onto the bench seat even as Phillips was reaching for the driver's side door. But he never found the handle. Instead, his open palm slapped into cold hard glass, and his fingers trailed down the window as the creature lowered its head toward his neck, mouth open, and ended the young steward's life.

THIRTY-NINE

"IT'S YOU," said Decker, jumping to his feet, keeping his pistol squarely aimed at his adversary. He had suspected this man was aboard ship—the same man he had seen in Mavendale months before—and now he had confirmation. "What have you done with her? Where's Mina?"

"I could ask you the same question," said the Man in the Black Suit, his gaze falling to the dead valet even as he kept his own gun trained on Decker. "After all, I'm not the one who got caught stooped over a dead body."

"I didn't kill this man. I found him like this."

"I believe you." The Man in the Black Suit nodded toward Decker's firearm. "It ill behooves us to engage in a futile standoff that will advantage neither party. I suggest you lower your weapon so that we may talk like civilized men."

"How about you go first," Decker replied. "I promise not to shoot you . . . yet."

"Very well." the Man in the Black Suit hesitated a moment, then lowered his gun and returned it to his inside jacket pocket. "Your turn."

Decker pushed his gun back into his belt.

The Man in the Black Suit stepped into the cabin and closed the door. He looked down at his colleague, then stepped over him and went to Mina's cabin. "She's gone."

"Yes. Not my doing, unfortunately. She was gone when I got here."

"So, if you didn't kill Mr. Clay, then who did? Mina herself, perhaps."

"No. Your valet was still alive, barely, when I got here. He was able to identify his killers. Vampires. Two of them. Male."

The Man in the Black Suit lowered his head. "Then my suspicions were correct." He sighed. "I believe I may have underestimated our enemies, Mr. Decker. I should not have left my valet alone with the girl for so long. It was an unfortunate oversight."

"Our enemies?"

"Why yes. I can assure you that the creatures who did this are as much your enemy as mine."

Decker knew he was right.

"They must have taken Mina."

"That would be a reasonable assumption."

Decker looked down at the dead man. "I suppose you are aware of what these creatures can do?"

"I am, which is a grave concern. I don't take many people into my confidence, but Clay knew of my plans by necessity."

"Which means the vampires probably know them now."

"Yes. This cabin is no longer safe to occupy."

"Why?" Decker asked. "They have what they came for. They took Mina, and they surely know about the mummy in the hold. What reason could they have to come back here?"

"Just one that I can think of." The Man in the Black Suit reached inside his shirt and withdrew a chain holding an amulet. Decker recognized it right away, even though the designs carved into it looked more Egyptian than those on Abraham Turner's trinket. "It belonged to Amenmosep and was the key to his power. I thought it prudent not to ship it along with the mummy, for obvious reasons."

"Amenmosep is still alive."

"Precisely, although in a deep gold-induced slumber, thanks to the ancient Egyptians. The archaeologist who discovered his tomb had no clue what he was meddling with."

"That archaeologist died in the theft you orchestrated," said Decker angrily. "He wasn't a part of this."

"His death was an unfortunate accident, and the man who shot him has been punished. I can assure you of that. I would also remind you that we lost one of our own men in that same theft simply because he went back to render assistance to the dying man. I suspect it was his death at the hands of those creatures that led the vampires to this ship."

"If they resurrect Amenmosep, it won't end well."

"You have a knack for stating the obvious, Mr. Decker. Amenmosep is one of the most powerful vampires that ever lived. He might even be the first of his kind. As such, he is supremely dangerous."

"And yet you chose to steal his mummy and transport it to America."

"If we hadn't, the vampires would already have it. They also tried to steal him from the museum but arrived too late. Besides, it was a risk we were willing to take. If our work is successful, we can rid the planet of these creatures once and for all."

"And do God knows what to Mina in the process." Decker felt like taking the gun back out and shooting The Man in the Black Suit where he stood. But he didn't, because right now that man was the only one who might know how to get Mina back.

"I understand your anger, Mr. Decker. I really do. But we

needed Mina in order to discover the vampire's weaknesses. We still do."

"You're not getting your hands on her again. I promise you that."

"That remains to be seen." The Man in the Black Suit shrugged. "But right now, we have a common goal. We both want to find Mina, and quickly. We also want to make sure those creatures do not get their hands on Amenmosep's amulet."

"That much, at least, we agree upon," said Decker grudgingly.

"Good. In that case, I propose a truce. Until such time as our mutual objectives are fulfilled and we are safely in New York, we should work together."

"The enemy of my enemy is my friend, you mean?"

"Something like that, although I doubt we will ever be friends."

"You're a perceptive man," said Decker. He didn't want to work alongside the people who had taken Mina, but he saw no other choice, at least in the short term. "If we are going to do this, we have to trust each other. I'll need to know your name. And don't give me the name you boarded the ship under. I already know that Charles Swan is a pseudonym."

The Man in the Black Suit smiled. "Charles Swan isn't totally fictitious. It was my grandfather's name on my mother's side. But you're right, if we are going to work together, there should be a measure of trust. I'll make the first move and hope that you will reciprocate should the time come. My real name is Ignatius Faucher."

"Thank you."

"You're welcome." Faucher crossed his arms. "Now we must address the next problem. What to do about the dead body currently soiling the floor of my cabin."

FORTY

DECKER DIDN'T KNOW how to respond to his new partner regarding the murdered man at their feet. The situation had spiraled out of control, and he was now in an impossible situation. If they reported the murder, there would be an investigation when the Titanic reached Queenstown. The police would come aboard, and the vessel would be held in port until a satisfactory resolution had been reached. That would delay the ship, and she would not cross paths with an iceberg and sink, altering history and causing the timelines to branch in order to account for the paradox—at least if Rory's hypothesis regarding how time travel worked was correct. That could have unknown ramifications on Decker's quest to save Mina and return home. On the other hand, Mina's arrival in the past and all that followed, including her hand in creating the Order of St. George, appeared to have been preordained and part of the original timeline. Since those events led directly to the current situation, he found himself in a rare moment of paralysis regarding how to proceed.

Faucher observed him with an unreadable stare. "I suppose

you are going to suggest that we report this tragic incident to the relevant crewmembers."

"I'm not sure what we should do," Decker admitted.

Faucher nodded. "My first inclination is to conceal the body, difficult as that might be, so as not to draw unwanted attention upon myself. But in this case, I'm not sure that would be a prudent course of action. Our silence will give the creatures who took Mina an opportunity to disembark in Queenstown and disappear. If that happens, neither of us will ever see her again. Likewise, they may try to offload Amenmosep, after trying to relieve me of his amulet, that is. But if we report the murder, the authorities will not allow anyone to disembark. Further, if we report Mina's abduction, they will initiate a ship-wide search which might return her to us. Either way, she won't be getting off the ship in Queenstown."

"You're kidding me, right?" Under different circumstances, Decker would have laughed. "The man who abducted Mina wants to report her abducted a second time from his own captivity?"

"Have you got a better idea?"

"Might I remind you, Mr. Decker, that we are traveling under meticulously crafted false identities that I assure you will hold up to scrutiny. As far as anyone on this vessel is concerned, my name is Charles Swan, an old money millionaire with friends in high places. They will take the murder of my valet and the abduction of my wife most seriously."

"And what happens if they find Mina and she disputes your story, which she undoubtedly will?" Decker asked.

"Trust me, we planned for the remote possibility that she might either converse with a member of the crew or somehow escape. Are you familiar with the work of the Swiss psychiatrist Paul Eugen Bleuler?"

"I can't say that I am. What does a Swiss psychiatrist have to do with any of this?" Decker asked.

"He classified Mina's condition. Or at least the illness we used as a cover story for her inability to leave the cabin during our voyage. We also thought the same fabrication would be useful in unforeseen circumstances, such as those we now find ourselves in. Have you heard of dementia praecox?"

Decker shook his head.

"It's an archaic term that was used as a catchall for several unfortunate conditions of the mind until Doctor Bleuler came along and refined the concept. In doing so, he provided us with a wonderful way to keep her sequestered in her cabin and explain any contradictions Mina might make with the pseudonyms under which we are traveling. Doctor Bleuler calls his new disease schizophrenia."

"No one's going to believe that Mina has a split personality," Decker said. "That's ridiculous."

"Is it?" Faucher's lips curled up into a condescending smile. "Her entire identity is already a fabrication. She didn't even exist before the 1880s when she arrived in London as a young woman in her early twenties. She hasn't aged perceptibly since that time. And even if she could explain those anomalies, she would sound crazy if she claimed to work for a secret government organization that chases monsters. So, you tell me, Mr. Decker, who is more likely to be believed . . . The woman with a fantastical story that can't be verified, or the loving husband who says she is sick with an illness of the mind?"

"You're forgetting one thing," Decker said. "I'll be there to back up her story."

"Ah, yes. I thought of that. But it would not be in your best interest to cause such trouble while we are still aboard the ship. Your own past is even murkier than Mina's. We've done our homework, and you didn't exist until four months ago. Think how that will look to the authorities in Queenstown, or when you try to disembark in New York, for that matter. So you see, staying quiet benefits you as much as it does I, and hopefully, Mina will see it the same way."

"You won't get away with this."

"I beg to differ, but who knows, maybe you're right. In the meantime, we are uncomfortable bedfellows. So what of it? Do we report this murder, or do we risk the Cabal taking Mina off the ship at the earliest possibility and losing her forever?"

Decker didn't have a good answer because he felt there wasn't one. If they reported the murder, he risked breaking the timeline, but if they didn't, he might never see Mina again. In the end, he shrugged, deciding that since Mina was probably destined to end up in this situation regardless, the best thing he could do was allow it to play out without interference and hope that the universe could cope. "You got us into this situation. You can get us out of it."

"Very well." Faucher cast a rueful glance toward the body. "Let us raise the alarm."

FORTY-ONE

THOMAS KING, Titanic's Master-at-Arms, and the closest thing to a policeman aboard the ship, stood with his hands on his hips and looked down at the corpse lying in front of him. Behind King, standing in the cabin's narrow access corridor, were two men of considerably higher rank. Bruce Ismay was the chairman of the White Star Line. William Murdoch was the ship's first officer and reported directly to the captain. Both men had been roused from their beds minutes after the murder in cabin C 20 was reported, and they now stood anxiously by while King conducted his preliminary investigation.

"You say this man's name is Stanley Burrows, and he was your valet?" King asked Faucher, referencing James Clay's pseudonym.

Faucher nodded slowly. "Yes. I spent the last several hours playing cards in the smoking room, and when I came back, I discovered him dead and my wife missing."

"And your wife's name would be?"

"Eleanor. We are traveling to the United States so that she can receive treatment for a condition of the mind. I fear that whoever killed my valet must have taken her."

"Or she heard the commotion and fled to avoid meeting a similar fate," King said.

"If that were the case, she would have contacted a member of the crew by now, surely," Faucher replied.

Decker stepped forward. Before calling for the Master-at-Arms, Decker and Faucher had stashed the handcuffs and their guns in Decker's cabin on A deck lest they be discovered. "I think it's unlikely she fled since several hours have passed, and there is no sign of her."

"I agree, but we must rule out the possibility before jumping to the conclusion she was abducted." King observed Decker with a wary gaze. "I didn't catch your name."

"John Decker."

"Thank you. Would you mind telling me how you became involved in this incident?"

"I'm a friend of Mr. Swan," Decker replied, then launched into the cover story he and Faucher had concocted while waiting for the Master-at-Arms to show up. "I crossed paths with him on his way back from the smoking room, and he invited me to his cabin for a nightcap. That's when we found the valet dead and his wife missing."

"Ah." King turned his attention back to Faucher. "Can you think of any reason why someone would want to murder your valet and abduct your wife, Mr. Swan?"

"I cannot." Faucher shook his head. "And right now, I'm more concerned with how you intend to handle the situation and the motives behind it. I would very much like Eleanor returned to me."

"I understand your concern." King rubbed his chin and glanced back down at the body. "The first thing we must do is report the incident to the authorities in Queenstown. We should leave the crime scene exactly as it is. Naturally, we will also initiate a thorough search for your wife."

"Look here, I think we should talk about this," said Ismay,

speaking for the first time. "A murder on board less than twenty-four hours out of port? That isn't going to reflect well upon the Titanic or the White Star Line."

"How would you suggest we handle it," asked King, turning to him.

"First off, I don't believe we should have this conversation here with the cabin door open. It is far too public, and although most passengers are asleep, we cannot preclude the possibility of someone overhearing us and learning of this unfortunate incident."

"You're right, of course. We should discuss this in private." King looked back at Faucher. "You know if anyone is occupying the third cabin in this suite?"

"It's empty," Faucher replied. "We booked all three cabins so that we would not be disturbed, even though we are only using two of them."

"Very good." King motioned for Ismay and Murdoch to follow him. "We'll take our conversation into the cabin next door where we cannot be so easily heard." He turned to Decker and Faucher. "I would like the two of you to remain here."

Decker nodded and stepped aside to let the three men pass. They cut a wide path around the body and disappeared into the second cabin, closing the door. Soon after, he heard muted voices, too low to understand.

Decker looked at Faucher. "Still think this is a good idea?"

"I think we're committed either way." Faucher watched the door with a concerned look on his face. "Although I suspect that Ismay and the first officer are none too happy about this turn of events. It won't surprise me if they try to keep it quiet."

"That won't be easy."

"On the contrary, we are in their domain, and they control the narrative. It will be exceptionally easy."

"You really think they would cover up a murder?"

"It wouldn't be the first time they have engaged in a cover-up. For example, there has been a large coal fire raging in the ship's belly since before the Titanic left Belfast. The fire is consuming coal at a frenetic rate and cannot be brought under control due to its size. Given recent events, namely the coal strike, which has surely left the vessel with less coal than they would normally carry, I would be surprised if they have enough fuel to reach New York without traveling at a reckless speed."

"And how would you know this?" Asked Decker.

Faucher smiled thinly. "I have my sources, Mr. Decker, just as you do."

"Then why did you board the ship if you knew this information?"

"Coal fires are common aboard vessels such as this, although they are not usually so large. And the added speed will allow us to reach New York quicker, which suits my agenda."

I wouldn't be too sure of that, thought Decker, but he kept the observation to himself. Behind him, the cabin door opened. Ismay, Murdoch, and King had returned. And they had apparently come to a decision.

King cleared his throat to speak, looking slightly uncomfortable. "It has been decided that we will defer this matter until New York. The police there are better able to handle a murder investigation. The body will be removed and placed in cold storage during the interim."

"You can't be serious," Faucher said. "I demand that you deal with this situation promptly and that you also find my wife."

Ismay took up the reins. "I assure you, Mr. Swan, that we considered all eventualities when coming to this decision. We will, of course, start a ship-wide search for your wife and alert all the stewards to keep their eyes open and report any suspicious activities. She is still on the ship, and we will find her. As for the murder of your valet, our decision has been made."

"And what if the killer disembarks in Queenstown?" Decker asked.

"There are only seven passengers scheduled to leave the ship in Ireland," said First Officer Murdoch. "We will, of course, scrutinize each of them to make sure they are not involved with this incident prior to their departure from the Titanic. We will also bar any other passengers or crew from leaving in order to preserve the pool of suspects."

Decker groaned inwardly. Only the seven passengers who held tickets as far as Queenstown would be allowed off the ship. That presented a problem. Even if he could locate Mina, they would have trouble disembarking. But he would deal with that problem when he came to it. Right now, there were more immediate matters to attend to, like figuring out how to work alongside Faucher without delivering Mina right back into his clutches and keeping Amenmosep's amulet out of the hands of those who would use it to resurrect him.

Ismay rubbed his hands together and addressed the Master-at-Arms. "I'm sure you are quite capable of taking care of the situation from this point onward."

King nodded. "That I am, sir."

"Excellent." Ismay turned to his first officer. "Well, the situation seems to be in hand, don't you think?"

Murdoch nodded. "I do."

"In that case, we shall retire to our staterooms." Ismay nodded at Decker and Faucher. "Good night, gentlemen." Then he turned with the first officer at his heel, stepped out of the cabin, and disappeared into the dark corridors.

Decker watched them go with a pit in his stomach. The

situation had taken a dire turn. Mina was in an even worse situation than before, and the ship was effectively locked down. Like it or not, he might find himself along for a ride that ended in disaster.

FORTY-TWO

MINA SAT and looked up at the two men who had come to the cabin where she was being held captive and killed her guard. They were monsters, just like Jack the Ripper. She knew this not only because of the way they had dispatched The Man in the Black Suit's associate but also because she sensed it. Ever since absorbing the energy and powers of Abraham Turner, she had been able to identify others of his kind simply by being close to them. She had learned of this unique ability while trailing the nineteenth-century version of Abraham Turner prior to sending Abberline and Finch to subdue him. Turner had sensed her, too. That was why she hadn't been present on the night they walled him up in his own basement. Now she had the same strange feeling, almost like a bad case of the chills, in the presence of these monsters.

That sixth sense, shared by the two men who now studied her, had probably saved Mina's life. If they had not recognized her as one of their own, they would have wasted no time dispatching her, just as they had her guard, who was killed before he could even draw his gun. A weapon they had subsequently removed from his body and held on her as they decided what to do with their unexpected discovery.

At first she thought they would simply cut her throat and drain her lifeforce just as they had that of the guard—Mina was not a full vampire and suspected she lacked their resilience to violent death—but they hadn't. Instead, they had removed her handcuffs and told her to get dressed, then led her away to their own suite of cabins, which, while still first-class, were smaller and less grand than those in which she had been previously imprisoned. Mina had allowed them to take her under the assumption that if they thought she was one of their kind, no immediate harm would befall her. On the other hand, resistance would likely lead to a swift death. She was stronger since absorbing Turner's powers, but no match for two full-blooded vampires.

"You feel wrong," one of the men said in a silky voice. "One of us, but also, not. What kind of creature are you?"

"I'm just like you," Mina said, holding up her arm and pulling her sleeve back to reveal the brand that had burned itself there on the night Abraham Turner's powers had flowed into her. Her new captors would both carry the same symbol on their own arms, because it was, for all intents and purposes, the mark of the vampire. "See?"

"That isn't true." The second man ignored her gesture. He reached out and cupped her chin, forcing her gaze up to his. "Tell us the truth, or it will be the worst for you."

"Very well." Mina had no intention of telling them she was responsible for Abraham Turner's disappearance and ultimate demise, but there was a version of the truth that might satisfy them. "I'm a victim of Jack the Ripper. His last victim, to be precise. He was killing me when two men showed up. They were carrying a knife made of gold, which they used to kill him. Because he was stealing my life force when his own existence was extinguished, the process reversed itself, and I took his instead. I became one of you."

"Impossible. We have an aversion to gold. It can subdue us, at least temporarily, but it cannot kill us."

"I beg to differ. This was no regular blade. It was of ancient Sumerian origin, made of the purest gold. It was also smeared with the blood of his previous victim to link the blade directly to him."

"That still wouldn't be enough to kill one of us."

"But it did. My best guess is that because Turner was stealing my life force when he got stabbed, it weakened him and threw the entire process in reverse. I took his life force instead."

"Which makes you complicit in his murder."

"Except I had nothing to do with it. I was his victim and did not know the men who killed him. Only afterward did I learn they were with a group called the Order of St. George."

"If that's true, how did you come to be here, a captive on this ship?"

Mina was taken aback. She had assumed the vampires had shown up because they had sensed her. However, it appeared they were unaware of her presence until they stumbled upon her in the cabin. "The men who saved me from the clutches of Abraham Turner were unaware of my transformation. They took me to a hospital, fearing I would die, but I quickly recovered thanks to my new abilities and escaped before they realized what I was. After that, I spent many years hiding before I fell afoul of the men you found me with. They are not from the Order of St. George. They are something much darker. They have kept me captive for several months and experimented on me, trying to learn the secrets of my condition."

"We know of these people and their goals. They stole the mummified body of a Founder. A man named Amenmosep who was one of the first of our kind. He was imprisoned millennia ago by the ancient Egyptians, who feared his power. Now he is in the ship's hold, and the men who captured you have his amulet."

"You want to resurrect him," Mina said, a chill running up her spine.

"Yes. We came to that cabin looking for the amulet. Instead, we found you."

"For which I am most grateful," Mina replied, doing her best to sound sincere. "I fear what they would have done to me had you not released me from their clutches."

"Don't rejoice yet," said the first vampire. "Your story intrigues us, but it is far from conclusive."

"And if it is true," said the second, "you were instrumental in the death of our brother."

"As I already told you, I had no hand in what occurred except to be in the wrong place at the wrong time." Mina wondered if she had made a mistake in twisting the truth to explain her circumstances. But what other choice did she have? "I did not ask for this nor did I plan for it, but regardless, Abraham Turner lives on inside of me and like it or not, I am now one of you."

"That much is true, which is why you are still alive. No vampire has ever been created in this manner before, and we were unaware it was possible. For that knowledge, we give you our thanks."

Mina wondered how the vampires did propagate their species. It would be valuable knowledge that might help in future encounters. But she knew better than to ask. Instead, she smiled and met the gaze of her latest captors with all the confidence she could gather. "If you don't mind, gentlemen, I would like to rest. I have been through a grueling ordeal, and I am in your debt for my newfound safety."

The vampires observed her for a moment, then one of them

spoke up. "Very well. You may rest for now. But be warned, the outer cabin door is locked, and we will be close by. Please do not mistake our benevolence for trust. That, you must earn."

"I understand and would do the same if the situation were reversed," Mina said. She needed them to trust her—or at least enough not to restrain her again—because the Titanic would soon arrive in Queenstown, and that was where she intended to disembark, leaving these monsters to their fate at the bottom of the North Atlantic, regardless of their ability to cheat death. But for now, there was time. The Titanic would not reach Ireland for many hours, and this was as good a place as any to hide from her previous captors and contemplate her new ones, while she formulated a plan.

FORTY-THREE

AFTER BRUCE ISMAY and First Officer Murdoch departed, Decker and Faucher found themselves alone with the Master-at-Arms, who turned to them with a grim look on his face. "I understand your frustration in waiting until New York to take care of this unfortunate situation. However, I assure you we made it with the best intentions."

"Don't give me that," Faucher said. "You just want to protect the reputation of this vessel and the White Star Line because it wouldn't look good to end up embroiled in a murder investigation before you've even gotten out of the English Channel."

"I assure you, sir, that is the farthest thing from our minds. The police in New York are better able to handle murder investigations than the small police force in Queenstown who are not used to such things."

"It doesn't matter," Decker said, turning to Faucher. "They've made up their minds."

"Yes, they have," Faucher replied bitterly. "My valet was a good man and didn't deserve to die in such a gruesome manner. I would also remind you that my wife is at the mercy of the fiends who did this."

"I'm well aware of the situation and will inform the victualing staff to keep their eyes and ears open. Have no fear, Mr. Swan, we will reunite you with your wife."

"Victualing staff?" Faucher snorted. "You're going to leave the recovery of my wife in the hands of a bunch of stewards, cooks, and scullions?"

"I assure you, we are more than capable of conducting a search for Mrs. Swan." If the Master-at-Arms was annoyed, he kept it from his voice. "Besides, there is no one else aboard ship who can handle the situation, and even if we reported the matter in Queenstown, I would rather not wait until noon tomorrow to find her."

"A word in private, if you don't mind," Decker said, placing a hand on Faucher's arm and tilting his head toward the other cabin.

Faucher nodded and followed silently. After entering the cabin and closing the door, he turned to Decker. "What is it you want?"

Decker spoke in a low voice so as not to be overheard. "It might not be in our best interest to force the matter with the Master-at-Arms. Don't forget who we are dealing with here. These are not normal people. They are vampires and will surely kill anyone who crosses their path and tries to liberate Mina."

"Are you saying we should do nothing?"

"No. I'm merely pointing out the danger of involving people who do not understand the situation. Since she was not killed at the same time as your valet, I am also of the opinion that Mina is currently safe. The vampires probably recognized her as one of their own, and if I know Mina, she will play to that. Besides, the crew of the ship will not find her unless they conduct a cabin-by-cabin search, since the vampires will undoubtedly keep a low profile. It's unlikely that Ismay and his first officer will agree to such an intrusive search because it would alarm the guests and raise questions they are not willing to answer."

"And we already know they're putting the company's reputation ahead of justice."

"Exactly. But we have an ace up our sleeves. The vampires want the amulet you are currently wearing around your neck. They will have to find us in order to get it, which gives us the advantage."

"Not much of an advantage if you ask me," Faucher said, glancing toward the door beyond which his dead companion still lay.

"But it is all that we have." Decker stepped back toward the door. "I suggest we wrap up our business here and turn our attention to more pressing matters, since there is nothing more we can do for your colleague."

"I suppose you're right," Faucher agreed grudgingly. He opened the door and stepped back into the cabin where the Master-at-Arms waited.

King raised an eyebrow when they reappeared. "Are you finished whispering among yourselves?"

"That we are," Faucher replied.

"Good." The Master-at-Arms looked harried. "I must make arrangements to get your valet placed in cold storage before the passengers begin to stir as I'm sure you understand."

Decker and Faucher remained silent.

King hesitated, as if expecting them to comment, before continuing. "And you won't be able to continue staying in this suite of cabins, I'm afraid. It's a crime scene and I need to preserve it for the police in New York."

"Naturally," Faucher said.

Decker didn't believe for one moment that the White Star Line would allow the NYPD to do much investigating. They would press for the incident to be kept quiet and for a quick resolution that would allow them to depart on their return journey without delay. Not that it mattered since he knew the ship would never make it to New York. As he had suspected, the universe, fate, or whatever else one might call it, had conspired to ensure the Titanic met its fate right on time despite a horrific crime. Even though no one would ever know it, this was just one more domino that fell in the right order to ensure the ship's destruction.

The Master-at-Arms clapped his hands together and turned toward the door. "If you would like to follow me, gentlemen, I will get Mr. Faucher settled into a new suite of rooms."

"There's no need for that," Decker said. "I have two rooms on A deck, one of which is unoccupied because my traveling companion could not make the journey. Mr. Faucher may take that room if he so wishes."

"That would be acceptable to me," Faucher said.

"Very well, then." King led them into the corridor and closed the door behind him, locking it with a master key. "Would you mind telling me your cabin number, sir?" he asked Decker. "So that we may inform you when we find Mrs. Swan."

"Certainly," said Decker, realizing that it was a risk. If the vampires got to the Master-at-Arms, they could extract any knowledge he possessed, including the location of Decker's cabin. But it was a calculated risk and Decker thought it unlikely that the vampires would locate the one person aboard who knew the location of Faucher, and by extension, the amulet. "I have cabins A 30 and A 32."

"Understood." The Master-at-Arms nodded, then addressed Faucher. "I will have a steward bring your belongings to you there posthaste."

"I would appreciate that," Faucher replied.

"Do either of you gentlemen have any questions before I bid you farewell to brief the overnight stewards on the situation regarding Mrs. Swan?"

"I have one question," Faucher said. "Actually, it's more of a request. I have an item of cargo in the hold. It is extremely valuable. I would like to check on it at your earliest convenience. Preferably right away."

"I'm sorry, sir," King said, shaking his head. "Passengers are not allowed in the cargo holds. It's for your own safety, you understand."

"Given the circumstances, I would expect you could make an exception just this once," Faucher countered.

"That won't be possible, sir. I assure you the cargo holds are secure, and any items within will remain safe until New York."

"I see." Faucher didn't sound happy. "In that case, I don't believe we have anything more to discuss until you locate my wife."

Then he turned and strode off down the corridor, leaving Decker to hurry behind, and the startled Master-at-Arms looking on.

FORTY-FOUR

WHEN THEY REACHED Decker's suite of cabins, Faucher grabbed his arm in a vice-like grip. "I have to check on my cargo regardless of what that buffoon of a Master-at-Arms says."

"You mean the mummy of Amenmosep, I assume," Decker replied.

"Yes. We can't allow the Cabal to find it."

"I agree. But you forget two things. First, we don't know which hold they put your cargo in. Second, Amenmosep is useless to the vampires without the amulet hanging around your neck because he won't be able to steal more years and rejuvenate."

"I know which hold the mummy is in." Faucher reached into his pocket and pulled out a brown slip of paper. It was a cargo receipt upon which was written the hold number. "And while I find it highly unlikely the vampires will go after Amenmosep while onboard ship, especially without the amulet, I would like to check on him anyway, just to reassure myself. If that creature were accidentally set loose, heaven knows what would happen."

Decker rubbed his neck. "I see your point." When Abraham Turner was released in twenty-first-century London, he had killed several people before reclaiming his amulet, even though those deaths did not rejuvenate him or prolong his own life.

"Are you going to help me?"

"We agreed to work together, at least in the short term, so yes," Decker replied. If nothing else, he wanted to make sure that Amenmosep's mummy was safe and where it should be. He was concerned about the consequences if it fell into the hands of the vampires, but he was equally concerned about the ability of Faucher's organization—which he did not know the name of yet, assuming it had one—to contain and secure the dangerous creature, which he knew was not strictly dead.

"Good. Then what are we waiting for?" Faucher went to a small wardrobe and opened it. He removed both of their pistols before slipping his own into his jacket pocket and handing Decker the other one.

"You want to go right now?"

"Can you think of a better time? It's almost three in the morning. There's nobody around."

"Unless we run into that Master-at-Arms again," Decker noted. "He would have to be an idiot not to suspect one or both of us are involved in the murder. For all he knows, you killed your wife and threw her overboard, then did the same to your valet and left him there to make it look like someone came into your room while you were gone and abducted her."

"Naturally, he suspects us of involvement. But he won't say as much since we are first-class passengers, and it would not be good form."

"If he or one of his crew sees us acting suspiciously in the middle of the night, he might change his mind. The last thing we need is more scrutiny."

"I fear we will be under his microscope regardless," Faucher said. "The best we can do is to be discreet. That said, I have no intention of waiting to check on the mummy. Until now, I wasn't sure the Cabal was on board. Now I know they are, and it is a concern."

"How are we going to find the cargo hold?" Decker asked. "This ship is massive, and we can't exactly ask for directions."

"On that score, I came prepared," Faucher replied. "But I will need my travel bags."

As if on cue, there was a soft knock on the cabin door.

Decker crossed the room, then hesitated. He kept the gun at his side. "Who is it?"

"Bedroom steward," came the reply. "I have baggage for the Swan party as per the Master-at-Arms orders. I'm sorry it's so late, but he said to bring it immediately."

Decker secreted the gun out of sight and opened the door just wide enough to confirm that it was indeed a bedroom steward. The man on the other side was gangly with slicked-back black hair and a youthful face. He looked to be no more than mid-twenties. Next to him was a cart, upon which were four large travel bags and one smaller bag. Decker opened the door wider and allowed the steward to enter, then watched as he unloaded the bags onto the floor.

"Would you like me to unpack them for you, sir?" The steward asked, looking between the two men because he was clearly not sure to which one the luggage belonged.

"No. That will be all," Faucher said, handing the steward a tip.

"As you wish, sir." The steward bowed slightly and retreated into the corridor.

Decker watched to make sure he departed, then closed the door. He turned to Faucher. "You were saying?"

"Ah, yes. The cargo hold." Faucher took one of the bags and lifted it onto the bed. He unbuckled it and rummaged inside before coming out with a long bundle of tightly rolled papers, which he proceeded to unravel. He spread the pages flat, holding them down to make sure they did not curl again, and leafed through them until he found the one he was looking for. "This will show us the way to the relevant cargo hold."

Decker moved closer and saw that the papers were actually blueprints. Deck plans for the Titanic. He raised an eyebrow. "How did you come by those?"

"I have my contacts. A friendly face at Harland and Wolff obtained them for me. I don't like leaving matters to chance and thought they might come in useful."

"It appears you were right." Decker leaned over the plans. "Even when we get to the hold, we won't know where to find Amenmosep, and depending upon how they stacked the cargo, the crate containing him might not be accessible."

"I'll know the crate when I find it," Faucher said. "And as for your second observation, we will have to wait and see, but I suspect it will be visible since I was most adamant that it be treated as fragile. I would be surprised if they stacked other cargo atop it."

"In that case, what are we waiting for?" Decker said as Faucher studied the blueprints and wrote their best route to the hold on a notepad he had removed from his pocket.

"What are we waiting for, indeed?" Faucher tucked the notepad back into his pocket and turned toward the door. "And bring your gun. I can't imagine there will be trouble, but you never know."

FORTY-FIVE

THE CABIN WAS DARK. Mina lay on the narrow bed provided by her new companions and stared up at the ceiling.

Sleep was impossible.

Beyond the cabin's connecting door, in the adjacent cabin, she could hear a murmur of indistinct conversation. Were the vampires talking about her or their plan to resurrect the ancient creature that went by the name of Amenmosep? To do that, they would need the amulet currently in the possession of the Man in the Black Suit. She had glimpsed it on a chain around his neck and recognized it right away. His life would now be in grave danger.

Not that Mina cared so much about that as she did about the carnage that would be caused by a ravenous vampire looking to rejuvenate itself after being imprisoned inside a tomb for thousands of years. Abraham Turner had cut a swath of destruction through twenty-first-century London after being restrained for only a fraction of that time. That Amenmosep had enough life force to sustain himself through such a long slumber without finally succumbing to death spoke of the incredible amount of victims who must have died at his hands.

After all, these creatures were not immortal. They merely extended their lives by stealing the remaining years of those they slayed.

Her most immediate concern, however, was escaping the ship before it embarked on the final leg of its journey to New York. Hours from now, the Titanic would drop anchor in Queenstown and provide her with that opportunity. Afterward, when she was safe, Mina would send word to London, and Thomas Finch, apprising him of the situation. If she were lucky, the pair of vampires who had rescued her from her captors, as well as Amenmosep, would be lost with the ship, but she could not take that chance. It would be bad enough if the vampires reached New York. It would be worse if the ancient creature in the hold were to do so. It was her job, and that of the Order of St. George, to prevent such a scenario.

But first, she must come up with a means of escape because she doubted the vampires would allow her to simply saunter out of the door and not come back. They had not physically restrained her, as The Man in the Black Suit had—she was not shackled to the bed—but she was hardly free. The vampires had made it clear they did not trust her, and although they had appeared to accept her explanation of how she became one of them and ended up on the ship, she had no proof to back up her claim—a story that was only partly true. For all they knew, she had actively taken part in the demise of Abraham Turner, which was closer to the reality of it. They must also wonder if Mina had killed Turner so she could steal his powers.

She rolled over in the bed and glanced up at the porthole above her head. All she saw was a patch of dark and starless sky. She didn't know what time it was or how many more hours she had to formulate a plan, but she knew that inspiration often came when she was not actively seeking a solution. Her best ideas materialized from deep within her subconscious when she allowed it free rein. The best way to do that was to relax. Not an easy task when you were on a doomed ocean liner under the distrustful gaze of creatures that would just as soon rip your throat out as engage in conversation.

Mina took a slow and controlled breath, then another, drawing the air in through her nose and out through her mouth. She had learned this relaxation technique while studying for exams in a London of the future before she knew anything about vampires, Abraham Turner, or even what John Decker really did for a living. It had served her well then, and she hoped it would do the same now.

She closed her eyes and cleared her mind, forcing the cascade of frantic thoughts that crowded it into submission. Soon, Mina achieved a sense of calm. The anxieties and fears of her situation fell away like an ocean retreating from the shore at low tide, and she was finally able to open her mind.

The voices beyond the cabin door had ceased, and she lay in silent darkness. With her mind cleansed of the ceaseless internal chatter that kept her awake, Mina felt herself drifting into a trance-like half-sleep where disparate thoughts and ideas surfaced unbidden, flared briefly into existence, then sank back into her subconscious to be forgotten. Each of these was evaluated by some internal cerebral mechanism that sorted the wheat from the chaff and eventually left her with a single idea that burned brightly and refused to fade.

She opened her eyes and sat up, examining the solution that had presented itself. It was half-formed, but she soon filled in the blanks and decided that, under the circumstances, it offered her the best chance of success. It was risky, though. If she failed, her true allegiances would be revealed, and she would find herself at the mercy of these vicious creatures who, even if they could not easily kill her, surely had the capability to make her life a living nightmare.

Mina considered the idea for a few minutes more, examining the pros and cons of her newly formed plan, and still came to the same conclusion. It was the most advantageous course of action under the circumstances. Satisfied that she had her answer, Mina slipped back down under the covers and closed her eyes again. Tomorrow, when the Titanic reached Queenstown, she would put her plan into action. Now, though, she would rest and gather her strength for what was to come.

FORTY-SIX

DECKER MADE his way through the ship with Faucher at his side. They moved quickly but carefully, keeping their eyes peeled for any members of the crew that might report their early morning trip back to the Master-at-Arms.

Every so often, Faucher checked the directions he had written on his notepad to make sure they were still heading in the right direction.

The stairs leading to the cargo hold were located on C deck, at the front of the ship. But that area could only be accessed from the outside by a set of stairs on B deck. They took the grand staircase down one level and headed toward the bow. After checking one last time to make sure no one was around to observe them, they stepped outside and took a set of metal steps down to the deck below.

The air was freezing, and a stiff wind buffeted them as Decker and Faucher crossed an open space between two huge electric cranes and past the bulkhead doors leading to the cargo hold many floors below. When they reached the door that accessed the interior crew areas at the front of the ship, they paused. This was the most dangerous part of their journey.

Beyond these doors were the seaman's mess, crew galley, and Fireman's mess, as well as the carpenter's store and ship's medical facilities.

"If anyone sees us, just say that we're lost," Faucher said, raising his voice over the howling wind that whipped across the ship's bow.

"I'm not sure they'll believe us," Decker hollered back. "A couple of first-class passengers wandering around an area that is clearly off-limits?"

"Have you got a better idea?"

"Not really," Decker admitted. He thought it unlikely they would encounter anyone at such an early hour of the morning, but unlike the passengers who were all tucked up in bed, Titanic's crew were required to work around the clock to keep the mighty vessel moving forward. The risk was real. "Might as well get this done."

Faucher nodded and opened the door, then stepped inside and waited for Decker to join him.

The corridor they found themselves in bore no refinement compared to first-class. It was utilitarian, with white painted steel walls and a ribbed metal ceiling. The deck boards were also painted white and already bore scuffs and dings from the passage of heavy boots. Bare bulbs in wire cages illuminated the corridor in a dim glow.

"The stairs we want are on the left here," Faucher said, once again referencing the notepad. He hurried forward and found the correct door, then opened it and ushered Decker inside. Once it was closed behind them, they both breathed easier.

Faucher grabbed a lantern that was hanging on a hook near the door and lit it. "There are crew areas on each level as we descend, so let's make this quick."

"I'm all for that," Decker said.

They descended the stairs and found themselves on a cramped landing. More crew quarters lead off to the left and right. In the center of the landing, about 10 feet apart, were a pair of spiral staircases.

Faucher went to the closer of the two. "Either of these will get us to the cargo hold," he said in a whisper before starting down.

Decker followed and they climbed steadily downward toward the ship's lower levels. As they went, their footfalls rang on the metal stair treads. The glow from the lantern played across the shaft walls, projecting their shadows and turning them into grotesque dancing caricatures.

Neither man spoke.

They passed through E deck, then F, and G, until there was only one more level to descend. Below them was the orlop deck, and the cargo hold within which Amenmosep's mummy waited. Unless the Cabal had gotten there first, that was.

And then they saw it, a faint glow filtering up from the shaft beneath their feet—another lantern.

Decker raised a hand and brought them to a halt. He turned to Faucher and spoke in a whisper that was barely audible over the thrum of the ship's engines on the other side of the bulkhead beyond the boilers. "There's a light. Someone must be down there."

"Why would anyone be down here?" Faucher replied.

Decker shrugged.

"Maybe someone just left a lantern burning," Faucher said under his breath. "We've come this far. I'm not giving up now. We might not get another chance."

Decker shrugged again and motioned for him to lead on.

Faucher pushed past him and put a foot on the top step of the final spiral staircase. At that moment, a voice drifted up from below.

"Hello? Who goes there?"

Faucher froze mid-step.

Decker tapped him on the shoulder and motioned upward. He mouthed a single word. Quick.

Faucher grimaced and withdrew his foot, then cast a frustrated glance down through the stairwell. But he wasn't foolhardy enough to try and continue on because he surely knew they would never be able to talk their way past the crewman who occupied the landing below.

Was the man there as a guard, Decker wondered? If so, who had posted him? The obvious answer was the Master-at-Arms, who probably didn't trust either of them one bit, even if he wouldn't say it outright. Faucher's request to visit the hold and check on his cargo when his wife was supposedly missing, and his valet was lying dead on the floor in his cabin would have done little to sway the Master-at-Arms in the other direction.

Not that it mattered why the guard was there, because it amounted to the same thing, regardless. They weren't getting into the cargo hold anytime soon.

"Hello?" the voice said again from below.

Now Decker took Faucher by the arm and pulled him towards the stairs leading back up.

"We have to go, now," he breathed into Faucher's ear. "Before we're discovered."

Faucher pushed back for a moment as if he were unwilling to give up their quest. His hand went to the amulet around his neck as if he wanted to make sure it was still there. Then his shoulders slumped, and he started to climb, much to Decker's relief.

Amenmosep would have to wait, at least for now.

FORTY-SEVEN

AN HOUR EARLIER, after assigning two crewmen to remove the corpse of Charles Swan's valet and take it down to the cold storage locker as surreptitiously as possible, Master-at-Arms Thomas King had went in search of another steward for a different task.

He didn't trust Swan or his friend Decker. There was something off about them, and it bothered him. He couldn't shake the feeling that they were up to no good and the dead body in Swan's cabin, coupled with his wife's disappearance, left him wondering if the valet's murderer was right in front of him all along. But naturally, he could not voice that suspicion openly. They were both first-class passengers and, as such, must be given the benefit of the doubt because if he was wrong, it could have serious ramifications for both his own career and the White Star Line. Better to conduct a discrete investigation and see where it led him.

High on the list of steps that would either confirm or discredit his suspicions was to inform the staff of the situation, or at least as much as they needed to know to keep their eyes peeled for any clues regarding Mrs. Swan's whereabouts. But there was one other thing he wanted to do.

Charles Swan had made a big deal about visiting his cargo in the hold to ensure it was safe. This struck King as a strange request under the circumstances. The man should have been more worried about his missing wife than some inanimate object he was carting to New York, regardless of its value. Which was why he intended to investigate Charles Swan's cargo and find out exactly what it was and why the man was so eager to check on it in the middle of a crisis. He also wanted to ensure that Swan would not go against him and attempt to visit the hold without permission.

The best way to do that was to post a guard at the door leading into the cargo hold. And that future guard was currently heading along the corridor toward King.

First-class steward Archie Drummond was empty-handed and no doubt on his way to the crew galley to snag a cup of hot tea. That would have to wait.

King intercepted him and instructed the unhappy-looking steward to follow him to the front of the ship, where they retrieved a pair of lanterns from the lamp store before proceeding down the stairs leading to the cargo hold access landing on E deck. Here a spiral staircase drilled through the ship all the way down to the orlop deck, where a metal door provided access to the hold within which Charles Swan's cargo currently resided.

When they reached the door, he explained the steward's new duties.

The man looked perplexed.

"I'm sorry, sir, but am I hearing you right?" he asked, surveying his surroundings, which were nothing more than an enclosed shaft through which the spiral staircase ascended with a small room at the bottom barely large enough to accommodate both of them. "You want me to stand here for the rest of the night?"

"That's exactly what I want you to do," King responded. "There has been an incident aboard ship which I am not at liberty to divulge. The incident may involve a piece of cargo in this hold, and I need to ensure that there is no unauthorized access. If anyone comes down here, you are to bring them to me immediately. Do you understand?"

The steward nodded. "Yes, sir."

"Very good. You can knock off at seven and go to your bunk. That should be enough time to make sure the hold is secure. Until then, look lively."

Again, the steward nodded. "Yes, sir."

Satisfied, King turned and started back up the spiral staircase. When he reached the top, he turned out the lamp and hung it on a hook so that it would be waiting for the next steward to be given the unfortunate task, then made his way back up one more level and finally emerged on C deck again.

He rubbed his hands together to warm them up. The bowels of the ship were freezing, and he was glad to be out of the claustrophobic shaft through which the spiral staircase wound. Then, without giving any further thought to the steward currently shivering next to the cargo hold far below, he made his way back to his office to investigate what Charles Swan was so eager to see.

FORTY-EIGHT

DEEP inside the dark and frigid hold, Amenmosep stirred. He felt strange. Ancient. The man he had killed should have sent life flowing back into him and restored at least some of the lost years—how many he did not know-that had been stolen by the Pharaoh and his elite guard. But it hadn't.

Worse, he was finding it hard to think. His mind was fogged, and he felt like he was stuck in a dreadful limbo state between sleep and wakefulness. He was acting on instinct, desperate to regain some measure of control, but it wasn't working.

The kill had been primal. He hadn't been able to stop himself. He had continued to shred and tear at the man even after he realized it would do no good. His amulet, which acted as a conduit to bestow the lifeforce of his victim upon himself, was missing. Without it, he could not rejuvenate and reclaim the years spent trapped in a dark tomb.

And he must do this quickly, because Amenmosep could feel the dregs of his life falling through the hourglass. He would not expire today, for sure, or even tomorrow. It would still take decades, perhaps even hundreds of years before the last vestiges of consciousness flickered out and death finally came for the man who had seen the fall of Mesopotamia, the rise of the pyramids, and the ocean of time reshape human civilization through millennia.

That was small comfort, though, because without the amulet his last gasp would be ignominious. A humiliation beyond words. He would continue to devolve, his mind fracturing as the beast within him took over. By the end he would be nothing more than a shriveled, walking carcass, the flesh desiccated and brittle. He would be driven only by a hunger he could never sate . . . And that need would drive him insane.

He was close to that already. The brutal and pointless killing had proven as much. Amenmosep had always prided his intellect. He had stayed one step ahead of his enemies by avoiding the wanton destruction that had doomed so many of his kind, even in an age where extreme violence was a way of life.

Then came the apparent civility of the Egyptians, and Amenmosep was able to leverage his intellect as others before him had wielded an axe. He was revered as a god for a thousand years or more. He drank the lives of others and added to his own. Until a man with greater ambition, a mortal creature full of fear and loathing for Amenmosep, finally got the better of him. He was overpowered—not an easy task—and buried under the shifting sands. And that was where he might have stayed, only vaguely aware of his imprisonment as the years and centuries passed by, thanks to the gold, always his weakness, that kept him locked in a terrible half-slumber from which he could not awaken.

Until now.

Amenmosep didn't know where he was, or why. His surroundings were strange and confusing. A vast metal chamber filled with wooden boxes and objects that defied logic.

And the noise . . . A steady rumble that vibrated under his feet and never ceased.

But he knew one thing.

The amulet was close by.

He had sensed it briefly, but then it had faded again almost as quickly.

Amenmosep made his way through the darkness toward the place where he had sensed the amulet, but found his way blocked by a smooth metal door. He touched the cold surface, ran his hand down the door, reveling in the lingering vibrations caused by the amulet's brief presence.

Then he shrank back into the darkness and waited. He would sense the amulet again. Of that he was sure. Then he would reclaim it and regain his wits. In the meantime, there was the hunger . . . always the hunger . . .

FORTY-NINE

DECKER AND FAUCHER returned to their suite of cabins on A deck.

No sooner had they entered, than Faucher slammed down into a chair next to the bed. "Well, that was a complete waste of time," He grumbled.

"Not entirely," Decker said. "It provides us with one important piece of information. The Master-at-Arms does not trust us."

"And how exactly did you come to that conclusion?" Faucher asked, raising an eyebrow. "We don't even know who was down there, let alone why."

"No, but we can make a reasonable assumption." Decker sat on the edge of the bed. He was tired and was finding it hard to keep his eyes open. He had barely slept more than a few hours over the last two days, and it was starting to take its toll. That was bad considering that his only chance to get off the ship with Mina, assuming there was even a way to do that now, given the circumstances, was fast approaching. "That man in the stairwell below us was not climbing up. Neither do I believe he was there to access the hold, since there was no indication that he was coming or going. It's more likely he was put there to guard the door."

"If you say so," Faucher mumbled, yawning.

"I do," replied Decker. "It's unlikely they post a crewmember to guard the hold under regular circumstances because that would be a waste of resources since the hold is such a low-trafficked and out-of-the-way area of little interest to anyone except those who have consigned items there for the crossing. That means he was ordered there with a purpose, and there's only one man who would have reason to do that."

"The Master-at-Arms."

"Yes. You probably shouldn't have been so eager to go down there at a time when you should be more concerned about your missing wife and dead valet. I would hazard a guess that it roused his suspicions."

"I'm a first-class passenger," Faucher replied. "I thought he would honor my request, regardless."

"Except the ship has rules the Master-at-Arms must abide by."

"Apparently. I bet he'd let Astor or Guggenheim down there."

"Maybe." Decker wasn't interested in discussing the pecking order of first-class passengers. "But they probably wouldn't ask in the first place. If they needed something, they would send a crewmember to retrieve it."

"Fair point." Faucher rubbed his temples. He stood up. "It doesn't look like we can do anything else tonight unless the man somehow locates Mina, which is unlikely even if he tells the crew to keep their eyes open since we have already decided that he won't search any cabins for fear of bad publicity."

"Nor do we want him to," Decker said. "It could very well end in a bloodbath, and I believe Mina is safe for the time being."

"Which is why I'm going to bed," Faucher said. He crossed

to the door connecting the two cabins and opened it, then turned back to Decker. "Don't get any bright ideas. Just because we're working together doesn't mean I trust you, and I'm a light sleeper."

"The feeling is mutual." Decker looked up at Faucher and suppressed a shudder. This man had taken Mina and kept her captive for months. He could only guess what she had been subjected to under his watch. "I might give you the same warning."

"Then we understand each other." Faucher stepped into the adjacent cabin and closed the door.

Decker let out a long breath, relieved to be alone finally. It had taken all his willpower not to throttle the man over the last few hours. For the moment, they needed each other, whether or not they liked it. But Decker knew that would change when Mina was found, which meant that he must be ready. Right now, though, all he wanted to do was catch a few hours of sleep. He lay back on the narrow bed without bothering to undress and closed his eyes. Soon, he fell into a light and fitful sleep, and dreamed of sanguine creatures with dull, dead eyes, prowling dark passageways looking for victims even as the ship they were aboard broke apart around them and icy cold water flooded in, eager to drag them all into the frigid, swirling depths.

FIFTY

FIRST-CLASS STEWARD ARCHIE DRUMMOND stood in the freezing stairwell next to the door leading into the hold and slapped his arms across his chest to restore some warmth to them. He blew on his hands, noting the fine mist of condensation that ballooned into the frigid air. It had been almost four hours since Thomas King, the Master-at-Arms, had sent him down here on this fool's errand, and so far, he had encountered no one trying to access the hold. At one point, early in his shift, footsteps had rung on the metal staircase above, and he had called out a challenge, but no one had answered. It was probably just a couple of firemen returning to their quarters buried deep in Titanic's bow.

Now, he wondered if the Master-at-Arms had lost his mind. He was a steward, not a night watchman. As a linen steward, he should have been many decks above making sure clean sheets were available for anyone who requested them, yet here he was, stuck in a dark hole with no one but himself for company. He toyed with the idea of leaving his post and returning to the warmth of the upper decks and the first-class stewards' stateroom, where he could climb into a bunk, pull the sheets up, and get some sleep. But that would mean disobeying orders, which could see him left on the dock in New York with no work and no way home. Drummond was not willing to take that chance, so instead, he froze and waited for the Master-at-Arms to either come to his senses or relieve him with some other unfortunate crewman who had been unlucky enough to cross Thomas King's path.

"Wish I'd never stepped foot on this damn ship," Drummond muttered under his breath, even though he knew that despite the hardship, it was the best job he could have landed since being thrown out of his lodgings for failure to pay his rent the previous week. After a couple of nights living rough, he had found himself on the docks standing in line outside the White Star employment office, eager to take whatever work the company was willing to put his way. And being a steward was better than being a stoker shoveling coal into the Titanic's hungry boilers. The pay was low, but he'd fallen on his feet and been assigned to first-class thanks to his previous experience on other ocean liners, including Olympic, the year before. That meant good gratuities. If he was lucky, he could save enough to find new lodgings when he returned to Southampton. But not if he disobeyed the Master-at-Arms.

Drummond stamped his feet and walked a circle in the cramped landing. The sun was probably coming up already, but here in this metal box with no portholes and only a pair of spiral staircases disappearing upward into darkness and down to the firemen's tunnel in the ship's keel, it might as well be an endless night.

He finished walking in circles and reached for the lantern that sat on the floor next to the cargo hold door. The flame had died to a low flicker, and the wick would need raising to keep it alight. But as he bent down, his ear close to the cargo hold door, he heard a noise on the other side.

It was nothing much. Just a faint scratching sound, barely

audible over the rumble of Titanic's massive engines. He wouldn't even have noticed it had he not been bending close to the door. But it made the hairs on the back of his neck prickle.

"It's just rats," he told himself, talking aloud just to hear his own voice. "All ships have rats. Get a grip."

But something told him it was not some furry rodent scurrying across the deck. It sounded more like—he didn't even want to think about it—claws dragging down the metal on the other side of the door.

Drummond picked up the lantern and raised the wick, relieved when the flame flared bright, illuminating the cramped stairwell with a warm orange glow. He reached out and touched the cargo hold door, then pressed his ear to it, listening as he held his breath.

Everything was silent now.

He stepped back from the cargo hold door and stood looking at it.

"Rats," he mumbled, more to convince himself than anything else. "Rats. It's always rats."

The loud crash that reverberated through the hold, not a moment after Drummond had spoken, made him jump back in fright.

He stared at the door, unsure what to make of this latest development, even as his racing heart slowed. Whatever had caused that noise was no rat. He knew that much. Drummond knew something else as well. He would have to go in there and find out what it was. Because if the Master-at-Arms discovered something had toppled inside the hold and that Drummond had failed to investigate and report any damage, he would be in about as much trouble as if he had deserted his post.

An image of the Titanic sailing away while he stood on the dock in New York and watched it leave, penniless and jobless, flitted through Drummond's mind for a second time.

He swore under his breath, then swore again for good measure. This was just his luck.

Drummond raised the lantern higher and approached the door. He drew back the latch and took a deep breath. Then he pulled the heavy door open with a grunt and stepped across the threshold into the Stygian darkness beyond.

FIFTY-ONE

DECKER AWOKE after seven a.m. as the first rays of morning sunlight were streaming in through the cabin window. He had only slept for a few hours, but he felt more refreshed than he had in days.

Swinging his legs off the bed and standing up, Decker went to a washbasin standing against the wall and splashed cold water on his face. This was the closest thing to washing facilities in his cabin, and it would have to do.

A quick glance toward the connecting door, where low rumbling snores emanated, told him that Faucher was still in dreamland. That was good because Decker wanted to speak with the Master-at-Arms and didn't want Mina's abductor there to hear it. Apart from anything else, the ship was only a few hours out of Queenstown, where Decker hoped to disembark with her—assuming Mina could be located, and the crew would let them leave. Neither one was a given, but if he was to have any chance, Decker must get on the good side of Thomas King.

He looked down at himself and his crumpled shirt. The same one he had been wearing the previous evening when he

215

had found the valet's body in the suite of rooms where Faucher had been holding Mina. Decker had arrived too late to rescue her, much to his chagrin. Now she was likely in the clutches of vampires like Abraham Turner. Her only advantage was a kinship with them, thanks to the strange process that had gifted her Abraham Turner's powers and longevity. Although Mina would probably disagree that it was a gift, Decker thought ruefully. Curse would be a more accurate description. Either way, he suspected it was keeping her safe for now.

Opening the narrow wardrobe next to the cabin door, Decker selected a fresh shirt. If he stood any chance of getting on the good side of Thomas King, he would need to play the part of an aristocratic first-class passenger. Crumpled clothing did not project that image. He slipped his shirt off and discarded it. Before putting the new one on, he went to the bed and withdrew the Model 1906 pistol from under the pillow. He had slept with it there as insurance against Faucher trying anything during the night. He tucked the gun into his belt, and put on the new shirt, closing it around the gun. While he was buttoning up, he heard a door open.

Decker turned to see Faucher standing in the connecting door between the two cabins. His arms were folded, and there was a curious look on his face.

"Going somewhere?" he asked, in a casual manner which nonetheless carried undercurrents of implied threat.

"The Master-at-Arms has not yet returned with news of Mina or provided us with an update on his efforts to locate her," Decker replied. "I'm fed up with waiting."

"So you intend to rattle his cage," Faucher said with a slight smile.

"I wouldn't quite put it that way." Decker finished buttoning his shirt and tucked it in, turned to the full-length mirror on the back of the cabin door to make sure he looked presentable. "I don't expect him to have any success in finding her. His methods are not thorough, and he doesn't want to alarm the other passengers."

"So why bother pressing him for answers if you believe it to be futile?"

"Because we have a cover to maintain. Don't forget that you are supposed to be the frantic husband whose valet has been murdered and wife abducted by persons unknown. You already roused his suspicions by insisting we visit the cargo hold last night instead of worrying about the fictional Mrs. Swan."

"A minor lapse of judgment." Faucher waved a hand. "It won't happen again."

"Pleased to hear it," Decker replied, taking his jacket from the wardrobe and putting it on. He reached into the pocket and removed the tintype photograph of Mina in a silver locket that he had taken from Finch back in London. "After I speak with the Master-at-Arms, I'm going to take a stroll around the ship and show Mina's photo around. Who knows, maybe I'll get lucky."

"It's unlikely anyone has seen her."

"And it's better than doing nothing." Decker stepped toward the cabin door. "I'll be back by noon."

"Not so fast." Faucher moved to block Decker's path with surprising agility. He put a hand on the door to stop it from opening. "You're not going anywhere alone. I'm coming with you."

Decker shook his head, thinking quickly. During the overnight hours, an idea had formed in Decker's mind regarding both locating Mina and an exit strategy for them both in Queenstown, but it would not involve Faucher for obvious reasons. Nor would it work if he could not speak to the Master-at-Arms alone. "That's not a good idea. The vampires are looking for that amulet around your neck. Right now, they have no clue where you are, but if you go walking around the ship, you might be discovered."

A look of indecision flashed across Faucher's face, quickly masked. "In that case, I shall leave the amulet here and there won't be any threat."

"That would also be unwise. The vampires probably know your face and could just as easily follow us upon our return to the cabin. We would then present them with an opportunity to attack us at our most vulnerable and in private. On the other hand, it is unlikely the creatures will recognize me since I am not a part of your organization or involved in the theft of Amenmosep from the British Museum. I shall speak to the Master-at-Arms alone, and you will remain here in the cabin."

"How do I know you won't betray me?" Faucher asked, with his palm still flat on the cabin door.

"You don't, just as I have no assurances that you will not betray me at the first opportunity. But right now, our goals are aligned, and we are facing an enemy more dangerous than either of us. Betrayal would not be in either of our best interests," Decker replied, hoping Faucher bought into his hollow words.

For a moment, Decker thought they were at an impasse, but then Faucher relaxed his hand and moved it from the door. "Very well. You can go. But if I so much as suspect that you are working against me, the vampires won't need to kill you because I'll do it myself without a moment's hesitation."

"Fair enough," Decker replied. Then he opened the door and slipped out, closing it behind him, before hurrying off to find the Master-at-Arms.

FIFTY-TWO

FIRST-CLASS STEWARD ARCHIE DRUMMOND stood at the entrance to the cargo hold and swung his lantern around in a wide, slow arc. This was the last place on earth that he wanted to be right now, but something had fallen, and it was his duty to investigate. Even so, he briefly considered retreating and to hell with the consequences. Neither the Master-at-Arms, nor the purser to whom he reported directly, might ever find out about it or that he had neglected to investigate, but he couldn't take that chance. Besides, if he found the dislodged cargo and could save it, he might earn a handsome reward from the rich passenger it belonged to. That alone was enough incentive to carry on, given his dire financial straits.

Drummond swallowed a trembling breath and stepped further into the hold, shivering as the darkness folded around him. Only the meager cocoon of his lantern's glow saved him from being completely consumed by it.

The hold was packed tightly with crates of all shapes and sizes, plus other items too big to be crated. For example, he knew that there was a Renault Type CB Coupe de Ville somewhere down here. The car was worth a small fortune and had been the talk of the steward's galley for the excess of its owner, a Pennsylvania millionaire who was traveling with his wife and two children in one of the largest suites aboard ship. But the fancy automobile was of no concern to Drummond at that moment. All he wanted to do was find the damaged cargo and get the hell out of there as quickly as possible. That would be no simple task. The stacked crates, cartons, and boxes towered above him and created a labyrinth of narrow man-made canyons that all looked the same, and he soon lost his bearings.

Drummond stopped to catch his breath and glanced around. He looked up at the stacked crates, the tops of which were lost in the gloom above his head. Likewise, he could not see the ceiling of the hold but knew that there were thousands of tons of steel between himself and the open sky. All except for the wide shaft that rose through the ship and ended at the now closed and secured bulkhead doors on deck. Next to these would be two large cranes, used to lower the cargo into the bowels of the vessel.

He suppressed a shudder and was about to move on when the scratching sound came again. It sounded exactly like before, except now it was louder and closer.

Drummond froze and swung the lantern in a wild arc, straining his eyes against the gloom, but saw nothing.

The sound repeated, like fingernails scratching across a hard surface. No, not fingernails. Claws. And now he realized why he couldn't find the source of the sound, because it was high above him in the darkness.

Something was crawling along the top of the crates, moving closer with each passing moment.

Drummond fought the urge to scream. He was alone, and it would do no good except to betray his position to whatever had made the sound. What that might be, he didn't know, but Drummond knew one thing. He didn't want to find out, because a primordial instinct for self-preservation had activated deep within him, and that instinct told him that whatever he shared the hold with was bigger than a rat. Much bigger.

That was all it took. Drummond didn't care about the cargo or a tip from some thankful millionaire. He didn't even care about losing his job anymore. All he wanted to do was get the hell out of there before whatever was crawling around the dark and frigid hold caught up with him.

Drummond found his feet. He turned and fled back in the direction of the cargo hold door. At least, he thought he was heading in the right direction. Every turn looked the same. Every stack of crates looked identical. While above him came that scratching of claws on the wood. And now he heard something else above the distant thrum of the ship's engines behind the watertight bulkheads—rasping breaths.

He was losing the race. Whatever was shadowing him atop the crates was closing the gap. But how, when even Drummond didn't know where he was? Then it occurred to him.

The oil lamp.

It was not only lighting his way but providing a beacon for whatever monstrosity was behind and above him. It was drawn toward it like a moth to the flame. Drummond came to a swift halt and fumbled with the knob that controlled the lantern's wick, turning it down as low as he dared and watching the comforting bubble of light shrink and fade. But he didn't extinguish it completely because he had no matches and would never get it lit again, and also because he needed the lantern in order to see his way. The meager amount of electric lighting in the hold had been shut off to preserve power because it wasn't needed at sea and could only be turned back on from the bridge.

Moving off again, Drummond fled through the tight aisles as quickly as his legs would let him. He tried to ignore the footfalls of whatever was stalking him as it abandoned all stealth and gave chase.

He turned a corner and then another, praying each time that he would see the bulkhead ahead of him and the cargo hold door. But each time he was met with another dark alley of crates. Worse, he was getting winded, and a stitch needled in his side.

From somewhere behind him, something smacked onto the deck.

Drummond didn't want to look but couldn't help himself. He slowed and half-turned, swinging the lantern around as he did so. And there, at the edge of the lamp's glow, was a shape that looked almost like a man except that it scuttled toward him on all fours, head lifted at an unnatural angle, mouth agape.

He could barely make out any other features in the darkness, but Drummond had seen enough. With a shriek of terror, he turned and pumped his legs faster, flying down the narrow space between the crates in a blind panic.

At his rear, he heard the creature giving chase.

Now it emitted its own shriek. A dry, rasping howl full of ravenous desire.

Drummond saw another intersection up ahead. He skidded around the corner without bothering to slow down. Then, as he stumbled to avoid losing his balance, the cargo hold door loomed large up ahead.

With a cry of utter desperation, Drummond put his shoulders down and barreled toward it, reaching the door, and dragging the latch back, then falling heavily through the hatch and out onto the landing beyond.

Without a moment's pause, Drummond turned to slam the door closed, then fumbled with the latch, but it was too late.

His pursuer slammed into it from the other side with a jarring thud.

The sudden impact was enough to send the door flying back

on its hinges, lifting Drummond from his feet and slamming him into the opposite bulkhead wall.

His head cracked against metal. His vision blurred. The lantern fell from his grip.

Something large and terrifying slunk through the open door and loomed over him, face close enough to his that a blast of foul breath caused him to gag.

Drummond whimpered and shrank back, his vision still wonky from the blow to his head. He felt hands on his shoulders and claws digging into his flesh. No, not claws. Fingernails sharp as talons.

He tried to twist free but instead was dragged back toward the cargo hold door. He reached out and gripped a railing on the spiral staircase, but he had no strength to hang on and it was soon ripped from his grasp. Then he was pulled through the door into the unforgiving darkness beyond as a final agonizing scream died on his lips.

FIFTY-THREE

THE MASTER-AT-ARMS STOOD in his cabin doorway dressed in a pair of Long Johns and glared at Decker, abandoning all pretense of deference to the first-class passenger who stood on the other side. "I'm not on duty for another two hours. This better be good."

"If my hunch is correct, it will prove better than good for both of us," Decker said. It had taken the better part of thirty minutes to find the Master-at-Arms. After stopping a steward in one of the passageways on A deck and inquiring, he learned that Thomas King had an office in the forward section of the ship on E deck's port side. But when he went there, he found it locked and empty. After finding and waylaying another steward who was hurrying toward the first-class accommodation with an arm full of towels, Decker was directed to Thomas King's cabin on the same deck, which was how he ended up standing in front of the disgruntled Master-at-Arms, who looked about as pleased to see him as if he had just stepped into a pile of dog poop left on the sidewalk.

"Let's hear it, then."

"I know how we can find Mrs. Swan," Decker said, referring

to Mina by the pseudonym Faucher had imposed upon her. "This vessel does not have regular room service. Is that correct?"

King looked blankly back at him. "Room service?"

"Sorry." Decker realized that in this day and age, room service was not yet a concept. Passengers could only receive meals in their room by prior arrangement because of an illness or other incapacitating event that prevented them from visiting the dining room. Faucher had brought Mina onboard anticipating this because he could not allow her out of the cabin and had fabricated a cover story that would also explain any outbursts or strange behavior on her part by claiming that she was suffering from an illness of the mind that made her delusional. "What I mean is that you only serve meals in the room under exceptional circumstances."

"That's correct."

"Mrs. Swan already had an arrangement in place due to her illness, I believe," Decker said. "Which got me thinking. The people who took her would want to keep a low profile. They would not allow her to go out on deck or visit the dining room. That means she would still need to take her meals in the cabin unless they intend to starve her."

"What of it?"

Decker sighed. Either the Master-at-Arms was being deliberately obtuse, or he was slow on the uptake. "These people would not have arranged to dine in their cabin ahead of time. All we need to do is look for passengers who request meals in their cabin without prior arrangement. Since it's unlikely that any other passengers will make such a request, the kidnappers will unwittingly reveal themselves."

"I see." King looked thoughtful. "You might be onto something, there. But it will take some time to find out. Mrs. Swan's alleged abductors would not have been able to make that request already as all such arrangements must go through the purser, who was already gone when the incident happened and will not be back on duty until nine a.m."

"Then you will inform him to be on the lookout?" Decker asked.

"That I will," King said, nodding. "I'll get dressed and go find him right away."

"Thank you. When you have news, you will find me in the reading room, where I will be for the next several hours. I would like to accompany you when you visit that cabin."

"The reading room?"

"Mr. Swan is beside himself, and I would rather not give him false hope. I don't intend to inform him of this unless it is successful."

"I understand." King's earlier combativeness had dropped away, and his professional manners had resurfaced. "Now, if you'll excuse me, I must get dressed and relay this information to the purser as quickly as possible."

"Of course." Decker stepped away from the door. He heard it close behind him.

So far, so good. But this was just the first part of his plan. Once they knew which cabin the vampires were holding her in, the Master-at-Arms would surely gather enough men to provide adequate backup and pay the room a visit. Decker intended to be among that group because the second part of his scheme would kick in once Mina was liberated. This was where things got tricky. It would require him to convince the Master-at-Arms that Mina had already been a captive when she boarded the Titanic. This would not be an easy task given Faucher's clever cover story, but he hoped Mina would be convincing enough to sway the Master-at-Arms, and with Decker's own testimony, they might stand a chance. Especially if Thomas King could be convinced to send a rush message via the Marconi telegraph machine to Scotland Yard, where Thomas Finch had an operative in the role of Detective

Inspector who would vouch for Mina's authenticity and the fact that she had been missing for the past four months. It was that very operative who had originally brought Decker's presence in London to light and delivered him to the Order of St. George.

Once that was done, hopefully, before the gangplank was drawn up in Queenstown, Mina and Decker would be allowed to leave the ship. What happened to Faucher or the vampires after that was of less concern. The Titanic would be on the bottom of the ocean in less than four days, and even if Faucher survived, which was unlikely, there would be a number of policemen on the docks in New York waiting for him thanks to unofficial arrangements that Decker was sure Thomas Finch had with the New York Police Department. The Order of St. George might be a purely British institution at this point in time, having not yet become CUSP, but even in 1912, their tentacles reached around the globe.

Feeling hopeful that he might actually find Mina and flee the Titanic before its grisly end was met, Decker made his way to the first-class reading room and settled in a chair near the entrance. He reached into his pocket and took out the locket containing the photograph of Mina. The one he had told Faucher he would show around to buy the time needed for his escape plan to succeed. He opened the locket and stared at the face looking back at him from the black and white tintype. Hopefully, he would see that face in real life very soon. With that thought in mind, Decker closed the locket and returned it to his pocket, then sat back, folded his arms, and waited.

FIFTY-FOUR

MINA SAT in the cabin provided by the vampires and went over her plan one last time in her head. It was a tenuous scheme at best and relied on several elements falling into place perfectly. And if it failed, she would end up revealing her true intentions to the vampires and would no longer be safe in their presence. But it was a chance she must take because the Titanic was drawing close to the Irish coast. When she looked out the porthole in her room, she could see the distant shoreline, including Roches Point, where the ship would soon drop anchor. Behind it, rising on the other side of the bay, was Queenstown itself, with brightly colored white, red, and orange buildings all sitting below St. Coleman's Cathedral, which dominated the skyline.

She took a deep breath and steadied her nerves. The time had come. Standing and going to the connecting door between the cabins, she knocked lightly and then stood back, anticipating an answer.

"What is it that you want?" said one of the vampires in a smooth yet dispassionate voice as he opened the door.

"I need to freshen up," Mina said.

"What for?" The vampire looked her up and down. "You look fine to me."

"I wouldn't expect a man to understand," Mina replied as matter-of-factly as she could. "But I have been wearing the same clothes since yesterday, and I'm uncomfortable. Not only that, but I have not had an opportunity to relieve myself since last night when you rescued me. There are no bathroom facilities in this cabin."

"There's a chamber pot under the bed." The vampire's eyes strayed from Mina into the room, then back. "Why didn't you use that?"

"Because I am a lady," Mina responded, drawing herself up to her full height and straightening her back. "A chamber pot might be fine for a common urchin or even a man, but not for me. I'm sure you understand."

The vampire sighed. "There's a women's lavatory behind the grand staircase. I can take you there if you so desire."

"That would be appreciated." Mina waited for the vampire to step aside before she breezed past him into the other cabin. The second vampire was sitting on a small couch with his legs crossed. He was wearing morning attire. A newspaper was spread across his lap. A cup of tea in a fine china teacup was in his hand, as if he had just taken a sip.

When she entered, he looked up and lowered the teacup. "I hope you slept well now that you have been liberated from the clutches of those evil men."

"Yes, thank you," Mina replied. She found it amusing that this vampire, who had likely killed hundreds, if not thousands, of innocent people just for the remaining years of their life, was describing her previous captor in such lurid terms. Not that she could argue, given all she had suffered at his hands over the last four months. "It was a most unpleasant ordeal."

"We already dispatched one. I assure you we will take care of the other. He won't bother any of us, ever again."

"Once we find him," said the other vampire, following Mina into the room. "Unsurprisingly, he appears to have moved to new accommodations."

"We'll find him soon enough." The vampire sipped his tea and gave a contented murmur. "And in the meantime, we shall revel in the lap of luxury. This really is the finest ship I've ever traveled on."

"Don't get too comfortable," said the other. "We're not here for pleasure."

"That doesn't mean we can't enjoy it." The tea-drinking vampire narrowed his eyes. "Where are you taking her?"

"She wishes to refresh herself."

"And use the lavatory. Women's issues," Mina said for good measure. Men of this era, even those who had been on the planet for centuries, were remarkably squeamish about such things.

The vampire observed her for a moment, then turned his attention back to the newspaper. "Don't be too long."

"I shall be as quick as I can," Mina replied, crossing the room.

As she reached the cabin door, her chaperone leaned close and whispered in her ear. "Just so you know, my reflexes are swift, and as one who has been on this earth for centuries, I can move faster than you would believe."

"Is that a threat?" Mina said, turning and meeting his gaze head-on.

"Nothing of the sort. It is merely a friendly warning should you decide to take your chances outside of our care."

"I shall keep that in mind." Mina pulled the door open and stepped into the corridor.

There were other passengers walking back and forth, some arm in arm, and most engaged in excited chatter. But Mina ignored them and weaved her way toward the lavatories with the vampire by her side. It would have been easy to raise the alarm here and cry for help, but she kept quiet because this was not her plan. The vampires were unpredictable, and one wrong move could cost the lives of innocent bystanders. She was not willing to have their deaths on her conscience.

They reached the lavatories.

Mina stopped and turned to the vampire. "I shall be a little while. Perhaps ten or fifteen minutes. If you would like to return to the cabin, I can make my own way back."

"I will stay here," the vampire said, taking a position near the wall next to the door.

"Very well." Mina shrugged as if she viewed his insistence on waiting as nothing more than a waste of time on his part. Then she stepped inside the lavatory and made her way to one of the sinks.

There were two other women present, both of them middle-aged and wearing large wide-brimmed hats with lace trim and shawls around their necks. They paid her little heed as they conversed and giggled over some private joke.

Mina leaned on the sink and steadied her nerves. Everything had gone to plan so far, but now came the trickiest bit. And the most dangerous. But she had come this far and must now continue if she hoped to survive.

Summoning all the angst that she could muster, and forcing tears from her eyes, Mina turned to the two women and grasped their arms. "Please, you must help me, for I am in a most dire predicament, and I fear for my life . . ."

FIFTY-FIVE

A COUPLE of hours after Decker had settled into his chair in the Titanic's reading room, a steward approached quietly and stopped with a subtle clearing of his throat.

Decker looked up.

The steward stood with his hands clasped behind his back. "The Master-at-Arms asked me to fetch you, sir. He said it was most important that you accompany me immediately."

"Has he found something?" Decker asked, setting aside the book he had been pretending to read and jumping to his feet.

"I really couldn't say, sir. He asked me to fetch you but did not take me into his confidence."

"In that case, lead the way."

Decker followed the steward back through the ship to the purser's office, where the Master-at-Arms was waiting with two stocky crewmen wearing knitted sweaters with the White Star Line name and burgee on the front.

"Have you found her?" Decker asked, closing the gap.

"That is my fervent hope, sir," replied the Master-at-Arms. "Only one cabin has requested meals to be taken in their room since departing Southampton. The request was made of the purser earlier this morning by a Mr. Fitzwilliam who occupies a suite on B deck. I am going there now but wanted to inform you of the situation first."

"I'm coming with you." Decker felt a surge of hope. Even though the Titanic had reached Queenstown, there was still time to get Mina off the ship.

"I think it would be better if we did this ourselves." The Master-at-Arms motioned for his crewmen to follow him. "It might not be safe, and I cannot put a passenger in harm's way."

"I can take care of myself," said Decker.

"No doubt." The Master-at-Arms was insistent. "But rules are rules."

Decker was having none of it. He could not afford the delay that would ensue if he were not reunited with Mina immediately. "I'm coming with you, and that's the end of it. Unless you would like me to inform the newspapers that your staff allowed a woman to be kidnapped on board the Titanic and held against her will?"

The Master-at-Arms looked momentarily indecisive as the ramifications of this dawned upon him. His superiors would, no doubt, be unhappy that he had involved a passenger in something so sordid as rescuing a kidnapped woman, but they would also frown upon the adverse publicity such an article would generate. In the end, his face relaxed. "Very well. You can come with us. But I warn you to stay out of our way. I cannot allow any harm to come to you."

"That's what I thought." Decker would have smiled if the situation were not dire. "What are we waiting for?"

"What indeed?" The Master-at-Arms turned, clearly frustrated that Decker had outmaneuvered him, and started toward the elevators.

They rode up one level, made their way through a set of baize doors, and followed the corridor until they came to a cabin that was obviously one of the most expensive on the ship, given how far apart the doors were spaced.

The Master-at-Arms brought them to a halt and knocked.

A moment later the door opened to reveal an older gentleman in black trousers and a silk shirt. An unknotted black bowtie hung loose around his neck. This was, no doubt, Mr. Fitzwilliam. "Can I help you?" he asked in a clipped British accent.

"That remains to be seen," replied the Master-at-Arms. "The purser tells me that you put in a request for meals to be taken in your room earlier today."

"That is correct." Fitzwilliam looked perplexed. "What of it?"

"Might I ask regarding the reason for that request?"

"You may not." Fitzwilliam looked past the Master-at-Arms toward the pair of crewmen and Decker. "What the devil are you people up to?"

"I'm afraid I am not at liberty to say." The Master-at-Arms looked decidedly uncomfortable. But he pressed on. "It will be most helpful if you would just answer my question."

"This is preposterous." Fitzwilliam's face grew dark. "I have never encountered such insolence from common staff." These last words were loaded with disdain.

The Master-at-Arms remained silent for a moment, as if thinking. "This is most unfortunate. I was hoping not to press the matter unnecessarily, but if you will not answer my question, I must insist that you allow me into the room for a brief inspection."

"Now listen here. I don't have to put up with this." Fitzwilliam put his hands on his hips. "You're not setting foot inside this room unless the captain is here to personally authorize it, which I assure you he won't."

The Master-at-Arms sighed. "I would rather not involve the captain, sir, but I will if necessary."

"Henry?" A female voice drifted from within the cabin. "Who are you arguing with?"

"It's nothing you need be concerned with, my dear," Fitzwilliam looked back over his shoulder. "Go back to your needlepoint."

"It is my concern when you are creating such a fuss." An elderly woman in an ankle-length dress that was buttoned to her neck appeared from within the cabin. She tapped Fitzwilliam on the shoulder. "Step aside."

Fitzwilliam, who was so full of indignation a moment before, did as he was told without uttering a word.

The woman pushed past him. "What is going on here?"

"Good afternoon," said the Master-at-Arms with a slight bow. "Are you Mrs. Fitzwilliam?"

"I should certainly hope so. But please, call me Adeline."

"Mrs. Fitzwilliam will do just fine."

"As you please." Adeline looked at the crewmen and Decker lingering in the corridor. She turned her attention back to the Master-at-Arms. "What brings you to our cabin in such a manner?"

"We are merely conducting an inquiry aboard ship. It is nothing to be alarmed about. We asked a question of your husband, and he was unwilling to answer."

"That sounds about right. He can be a cantankerous fool. What is it you need to know?"

"We merely wished to ask the reason your husband requested the purser to arrange for dining in your room."

"That was all you wanted to know?" Adeline shot her husband a withering look. "The meals are for me, because I have been feeling under the weather since we boarded. I'm afraid it might be a touch of influenza, and I did not wish to spread it around the ship."

"Ah. I see." The Master-at-Arms nodded. "That makes

sense. I have just one more question. Are you sharing the room with anyone else?"

"No." Adeline shook her head. "We are traveling alone. Why?"

"Just a routine inquiry. We received word of a stowaway coming aboard in Cherbourg," the Master-at-Arms lied. "It looks like the information might have been false."

"I see. And you thought we might be harboring this person?"

"Not at all. But we are required to be thorough." The Master-at-Arms stepped back from the door. "I'm sorry for the intrusion. I shall have a steward bring champagne and caviar when you are feeling better by way of an apology."

Adeline Fitzwilliam nodded, then stepped back into the cabin and closed the door.

Decker looked on, disappointed. These people were obviously not holding Mina hostage. Nor were they vampires. His window of opportunity to rescue Mina and escape the ship was swiftly evaporating, and he didn't know what to do next.

FIFTY-SIX

THE TWO WOMEN in the bathroom looked at Mina with startled expressions.

Mina wasted no time in getting to the point. "There is a man outside who is most disagreeable. He has been following me, and I fear he wishes me ill."

"Oh, my. What kind of a man?" The closer of the two women, obviously well-bred with porcelain features and dark hair styled into a short bob, raised a hand to her mouth in alarm.

"An unwanted suitor," Mina said, thinking fast. "I boarded the Titanic to escape him and return to New York, where I was raised, but he must have discovered my intentions and followed me. Now he is trying to force me off the ship in Queenstown. I fear that if he succeeds, my life will be worthless, for he is an ogre who cares not for my feelings."

"Well, we can't have that," the other woman said, putting her hands on her hips and looking past Mina toward the door. "Tell me, how will I know this man?"

"He's lingering in the corridor and will be close to the door. You will know him by his dark gray morning suit. He has an antique silver pocket watch also, which he carries in his upper breast pocket." Mina waited a moment for this description to sink in. "I'm so sorry to involve you. I came in here because it is the one place I thought he would not follow me. But as soon as I leave, he will be up on me."

"Don't give it a second thought," the woman said. "My name is Margaret, but everyone calls me Molly."

"Catherine," said the other woman.

"Pleased to meet you both. I'm Helena," Mina replied, saying the first thing that came into her head.

Molly took a step toward the door. "Both of you, stay here." She turned to Mina. "I shall take care of the situation, and then we will spirit you away."

Mina watched her leave, hoping she had not placed the woman in mortal danger. She looked at Catherine. "What do you think she will do?"

"Molly is well known aboard ship. She is friends with Mr. Astor and dined with the captain last night. She will summon help in short order, I am sure. Your unwanted suitor will be detained, at least long enough for you to affect and escape, although I cannot say what will happen after that."

"My immediate situation is of the most concern right now," Mina replied. She could hardly believe her luck in running into this pair of women. She had figured there was a fifty percent chance that anyone she encountered in the lavatory would be unwilling to get involved in a domestic situation. Instead, she had found a champion who had no qualms about going head-to-head with a man and was more than willing to help her escape his clutches. Although that might not have been the case had Molly known the true nature of this man, which was why she could not relax until the door opened again several minutes later and her savior returned with a glint in her eye.

"If you leave now, your suitor will be unable to follow,"

Molly said with a flourish. "He is explaining himself as we speak."

"You're a lifesaver," Mina said with gratitude. She would have hugged Molly, but she feared that might be viewed as inappropriate.

She needn't have worried. Molly stepped forward and wrapped her arms around Mina in a quick embrace, then pulled away. "You are welcome." Then she took off her hat and placed it on Mina's head before removing her shawl and wrapping it around Mina's shoulders. She stepped back. "A perfect disguise, just in case."

"This is too much," said Mina. "How will I get them back to you?"

"Keep them. I have plenty more," Molly replied with a smile. "But if you run into any more trouble and need a hand, come and find me. I'm in cabin E 23."

"I'll remember that," said Mina.

"Make sure that you do." Molly looked at her companion. "Get this young lady to safety. I shall stay here to ensure she is not followed."

Catherine nodded a silent acknowledgment, then took Mina by the arm. "Come along."

They went to the door and opened it a crack, peeking out. The vampire was in heated conversation with two stewards who had cornered him and were now blocking his path. A third steward stood some distance away, watching.

"Just follow my lead and act like you are perfectly giddy with joy. Pay no heed to that man as we leave," Catherine said. "Do not look back over your shoulder, whatever you do."

"I believe I can do that," Mina replied.

"Wonderful." Catherine took Mina's arm in her own, then pushed the door open and stepped out. She turned hard left and started away from the vampire, raising her voice as she did so. "And then, Mr. Astor said that I should winter in Marseille.

Well, I said to him, Marseille is fine, but Nice is nicer." She followed this with a flamboyant laugh.

Mina resisted the urge to glance back at the vampire and followed suit with a laugh of her own.

They reached the grand staircase and turned toward it.

When they were out of sight, Catherine released Mina's arm. "That went splendidly, I do believe."

"How can I ever thank you?" Mina asked, breathless.

"Stay well away from that oaf." Catherine grinned. "And remember, men might think they're smart, but they have nothing on us. Now hurry and leave before your unwanted suitor talks his way past those stewards."

Mina thanked the woman again, then hurried away. The ship had surely dropped anchor off Queenstown by now, and she wasted no time in asking directions to the gangplank. An hour from now, she would be back on terra firma and free of both the vampires and The Man in the Black Suit.

FIFTY-SEVEN

DECKER FOLLOWED the Master-at-Arms back to the purser's office. After the two crewmembers went their separate ways, he followed Thomas King inside and closed the door, then he turned to the purser. "Has anyone else requested meals in their room?"

The purser shook his head. "No. Just Mr. Fitzgerald. But that doesn't preclude the possibility of a meal being collected in the dining room and brought back to a cabin by one of the guests. Likewise, there is an à la carte restaurant on board with a buffet."

"I know. I ate there last night," Decker replied.

"Then you will know how easy it is for a passenger to collect food from the buffet and take it to their cabin."

"Is there a way to find out if any of the passengers have done that?"

The purser shook his head. "Afraid not. We have no prohibition on passengers taking food back to their cabins, and although the bedroom steward might remove the empty plates, it will be impossible to find out which of them has done so."

"I see." Decker was frustrated. He didn't know how long

the Titanic would be anchored in Queenstown, but he was sure the captain would be eager to depart as soon as possible.

"I'm sorry your hunch did not prove correct," the Master-at-Arms said, standing to Decker's left with his arms folded. "We have instructed the gangplank crew not to allow anyone off the ship who is not scheduled to depart today and shall continue to look for Mrs. Swan. We will find her, I promise."

"Thank you," Decker said, although he knew that Thomas King's words were spoken more to placate him than because the Master-at-Arms had any idea what to do next. The problem was, Decker didn't know how to proceed, either.

"And now, if you will excuse me, I have other duties I must attend to," said the Master-at-Arms, turning toward the door. At the threshold, he stopped and looked back at Decker. "When I have news, I shall inform you immediately."

Decker didn't reply. What was there to say? He watched the Master-at-Arms step out onto the first-class landing and disappear along the corridor, then thanked the purser for his help and followed behind.

FIFTY-EIGHT

MINA HURRIED through the first-class corridors to the other end of the ship, where a second staircase would take her down to E deck. After that, she backtracked through the ship toward the gangway door where the tender from Queenstown waited.

Along the way, she passed a gaggle of newly boarded third-class passengers looking for their steerage accommodation with knapsacks and canvas bags over their shoulders. They looked a world apart from the gentry hobnobbing on the promenade deck above. As she passed them, she couldn't help but wonder how many of these unfortunate souls would drown three days hence, in the unforgiving waters of the North Atlantic.

Her throat tightened, and she pushed the thoughts away with great effort. She could do nothing for them. The timeline was set, and she must not interfere. Any change now could have drastic ramifications in the future. Her actions to this point had not caused ripples—so far as she could tell—because the chain of events that had led her here created a loop that was always meant to be, but if she deviated from that and attempted to avert a disaster such as the Titanic sinking, the future might be altered in ways she could not imagine. The universe would cope with this by creating an alternate reality, which she could then end up trapped inside. With that in mind, she rushed past the doomed passengers and tried not to look into their eyes as she made her way to the gangplank.

When she got there, Mina found only a small number of people waiting to disembark, including a man of the cloth who smiled at her and introduced himself as Father Browne.

In his hand was a small box camera, which he raised. "Would you mind?" he asked in a light Irish accent.

Mina stiffened and thought quickly. She did not want her photograph taken. "I'm sorry, Father, but I'm in no condition to be photographed. I fear that I look positively green around the gills and have been feeling seasick."

"I understand, young lady." The priest smiled thinly and lowered the camera. "It is a shame that you could not enjoy the crossing from Cherbourg."

"Indeed." There were no more passengers leaving the tender now for the crossing to New York. Those waiting to disembark shuffled forward and started down the gangplank in a single file. Two stewards and an officer in a peaked cap with a gold braid stood aside and checked their tickets as they went.

When it was Mina's turn, she realized that she did not have a ticket. However, she thought they would have no reason to stop her. After all, she was a first-class passenger and had every right to disembark the ship whenever and wherever she pleased.

She was wrong.

One of the stewards stepped into her path. "I'm sorry, ma'am, but I'll need to see a ticket from either Southampton or Cherbourg to Queenstown in order to let you off the ship."

"That's ridiculous," Mina said in the most authoritative voice she could find. "I've not been feeling well and do not wish to continue on the journey. I fear my sea legs are not what I imagined them to be."

"Be that as it may," the steward replied. "We are under orders to allow only those passengers scheduled to depart at Queenstown onto the tender. The Master-at-Arms was most specific."

"Is there a problem here?" asked the officer, stepping forward.

"Yes," Mina replied. "I wish to disembark, and this man is preventing me."

The officer turned his attention to the steward. "Perhaps you would like to check the list and see if this young lady is on it."

The steward shrugged. He looked at Mina. "Name?"

A sudden panic seized Mina. She could not give her real name, under which she was not traveling, and the false name provided by her captors would not be on the steward's list of disembarking passengers. But what other choice did she have? "My name is Eleanor Swan."

The steward nodded and ran a finger down a list attached to a clipboard. He looked up at her, and his eyes narrowed. "I think you had better come with me, Mrs. Swan."

"That won't be necessary." Mina realized she had made a tactical mistake. She did not know what was going on, but it was clearly bad. "If you would be so good as to let me disembark, I would be forever in your debt."

The steward waited for one of his companions to step up next to her, then he turned and conversed in hushed tones with the officer. When he turned back to her, the look on his face suggested that he had no intention of allowing her off the ship.

"Mrs. Swan, I shall ask again. Please accompany me." He stepped toward Mina.

She backed up and decided that it was time to leave. But her way was blocked by a third steward, who had approached quietly from her rear.

"Please, do not make a scene," said the officer. "You have not been well, Mrs. Swan. Let us take care of you."

"I'm fine," Mina snapped, dropping the pretense of civility. "Let me off the damn ship right now."

The officer nodded to his men without replying. The muscle under his right eye twitched. He was clearly not used to dealing with such combative passengers, especially when they were from first-class.

Two of the stewards approached from different directions and took her by the arms. At first, she resisted, but their grip only tightened as they led her away. The officer followed behind.

They led her back toward the grand staircase and all the way up until they reached A deck. Mina did not know where she was being taken, but it was clearly not to the Man in the Black Suit's cabin, which was on C.

She relaxed a little despite her anger at being detained in such a disrespectful way.

They made their way through a first-class corridor near the bow of the ship and came to the cabin. The officer stepped around his men and knocked.

The door opened.

Mina recoiled at the man who stood there.

"Well, well. You found her." A smile broke on Faucher's face. He stepped aside. "Please do bring her in, and I shall make sure she does not escape my supervision again."

FIFTY-NINE

DECKER LEFT the purser's office and proceeded to the grand staircase nearby. He climbed up to A deck, then stepped out onto the promenade deck. The Titanic was anchored far from shore at the mouth of a wide bay across from which he could see Queenstown and the rolling Irish hills beyond. The sky was a leaden gray, and there was a hint of rain in the air. Far below him, moving across the water with slow determination, was a small vessel. A cluster of people huddled on the open deck with their baggage spread around them. These must be the passengers that were scheduled to disembark in Ireland. Even though they were a good distance away, he studied the faces but saw none that resembled Mina. If nothing else, the vampires had not spirited her off the ship.

He watched the tender chug toward the docks, taking with it his last hope of escape before the Titanic hauled anchor, turned her bow westward, and steamed into history. Then, with a heavy heart, he walked slowly back along the promenade deck with his collar turned up against the biting wind and stepped back inside. His room was close by, but he could not face Faucher again just yet. He had failed to locate Mina and disembark the Titanic and he was overcome by a sense of hopelessness darker than any he had experienced since arriving in London many months before.

He made his way toward the back of the ship and found himself in the first-class lounge where he settled on the sofa.

A steward in a white jacket approached, carrying a silver tray. "Can I fetch you a drink, sir?" he asked.

Decker thought about this for a moment, then shrugged. "Why the hell not? Whiskey neat on the rocks."

"Very good, sir." The steward hurried away and returned a few minutes later with a rocks glass full of amber liquid.

Decker took the drink, tipped the man, and watched the steward beat a hasty retreat. He swirled the liquid around in the glass, staring down into it morosely. He had achieved nothing since setting foot on board. Maybe he shouldn't have stopped Finch from coming along. Perhaps together, they could have found Mina and made their escape. Not that it mattered now. Finch was hundreds of miles away in London, and Decker was committed to whatever fate lay in store.

He sipped his drink and looked out through the teak-framed windows onto the deck beyond. Passengers strolled back and forth. Some of the women carried parasols over one shoulder. Others walked arm in arm with their beaus, flowing dresses tugged by the wind. All wore fashionable hats that would have been suited as much for Ascot as a transatlantic cruise. The men sported heavy jackets and top hats over their morning suits. They greeted the other passengers with polite nods. Most of these people, Decker thought, would soon be dead.

The steward returned and hovered over Decker's shoulder. "Can I get you another drink, sir?"

Decker glanced down and realized that his glass was empty. He had finished the drink while lost in maudlin thoughts. "Sure, why not?"

The steward nodded and hurried away. A few minutes later, a figure approached and stopped a few steps away.

Decker looked up, expecting to find his whiskey waiting, but it wasn't the steward standing there. Decker stood and approached the man. Then, after a brief conversation, he followed his visitor from the room, all thoughts of the drink abandoned.

SIXTY

DECKER HURRIED BACK to his cabin. His heart was racing. The gun tucked into his belt felt heavy. At the door, he paused to gather his wits and slipped the weapon out. Then he opened the door, took a deep breath, and stepped inside.

The first thing he saw was Faucher standing by the connecting door with one arm around Mina's waist, holding her close. In the other hand was his own weapon, the muzzle pressed to the side of her neck. When she saw Decker, Mina's eyes flew wide in surprise, but she remained silent.

"I'm so pleased you could join us," Faucher said, a thin smile touching his lips. "Why don't you be a good lad and put that gun down."

"What are you doing?" Decker asked. "We were supposed to be working together, or did you forget?"

Mina's face turned from surprise to shock. "What? You've been working with this man all along?"

"It's not what you think." Decker gripped the gun tighter than ever. He looked at Faucher. "Let her go."

"So that you can get a clear shot at me? I don't think so."

Faucher gripped Mina tighter. "Now, do as I say and drop the gun."

"Or what?" Decker was pressing his luck, but he had no choice. "You won't shoot her. You need Mina alive and well for your experiments."

"You have a point. It seems we are at an impasse, at least temporarily."

"That would appear to be so. Tell me, how do you think this is going to work from here on out?" Decker asked. "After all, your fake valet is dead, and you've drawn too much attention to yourself now. Mina will never go along with the lie that she is your sick wife. And you can't get rid of me. A second body in the space of twenty-four hours would be too hard to explain. It's over. Release Mina, and we can talk."

"It's not over. As far as anyone else on the ship is concerned, Mina is still my wife, and I have plenty of drugs left to keep her sedated until we reach New York. Might I remind you . . . I didn't kill my colleague. I am the victim here, at least in the eyes of the Master-at-Arms and his lackeys. The only variable not accounted for is you."

"Which is a shame because I'm not going anywhere."

"I wouldn't say that." Faucher maneuvered himself behind Mina. He removed the gun from her neck and pointed it toward Decker. "I've changed my mind. We really aren't at an impasse. I hold all the cards. Put the gun down, or don't. It's of no concern to me because you won't risk injuring Mina. That is your weakness. I, on the other hand, don't have a similar Achilles heel. Here is what's going to happen. I will shoot you dead. After that, I will make sure Mina is suitably sedated before calling that dimwitted Master-at-Arms to the cabin and informing him it was you who abducted Mina and killed my valet, then tried to blackmail me for my wife's return. When I refused your demands, you came at me with a gun, and I was forced to shoot you."

"That's ridiculous," said Decker. "No one is going to believe that given the circumstances."

"I disagree. The people who own this ship will do anything to avoid negative publicity on her maiden voyage. They won't bother to look past an easy scapegoat if it means the matter is solved prior to reaching New York and involving the authorities. That was what they hoped would happen all along, which is why they didn't involve the police in Queenstown."

Decker knew he was right, but he knew something else, too. Faucher wasn't in possession of all the facts. He met Mina's gaze, and an unspoken message passed between them. Then he looked past Faucher toward the connecting door between the cabins. His adversary had forgotten one thing. Each cabin had its own point of entry. The Master-at-Arms had quietly let himself in and silently maneuvered into position behind Faucher, where he overheard every word. In his hand was a Colt revolver, which he now raised.

Decker gave Mina a slight nod.

Fast as lightning, she twisted sideways and knocked the gun down toward the floor to prevent him from shooting Decker even as the Master-at-Arms stepped up behind Faucher and pressed the revolver's muzzle to his head.

"That's quite enough," said the Master-at-Arms. "One wrong move, and I'll put a bullet in you."

Mina turned and glared at Faucher, who was standing with the gun at his side, barely moving a muscle. She reached down and plucked the weapon from his hand. "I'll take that if you don't mind."

Faucher met Decker's gaze. "Well played."

"Well played, indeed," said the Master-at-Arms, looking at Decker. "I wasn't inclined to believe you, but I'm glad that I did. Mr. Ismay will be positively thrilled to have this mess cleaned up."

"Pleased I could be of service," said Faucher sardonically.

"I bet you are." The Master-at-Arms produced a pair of handcuffs. "Your hands behind your back."

Faucher hesitated a moment, then complied. "The people I work for have powerful friends. None of this will stick. I'll be free the moment we dock in New York. You'll see."

"Maybe, maybe not. But in the meantime, your new accommodations on this vessel will be a little less salubrious." The Master-at-Arms slipped the handcuffs on Faucher's wrists and clicked them closed. Then he chuckled. "Dimwitted, am I?"

Faucher didn't respond.

The Master-at-Arms chuckled again. Then he turned and marched Faucher to the cabin door, where two men were waiting, and handed him over, before issuing a terse command. "Take him to the brig and make sure he's locked up tight."

"Wait." Decker nodded toward Faucher. "There's a pendant on a chain around his neck. It doesn't belong to him. It belongs to Mina."

"Is that true?" King turned to Mina.

She hesitated, casting a quick glance toward Decker, then nodded.

The Master-at-Arms nodded to his men. "Search him and remove the pendant."

"No. The amulet belongs to me." Faucher struggled in the sailors' grip.

But it was useless. They soon found the amulet on a silver chain around Faucher's neck, and removed it, then handed it to King.

"You can't take that." Faucher's face contorted in anger. "It's mine."

"We'll see." King waved a hand toward the door. "Get him out of here."

The seamen nodded and bustled Faucher away. Then the Master-at-Arms turned back to Decker and Mina. He held the amulet up and studied it. "There seems to be some disagreement regarding the ownership of this item."

"It was taken from Mina," Decker said. "We would be most grateful if you would give it back."

"I don't think so." The Master-at-Arms slipped the amulet into his pocket. "I'll put it in my office safe, where it will be out of harms way until we reach New York. At that point, if what you say is true, it will be returned."

"You don't understand." Decker took a step forward.

"I would think hard about what you say next, Mr. Decker. I have been instructed to provide assistance, but this is still my ship. The pendant goes in the safe."

"It's fine." Mina placed a hand on Decker's shoulder. "We'll deal with it later."

Decker raised his hands and stepped back.

"That's better." King folded his arms. "Now, it's time for some answers."

SIXTY-ONE

AN HOUR LATER, Decker and Mina sat in the office of
Master-at-Arms Thomas King, who wanted a more in-depth
explanation of the events that had unfolded. They had missed
their opportunity to depart the ship. By the time they dealt with
Faucher, the Titanic had already pulled anchor and left Roche's
Point far behind and they were assured that it was now
impossible to dispatch a tender to collect them. Like it or not,
Mina and Decker were along for the ride.

Earlier, as Titanic was preparing to leave Queenstown, King
had sought Decker out in the first-class lounge to tell him that
Mina—or rather Mrs. Swan as she was then thought to be—had
been stopped while trying to leave the ship and was safely back
with her husband. This was the last thing Decker expected, and
it put him in an awkward position. He was forced to take the
Master-at-Arms into his confidence, although he left a great
deal of details out. King was skeptical, but a hastily sent
message to the telegraph office back in London soon yielded
results. After a wait of thirty minutes, which felt like an
interminably long time to Decker, an answer had come back. It
was from Thomas Finch who confirmed Decker and Mina's

identities and instructed the Master-at-Arms to do as Decker said, by direct order of his Majesty.

The message was necessarily short and lacking in detail, but it had forced King's hand. He grudgingly listened when Decker told him that Mina had been a captive aboard ship all along, and that there was more going on than he could comprehend. There was also no time for a lengthy explanation. Mina must be liberated from the man King knew as Mr. Swan, and quickly. Swan must then be apprehended and held until they reached New York, which, of course, Decker knew would never happen. After cobbling a hastily conceived plan together, Decker had made his way back to the cabin.

Now, Mina and Decker sat opposite the Master-at-Arms and did their best to explain the complicated situation without revealing more than King needed to know. A second telegraph had come in and was waiting for them when they got to the office. This one was longer and instructed the Master-at-Arms to assist Decker and Mina as required going forward. It also reiterated that they were to be allowed unfettered access to all parts of the ship. Finally, it confirmed them as agents of the Crown acting directly on behalf of his Majesty.

"This whole situation is damned confusing," grumbled the Master-at-Arms, rubbing his temples. "You're trying to tell me that the people who brought Mrs. Swan—I'm sorry, Mina—aboard this ship are agents of a nefarious organization that seeks to overthrow the British government, and that those who subsequently abducted her and killed that valet are a rival organization with similar goals?"

"That is exactly what I'm saying," Decker said. He had concocted a cover story that would allow them to operate freely on the ship while not revealing the true nature of the threat, which Decker felt was now mostly contained. This was partly because he did not wish to reveal the Order of St. George, but also because he felt the Master-at-Arms would struggle to believe that Mina was a chimera, part vampire and part human, who had been abducted so that Faucher and his cronies could experiment upon her. That there were more vampires roaming the ship, seeking to stop Faucher and take possession of a slumbering creature currently in the vessel's hold, would further stretch King's sanity. In short, a simple explanation would suffice.

"And as for you," King said, turning his attention to Mina. "Why would either of these groups of people wish to keep you captive? It doesn't make sense."

"And it will have to stay that way," Mina responded coolly. "I regret we cannot take you fully into our confidence. I realize it is a lot to ask for your cooperation based on trust alone but rest assured that you are doing the right thing."

"And the man I just put in my brig?"

"His real name is Ignatius Faucher," Decker said. "He is to be held there until New York, at which point the people we work for will arrange for his removal. I warn you he is a most persuasive man, with whom your crew should not engage in conversation."

"I'll keep that in mind." King leaned back in his chair and folded his arms.

"And the other miscreants running around my ship?" King asked. "They killed that valet, didn't they?"

"Yes. But you must let it be. There is nothing more you can do."

"You want me to turn a blind eye to murder?"

"That is exactly what I want you to do. As I already mentioned, they are more dangerous than you could ever imagine. Apprehending them would put your men in mortal danger. We will deal with the situation in New York."

"And in the meantime?"

"I suspect they will keep a low profile and will not cause any further trouble under the circumstances," Decker replied.

"Besides, I don't even know where they are or which cabin they are in," Mina said. "I was still under the influence of sedatives when they took me. I've only recently regained my senses."

"Yet you escaped from them," said King, sounding incredulous.

"My recollection of the entire event is hazy, to say the least."

"Memory loss is common when dealing with such strong drugs. The effects can last for days afterwards," said Decker. "Sometimes weeks."

"That's a shame," said King. "It's going to be hard enough to explain this mess to the powers that be as it is."

"I'm sure you'll do just fine," said Decker. He pushed his chair back and waited for Mina to do the same. "Now, if you don't mind, we shall take our leave. We are not at liberty to discuss anything else, and I'm sure my colleague is tired and hungry."

"Wait," said the Master-at-Arms as Decker and Mina stepped toward the door.

Decker looked back. "Yes?"

"The young lady will require new accommodation since the cabin she was originally booked into is indisposed. I'll inform the purser to make the arrangements. Stop by his office in an hour or two and he should have a cabin ready."

"Thank you, we'll do that."

"You're welcome. And one more thing—a courtesy if you will," King said, looking up at them. "Keep me informed of your movements from here on out. I want no more shenanigans on this ship without my knowledge. Got it?"

"You have my word on that," said Decker, not meaning it for a second. "I have a request in return. If you see or hear of anything out of the ordinary, please inform us immediately, no matter how trivial you deem it."

King nodded his agreement.

"Thank you," Decker said, then he turned and strode from the office with Mina at his side and started down the corridor.

When they were out of earshot, Mina gripped Decker on the shoulder and brought him to a stop. Anger flashed in her eyes. She glared at him. "Now we've taken care of that, you have some explaining of your own to do. Not least of which is what the bloody hell you're doing aboard this ship and why you were working with the man who kidnapped me."

SIXTY-TWO

DECKER TURNED ON MINA. "This is not the place. We should have this discussion in private. Let's go back to the cabin."

"No. I want answers right now," Mina growled. "Otherwise, I'm not going anywhere with you."

"Don't be ridiculous." Decker took Mina by the arm and steered her into a side corridor where they could be afforded more privacy. He spoke in a low voice. "I came aboard the ship to rescue you after we discovered you were being moved out of the country by Faucher and his associates. We would have rescued you earlier, except the man we interrogated didn't know where you were being held."

"Some rescue," Mina scoffed. She clenched her jaw. "I ended up in the clutches of a whole other group of monsters."

"You're safe now, aren't you?" Decker could not begin to imagine what Mina had endured over the past four months, and he wouldn't find out anytime soon. The anger and fear she had bottled up for so long was rushing out like water from a crumbling dam. And with no one else to be mad at, he was in the line of fire. "Take it easy."

"Don't tell me to take it easy. And I'm far from safe. In seventy-two hours, this ship will hit an iceberg and sink. We'll probably both freeze to death in the Atlantic or get trapped below decks and end up as frozen corpses at the bottom of the ocean. Our last opportunity to escape that fate is gone, and we can't even warn anyone because it will break the timeline."

"Assuming they would even believe us." Decker reached out to take Mina's hand. "I understand you've gone through a dreadful ordeal, but I'm not your enemy."

"Really?" Mina pulled her hand away. "Then why were you in league with that man?"

"He left me no other choice under the circumstances. I found out which cabin he was holding you in and came to free you. When I got there, his valet had been murdered, and you were gone. Faucher showed up moments later while I was examining the body. He recognized me from Mavendale, and I, him. Since you were missing, our goals were temporarily aligned. I felt it was better to keep him close so I could watch him than the alternative. I had no intention of letting him get his hands on you again. I was going to take him out the minute we found you."

"You weren't working with him back in London?"

"How could you even think that?" Decker was genuinely shocked.

Mina shrugged. "I spent the last four months being experimented on in ways you cannot imagine. It was a living hell. I also had a lot of time to think, and I came to the conclusion that my abduction must have been orchestrated with help from within."

"It was," Decker replied. "A man named Daniel Garrett."

"Garrett?" Now it was Mina's turn to be shocked. "He's been with the Order for years. He was one of our best operatives. Thomas recruited him personally."

"I know. And I'm sorry. I also found it hard to believe

anyone from within the Order would betray us. But given the circumstances, I came to the same conclusion as you and started investigating everyone with the means and opportunity. It paid off when I followed Garrett to an illicit meeting above a rundown shaving parlor in the East End. We questioned him, and Garrett refused to talk, at least at first. Finch sent me home to get some rest and persuaded him to talk after I'd gone. Don't ask me how he did it."

"He has his ways," Mina said. "Sometimes it's better not to know." She sighed. "I really wish you had gotten off when you realized how hard it would be to find me. Or even better, hadn't come aboard at all."

"You're lucky it's just me," Decker said. "Finch was adamant about accompanying me. It was all I could do to stop him."

"That sounds like Thomas." Mina let herself smile. "You must have been very persuasive for him to stay behind."

"I was," Decker replied solemnly. "With a little help from some chloroform. Then I locked him in my bedroom and dismissed his driver before catching the boat train."

"You drugged him?" Mina's smile turned into a grin. "I wish I was there to see that. He must've been mad as anything when he woke up and realized what you'd done."

"I'm trying not to think about it," Decker admitted. "He'll probably throw me back in that jail cell where he found me if I ever go back to London."

"That's if you're lucky." Mina's anger had faded away. She looked up at Decker with wide eyes. "I'm sorry I yelled at you. I should have known you would never betray me."

"And I should have known you would find a way to escape those vampires."

"Yes, you should." Mina hesitated. "I almost made it off the ship. I got all the way to the gangplank, but they stopped me from getting into the tender because I wasn't scheduled to disembark."

"That was kind of my doing," Decker admitted. "I didn't want the vampires taking you off in Queenstown because I might never have found you again. The Master-at-Arms was all too happy to stop any unauthorized departures considering he had a dead body on his hands and a murderer running around the ship."

"So here we are," Mina said. "Trapped together on one of the most famous ships in history and heading towards disaster."

"Yup."

"Figures." Mina shrugged. "Funny thing is, I'm not sure this is even the worst situation we've ever been in."

"It's at least in the top three," Decker said with a grin.

"You know, we've got a couple of days before we're due to hit that iceberg. Might as well make the most of them. After all, we're on the Titanic. It's terrifying, but at the same time, you have to agree it's freaking cool."

"What did you have in mind?" Decker asked.

"Well, for a start, they had awesome food on this floating deathtrap, and I'm starving. Where's the restaurant?"

Decker gave Mina the once over. "You must've been wearing those clothes for days. Maybe we should find you a fresh outfit first."

"My captors didn't exactly pack me a suitcase. This is the only dress I have."

"That might be a problem. This isn't like the cruise ships of the twenty-first century. There are no chic boutiques here."

"Don't worry, I know a place where we can get what I need. Cabin E 23."

"Who's in cabin E 23?" Decker asked.

"A friend," Mina said, smiling. "But first, let's eat."

Decker grinned. He held an arm out for her to take. "Whatever you say. The restaurant has a fantastic filet mignon. Melts in your mouth. I'll treat you."

"Damn right. I still haven't forgiven you for following me on this ship. It was a foolish thing to do. But if I have to hit an iceberg and sink with anyone, I'm glad it's you."

SIXTY-THREE

LATER THAT NIGHT, Decker sat in a chair next to the bed inside the suite assigned to Mina earlier that day by the purser, which had not only a bedroom but also a small sitting area with a sofa and table. It was almost midnight, and Mina was asleep, but she had asked him to stay and watch over her. A lamp next to the sofa was on, casting an orange glow about the room.

Decker thought back to the events of the day. After leaving the Master-at-Arms and reassuring Mina that they were still on the same side, she had insisted that they visit Titanic's sumptuous restaurant, where she ate not one but two filet mignon steaks and washed them down with half a bottle of 1908 vintage Chateau Filhot Sauternes, an intensely flavored sweet white wine. She had originally asked for a Cabernet, but the waiter had informed her that their stock was small due to the problems of storing red wine aboard ship where the movement would disturb the sediments. He had suggested the Sauternes instead, and Mina had graciously accepted. After her ordeal, she was not in the mood to argue.

Later, they visited the room of Mina's new friend, Molly, where Mina introduced Decker as her brother, who was helping her escape. She explained her lack of clothing by saying that her own wardrobe had been slashed with a knife and destroyed in an act of revenge by her jilted suitor during his attempt to remove her from the ship in Queenstown. The woman was aghast and wasted no time in organizing a suitable wardrobe for a first-class lady aboard ship. Molly's own clothes were several sizes too big, but her friend, Catherine, was a more adequate fit, and now Mina had four fresh dresses hanging in the wardrobe and two new hats.

Decker leaned back and closed his eyes, overcome by exhaustion. Even though he had slept for a few hours the night before, it was a light and guarded slumber, given the man who occupied the cabin next door.

"John?" Mina had rolled over and was looking at him.

Decker opened his eyes and looked at her. "I thought you were asleep."

"I was for a while. Thank you for staying with me."

"You're welcome." Decker was just glad to be reunited with her. "What's bothering you?"

"The amulet that Thomas King took from Faucher. It's what the vampires want. Without it they can't rejuvenate that creature down in the hold. King doesn't know the danger that he's in."

"We'll be fine. The amulet is locked in the Master-at-Arms' safe, and neither of the vampires that took you are linked to it through blood, which means they can't sense it. Only Amenmosep has that ability because it was his amulet."

"That doesn't mean the Master-at-Arms is safe."

"The vampires don't even know that he has it."

"And Amenmosep?"

"He's incapacitated, just like Abraham Turner. At this point, he's nothing more than a shriveled carcass locked in a crate in the hold. And even if he weren't, I doubt he could sense it."

"I don't follow," Mina said sleepily.

"Paint of this era contains lead. The one element that can shield the amulet," Decker said. "There must be lots of it on this ship. Not to mention, all the plumbing is probably lead, too. He'd have to be right on top of it before he felt the slightest tingle."

"I hope you're right."

"I am. And in a few days, the amulet will be at the bottom of the ocean, three miles down, still locked inside the safe in the Master-at-Arms' office.

"And Amenmosep will be right there with it, still stuck in the hold."

"Exactly."

"What if the vampires try to resurrect him before then, even without the amulet?"

"It's unlikely. There are six holds on this ship, and they are huge. The vampires could never find the correct crate among the other cargo. My guess is that they plan to intercept the crate after it's offloaded in New York. Right now, their goal is the amulet and nothing more. Don't forget; they are unaware the ship will sink."

"Now I just need to stay away from them," Mina said. "I can't imagine it pleased those vampires that I gave them the slip."

"Probably not. But this is a large ship, and we know which area to avoid."

"They might be looking for me."

"Maybe. Or they might have assumed that you disembarked in Queenstown. Either way, they won't risk drawing attention to themselves in public. As long as we're careful, it will be okay."

"At least until the ship sinks."

"Yes, until then." The Titanic's fate had hung over Decker like a cloud ever since they left the Irish coast, but it was a situation they could not tackle until it happened. All he could hope was that their foreknowledge gave them an advantage, even if they could warn no one else.

Mina must have been thinking the same thing. "Titanic hit the iceberg a little before midnight on the fourteenth. It took about two and a half hours to sink, but to begin with, nobody believed it would go down. They lowered the first lifeboats at less than half capacity."

"How do you know all this?" Decker asked. He knew the ship sank, of course, but not the details. He couldn't remember the date it went down except that it was at night, and there was confusion among the passengers and crew.

"Are you kidding me? The Titanic always fascinated me," Mina said. "I used to read books on it and watch documentaries when I was growing up. Of course, I never imagined I'd actually be on it. That isn't quite so much fun."

"You can say that again." Decker was silent for a moment. "If the first lifeboats weren't full, there's an opportunity for us to get off."

"Yes. But we have to make sure we are in the right place. When Captain Smith called for women and children to board the lifeboats, the order was taken differently depending on who was in charge of a particular boat. The officer in charge on one side of the ship interpreted it as women and children first. In contrast, the officer on the other side refused to let men onto the lifeboats regardless of open seats, even if there were no more women and children in the vicinity willing to climb aboard."

"I don't suppose you remember which side allowed men on?" Decker asked. While he had no intention of taking the place of a woman or child, he saw no reason not to climb aboard a boat that would depart half-empty, anyway.

"Sorry," Mina replied. "I guess I should've paid better attention."

"Hey, it's not like you could have known it would ever be

important," Decker said. "We have a fifty percent chance of getting it right the first time. Those are good odds."

"Not good enough. More than half the people aboard will be dead in seventy-two hours. That number could very well include us."

"I know."

Silence fell between them as they contemplated this. Neither one wished to continue the conversation because there was no good resolution. After a while, Decker heard Mina's breathing become rhythmic and interspersed with light snores. Overcome by exhaustion from her ordeal, sleep had overcome her despite the horrors that lay ahead.

Decker watched her for a while. His own cabin was not far away, but he had no intention of leaving Mina alone. Not when they were so recently reunited. He settled back in the chair and closed his eyes. Soon, he also fell into a light and restless sleep.

SIXTY-FOUR

IGNATIUS FAUCHER SAT on the floor in a padded room near the bow of the ship with his arms folded. Titanic didn't have a brig in the traditional sense. There were no cells with bars across the front or narrow beds to lie on. Instead, what it possessed was a small square room next to the ship's hospital that more resembled the sort of accommodation afforded to a patient in an insane asylum.

The walls were covered with padded cloth, as were the floor and ceiling. Even the inner surface of the door was padded. There was no furniture. The only illumination came from one small bulb mounted in a recessed alcove high above.

That the Titanic possessed only this one barely suitable room within which to confine a prisoner would have amused Faucher under other circumstances. It said a lot about the sensibilities of those who owned the ship that they considered it more likely a passenger would lose their mind than commit a crime.

Still, at least it was comfortable, Faucher thought. And even if he was forced to spend the next four days confined to this room, he would walk free the minute they reached New York.

Of that, he was certain. And although he had lost Mina, at least temporarily, he still possessed another important item.

The Master-at-Arms had taken the amulet from around his neck, thanks to Decker's meddling, but it was of no concern. The silver chain and the loop that held the amulet were genuine and had spent millennia at the bottom of a canopic jar in Amenmosep's tomb. But the amulet itself was a fake and would do them no good.

Realizing the danger posed by the vampires who had shown up at the British Museum, and concerned they might follow him aboard ship, Faucher had possessed the forethought to have the amulet copied. This had been no simple task, but a visit to a local stonemason who had fallen upon hard times solved the problem. For a ten pound note—equivalent to about three weeks of pay—and a promise to remain silent about his task, the stonemason had fashioned a convincing enough copy of the amulet and aged it with the help of soot, and other materials rubbed into its surfaces. He had even carved the same symbols into the small stone disk, although the rendition was crude compared to the original. For this task, he had been given twenty-four hours and had not disappointed. The amulet did not possess the power of the original, but it would pass all but the most rigorous inspection, especially since no one had seen the genuine amulet in thousands of years. If the vampires found and took the copy, even if they killed him in the process, the original would be safe. Only Amenmosep himself would be able to tell the difference because each vampire was linked to his own amulet, and it would call to no one else. So long as the ancient creature remained safely inside his crate down in the hold, there would be no problem.

Faucher opened his coat and ran his fingers along the seam. They brushed over a slight bulge that would be unnoticeable to anyone who didn't know it was there. This was the genuine amulet, removed from its chain and sewn into the jacket where it would not be found. Even if the worst happened and Faucher was killed, his associates waiting in New York could retrieve the jacket from his body and take possession of the amulet. While not a hundred percent foolproof, it was about as close to an insurance policy as Faucher could get. Thankfully, the vampires had failed in their bid to kill him, and now he was in the one place they could not easily reach. All in all, apart from temporarily losing Mina and enduring less comfortable digs for a few days, things had worked out quite well.

Faucher closed his jacket again, content that the amulet was still there, and leaned against the wall. He didn't know what time it was because there were no windows in his padded cell, and they had removed his watch along with anything else the Master-at-Arms deemed unsafe for a prisoner to possess. They had even taken his shoes and bow tie. But he guessed it was sometime in the middle of the night, judging by how long he had been confined and the fact that he had been brought a light supper of bread and soup many hours earlier. It was hardly the lavish banquet he would have enjoyed in the first-class dining saloon, but it was better than nothing.

Faucher took a deep sigh and closed his eyes. The cell was cold, and he wished there was a blanket. But in at least one respect, the frigid temperature had worked in his favor. The sailors who threw him in here had let him keep his jacket, within which the amulet was secreted, for warmth. But despite this, his extremities felt frozen. The thin dress socks on his feet were no match for the bitter North Atlantic air.

He ignored the chill and tried to sleep, but it proved elusive at first. Then, just as he was finally drifting off, a noise came from the other side of the cell door.

Faucher opened his eyes and sat up straight. Could it be breakfast time already? He didn't think so.

The noise came again, and the hair on Faucher's neck stood up. This didn't sound like some steward bringing him refreshment. He could hear rasping breaths that sounded almost animalistic.

Something scratched on the outside of the door, like fingernails raking on the metal.

Faucher shrank back, a small whimper escaping his throat.

The sound came again, followed by what could only be the rattling of the door handle, although Faucher could not be sure because there was no handle on the inside of the cell door.

He pressed himself against the back wall, watching the door in wide-eyed fear. Then he heard the unmistakable sound of barrel bolts being drawn back—one at the bottom of the door and another at the top. A moment later, the door swung inward, and Faucher got a good look at his visitor. He would have screamed in terror, but there was no time.

SIXTY-FIVE

WHILE IGNATIUS FAUCHER contemplated his situation many decks above, Amenmosep huddled in the darkness inside the hold, his wasted body pressed into a small alcove between two crates. He had been this way for almost twenty-four hours after killing the steward guarding the door. Even dispatching two victims in quick succession had not reinvigorated him because the deaths meant nothing without his amulet.

He had sensed it briefly many hours ago, but then it faded before he could pinpoint its position, and he had been too weak to follow. Exhausted, Amenmosep had found a concealed place to hide and rest, hoping that the passage of time would restore at least a little of his previous vigor. But he had been buried under the Egyptian sands for too long, and no amount of rest would help. There was only one way he was going to regain his strength and youth. He must find the amulet and reclaim it.

Amenmosep gathered what little strength he had remaining and crawled from concealment. He tried to stand on two legs, but they would not support him, so instead, he dragged himself along on all fours until he reached the hold door. He was still not sure of his exact location but had concluded that he must be in the bowels of a ship, judging by the unsettling sway that upset his equilibrium. If he was right, it was a big ship constructed of metal. Vessels of Amenmosep's day were built of wood. Planks shaped and lashed together. They were also powered by sails, but the constant throbbing rumble that vibrated through this unbelievably large ship's belly suggested another means of forward motion, although he couldn't begin to guess what it was.

Amenmosep reached the door. It was standing open just like it had been when he dragged his hapless victim back into the darkness and tore at him with hungry desperation. Beyond the door was a small oblong space that rose into more darkness. Twisting steps made of iron wound their way through this shaft, going so high that he could not see where they ended. But he knew one thing. They went somewhere better than this.

Placing a foot on the bottom rung, Amenmosep tested it, then put his other foot on the next rung. He continued on like this, using his hands to clutch at the higher rungs lest he toppled backward. He soon came to a landing with doors leading off. There were men here in the rooms surrounding the staircase. But he did not sense the amulet and let them be. Senseless killing would only drain his strength faster.

He climbed higher, coming to another landing, then a third. In each instance, he felt the presence of humans all around him, but as before, the amulet remained elusive.

Finally, after what felt like a long time, Amenmosep reached one final staircase. This one was not a spiral. The ship's sway was more pronounced here. The sound of wind howling above reached his ears. And now he sensed it. Nothing more than a faint tingle.

The amulet.

It was close at hand. Amenmosep scurried at the last set of stairs and threw open the doorway at the top, the exertion leaving him exhausted. But it was worth it. He could feel the amulet calling to him like a long-lost friend. It was so close now he almost fainted with joy. He turned his head one way, then the other. The corridor that he now found himself in was empty. He stepped out and paused, focusing on the amulet. Then he turned toward the door several feet away on the other side of the corridor.

It was there. He knew it.

Amenmosep went to the door and touched it. He placed his head close and felt a throbbing pull from beyond. The ancient brand on his wrist, a symbol burned there for as long as he could remember, tingled in anticipation.

He looked down. There was a curved handle, but when he tried it, the door would not open. Then he saw the small metal rods holding the door closed. One at the top and one at the bottom. He heaved himself up on legs, barely able to support his own weight, and drew back the top bolt. Slumping back down, he did the same with the bottom one. Then Amenmosep pushed the door open.

Huddled at the back of the room beyond the door was a thin man dressed all in black. When he saw the nightmare creature in front of him, he shrank back in terror.

The amulet was practically screaming at Amenmosep now. It made every fiber of his body come alive and dance. He drew in a long, rattling breath. Then, unable to resist any longer, he leaped forward with arms outstretched, all thought of weakness gone.

SIXTY-SIX

STOKER FRED BARTLETT'S shift had finished twenty minutes earlier. He was dirty and tired after a four-hour shift shoveling coal into Titanic's hungry furnaces. His workday was necessarily short because of the extreme heat in the boiler rooms. Any more than that, and he would risk death due to dehydration, which was why he would not return to his station for eight hours. Now, all he wanted to do was climb into his bunk in the dormitory he shared with fifty-three other stokers, also known as firemen, in the Titanic's bow, far from the passenger accommodation and deliberately out of sight. But first, he wanted to visit the Fireman's mess a level above the dormitory on C deck, where a steaming mug of tea would be waiting.

He made his way through the ship and up the crew stairs, then hurried across the open forecastle deck between the hulking cranes and around the cargo hatches to the crew areas tucked into the front of the ship. Above him was a tall mast. Halfway up, in the crow's nest, he could make out a figure leaning forward and peering out into the night. There would be another crewmember there, too. The ship had six crewmen employed as lookouts who would swap out every two hours because to spend any longer exposed to the elements so high on the mast would risk frostbite.

Bartlett's job might be hot and dirty, he might spend hours on end at the bottom of the ship hauling coal with a shovel, but he would rather do that than climb the narrow ladder inside the mast and step out fifteen meters up into a flimsy basket to stare out the horizon. That, thought Bartlett, might be the worst job on the ship. At least in his opinion.

He lowered his eyes from the crow's nest and hurried back inside, closing the door behind him to keep out the worst of the chill because the crew accommodations in this part of the ship were not heated. His life was a constant swing of the pendulum between excessive heat and bitter cold, thought Bartlett morosely as he headed for the mess room. Still, it was better pay than being a steward, although at times, he thought the trade-off was not worth it. But he'd worked boiler rooms all his life, starting on White Star ships like the Germanic and Majestic. Smaller vessels than the one he currently served on, but no less demanding. It was all he knew and probably all he would ever know.

Bartlett made his way along the corridor. The fireman's mess was up ahead on the right, but another door stood open on the left next to Titanic's small hospital facility, which was really only two rooms with a bed in each. One that should not have been open.

He slowed and looked around, wondering if the Master-at-Arms was somewhere nearby. The open door led to the vessel's only jail cell. That was strange. It was supposed to be shut and locked, even when it was not occupied.

He didn't see the Master-at-Arms anywhere. The corridor was quiet and empty. Not even a murmur of conversation from the mess further down the corridor reached his ears. It was the early hours of the morning, and most of the other firemen on his shift had opted to go straight to their beds rather than seek a warm cuppa.

He approached the door, then he heard it. A slurping, lapping sound, similar to the one his dog back in Southampton made when drinking from a water bowl. But there were no dogs on the ship, and certainly not in the crew areas.

Bartlett stopped before he reached the threshold. Now that he was closer, he wasn't so sure he wanted to know what was in the padded room. A tingle of apprehension wormed its way up his back. Some ancient sixth sense told him to run. Turn around and get the hell out of there.

The lapping had stopped now as if whoever was making the noise had realized he was there. Bartlett strained his ears, but all he heard was the faint sound of water breaking against the ship's bow and the wind buffeting over the deck.

"Just my imagination," he muttered, trying to convince himself that all was right, mostly because he knew what he had to do next. He couldn't turn and run because there might be an injured crewman in the room or, worse, a guest.

Bartlett took a deep breath, steeled his nerves, and stepped into the doorway.

The sight that greeted him froze the blood in his veins.

A man lay on the floor with his neck ripped open. Blood had spread around him like a crimson halo. The man's clothes were ripped and shredded. His jacket lay a few feet away, torn apart at the seams. Crouching above him was another man, naked and skeletal, with ashen gray skin and tufts of wiry hair attached to his mottled scalp. Blood rimmed his mouth. In his hand, this barely human creature gripped a disk made of stone. This, too, was streaked with blood.

The creature's head snapped around. It fixed Bartlett with milky eyes that somehow still shined with an impossible intensity.

A gasp of surprise laced with fear escaped Bartlett's mouth.

He took a step back, unable to tear his eyes from the grisly tableau.

"What is this?" he bellowed, barely aware of his own words.

The creature stood and stared at him. Then his mouth pulled back into a rictus smile to reveal stained and yellow teeth.

Bartlett found his feet. He turned to run.

He never got the chance.

The creature lunged forward, gripped his collar before he could even take a step, and dragged him back into the cell.

He would have screamed, but his throat was the first to go.

SIXTY-SEVEN

THE TINY CELL had been transformed into a slaughterhouse.

The Master-at-Arms shook his head in disbelief and turned to Decker. "What could do a thing like this?"

"You wouldn't believe me if I told you," Decker said, looking at the carnage in front of him. It was nine in the morning, and he had been roused thirty minutes earlier by a frantic steward who had checked his cabin, then made his way to Mina's suite where Decker was still sleeping in a chair.

"Try me." King rubbed his temples. He shook his head. "This is a disaster. And on our maiden voyage to boot. We're not even halfway to America and already we have three bodies."

Beside Decker, Mina tensed. She touched his elbow and whispered. "Can we talk?"

"Give us a minute," Decker said to King.

"Why not." King looked at the two dead bodies littering his padded cell. "It's not like either of these chaps are going anywhere anytime soon."

Decker followed Mina out onto the forecastle deck. He turned to her. "I know what you're going to say."

"We can't tell him the truth."

"I don't think we have a choice."

"Yes, we do. We say nothing and leave the crew of this ship to investigate on their own. In less than three days it won't matter either way."

"And what about the people that might die if we stay silent?"

"They're going to die anyway," Mina said. "In our time, this has already happened. Everything we do on the ship is preordained."

"I don't remember anything about vampires being aboard the Titanic," Decker replied. "Let alone ripping people apart. Do you?"

"That's my point." Mina's face was hard as stone. "You can't change history. This has already happened, and no one found out about those murders, or anything else that will occur between now and the sinking. At least not as it relates to vampires."

"I can't do it," Decker said. "What if our inaction changes history? Have you thought about that?"

"It won't."

"You can't be sure."

Mina's shoulders slumped. She blew into her hands to warm them. "You're right. But do you really want to tell that man that he's dealing with vampires?"

"Maybe."

"He won't believe you."

"He'll believe his eyes. No normal man could rip Faucher and that crewman apart like that."

"Which brings me to my next question," Mina said. "Do you think it was the vampires that did this, or something else?"

"You mean Amenmosep."

"Yes. You saw Faucher's Valet. He wasn't torn apart like that. These killings . . . They're savage. Uncontrolled. That doesn't sound like the creatures that took me. They were the exact opposite. I'm telling you; this wasn't them."

"Which is even more reason to tell King what's going on." Decker was just as loathe to tell the Master-at-Arms the truth as Mina, but the alternative might be so much worse. "And like you said, in a few days, it won't matter. Most of these people will be dead."

"That's harsh."

"It's the truth. Unless you want to find the captain and tell him what he's steaming toward."

"You know we can't do that."

"Then let's give the Master-at-Arms a fighting chance to protect lives while he can," Decker said. "We'll tell him in private and swear him to secrecy."

"I still don't like it."

"We'll also confirm our suspicions before we say anything. If Amenmosep is still in the hold then we'll revisit this conversation." Decker took Mina's hand. "We have to be in agreement before we tell him anything."

Mina said nothing for a moment. She walked to the railing and looked out over the cold gray ocean. "I thought the worst thing we had to worry about was getting off the ship alive after it hits that iceberg."

"I know." Decker came up behind her. He leaned on the railing. "We'll deal with this the same way we do everything else."

Mina nodded. Her hair blew in the wind, whipping around her neck. "We should go back in there. I want to take a closer look at those bodies." She turned and headed toward the door.

Decker followed her back inside.

When they reached the cell, King glanced their way. "Anything you want to tell me?"

"Not at the moment," Decker replied. He stepped into the padded room with Mina at his side and approached the pair of eviscerated bodies. He kneeled next to Faucher. "Why come after him?"

"That's what I was wondering," Mina said.

The Master-at-Arms had followed them in. He stood with his hands in his pockets and looked down at his erstwhile prisoner. "You think this man was the target?"

"Why else would he be dead?" Decker said. "He was in a locked room. There were plenty of easier victims, just one deck below in the fireman's quarters. There were plenty of people walking around the ship. The killer came here for Faucher." Decker turned to look at the dead stoker. "This man was just in the wrong place at the wrong time. He probably stumbled across this on his way down below."

"The jacket," said Mina, looking at the discarded garment lying a few feet away. She stepped over the body, careful to avoid the blood, and picked it up. "The seam has been ripped open. Why would the killer bother to take Faucher's jacket off him and do that?"

"Because he's crazy?" asked King.

"Or because our killer was looking for something." Mina ran a finger along the torn inner lining. She looked at Decker. "Something was concealed here."

Decker stepped closer and looked at the jacket. There, imprinted within the silk of the lining, was a round indentation. "I have a bad feeling about this."

"Me too." Mina turned to the Master-at-Arms. "We need to see the amulet in your safe right now."

King looked perplexed. "Are you serious? We have two mutilated bodies on our hands. There are more important things to do."

"No," Decker said, shaking his head. "There aren't. Take us to your office this instant. We have to check that safe. It might explain why these men are dead."

SIXTY-EIGHT

AMENMOSEP LAY on the bed with his eyes closed and his hands clutched over his stomach. Next to him, on the sheets, was the small stone disk that played such an integral part in extending his life over eons. The silver chain and the holder that held it around the rim were gone, but it was of no concern. He had what he needed and would soon be at full strength.

The first-class cabin was opulent. Actually, it wasn't so much a cabin as a suite of rooms, and it would provide an excellent place for Amenmosep to recover his strength before he ventured out in search of more tantalizing prey.

On the floor, pushed up against the wall, were the original occupants of the room, their throats cut open by a knife he had found in the room next to the one where he had recovered his amulet. He didn't know their names, and he didn't care. They were a means to an end, nothing more.

After killing the two men in the strangely padded room, he had decided it would be best to keep a low profile, at least for the moment. The animalistic urges that had racked him during his first kills down in the vessel's hold had all but vanished. He felt stronger. He felt more like himself. This was partly due to

286

the knowledge he had ingested along with the remaining life force of Faucher and the stoker. He knew where he was and when he was, although that last fact left him reeling. Had it really been so many centuries since he had last walked the earth? Apparently so.

But this new age that he found himself in was better. The people were meek and soft. It had been easy to find a solitary passenger roaming the first-class hallways in the middle of the night. The old man had been returning from a poker game that had gone on into the early hours inside another cabin. Amenmosep had followed a little way behind and struck when the man was fumbling with his key to open the cabin door, a little worse for wear thanks to a bottle of brandy that would have cost a third-class passenger three months of wages.

Ten minutes later, after taking care of both the man and his terrified wife, Amenmosep had not only extended his own life by many more years—although not as many as he would have liked considering their ages—but had also found a place to hide and absorb the years he had stolen. Not only that but there was a full wardrobe of clothes that would allow him to blend in with the other passengers once his desiccated skin had healed and he was feeling more like himself.

How long this would take, he did not know, but given the inordinate amount of time he had spent in forced slumber, he suspected it would be at least twenty-four hours and maybe more. He could feel the energy racing through his body and repairing his brittle bones and shriveled organs, but he was by no means restored. Not yet.

When he was, Amenmosep knew exactly what to do next.

The man in the padded room had not just returned his amulet and provided him with many more years of life, but he had passed on a particularly interesting piece of information, albeit unwillingly, as his life force flowed from him into its new host.

There were more vampires on the ship.

Three of them.

Amenmosep had never been squeamish about killing his own kind, especially when it benefited him. And the other vampires on this ship would benefit him greatly. The stored lives that they carried within them would rejuvenate him faster than killing all the other passengers. And now that he had the amulet, he could do that. Most vampires didn't even know it was possible to kill one of their own kind and absorb their energy. And ordinarily, it wasn't. But Amenmosep was no ordinary vampire. He was one of the first and purest. To him, most other vampires were nothing more than rodents. Maybe one step above the rest of humanity, but vermin, nonetheless. They were half-breeds, and that was their weakness. They could not kill him, but he could easily kill them.

That thought sent a shiver of pleasure through him.

Soon, when he was strong enough, he would emerge from this cabin indistinguishable from any other first-class gentleman on the ship, and then he would hunt.

Three vampires.

He could hardly wait.

Amenmosep let the thought linger in his mind as he rested, and then he smiled. In Egypt, he had been a god. He saw no reason why he could not be one again.

SIXTY-NINE

"LET ME SEE THE AMULET," Decker said. He was standing in Thomas King's office with Mina at his side.

The Master-at-Arms looked visibly shaken but had agreed to accompany them to the office, leaving his men to deal with the mess in the padded cell, although he was far from happy about it.

"I can't imagine why you're so obsessed with a piece of jewelry when there are two men lying dead, not a stone's throw from here," King said.

"I assure you, it's of the utmost importance that we examine that amulet." Decker wasn't sure what he was looking for, but he hoped they would know it when they saw it. If his hunch was correct, they were in a world of trouble.

"Ridiculous, that's what it is," grumbled the Master-at-Arms, crossing to the safe and dialing in the combination before pulling the heavy door open. He reached inside and withdrew the amulet, still on its silver chain, then placed it on the desk. "There you go, for all the good it will do you."

Decker picked up the amulet and looked at it. He didn't know what he was expecting to see, except that it belonged to an Egyptian who had lived thousands of years before, which meant that it was old. Ancient, in fact. He held it in front of his face and studied it. The pitted and scarred surface was covered in markings he couldn't interpret. Giving up, he handed it to Mina. "What do you think?" .

"I don't know." Mina turned the amulet over in her hand. Then she turned her attention to the chain and the thin metal loop that hung from it surrounding the stone disk. She fumbled for a moment, and then the loop sprang apart, released by a hidden catch. Removing the stone disk, Mina set the chain down on the table. "This isn't right."

"What do you mean?" Decker asked.

"The stone this is made from. It's too soft." Mina held the amulet between her thumb and forefinger and slammed it into the edge of the desk with all her might. A piece of the rim chipped off and fell onto the floor.

"What are you doing?" Decker exclaimed, aghast.

"It's made of sandstone. And not a particularly durable composition at that. It has a low quartz content. There is no way this would have survived thousands of years. The real amulet would be crafted from something much harder and durable."

"Then we were right, it's a fake."

"Yes. Look at the rim where that piece chipped off. The stone inside is clean. All the dirt and weathering are on the surface with no penetration. It's an excellent copy, but a forgery nonetheless."

"Faucher swapped out the real stone for a fake and sewed the genuine one into the lining of his jacket as an insurance policy. He knew someone might come looking for it."

"Precisely." Mina put the amulet down on the desk. "Which makes it even more likely that it wasn't those two vampires that killed him and took it. Not only would they be unaware that he had been arrested, but they wouldn't be able to sense the amulet. Only Amenmosep could do that."

"Hold on a gosh-darned minute," the Master-at-Arms said, looking confused. "What's all this talk about vampires? You're joking, right?"

"I'm afraid not," Decker said. "I hate to be the bearer of bad news, but there are at least two vampires on board, possibly more. I also believe that a particularly dangerous creature has escaped from your hold."

"What kind of a creature?" The Master-at-Arms didn't sound like he believed a word of it.

"A vampire of ancient origin."

"Probably much more powerful than the ones that abducted me," Mina said.

"So now it was vampires that abducted you, was it, Miss?"

"Yes." Mina nodded.

"The pair of you have lost your marbles. Either that or you've been into the sherry." The Master-at-Arms shook his head. "I've had enough of this charade. Two more men have been murdered on my ship, and here you're spinning me fairytales. I won't have it, I tell you."

"This is no fairytale," said Decker. "We must visit hold number three at your earliest convenience."

"Does this have something to do with that cargo your erstwhile colleague was so keen to check on?"

"Yes, it does." Decker was growing tired of this back-and-forth. "Time is wasting. We need to go right now. More lives may be at stake."

"Very well. I'll take you down to the hold. But not because I believe a word of your vampire tale. I want to see what that man was so desperate to see. Maybe it has something to do with his death."

"A shrewd deduction." Decker glanced toward the door. "There's no time like the present."

"The pair of you are going to be the scourge of me," King grumbled, rounding the desk and stepping out into the corridor. "Well, come along."

They made their way to the front of the ship, crossing over the forecastle deck and entering back into the crew compartment on the other side. There was still activity around the padded cell, with men coming and going as they cleaned up the mess within.

King ignored the activity and went to a nearby door marked 'lantern store'. He stepped inside and grabbed three lanterns, handing one to Mina and another to Decker.

"It will be dark down there. You'll need these," he said, lighting his lamp.

Decker nodded and took the lantern, then followed the Master-at-Arms to a door further along the corridor. Decker had been here once already, when he and Faucher had tried to sneak down to find Amenmosep. A flight of stairs led down to the deck below. Here a pair of spiral staircases wound all the way down to the cargo level.

They descended in single file with King in the lead. When they reached the landing outside the cargo hold, the Master-at-Arms came to a stop. The door was standing open.

"This isn't right," King said, looking at the door. He stepped across the threshold, holding his lantern high, and waited for the others to join him before picking his way past the closest crates. Then he came to a sudden stop with an exclamation of surprise.

Decker stepped around him and followed his gaze.

Propped up against a crate, his face frozen in a mask of terror, was a steward. Or at least what was left of him.

SEVENTY

THE PAIR of vampires who had followed Ignatius Faucher aboard the Titanic had done nothing to draw attention to themselves since Mina had slipped away from them the previous day. They were unsure what to do about her, given that she was technically one of their own. Under different circumstances, they would simply have found and killed her, but no vampire in thousands of years had dispatched one of their own, and they were not even sure how to go about it. Besides, they had no proof she was even a threat.

Simeon, the younger of the two, sighed heavily. Other than orchestrating a distraction outside the ladies' lavatory so she could make her escape, which he had easily talked his way out of, Mina had made no further moves against them.

Then there was Amenmosep and the amulet. It had been a mistake to kill the valet when they realized Faucher was not in his room. It had been an even bigger mistake to free Mina and leave without waiting for Faucher to return. A quick search of the cabin had not turned up the amulet, which meant Faucher must have had it about his person. But Mina's presence had caught them by surprise, and they had acted out of instinct.

Now they did not know the location of either Faucher or the amulet, despite their best efforts. His cabin, where they had killed the valet, was empty and the luggage was gone. They didn't dare ask the purser which room he had been moved to for fear of arousing suspicion, so they were forced to wander the public areas, hoping he would emerge. So far, those efforts have been futile.

But all was not lost. They had never intended to snatch Amenmosep while still aboard ship. After the Titanic reached New York, its cargo would be transferred to a dockside warehouse where the owners could claim it. Faucher and the organization he worked for would never get the opportunity. The crate containing the ancient vampire would be spirited away the moment it arrived at that warehouse, thanks to others of their kind who were waiting there under the guise of dockworkers.

The amulet was a bigger problem. If they couldn't find Faucher before the ship reached America and retrieve it, the Cabal would be forced to make a move on him after he disembarked. This would be more dangerous. The organization that Faucher worked for had already stolen the amulet and Amenmosep from under their noses. They had also captured Mina. Farouk worried that more of their kind might end up the same way. He would rather not risk such an outcome by trying to intercept Faucher either on the docks, or sometime after. Even so, he had sent a coded telegraph ahead to New York, advising the Cabal of the situation.

Now all they could do was keep looking for Ignatius Faucher and avoid drawing any unnecessary attention to themselves in the process. There could be no unnecessary killings or further abductions. Enough mistakes had been made already. Farouk sighed again. This entire operation had gone wrong almost from the start, but it would all be worth it. Amenmosep was a Founder. One of the original vampires and the oldest of their kind. No one knew what had befallen the rest of them, because none had ever been found—until now.

And once resurrected, Amenmosep would restore the vampires to greatness. He would share his purity and make them strong. Then, the vampires would rise and take their place once more as the apex species on earth, and the rest of humanity would be nothing more than cattle to be slaughtered at will.

Simeon smiled and savored that thought. After so many centuries of hiding in the darkness, it would feel good to step back into the light. Very good indeed.

SEVENTY-ONE

"NOW DO YOU BELIEVE US?" Mina said, turning to the Master-at-Arms.

"I believe there's a killer loose on the ship," King said, staring at the body of steward Archie Drummond. "And not a particularly genteel one at that. I can't imagine what Mr. Ismay is going to say."

"You should worry less about the people who own the ship and more about the passengers whose lives are at risk," Decker said, realizing the futility of his words even as he said them. One vampire, even an ancient and vicious creature like Amenmosep, could take nowhere near as many lives as the frozen chunk of ice currently drifting down into the shipping lanes that would ultimately doom the vessel.

"Easy for you to say," King replied. "A scandal like this could harm the ship for years."

"This conversation is irrelevant," Mina said, stepping between the two men. "The steward is dead, and the threat is real. Nothing is going to change that. Right now, we have to find that shipping crate and confirm who or what is doing this."

"You're still convinced that a monster escaped my hold?" King shook his head in disbelief. "Whoever did this is human, not some mythical creature from a horror novel."

"You still don't believe the proof of your own eyes?" Decker asked. "A regular man would not have the strength to tear a person apart like this with their bare hands. Look at the wounds. They were not inflicted by a knife or some other instrument. This man has literally been ripped apart."

"Who are you people anyway?" King asked, looking between Mina and Decker. "The telegraph said you worked for his Majesty, but you sound crazy, talking of monsters and vampires."

"We work for an organization that deals with such threats," Decker replied. "It was founded during the reign of Queen Victoria to tackle that which the regular police force could not. I assure you that those monsters you talk of are quite real. And not just vampires, but all manner of creatures that hide in the shadows. We live in a strange world of which science only understands a fraction, Mr. King, and you would do well to remember that. Now, we're wasting time here. We can do nothing more for this man, but we can confirm who or what we are dealing with and maybe save others."

"Fine. We'll go see your bloody crate. After that, I'm going to search for this killer in the real world, and you may do as you please."

"As you wish," Mina said.

The Master-at-Arms lingered a moment, his gaze resting upon the corpse of his steward, then he turned and picked his way between the crates. "The cargo you seek belonged to a passenger. It will be in the right front quarter of the hold. Everything else is commercial cargo or larger items such as motor cars and machinery."

"That narrows it down," said Decker.

"It still leaves a large area to search, and we don't know what this cargo looks like other than being a crate."

"If my hunch is correct, we will know it as soon as we see it." Decker followed behind King and Mina. They walked in single file, because there was no other option, and soon arrived at the area in question.

The Master-at-Arms was right. There were hundreds of items stacked several crates high. They towered around the trio with only cargo numbers stenciled on them to identify the contents and owners once the ship reached New York. Without Faucher's cargo slip, which was probably still in his jacket, they would not be able to tell which crate contained Amenmosep. Worse, if he was buried deep within a stack of cargo, they might not even be able to find the correct crate, even with its corresponding number. Unless the creature had broken free, that was.

"This will be quicker if we split up," Mina said, looking around.

"I'm not sure that's a good idea with a killer on the prowl," King said.

"The killer is long gone, at least from the cargo hold," Decker told him. "That steward was killed many hours ago. Rigor mortis has set in. He died some time before Faucher and the stoker."

"Which means the killer is up there somewhere while we are wasting our time down here," grumbled the Master-at-Arms.

"I assure you this is not a waste of time," Decker replied. "And Mina is right. This will go much faster if we split up."

"Very well," grumbled the Master-at-Arms. He started toward a narrow passageway between crates. "I'll go this way. We'll meet back here in half an hour if we don't find anything, and then I'm done with this wild goose chase."

"If you come across anything out of the ordinary, shout and

we will find you," Decker said, starting toward another passageway while Mina continued along the one they had been traversing, her lamp held ahead of her to light the way.

Decker searched for twenty minutes, weaving back and forth between the crates with little to show for his efforts. He was about to give up, wondering if his suspicions had been unfounded, and Amenmosep was still tucked safely away inside his temporary coffin made of rough wood planks. But then, as he circled back around to check further afield, a shout reached his ears.

It was Mina. "I've found it."

Decker turned and hurried back toward her. "Keep talking, and we'll follow your voice."

Mina responded, and it took Decker less than a minute to locate her.

Soon after, the Master-at-Arms came running, breathless, through the stacks of crates. He stared at the scene in front of him. An oblong crate stamped fragile in red ink underneath the cargo number. One end was crushed as if it had been dropped. The lid was gone and lay several feet distant, the nails that once held it in place sticking up out of the wood. Straw, used to pack the cargo within, had spilled onto the deck. But the ultimate proof that Amenmosep had escaped was right in front of them. The shreds of bandages that had once wrapped the mummy were scattered all around as if the creature had clawed its way out of them to get free.

Decker looked at Mina. "We have our answer."

"Amenmosep is roaming the ship," Mina replied, her face ashen. "And he has the amulet."

SEVENTY-TWO

THE MASTER-AT-ARMS PACED BACK and forth in his office, a worried expression creasing his face. "I'm still not inclined to believe that there is a creature of supernatural origin on my ship, but I also agree that it would require an incredibly determined human of impossible strength to kill a person in the way those men died. Regardless of my beliefs, someone or something is loose, and I need answers. I need them fast. How can we stop these slayings?"

"I'm not sure that we can," Decker said. "We don't even know where Amenmosep is, let alone how to contain him."

"And these other . . ." The Master-at-Arms paused and shook his head as if he couldn't believe what was about to come out of his mouth. He looked at Mina. "These other vampires that you claim held you captive; how worried should I be about them? Do we have more than one set of killers aboard ship?"

"Yes and no," Mina said. "The vampires did kill Faucher's crony, who came aboard to guard me and posed as his valet. But the crime was targeted and undertaken with a specific aim.

Since Faucher is now dead, and the amulet is in the creature's possession, it is unlikely they will kill anyone else. The same cannot be said for Amenmosep. He has been hibernating, so to speak, for thousands of years. It's amazing that he didn't use up his life force and die during that time. Regardless, he's going to be desperate. He will need to kill many more times in order to regain the lifespan he once possessed."

"This is a nightmare." King groaned. "He could strike again at any time. There are thousands of people aboard the Titanic. Given what I've seen of this killer, it could be a bloodbath. How can we ever keep them all safe?"

"You can't," said Decker, realizing that his words were prophetic on more than one level. "Amenmosep will want to stay out of sight when he's not looking for victims and could go to ground anywhere. Our only clue to his presence will be the dead bodies that he leaves behind."

"Assuming he leaves any," said Mina. "He might kill again ten minutes from now, or he might hide and bide his time. He may even decide to wait until the ship reaches its destination and make New York his new killing ground."

"Then he has us at a horrible disadvantage." King stopped pacing and leaned on the desk. He took a trembling breath. "Our only viable option is to hunt him down now before he kills again. But this vessel is enormous. The biggest ship ever to plow the waves. Even if I had the staff, which I most certainly do not, it would take days to search every deck and all the cabins on each. There are a thousand hiding places, big and small. We would almost certainly be in New York before the job was done."

"Regardless, I'm not sure a ship-wide search would be advisable." Decker understood King's frustration, but he also knew that their adversary was more deadly than the Master-at-Arms could ever begin to comprehend. Even in the twenty-first

ANTHONY M. STRONG

century, with Colum and Rory at his side, and all the resources of CUSP, this situation would be a challenge. The last time they had gone up against one of these creatures, Mina had almost died. Abraham Turner was a formidable foe, but Decker suspected that Amenmosep was both bolder and more desperate. "The creature that killed Faucher and your crewmen would not hesitate to dispatch any searcher who crossed his path. Conventional weapons will be useless against him, and he will be stronger than you could ever imagine, even in his weakened state."

"Especially if he has killed again since this morning," Mina said. "With each fresh victim, he will restore his strength and become more human. He will also gain more insight into this strange new world that he finds himself in and become more cunning. Before long, he will be able to come and go at will, indistinguishable from any other passenger."

"Just great," King said. "And what about when we dock in New York? Are we to just let this sadistic killer walk off the ship scot-free?"

"Unless you have a way to identify him that we have not thought of, that may be your only option. Of course, you could inform the authorities and have them detain every passenger until he is found," Decker said, knowing full well that the question was moot. By the time Titanic's surviving passengers reached New York, detaining them to look for a killer would be the last thing on anyone's mind, assuming anyone who knew about the killings had even escaped with their lives.

"I'm not sure Ismay and the rest of the board would like that idea. No, not at all."

"Probably not," said Decker.

"Yet we can't allow a killer to run loose aboard ship," King said, his face a picture of desperation. He looked at Decker. "What should we do?"

"I'm not sure there's much we *can* do," said Decker.

"Except to wait," said Mina. "Eventually, this creature will strike again."

"And when he does?" King asked.

Mina hesitated a moment before answering. The anguish on her face was plain to see. "I don't know."

SEVENTY-THREE

DECKER SAT on the sofa in the small lounge area that made up one half of Mina's newly assigned stateroom aboard the Titanic and observed the glass of wine in front of him with indifference. The bottle, another 1908 vintage Sauternes, sat nearby. It was late on the evening of the twelfth, and the rest of the day had passed with no further incidents and no more bodies, for which he was grateful. Even so, Mina had insisted that he stay in her cabin, rather than sleep in his own. Amenmosep, she said, would know the whereabouts of Decker's cabin now he had killed Ignatius Faucher, and Decker would no longer be safe there. Decker had agreed willingly, and was secretly pleased, because he did not wish to leave her alone.

Mina sat perched on the other end of the sofa with her own wineglass held in one hand. The other hand rested on her lap where she drummed her fingers absently against her knee. She looked at Decker's glass before glancing toward him with raised eyebrows. "Are you going to drink that?"

"I think I'd rather keep a clear head," Decker said. "You

never know when our good friend Amenmosep will strike again."

"One glass is not going to make a difference," Mina replied with a thin smile. "And you really should make the most of this. Do you know how much it would cost to buy a drinkable 1908 vintage Sauternes in our own era?"

"Since when are you such an expert on wine?" Decker asked with a laugh, unable to hide his amusement despite the feeling of unease that had lingered ever since they departed Queenstown.

"I've had a long time to refine my tastes." Mina sipped her wine with obvious gratification. "I know you don't want to hear this, but I am not the headstrong and impulsive girl I used to be. I might look outwardly the same, but the passing years have tempered what lies inside me with the wisdom of age."

"I'm sorry. It's sometimes hard to remember how long you have spent trapped in the past before I showed up," Decker said. Despite everything, he was glad for this momentary respite that allowed them to reconnect. He had barely had a chance to sit down with Mina since they were briefly reunited many months before.

"Only to end up on a doomed ocean liner along with the same creatures who bestowed this curse of hellish longevity on me in the first place." Mina chuckled, but the laugh was hollow.

"Without that longevity, you might not have so easily survived until an opportunity to return home presented itself."

"If an ability to remain young were all of it, my affliction would not be so bad," Mina said, taking a larger gulp of her wine this time. "But don't forget, I have all of Abraham Turner's memories, along with the combined knowledge and recollections of all those whose lives he cut short. They crowd my head like a thousand voices that won't cease their jabbering. I dream of their lives and have nightmares of their deaths. They haunt me night and day." Mina took a deep breath and finished the last of her glass. "Then there's the hunger. Even without Abraham Turner's amulet, I constantly fight against his darker urges, inherited along with the memories and lifespan. The urge to add more years to those he had already gathered is always there, bubbling beneath the surface."

"I had no idea it was this bad," Decker said, moving closer to Mina. "I'm sorry."

"Don't be." Mina snatched up the bottle and refilled her glass. "It's my burden to bear, and it hasn't been all bad. There are things I would not trade for the world. People I would regret never having met if I could go back and change my fate."

"You mean people like Thomas Finch?" Decker asked, wondering if he was stepping onto dangerous ground. He still remembered the conversation between the pair several days before when Finch told him the real reason for his insistence upon joining Decker aboard the Titanic.

"What do you know of that?" Mina's head snapped around.

"Enough to understand why Finch would risk his life boarding the ship to get you back, even after I warned him of the mortal danger he would find himself in."

"Daisy." Mina's shoulders slumped. "You know about Daisy."

"Yes. He told me." Decker paused a moment, gathering his thoughts. When he spoke again, his voice was low. "At least, he told me enough to understand his motivations. What I don't comprehend is why your daughter is being raised by her father and another woman."

"I made a choice long ago to do what was best for both Daisy and her father. It wasn't an easy choice, and I have often wondered if it was the right one, but it had to be made."

"You want to talk about it?" Decker asked although he suspected what the answer would be.

Mina shook her head. "I don't think so. That part of my life is behind me, and I have moved on, as has Thomas."

"He still cares for you," Decker said.

"I have no doubt. And now, I shall say no more on the matter. Please respect my wishes."

"Very well." Decker had pushed about as far as Mina was willing to go. He changed his mind and picked up the wine. It was sweet and fruity, lingering pleasantly on his palate. "This isn't half bad," he said, taking a second sip.

Mina smiled. "That would be the noble rot."

"Huh?" Decker was mystified. Rot was hardly a term he would have associated with fine wine.

"Sauternes is made from Sauvignon Blanc, Sémillon, and muscadelle grapes, the latter of which has been affected by a fungus known as noble rot. That's what makes certain vintages better than others, depending on the harvest."

"I see." Decker stared at the wine with new appreciation. "You really have become quite the refined woman and an apparent wine connoisseur."

"When I'm not chasing monsters," Mina said with a grin. "Although even after several decades, I find the clothing of this era far too restrictive. What I wouldn't give for a T-shirt and a decent pair of Levi's."

"If we can survive Amenmosep and get off the ship without drowning in the process, I might be able to make that happen," Decker said. He hesitated a moment before speaking again, almost nervous to say the words out loud for fear of jinxing them. "I may have found a way back home."

Mina's eyes widened briefly, but then she regained control. "Really?"

"Yes. I don't want to get your hopes up because there are still a lot of obstacles in our way, but if all goes well, we might be back on Singer Cay and reunited with our friends sooner than you would think."

"That would be nice," Mina said, with less enthusiasm than Decker would have expected. "How about you tell me all about it when we get to New York."

"You don't want to hear about it now?"

Mina shook her head. "I would hate to get my hopes up and then end up at the bottom of the ocean. Let's focus on surviving the Titanic, and then you can tell me the rest."

SEVENTY-FOUR

DECKER SPENT the night in Mina's cabin for a second night.

It was now the thirteenth. An unlucky number for sure, but in the case of the ship they were now on, the fourteenth was a much more disastrous one.

He rose, went into the bathroom, and dressed.

When he came out, Mina was awake. She smiled. "Good morning."

"Good morning to you, too," Decker said. He walked to the cabin door. "I'm going to take a stroll so that you can dress in peace. I'll meet you downstairs for breakfast?"

"Sure." Mina nodded. "Half an hour?"

"Sounds good." Decker stepped out into the hallway and made his way to the promenade deck. He stood at the rail watching the waves roll past the ship for a while before completing a circuit around the deck. The day was bright and clear, with only a slight breeze. He passed other passengers out enjoying the unseasonable weather, then headed back inside and down to the first-class dining saloon, where he found Mina waiting at a table near the door.

He took a seat opposite her and ordered from the waiter, who scurried across eagerly to serve him. That conversation from the night before appeared to have been forgotten, or at least, Mina did not wish to acknowledge it. Decker wanted to press her further on her relationship with Thomas Finch but sensed that he would not get anywhere. For whatever reason, Mina wished to keep her past private when it came to Finch and the daughter they shared. He could only hope that at some point in the future, she would be more forthcoming.

Besides, there were more pressing concerns. Like the two vampires who had abducted her from under Ignatius Faucher's nose, and the creature that had escaped from the hold and who might even now be rejuvenating himself and learning enough about his surroundings to hide in plain sight. But there was nothing either of them could do at that moment, so Decker chose to put his fears aside and deal with Amenmosep if and when and it became necessary.

Now, he sat opposite Mina and observed her, wondering what other secrets she held besides the daughter that Thomas Finch was raising with another woman. He couldn't help but wonder why Mina had walked away and how much she had changed since they were together on Singer Cay.

He felt partly responsible for all that had befallen her. Actually, that wasn't true. He felt totally responsible. He was the one who had first gotten her involved in the world of monsters and vampires. Back in Alaska, where they first met, he had allowed her to risk her life. Then, in London, when they went up against Jack the Ripper, he had failed to draw a line when she muscled in on his and Colum's mission. That failure to protect her had led directly to her brush with death, subsequent transformation, and the situation they were now in.

On the other hand, if he had not made the choices that he had, the entire timeline would be broken. Mina would never have traveled back in time and become a founder of the Order of St. George, and by extension, CUSP would not exist. Which meant that Decker would never have been in a position to initiate the entire chain of events because he would not have been employed by them and sent to London.

In the end, despite his feelings of guilt, Decker decided that the past, or in his case, the future, was part of a vast scheme of interrelated events he could not even begin to comprehend and that second-guessing actions he could not change would do no good. the Order of St. George, and later on CUSP, had saved a lot of lives, and who was he to question that?

"Hey, you okay over there?" Mina asked, watching him from the other side of the table.

"Sorry. Lost in a world of my own." Decker shook off the rare moment of self-pity.

Mina observed him for a moment, then leaned forward and spoke in a low voice. "We need to come up with an exit strategy in case one of us doesn't make it to the lifeboats."

That same thought had occurred to Decker. "You have something in mind?"

Mina shook her head. "I wish I did. But unlike everyone else on the ship, we know what is going to happen. That has to count for something."

"I don't see how," Decker said. "Pretty much everyone who survived was in a lifeboat, and there aren't enough for even half the people on this ship. Not only that, but as you said, depending on which side of the ship they were on, men were barred from getting on the lifeboats even if there were seats available. The captain's orders were interpreted differently by individual crewmen. The way I see it, we have a fifty percent chance of being on the correct side of the ship for both of us to get on one, and even if I can get into a lifeboat, it doesn't feel right to leave so many other people to their deaths."

"You can't do anything about that," Mina said. "The history of this ship has already been written as has the fate of everyone aboard. We just happen to know it ahead of time from our current perspective. Using that knowledge to save ourselves is not a crime. Nor is it morally wrong considering that we cannot share our knowledge of future events with anyone aboard."

"I know," said Decker. "Doesn't make me feel any better."

"Me either," said Mina. "But trust me, I spent decades grappling with the knowledge that I could change future events. For example, we could intervene and stop two massive world wars that will take the lives of untold millions. There were over twenty million deaths in World War I alone. World War II was even worse. But that is not our place, and if we did it, the universe would compensate by creating an alternate timeline. We would save no one in our own reality."

"I understand what you're saying," Decker said. "But it doesn't change the fact that even if we use our knowledge of what will happen to the best of our abilities, it doesn't mean we will both survive."

Mina was silent for a moment. She looked at Decker with tears in her eyes. "I know."

SEVENTY-FIVE

AROUND NOON, Amenmosep opened his eyes and sat up.

He looked about, momentarily confused by his surroundings, until the memories of his long-overdue return to the land of the living snapped back in place.

Bright sunlight streamed in through a porthole and cast dapple patterns on the carpeted floor. The sound of waves breaking against the side of the ship reached his ears. Faint voices drifted into the stateroom from the deck beyond.

He had spent part of the previous day and all that night into this morning slumbering in the 'borrowed' stateroom. Long enough that his decimated and time-ravaged body was able to start healing thanks to the life force donated by his victims, including the pair that now lay dead and discarded on the other side of the room in a pool of their own blood.

He stood and stretched, then went to the mirror hanging on the wall next to the cabin door and looked into it, examining his face. Gone was the pallid sheen of death that had hung over him, replaced by a vitality that, even if it didn't convey youth, was more than enough to blend in with the crowd of well-heeled first-class passengers that strolled the promenade decks and ate in the restaurants of the greatest ship on earth.

He reached up and touched his jaw, felt the elasticity of his skin. How long had it been since he last felt truly alive? A long time. Millennia. His last memories were of the Egyptian Royal Guard descending upon him in the temple like a pack of ravaged wolves, eager for the kill. Yet he was here, and each and every one of those guards had died long ago and were now nothing but dust blowing in the wind. The same could be said for Pharaoh, who was so afraid of Amenmosep that he risked everything to destroy him. In fact, the entire civilization that had subdued him had now been gone longer than Amenmosep had walked the earth prior to their brutal assault upon him. He took some measure of satisfaction in that.

And now here he was, with the knowledge of Ignatius Faucher, the man who desired to use him against his own race, tucked neatly inside his head. Not to mention the combined experiences and memories of the unfortunate sailors he had killed.

And there was something else, too. A final gift given to him by the man who called himself Ignatius Faucher. Three vampires who were on this very ship. Two of them traveling together, and a girl who presented something of a mystery. Part vampire, part human. He would enjoy sucking the life from her and learning her secrets. And he knew where to start looking. The cabin of her associate and friend. A man named John Decker. He would surely know her whereabouts.

First though, he would find the pair of vampires who had followed Faucher onto this wondrous vessel. Their deaths would draw no attention whereas Decker and girl might quickly be missed, making it more difficult to stay hidden. Best of all, the two vampires would not see the threat he posed until it was too late, because they would never imagine that one of their own would ever dispatch them and take their life force.

But they were nothing more than sacrificial lambs in his eyes. Why bother killing a thousand people when he could kill those vampires and inherit a thousand years of life from each?

Amenmosep turned away from the mirror.

If only he knew which cabin they were in, he could make short work of them. Instead, he would be forced to wander the decks, waiting for that tingle of recognition as they came within range of the sixth sense all vampires possessed regarding their own kind. They would recognize him as one of our own, too, of course. And that was their weakness. By the time they realized the danger, they would be dead.

Amenmosep shuddered with anticipation. How good would it feel to absorb their essence and be truly reinvigorated? He had come so close to death that he could taste it. Had that Egyptologist not dug him up and removed his body from the cold dark rock beneath the sands of the Valley of the Kings, he would have flickered out and ceased to exist, the stolen years that sustained him having finally run out.

Amenmosep stepped past the corpses heaped against the cabin wall under the porthole and withdrew a morning suit from the slim wardrobe beyond. He dressed quickly and slipped on a pair of patent leather shoes. They felt loose on his feet and his benefactors clothing hung on him, but it would do.

He went to the stateroom door and opened it, peering out into the hallway beyond. Passengers came and went along the corridor, paying him no heed.

Amenmosep smiled. His long hours spent recuperating had been worth it. He was no longer a disfigured monster, acting only on instinct. He was himself again, albeit centuries removed from his last point of reference.

He tugged at the hem of his jacket, or rather the jacket of the man now lying dead in the room behind him and stepped out into the corridor.

No one gave him a second glance.

Amenmosep closed the door behind him and made his way toward the first-class dining room. It had been so long since he had last eaten real food that he could barely remember the taste of it, and even vampires could enjoy the pleasure of the senses. He would gorge himself, taking advantage of all the amenities this floating palace had to offer, and then, once his belly was full and he had indulged himself to the limit, he would go in search of a different sustenance.

And who knew? He might even stumble across those two vampires in the dining room. Wouldn't that be a stroke of luck?

Amenmosep licked his lips at that thought and said a silent thank you to Ignatius Faucher, whose death had provided him the knowledge of their presence aboard the ship. And at that moment, as he weaved through the throng of passengers making their way back and forth with nary a sideward glance toward him, he felt a rush of hope for the future. This vessel was traveling to a brave new world ripe for the picking, and Amenmosep intended to make the most of it.

SEVENTY-SIX

WITH NOTHING better to do and no more incidents aboard ship, at least as far as they were aware, Mina and Decker strolled the promenade deck during the afternoon hours and soaked up the sights and sounds of the historic ocean liner. Decker still found it hard to believe where they were, and more than once resisted the urge to pinch himself and make sure he was not dreaming, but their surroundings were all too real. And all too frightening.

In the early evening, they made their way back toward the focal point of the ship's first-class public spaces—the grand staircase. Decker took the opportunity to broach a subject that had been on his mind since lunchtime.

"I've been thinking about the two vampires that abducted you," he said, tilting his head slightly toward Mina so that his words were not carried to the surrounding passengers. "What are the chances that they will come looking for you?"

Mina shrugged. "I don't know. I'm sure they weren't happy when I gave them the slip, but they do still think me one of their kind, so any aggression they might have toward me will be tempered by that viewpoint. Given the short time left to us before disaster strikes, a little over thirty hours, I would say it's unlikely we will need to worry about it."

"Unless they find a way off the ship just as we are hoping to," Decker said. "And then we will all end up aboard the same rescue ship."

"The Carpathia," Mina said. "But don't forget, we have a knowledge of events that they do not possess, which gives us the upper hand."

"I haven't forgotten." Decker held the deck door open for Mina to step inside, then followed her. "But it's worth considering what will happen if you make it onto the Carpathia, and I do not. Because there are not two, but three, vampires aboard the ship, and the third one does not appear to care about leaving a trail of bodies behind."

"Don't talk like that," Mina said. "We're both getting off the ship. That's all there is to it."

"I admire your confidence, but history has stacked the cards against me."

"If those vampires, any of them, show up on the Carpathia, then I will deal with the matter at that time. But like you said, the cards are stacked against the men aboard this ship, so there's a good chance they will end up going down with her. I agree that we should have a plan, but in this case, it's impossible to count the variables, and even if we could, we have limited resources at our disposal. I hate to say it, but this is one we are going to have to play by ear."

Decker nodded solemnly. "There's something else I want to ask you. A favor for if I don't make it."

"You want me to deliver a message to Nancy."

"Yes. She deserves to know what happened to me in the past, and immaterial of whether you find a portal back to the twenty-first century, your longevity will eventually deliver you there, regardless. It's a lot to ask, I know, but given our present situation, there is no other way that I can guarantee to reach her."

"Decker . . ." Mina's voice trailed off. She choked up, a tear rolling down her cheek. "I asked you not to talk like that. You have to make it off the ship and survive. Not just for Nancy, but for me. You know how I grew up and what I went through. You're the closest thing to a real father I've ever had."

"Which is ironic considering that technically you're older than me now," Decker said, forcing a smile.

"Don't make this into a joke." Mina wiped away the moisture from her eyes. "All the time that I've been trapped here, the thing that kept me going most was the thought that you were out there and would never abandon me. Even when that man took me and locked me in his dreadful house so that his sadistic doctor could experiment on me, I knew you would eventually find me and stop him. That's what you do—find a way. Nancy feels the same, I guarantee it. She's waiting for you, so don't give up now. You'll get home, then you can tell her about all of this in person after the wedding."

"I appreciate your optimism, but we both know how this will end. I am far from guaranteed to survive, and I'm begging you to grant me this one favor."

Mina was silent for a moment, then she nodded. "You know I would never leave Nancy wondering what happened to you. But it's all academic. Neither of us is dying on the ship."

Decker said nothing. After all, what more was there to say? He would either live, or he wouldn't, and the answer lay a day and a half in the future. No amount of discussion would change that.

They came to the grand staircase. Mina kept going toward their cabins, but Decker made for the stairs instead. "Go ahead to your stateroom. I'll meet you back there in a little while."

She turned, surprised, and walked back to him. "What are you doing?"

"I want to go check out those two vampires that snatched you away from Faucher and see where their cabins are."

"Why?" Mina's surprise turned to concern. "I thought we were going to steer clear of them."

"You are. But they've never seen me. They have no idea who I am. I'd like to know exactly where they are located, just in case."

"You don't need to worry. They won't get close to me, because I'll feel them coming if they try."

"They'll feel you, as well. They might even notice you first. After all, you aren't actually one of them, at least not fully, and your senses might not be as acute."

"I don't like this," Mina said.

"It's fine. I'll be thirty minutes. Forty-five at the most. Go back to the cabin and stay there until I return." Then he turned and descended the stairs before Mina could argue further.

SEVENTY-SEVEN

AMENMOSEP WANDERED THE SHIP, marveling at its construction and size. It was like nothing he had ever seen before. The boats of his day were small skiffs made of papyrus or short planks of wood and held together with ropes. Most were powered by oars, but some caught the wind with rudimentary sails.

This vessel was worlds away from that.

He was aware from the combined knowledge of those who he had recently killed, that the Egyptian civilization he knew was long gone, their monuments and temples crumbling into the desert and covered by sand. He was also aware of the magnificent and wondrous civilizations that had arisen after that time, not least of which was the one that had constructed this unbelievable feat of engineering upon which he now stood. And across the vast ocean, waiting for him, was what they called the New World. A blank canvas within which to hunt and steal even more lives.

But right now, he was more concerned with self-preservation. Namely, finding those two lesser vampires and the half-breed young woman called Mina that were even now traveling aboard the same ship. He didn't know within which cabins any of them were, but he would sense them before they sensed him. Of that, he was sure. His abilities would be so much greater than theirs just by virtue of his purity and how long he had walked the earth. Eventually, he would find them, and when he did, they would sacrifice themselves so that he could go on. Whether that sacrifice was willing would be up to them. Either way, they would not be stepping off the ship alive.

The only problem was, there were so many decks and hundreds of people milling around at every turn. He had been wandering the narrow passageways for hours, moving between decks at intervals, and so far, had sensed not a single vampire.

That was disappointing. Any of them could have extended his life by hundreds of years, perhaps thousands. Much better than the slow process of killing humans one by one. But he had to admit, the desire to spill blood was great, and with each new kill, he felt stronger. This was why, after several hours of fruitless search, Amenmosep decided that until he found more satisfying prey, he might as well avail himself of the pathetic humans swarming around him.

Then he saw her. A slender little thing with shoulder-length hair and a trim waist. She was a servant, that much was clear. Or as they called them aboard the ship, a stewardess. She was coming out of a cabin and moving away from him down the passageway.

Amenmosep quickened his step as best he could—he was still weakened by the centuries spent trapped and incapacitated in that dark tomb beneath the Egyptian sands—and followed her.

If he was lucky, she would lead him into a less-trafficked area where he could strike with impunity. A tingle of anticipation rushed through him. He liked the girls most of all. Their life force always tasted so . . . sweet and innocent. He also liked the way they trembled before him, exposed and vulnerable. Sometimes, back in his heyday, he had taken a sacrificial offering and kept her alive for days, toying with her and enjoying all that her body had to offer, before finally giving her the honor of extending his life.

He wouldn't be able to go that far with this one, for sure, but just the act of slicing her throat and drinking the years of her youth would be enough. When he reached the New World and established himself there, he would have plenty of time to indulge in more leisurely kills.

But he would have to be careful now. There could be no more uncontrolled feeding frenzies. He would have to be more discreet in the future. His previous acts had surely been discovered. At least, the ones in that strange, padded room and maybe even one or both of the stewards down in the hold. The older couple that had provided him with a cabin in which to sleep, would not have been, especially since he had informed the bedroom steward responsible for his own cabin and those around him, that he would require no further assistance and wished to be left alone. He had sensed no confusion from the man. No recognition that Amenmosep was not the original occupant. No one would venture into the cabin or challenge his right to be there. Amenmosep was sure of it.

Up ahead, the girl had quickened her step. Amenmosep increased his own pace to keep up, all his attention now focused on the kill. Hidden within the folds of his jacket was a pocketknife he had found upon the unfortunate stoker who had stumbled upon him while he was dispatching the man named Faucher. He slipped a hand into his pocket and felt around for the weapon until his fingers closed upon it. The four-inch blade was folded back into the handle. He let it stay that way for now. It would feel the flesh of the young woman's neck soon enough, and then Amenmosep would satisfy his urge to kill. At least for a little while.

SEVENTY-EIGHT

DECKER WATCHED Mina set off toward her stateroom, then he descended the grand staircase. Once again, as he made his way down, he couldn't help but marvel at the exquisite craftsmanship on display all around him. The sweeping curves and balustrades intermingled with finely detailed iron scrollwork depicting foliage and flowers tinged with bronze accents were a sight to behold. Richly detailed oak paneling enclosed the space beneath the curve of a glass dome that flooded the staircase with an almost ethereal light. It reminded Decker more of something one might find in a grand country house or maybe even an antebellum mansion than the interior of an ocean liner. It was a shame, he thought as he descended, that all of this would soon be at the bottom of the ocean, where it would not be seen again for almost three-quarters of a century. By that time, the dome would be gone, along with most of the wood. All that would be left was a cavernous gaping hole down through the slowly decaying ship, with only the ghost of its former glory left to behold.

Decker paused when he reached the C deck landing and looked back up, lost in the majesty of his surroundings. Then he shook off the sense of awe and continued on, making his way along the corridor toward the ship's stern and the cabins where Mina said she was held by the two vampires.

When he got there, Decker slowed and walked past at a more leisurely pace. The door was closed and there was no sign of anyone coming or going. He wasn't sure exactly what he expected to find and would not have recognized the vampires even if he saw them, but he wanted to know where his—or rather Mina's—enemies were hiding. If anything happened and they took her again, he would know where she was.

His curiosity sated, Decker picked up the pace and continued, nodding an occasional greeting to other passengers as he passed them.

At the end of the corridor, he arrived at a door leading to the second-class promenade deck and library. Here he turned and retraced his steps, slowing a second time as he passed by the vampires' cabin. At the grand staircase, he climbed back up to A deck and headed toward Mina's cabin.

When he stepped inside, she looked up. "Satisfy your curiosity?"

Decker nodded and sank down onto the sofa.

"What were you looking for?" Mina asked.

"I don't know," Decker admitted. "I think the waiting is getting to me. There's been no sign of Amenmosep, and the other vampires appear to be keeping a low profile, just like we thought they would. I hope there won't be any more killings before tomorrow night, but there's still one deadly event looming in our future that we can't avoid. Sitting around and waiting for it is getting on my nerves."

"That's the problem with knowing what's going to happen," Mina said. "Especially when you can do nothing to change it."

"I suppose." Decker lapsed into silence because he could think of nothing more to say.

SEVENTY-NINE

FIRST-CLASS STEWARDESS BETTY O'SHEA left the B deck cabin of passenger Eliza Bean, who she had helped into her corset, petticoat, and two-piece silk dress, and made her way along the corridor toward the crew stairs. She was one of only eighteen stewardesses aboard the ship, compared to eight times as many male stewards. Her job included dressing the fashionable first-class ladies, running baths for them in the communal bathing facilities, and dealing with any other matters too delicate for a male steward to handle. Her destination was another cabin on D deck, and yet another lady who needed help to get into her clothing so she could stroll the promenade deck and show off her wealth. This was Betty's life. Going from room to room and dressing the wives of rich businessmen and aristocrats in skirts and frocks that she herself could never hope to afford.

Betty's feet hurt, and all she wanted to do was return to her crew quarters, but she still had four hours left before she could do that, and she might even have to work longer if too many passengers requested the services of a stewardess. With so few on board, she worked three times as hard as a male steward and received less than two-thirds of the pay. But it was still better than working in a factory back in England. At least here, her meals were covered, and she had somewhere to sleep at night that didn't eat up half that pay.

She passed a pair of first-class passengers strolling along the corridor with their arms locked together. They did not move as she approached, and Betty was forced to turn sideways to avoid them. As she passed, the male passenger fixed her with a disapproving glare. She said nothing despite the anger that bubbled up inside her—it was not her place—but could not help casting an irritated glance back toward the two as they moved away from her.

It was then that she noticed the other passenger.

He was tall and rakish, with a swarthy complexion that didn't look entirely healthy. His eyes were two dark coals set into their sockets. His clothing appeared loose on his frame, the jacket too wide and the shirt billowing. He must be a first-class passenger for sure, but he did not carry himself with the swagger of wealth or the assurance of title.

He moved slowly, walking with a stiff gait. His arms hung at his side, limp and unmoving. Then she noticed his fingernails. They were long. Unnaturally so for a man. They curved out of his fingers to pointed ends, almost like talons. And they were a sickly shade of yellow.

Betty shuddered and turned her attention forward again. She picked up her pace, eager to put some distance between herself and the unusual passenger.

When she reached the crew stairs, she pushed the door open with relief and stepped out of the corridor, then started down to the deck below. Her racing heart slowed a little. At least until she heard the door open again above her and footsteps ringing on the uncarpeted metal stairs.

Maybe it's just another steward, Betty thought, not wanting to look back and see. But she had to know, because the crawling feeling of unease was back. She gripped the handrail running along the wall next to her and cast a glance over her shoulder.

Her breath caught in her throat.

It was him.

He was descending behind her, his gaze fixed unerringly forward.

Betty resisted the urge to scream. She turned forward once again and moved even faster, her feet pounding the stair treads as she raced toward the deck below. She reached the landing—which also doubled as the maids' and valets' pantry with storage lining the wall opposite the stairs—and tugged at the door leading back out into the passenger areas. At first, it didn't open, and a knot of fear twisted in her stomach. She looked back at the stairs where the stranger was drawing ever closer, descending with a leisurely sense of purpose that was somehow more menacing than if he had simply chased her.

"Come on," she said to herself, overwhelmed with panic. "Open damn you."

Then she realized that in her haste, she had not turned the handle. She pulled the door open, raced along a short service passageway, and out into the corridor beyond, where she almost collided with a pair of women wearing long, flowing dresses. Only a quick reaction prevented Betty from bowling them over.

"So sorry," she gasped, as they turned their gaze toward her in annoyance. Then she stepped deftly around them and hurried away toward the grand staircase and the front of the ship, even as one of the women commented on her impertinence.

But Betty didn't care. The strange man with the swarthy complexion and ill-fitting clothes was surely right behind her.

She slowed and risked one more backward glance, then breathed a sigh of relief. There was no sign of the menacing stranger in the corridor behind her. He had been almost close enough to reach out and grip her by the collar when she was struggling with the access door, so he should be in sight by now.

Betty slowed her pace, aware of the curious looks she was receiving from the passengers. She felt safer now, anyway. Why had she ever ducked into the crew stairs to begin with? It left her alone and vulnerable. But she had never thought that a passenger would follow her there. After all, why would they? Unless they meant her ill.

Betty gathered her wits and continued on, contemplating the motives of the copper-skinned gentlemen, and what might have been, even as a trickle of fear crept up her spine. She cast one more furtive glance back along the corridor, but there was still no sign of him. Breathing a sigh of relief, Betty turned at the grand staircase and crossed over the first-class landing toward the starboard side of the ship, then took a right and doubled back along another corridor, running parallel to the one on the port side.

Up ahead was her original destination. She reached the first-class stateroom and came to a stop, then knocked lightly, identifying herself. When the door opened and a lady with porcelain features and straw-colored hair tied back into a bun let her inside and closed the door behind her, Betty finally felt safe again.

EIGHTY

AMENMOSEP FOLLOWED THE YOUNG WOMAN, keeping far enough behind that his actions would not draw undue attention. When she turned and disappeared through a doorway, he did the same, closing the door behind him. A narrow staircase descended to the decks below. The stewardess was hurrying down as fast as she could. She glanced back over her shoulder, and her eyes grew wide with fear.

Amenmosep smiled. This enclosed stairwell would be the perfect place to feed. The only problem was that in his weakened state, the stairs were proving more of a challenge than he expected. He gripped the handrail to steady himself and continued down as fast as he dared.

The young woman had reached the landing below. But she was having trouble with the door.

He closed the gap between them, a surge of excitement washing over him as he drew close. Perhaps he would catch her, after all.

But then she succeeded in opening the door, and raced through, slamming it shut behind her.

Amenmosep felt a flicker of disappointment. This empty

dark space would have been perfect for his needs. But no matter. He would still catch her, and there were plenty of places where she could be killed away from prying eyes.

He reached the landing and pulled the door open, stepped out, then made his way along the corridor to the main passenger thoroughfare. He emerged and saw the stewardess hurrying along at a brisk walk. Now that he was up the stairs, Amenmosep felt stronger. He would catch her in due course and add her own life force to his.

He started after her, reveling in the chase and ignoring the glances of curious passengers alarmed by his appearance. It would have been easy to turn and snatch any one of them, open their throat right there in front of everyone, but that would be foolish. Besides, he wanted the girl and no one else.

At least until he felt a familiar tingle of recognition.

Amenmosep stopped mid-stride. There were vampires here. He could sense them. But not in the corridor. The sensation was not that strong. This was coming from one of the cabins to his left.

Smiling, he stepped from the main corridor into the passage leading to the cabins and followed his intuition to one cabin in particular, where he stopped.

It was ironic, Amenmosep thought, that after spending most of the day in a fruitless search for others of his kind and giving up, the young woman had led him straight to them, unaware of just how close to death she had come.

He slipped the amulet from his pocket and kept a grip on the pocketknife in the other. He was about to knock on the cabin door when it opened to reveal a slender gentleman dressed in a gray morning suit. Another man lingered behind, looking over his companion's shoulders with an expression of awe on his face.

Apparently, his approach had also been sensed.

Without waiting for an invitation, Amenmosep stepped across the threshold and pushed the door gently closed.

Fifteen minutes later, feeling remarkably refreshed and brimming with thousands of stolen years, he reentered the corridor, giving no more thought to the stewardess that had led him here, and started back toward his own cabin. That two of his own kind now lay dead was of no concern. They had served their purpose, as would many more, he was sure. But for now, he would rest and absorb the unwilling gift their deaths had given him. Then he would go in search of the final vampire roaming the ship. The half-breed who went by the name of Mina.

EIGHTY-ONE

THE LAST EVENING before Titanic's date with an iceberg was a muted affair for Decker and Mina. They did their best to ignore the black cloud that hung in their future, but try as they might, their thoughts invariably turned to what lay ahead.

At seven, alerted by a bugler playing on the landing near the grand staircase that dinner was about to be served, they made their way to the first-class dining saloon where a ten-course meal awaited. Decker wasn't sure what to expect, since they had only taken their evening meals in the à la carte restaurant so far. This proved to be a much more laborious process, with the various courses served over a three-hour period. Waiters in white jackets scurried around the massive room, which was, apparently, the largest enclosed space on the ship, and brought plate after plate.

Afterward, having been unable to consume even half the food on offer, Decker followed Mina back to her cabin.

After they stepped inside, she turned to him. "I was thinking . . . I should send a telegraph to Thomas in the morning." She went to the couch and sat down. "I don't know

ANTHONY M. STRONG

what is going to happen, but it might be my last chance. What do you think?"

"I think that if you have something to tell him, you should take the opportunity while you can." Decker's thoughts turned to Nancy. He had asked Mina to relay a message from him when she reached the future. A last goodbye if he didn't make it back. He wished it were as easy as sending a telegraph. Given the years that separated them, Decker could never guarantee that Nancy would receive any message he sent. So much could happen in the meantime to prevent Mina from ever delivering it.

"I'll go to the telegraph room first thing in the morning."

"You need to be careful what you say."

"I know. I won't reveal anything regarding Titanic's fate."

"And Daisy?" Decker asked.

"What about her?"

"You should send a telegraph to her via Finch, too."

"She isn't aware that I'm her real mother," Mina said, a brief look of anguish passing across her face before it vanished again. "I'm not sure it would be appropriate."

"She might not know about you now, but that doesn't mean that she won't learn the truth at some point in the future." Decker sat down next to Mina. "Depending on what happens tomorrow, it might be your only opportunity to tell her how you feel."

"I hope she never learns about me." The look of anguish was back now. "I made Thomas promise never to tell."

"Why would you do that?" Decker asked, aware that she would probably not answer him.

She looked away. "It was for her own good."

"Wouldn't you want to know if you were in her place?"

"I really don't want to talk about this right now."

"Fair enough. If you ever do want to talk about it, I'm happy to listen." Decker stood.

Mina didn't reply. Instead, she yawned. "It's late, and I'm tired. I think I'll go to bed, although I can't imagine I'll get much sleep under the circumstances."

"Me either," Decker replied. "But we should try. Tomorrow will be a long day and an even longer night."

"I know." Mina headed toward the suite's small bathroom to get ready for bed. In the doorway, she paused. "I don't usually admit this, but I'm scared."

Decker met her gaze. "I know. Me too."

Mina was silent for a moment, then she closed the bathroom door. Ten minutes later she stepped back out in her borrowed nightgown. She climbed into bed, then turned off the light on the wall above the headboard, leaving only the dim lamp beside the sofa burning. "Good night, John."

"Good night." Decker sat awhile, until he heard her softly snoring despite her claim that sleep would be elusive, then he stood and went to a small chest of drawers standing next to the door. Atop this were several sheets of paper with the White Star Line emblem at the top.

He removed a fountain pen from his bag and settled back on the sofa. There was no hard surface on which to write, so he took a book that Mina had been reading and used it as a makeshift desk on his lap. He looked down at the blank sheet, suddenly lost for words, then, after a few minutes, he began to write.

When he was done, Decker folded the sheet of paper and slipped it into an envelope, which he sealed. On the front, he wrote a single word. Nancy.

He set the book and pen aside and held the letter in his hand, staring at it for the longest time. Tomorrow he would give this envelope to Mina and ask her to keep it safe over the decades until she finally made it back to the twenty-first century. By then, the ink would have turned brown and the paper brittle, but if he didn't survive what was to come, it would be his final message to the woman he loved.

He told her how much he loved her, and how he thought about her every day since becoming trapped in the past. She was the last thing on his mind at night and the first thing on his mind in the morning.

Decker put the letter down next to the book and pen but still did not move. Then a thought occurred to him. He picked up the book and pen once more, took another sheet of paper, and wrote a second letter, which he sealed in its own envelope and set next to the first.

That done, he turned off the lamp and lay back on the sofa with a pillow under his head. When he closed his eyes, Nancy's face was waiting. He focused on that image. The way she smiled, and how her eyes sparkled when she was happy. He hoped that against all the odds, he would get to see that smile again, and look into those eyes, but he couldn't shake the feeling of foreboding that had settled upon him. Tonight, he was sure, would be one of the longest of his life.

EIGHTY-TWO

FIRST-CLASS BEDROOM steward Lawrence Hayward had only just started his shift at eight a.m. on the morning of April fourteen when the door to cabin C 146 flew open and a middle-aged woman in a purple brocade dress stuck her head out, her expression a picture of distress.

Her gaze alighted on him, and she appeared to relax. "I say, steward."

"Yes, madam?" Hayward turned toward her. "What can I do for you?"

"I'm afraid my cabin has sprung a leak of the most noxious variety," replied the passenger. "All was fine when I retired to my bed last night, but when I awoke, it was there, on the floor near the washbasin. I wonder if you would be so good as to take a look."

"Certainly, madam." Hayward changed direction and stepped into the cabin, expecting to find a puddle of water on the floor. But what he saw was anything but. A crimson stain had spread several inches across the floor on the far side of the cabin, near the wall. When he drew closer, Hayward saw that it had not come from the washbasin, as he would have expected, but had instead oozed from under the connecting door that could be unlocked to expand the cabins into larger accommodations. Another connecting door on the other side could further extend the suite of rooms to encompass the cabin two berths away.

He tried the handle and found it locked.

"Do you know the occupants of the cabin next door?" he asked, turning to the woman.

"No, I'm afraid not." She shook her head. "I'm traveling by myself and have no need for more than a single cabin."

"I see." Hayward stooped next to the mystery spill and touched it with his finger, noting the viscous consistency. He touched his fingers together and found them sticky. When he lifted the gooey liquid to his nose, he noticed a sickly-sweet metallic odor that was most unpleasant. A shudder of revulsion ran through him. There was only one substance he could think of that looked and smelled like that.

He straightened and quickly rinsed the noxious substance from his hands, then strode toward the door. "I'll be back in a moment."

"Is everything all right?" Asked the passenger, following him to the door.

"Please, just wait here. Don't touch the stain." Hayward made his way to the next cabin and knocked.

He waited for almost a minute but received no answer.

He knocked again. "Cabin steward. Is everything okay in there?"

There was still no answer.

Hayward was unsure how to proceed. He had worked on ocean liners for the better part of twelve years, and never encountered a situation such as this. He considered fetching either the purser–who would have a key to the room—or the Master-at-Arms. Maybe even both.

But what if someone was injured and needed immediate

attention? The blood seeping into the cabin next door certainly pointed to that. There might not be time to summon further help.

Still, he was loath to break down the cabin door when there might be a simple explanation for the blood, even if he could not think of what that might be.

But he didn't need to.

When Hayward tried the knob, he found the door unlocked.

He pushed it open and lingered in the doorway. "Hello? Can anyone hear me in there?"

Silence was his only answer.

Hayward took a deep breath and gathered his courage, then stepped across the threshold.

The cabin he now stood in contained two beds separated by a short sofa. A connecting door to his left stood open, leading into another cabin. The connecting door to his right was closed. Beyond this was the cabin belonging to the woman in the brocade dress. It was from under this door that the crimson leak spread. And now Hayward saw why.

Lying crumpled against the door, their faces frozen in death, were the bodies of two men dressed in morning suits. Their throats had been slit. A pool of blood surrounded them like a dark cherry-colored lake.

From behind him came a gasp, then a terrified scream.

Hayward turned to see the passenger who had summoned him standing in the doorway, her hands clasped to her mouth, eyes wide with terror.

She stumbled backward, a second shriek bubbling up.

Hayward followed, retracing his steps, and shut the cabin door to block the ghastly sight from view. Then he barked an order to a second steward, drawn by the woman's hysterical wails.

"Get the Master-at-Arms. Bring him here right now."

The steward nodded without questioning the authority of

ANTHONY M. STRONG

his peer, perhaps because he noticed the look on Hayward's face. Then he turned and sprinted back the way he had come, weaving around the startled passengers who were emerging, bleary-eyed, from their staterooms to see what all the fuss was about. And all the while, the woman in the brocade dress kept shrieking, despite Hayward's best efforts to placate her.

EIGHTY-THREE

DECKER STOOD in the cabin and looked down at the pair of bodies. It was ten a.m. He had been summoned less than thirty minutes before by Thomas King, the Titanic's Master-at-Arms, who had sent a solemn steward to deliver the news of these latest deaths. After finding no one in Decker's cabin, the steward went to Mina's quarters. After that, he led them down two decks to a suite of cabins Decker recognized all too well because he had scoped them out only the evening before.

Mina now stood next to him, observing the scene in front of her with a look of mild disdain. Completing their small group was the Master-at-Arms, who had ushered everyone else from the room and posted a steward on the door to ensure they were not disturbed.

"These are the two men who took me from Faucher's cabin," Mina said.

"The vampires." Decker kept his voice low to avoid being overheard.

"Yes." Mina motioned toward the open door that led into a second cabin. "They put me in there."

"I thought these creatures were almost impossible to kill,"

Decker said. His final battle with Abraham Turner was something he would never forget. If it hadn't been for the Sumerian knife with the gold blade that Adam Hunt had managed to borrow from the British Museum, both he and Detective Inspector Mead—a British police officer who had become embroiled in the affair—would probably be dead and Turner would have escaped having stolen Mina's life force.

"Well, someone managed it," said King. "And they made a hell of a mess in the process."

"Amenmosep." Mina's gaze was fixed on the slicing cuts across the vampires' necks. "No one else could have got close enough to do this, and even if they had, those wounds would not have been fatal."

"Not fatal?" The Master-at-Arms raised an eyebrow. "I defy any poor bugger to survive with their neck slit open like that."

"Remember, Mr. King, that these were not normal people. They were vampires and would quickly heal from all but the most egregious assaults. Very little can kill them, and it would take immense strength even to inflict the cuts we see here. They died not because of blood loss but because their life force was stolen even as they bled. They had no ability to recover." Mina leaned down toward the closest body, where a semicircular impression was imprinted into the dried blood above the cut. She pointed to the neck. "Also, look here. Amenmosep's amulet. He pressed it against this man's neck as he was dying, and it left an impression. There is no doubt."

"Which means he'll be even more powerful than before," Decker said.

Mina nodded. "And he will be rejuvenating. Probably at an accelerated rate. We won't be able to distinguish him from any other passenger."

"Is that bad?" The Master-at-Arms looked between them.

"Very." Mina looked at Decker. "Our only advantage is that he will not have long to avail himself of his newfound youth."

"Because we dock in New York in three days?" Asked the Master-at-Arms.

"Something like that," said Decker to King without elaborating. "Tell me, what did you do with Ignatius Faucher's gun?"

"It's in the safe in my office, along with that pendant you wrecked yesterday."

"I'm going to need it."

"Don't you already have a gun?" Mina asked.

"Yes. But Faucher expected the vampires to follow him on board the Titanic. He would have taken precautions. One of those might have been the bullets in his gun. I need to look at them."

"You think he—"

"Maybe," said Decker, cutting Mina off. If his hunch was correct, the bullets in Faucher's gun would either be cast from a gold alloy or be plated in it. The precious metal was the only thing that could slow down a vampire. "Like a werewolf, only a different metal."

"Someone care to fill me in?" Asked King, looking confused.

"Not really." Decker glanced toward the door. "The gun?"

"You want me to get it for you right now?"

"Can you think of a better time?" Decker replied.

"You realize there are two dead passengers on the floor in front of us with their throats cut open, right?"

"I can see that. But the operative word is dead. We can do nothing more for them. Even if we could, I'm not sure I would be inclined to do so, given the threat they posed to Mina and the other passengers on the ship."

"Back to the vampire thing again." King shook his head. "You know, I can't decide if I believe you or if the pair of you belong in an insane asylum."

"I don't care if you believe us or not. Either way, there's a sadistic killer on the ship, and there will be more deaths unless you do as we say."

"All right. Come with me. I'll get the gun." The Master-at-Arms started toward the door. He pulled it open and stepped through. He waited for Decker and Mina to exit before closing the door, then turned to the steward standing on the other side. "Make sure no one enters this room except the three of us. You understand?"

The steward nodded. "Yes, sir."

"Come along then," King said, motioning for Decker and Mina to follow him. He led them through the ship's corridors and down to his office, then unlocked the door and hurried inside. He went to the safe and dialed in the combination before pulling the door open. Withdrawing Ignatius Faucher's gun, he offered it to Decker. "I hope you know what you're doing."

"So do I." Decker took the weapon and turned it over in his hand.

Mina inched closer to him to look at the gun. "Well?"

Decker checked the magazine. He palmed a round, then held it up between his thumb and forefinger. The bullet glittered yellow. He studied it, noting the weight. "Just as I thought."

"Gold," Mina said.

"Not quite," Decker said. He slipped the bullet back into the magazine. "It's too light. I suspect the bullet is only gold-plated, which would make sense. An entire bullet of pure gold would be too heavy to fire effectively and might not even make it out of the gun barrel."

"That might not be enough against Amenmosep," Mina said, looking worried.

"I know," Decker replied. "But it's better than nothing."

EIGHTY-FOUR

"I THINK it's time you informed the passengers and crew of the danger they are in," Decker said. They were still in Thomas King's office, facing the Master-at-Arms, who looked decidedly unsure of himself.

"I don't agree," King said. "Informing the crew and passengers at large of the murders on board will only cause unnecessary panic. Better to take a small contingent of the crew and search for the killer."

"You won't find him," Mina said. "Amenmosep will have absorbed the life force of those two vampires by now. Even if he didn't before, he will now blend in with the other passengers and have enough knowledge of this century to fit in. It will be impossible to find him, considering you don't even know what he looks like."

"I still can't decide if the pair of you are delusional, but it makes no difference. Vampire or human, a flesh and blood killer is walking the hallways of this vessel, and sooner or later, they will make a mistake."

"I'm not so sure that you understand—"

Decker cut Mina off. "You must do what you think best, Mr.

King. The welfare of those aboard this ship is your responsibility, and I'm sure you will not take that duty lightly. All I would ask is that you proceed with caution. Regardless of your belief in the supernatural nature of the killer, he is supremely dangerous and will not hesitate to take the lives of your men."

"My men can take care of themselves," the Master-at-Arms said, a light scowl creasing his forehead. "I don't suppose you intend to give that gun back?"

"No. I don't."

"That's what I thought. I must say, it doesn't thrill me to have armed passengers running around my ship. But since it has been made clear to me that the pair of you work for his Majesty's government and are to be given free rein, there isn't much I can do. That's the only reason I didn't confiscate your own weapon when we arrested Ignatius Faucher. Considering there will be two guns at your disposal now, please try not to shoot any innocent people."

"It hasn't happened yet," Decker said.

"Good. Make sure that it doesn't."

"We'll do our best." Decker moved toward the door, motioning for Mina to follow. "I think it's time we took our leave and let this good man get back to work."

Mina looked momentarily stunned, but then she followed Decker into the corridor.

When they were out of earshot, she turned to him. "What was all that about?"

"All what?" Decker asked.

"You backed down way too easily in there. You know as well as I do that he's not going to find Amenmosep, and even if he did, would not be able to stop him."

"What else would you have had me do?" Decker made his way toward the grand staircase. "Even after everything he has seen and all that we have told him, the Master-at-Arms still doubts the validity of our claims. He doesn't believe for one moment that there's a genuine vampire loose on the ship. He's humoring us. He'll never inform the passengers of the danger they're in because it would tarnish the ship's reputation on its maiden voyage."

"If only he knew what lies ahead, he might not be so worried about it."

"Exactly. Which is my second point. The men and women who survive this sinking are written in stone. History cannot be altered. Two-thirds of the people on the ship will be dead in a little over twelve hours, and that is an immutable fact. At this point, it matters little whether they perish at the hand of Amenmosep or succumb to the freezing waters of the North Atlantic. Their fate is sealed."

"That's harsh."

"But true." Decker was walking briskly now. "At this point, our only concern is keeping a low profile until the ship impacts that iceberg and we have our chance to escape. Amenmosep will surely be looking for you, and I don't intend to make it easy for him."

"Meaning?"

"Meaning we go back to your cabin and stay there until zero hour. When is that precisely?"

"About twenty minutes before midnight," Mina replied. "That will give us about half an hour to get on deck before they start loading the lifeboats."

"I intend to be on deck and waiting when the collision occurs." Decker hurried up the grand staircase with Mina keeping pace beside him. "Since we cannot interfere in the events around us, I intend to be in one of the first lifeboats. Our presence won't displace anyone who should have lived."

"I hate this," Mina said. "My biggest struggle since arriving in the past has been to stand on the sidelines and let history run its course for better or worse. But this time, I'm caught in the middle of it."

"I know." Decker reached the top of the staircase and turned toward the first-class cabins. "But you have to keep in mind that if we depart from the accepted timeline, we will end up creating an alternate reality, at least if Rory's hypothesis is correct about how time travel works. Since we don't know how being stuck in an alternate timeline would affect our attempts to get home, we cannot take the chance."

"Doesn't make it any easier."

"No, it doesn't." They had reached Mina's cabin now. Decker stepped aside to let her unlock the door. They hurried in and closed it behind them.

Decker breathed a sigh of relief. "So far, so good."

"We're still in danger from Amenmosep," Mina said. "We might be out of sight, but if he passes too close to this cabin, he can still sense me."

"Then we'll have to hope that he doesn't get close enough," Decker replied. He took the gun from his jacket pocket. "And if he does, we had better hope these gold-plated bullets do more than just irritate him further."

EIGHTY-FIVE

AMENMOSEP HAD SLEPT for what felt like days. The incredible number of years stolen from the two vampires he had killed the afternoon before had been overwhelming. He had stumbled back to the cabin he had made his own, giddy from the amount of energy released into his body. The feeling was akin to a heavy night of drinking, except the effects were much more intense.

He flopped down on the bed and closed his eyes.

That was all he remembered until now.

He sat up and looked around. Daylight streamed in through the porthole to his left and he could see a patch of blue sky. He wondered what time it was. The man who had previously occupied this cabin possessed a pocket watch, but Amenmosep had not touched it because the case was made of gold, so it remained tucked into the dead man's breast pocket.

He swung his legs from the bed and stood up, overcome by how useful he felt. Compared to those he had previously killed since reawakening, the life force he had taken from the two vampires had invigorated him a thousandfold. He hadn't felt this alive since Narmer, the first Pharaoh of Egypt, sat on the throne.

Amenmosep was still wearing the same clothes that were on his back the day before. Now he changed into a fresh shirt, then left the cabin and made his way through the ship toward the grand staircase. He ascended to A deck, noting the clock on the oak-paneled wall. It was four in the afternoon. He had slept for far longer than he expected—almost twenty hours. But what a sleep it was. No one even gave Amenmosep a second glance as he turned down the first-class passageway toward the room occupied by the man named Decker.

He stopped outside the door, hoping he would sense the vampire named Mina, but he felt nothing. No matter. He would kill her friend and steal not just his life force but the memories inside his head. Then Amenmosep would know precisely where Mina was, and she would be next.

He slid a hand into his pocket and withdrew the folding knife—the same one he had used to kill the vampires the previous day. From his other pocket, he slid the amulet. Then he knocked on the door.

There was no answer.

Amenmosep let twenty seconds pass, then knocked again with the same result.

John Decker was not there. That didn't mean he wouldn't come back.

Returning the amulet to his pocket, Amenmosep opened the knife blade and inserted it between the doorframe and the door, applying gentle pressure until the latch gave way. He pushed the door open and stepped inside, looking around. There was a bed against one wall, the sheets rumpled as if someone had slept there recently. A connecting door led into a second cabin with another unmade bed. But it was what Amenmosep didn't see that left him momentarily frustrated.

There was no luggage. No sign of habitation beyond the

unmade beds. If John Decker had been here, he wasn't any longer.

Amenmosep retreated to the door and stepped into the corridor, closing it softly behind him. Had Mina expected that he would come after her, or was there another explanation for John Decker's sudden disappearance? Amenmosep didn't know, but it was of no concern. Sooner or later, he would find both of them.

And he would start looking right now.

Amenmosep made his way back along the corridor toward the first-class landing. What better place to start his hunt than the ship's vast public areas? If the vampire and her friend did not realize he was looking for them, they might very well spend time there.

Up ahead was the first-class reading and writing room, and beyond that, the lounge. Amenmosep strolled casually through the writing room, hoping to feel that tingle of recognition, but he found it mostly empty. The first-class lounge was busier but occupied mainly by men who sat around deep in conversation or reading the three-day-old newspapers brought aboard in Queenstown while they sipped brandy and whiskey from fancy glasses.

The smoking room beyond was no better, except there wasn't a single woman to be found. The thick pall of cigar smoke hanging in the air made him cough, and he beat a hasty retreat.

Returning to the first-class landing, Amenmosep rode the elevator behind the grand staircase down to B deck and made his way aft toward the à la cart restaurant.

And then he saw her.

The stewardess that had escaped him the day before.

She was coming out of a first-class cabin and humming softly to herself. She didn't even notice his approach.

Amenmosep smiled. Mina and her friend could wait a while

longer because he had unfinished business. The maid had escaped him once but would not do so again. Not now that he was brimming with life and had all the time in the world. When he first followed the stewardess the previous day, his intention had been to end her quickly. A flash of his knife and it would all have been over—a quick death, if not an entirely painless one. Now a more intriguing possibility occurred to him.

Amenmosep quickened his step and closed the gap between them.

He slipped the knife from his pocket and opened the blade.

The stewardess still hadn't noticed him. She was reaching back for the door handle to close it.

Like a hawk descending upon its hapless prey, Amenmosep drew level with her, and in a motion so quick she didn't even register what was happening until it was over, he pushed her back into the cabin, or rather a short internal corridor that led to the cabin, and kicked the door closed.

His free hand covered her mouth to stifle the scream she was surely about to utter.

"Remain silent, or I'll kill you here and now," he whispered, his mouth inches from her ear.

From within the cabin came a sound of movement. A figure appeared, short and plump, wearing a hideous pink gown.

The woman's eyes flew wide. "Whatever is going—"

Amenmosep didn't let her finish. He pivoted on the ball of his foot, still holding the terrified stewardess by the chin. His other hand sliced sideways in a deadly arc, with his arm fully extended. There was a moment of resistance as the knife blade met the woman's neck.

She stumbled backward, her hands rising to her throat in a vain effort to stop the bleeding. Her mouth opened and closed as if she were a goldfish. Her eyes bulged in their sockets.

Amenmosep stepped past her and pushed the stewardess down onto the bed. "Is she the only occupant of this cabin?"

The stewardess said nothing. She was paralyzed by fear.

"Answer me."

The stewardess nodded.

"See, that wasn't so hard." Amenmosep turned back to the stricken woman. She was on her knees now, the ghastly dress turning from pink to bright red. He slipped the amulet out and kneeled next to her. This was a bonus.

When he was done, Amenmosep stood and looked at the stewardess, still lying where she had landed with the bed sheets clumped around her. She looked small and frightened. Her mouth was moving, but no sound came out, as if she were silently pleading for mercy.

Well, she wouldn't get any of that today.

Amenmosep approached the bed and leaned over the terrified stewardess. All thoughts of Mina were gone. There was plenty of time for that later. First, he would enjoy all this little thing had to offer before his knife found her throat. If he was lucky, it would take hours.

EIGHTY-SIX

IT WAS thirty minutes to midnight. Beyond the porthole in Mina's stateroom, was nothing but inky blackness. Even the sounds of the waves lapping against the Titanic's hull had gone silent. It was as if they were sailing through an endless void. But Decker knew the truth. Somewhere out in that insidious darkness, death was waiting. A frozen killer that was now mere minutes from striking.

He fought back his unease and looked at Mina. "It's time. We should go up on deck."

Mina was lying on the bed with her hands clasped across her belly, staring at the ceiling. She had remained quiet for most of the evening, lost in thoughts of what was to come. Decker had been occupied with his own thoughts. Of home and Nancy, and if he would ever see either of them again.

Now, Mina swung her legs off the bed and stood. She straightened her dress. "This would not be my first choice of clothing in which to escape a sinking ship."

"But it's all that we have," Decker said, picking up Faucher's gun and pushing it into his pants belt before letting his jacket fall back over it. He went to the wardrobe and took out his own gun, then offered it to Mina. "You should take this."

She shook her head, declining. "What good would it do? The bullets won't stop Amenmosep, and those in Faucher's gun are the wrong caliber, so we can't even divide them between us. Besides, I don't like guns."

Decker shrugged and put the gun back. He went to the door. "We need to go, right now."

Mina nodded and grabbed a shawl which she wrapped around her shoulders because it would be freezing up on deck.

They slipped from the cabin and made their way toward the grand staircase and the first-class landing. The ship was eerily tranquil given what was about to happen, but of course, Decker realized, no one knew of the imminent danger they were in. Not quite yet, anyway.

When they stepped out onto the starboard first-class promenade deck, the bitter chill hit them like a slap in the face. There were a few other people around, one or two couples taking in the late-night air. Decker went to the railing and leaned over, peering toward the ship's bow.

Now the full effect of the moonless night and calm ocean was clear. He might as well have been staring into a void. There wasn't even a single star to light the sky. It was a strange and unsettling feeling.

He took Mina's hand and guided her along the Promenade as far as they could go. On Titanic's bridge above him, it must already have been pandemonium as the ship's quartermaster tried in vain to steer the colossal ship away from disaster. But standing there on the empty and silent deck waiting for the inevitable, Decker wondered if something had changed, and they would miss the iceberg after all.

Then he felt it.

A shudder that worked its way up from the ocean below,

accompanied by a tortured grinding sound that sent the hairs on Decker's arms standing on end.

He felt Mina's hand grip his own just a little tighter.

A shape loomed from the darkness in front of them. A wall of Arctic blue slid gently by so close that Decker felt he could reach out and touch it. Chunks of ice landed on the deck, big and small.

"Come on," Decker said, dragging Mina toward a set of steps that, according to a sign on the wall, led to the boat deck. "We can't stay here. We need to find the lifeboats."

He took the steps two at a time, ignoring the startled looks from a pair of passengers who were descending toward the promenade. He briefly thought about shouting a warning but changed his mind. If they were meant to live, they would do so, just like all the other passengers who even now were in their cabins, either recently awoken by the collision or still sleeping. Most would not even realize anything was wrong until the bedroom stewards started going door to door and rousing them. Even then, some would ignore the frantic stewards until it was too late.

"Which side do we want?" Decker asked as they reached the boat deck. To his left, he could see the lifeboats hanging in their davits. There would be an equal number on the other side of the ship. Fourteen of them in total. To his right, down the middle of the ship, were four enormous funnels. Deck chairs that would never be used again were stacked against the walls. "Port or starboard?"

"I don't remember." A flash of panic crossed Mina's face.

"It's fine. We'll stay here. If they won't let both of us on, we will go to the other side and take our chances." Decker made his way toward the nearest lifeboat. He glanced at his watch. It was almost midnight and there was no sign of anyone coming up on deck yet.

He ducked under a galvanized steel line running from the

deck to the top of the nearest tunnel—part of Titanic's rigging—and went to the railing. The iceberg was no longer visible, having melded back into the blackness as if it had never been there. But far below them on the ship's lowest decks, he knew that water was even now pouring in through the buckled hull plates. Titanic was slowly dying.

"Where the hell is everyone?" Decker said, stomping back to Mina. He rubbed his hands together to keep them warm.

"They'll come," Mina said. "Just be patient."

As if to prove her right, a solitary crewman appeared from the stairs further along the boat deck. A second emerged from the deckhouse underneath the closest funnel.

"Oi," exclaimed the closer of the two men, hurrying toward Decker and Mina. "Step aside, please."

More people were appearing now. Many of them wore White Star Line uniforms, but passengers were milling about the deck, too.

With so many lifeboats to choose from, Decker wondered about their chances of survival. He watched the two crewmen tugging at the ropes that secured the lifeboat's canvas cover. Several minutes later, they pulled the cover back and discarded it.

More passengers were arriving on deck now. Some of them looked annoyed as if they resented being sent up on deck at such a time of night. He heard more than one gripe about the ridiculous nature of the emergency. After all, Titanic was unsinkable. Others, though, looked positively shellshocked. One woman, wearing a lace nightdress under a heavy coat, wandered past them. Another carried a baby in her arms, the infant bawling in the frigid air. But the mood on deck was changing. Decker could sense it. While most of the passengers, more of whom were appearing with each passing minute, remained certain the ship would not sink, a minority had started to believe otherwise. He could hear it in their hushed conversations and see it in the way they watched the crew preparing the lifeboats.

And then he heard the music.

Titanic's band had taken up position near the entrance to the grand staircase and were blithely playing as if nothing was wrong.

For some reason, that scared him more than anything.

EIGHTY-SEVEN

AMENMOSEP STEPPED out into the corridor feeling pleased with himself. The stewardess had proved to be most entertaining, and he had spent many hours enjoying her company, even if she could not say the same. But all good things must come to an end, and eventually he had grown tired of her pathetic whimpers and drew his blade across her throat, ending her misery.

He closed the cabin door gently behind him and turned toward the front of the ship, the half-breed once again on his mind. He doubted he would find her now. It was after midnight, but tomorrow . . .

Then he noticed the commotion. Passengers that should be fast asleep in their beds appeared in the hallways. They shuffled along like a pack of dazed sheep, heading toward the staircase and the boat deck above. Amenmosep's curiosity was piqued.

Instead of turning against the tide and heading down to his own cabin one deck below, he followed along with the crowd and soon emerged on deck. By that time, enough snatches of conversation had reached his ears to know that the ship was in trouble. The engine room and lower decks were filling with water and the bedroom stewards were racing along the corridors, waking people and sending them topside.

This was an unexpected turn of events.

The chill night air hit Amenmosep the moment he stepped outside. Crewmen were manning the lifeboats, desperately turning the cranks that would swing the davits out over the side of the ship. The air was thick with noise. The roar of steam escaping the ship's funnels was loud enough that it forced the crew to shout orders at the top of their voices.

The horde of passengers ushered onto the boat deck now milled around in confusion. Meanwhile, somewhere close by, a band was playing.

Amenmosep stood for a while, observing the chaos, then he turned and strolled casually toward the ship's bow. A panicked young woman cut in front of him, and he swiped her out of the way with an irritated growl. A man dressed in a black tuxedo observed the assault and strode toward him, face creased with indignation.

"Now look here, old chap, what the devil do you think you're doing?"

Amenmosep didn't answer. Instead, he waited for the enraged passenger to draw close enough, then whipped out his knife and thrust it upward into the soft flesh beneath his ribs.

The man's angry expression turned to one of shock and pain. He grunted and staggered toward the rail, gripping it even as his shirt turned crimson.

Amenmosep veered sideways and gripped the distressed passenger, then tossed him over the railing in a quick, fluid movement, as if he were no heavier than a feather. If the man screamed on the way down, his terror was lost in the general cacophony.

Satisfied, Amenmosep kept going without breaking stride and resumed his original course, confident that everyone else on deck was so wrapped up in their own drama that they had not even noticed the swiftly executed murder.

Up ahead, he could see a small cluster of passengers gathered around a lifeboat that was already swung out over the side. A pair of crewmen were trying to stop the boat from swaying, pulling on lines to draw it close to the rail.

And amid this group, he spied a solitary young woman, waif-like in appearance, and dressed in a heavy coat. He smiled because he knew exactly who she was. He could sense it.

And when she turned and looked at him, a look of horror flashed across her face, and he knew she had sensed him, too.

EIGHTY-EIGHT

"WOMEN AND CHILDREN." The closest crewman to Decker and Mina shouted at the top of his voice, trying to be heard over the roar of angry steam escaping from the funnels overhead. The musicians playing an upbeat ragtime number at odds with the grave situation unfolding didn't help matters. Behind him, close to the railing, was a lifeboat waiting to be filled. "Captain's orders. Women and children first."

Mina edged through the throng and grabbed the crewman by his arm. "What about men?"

"If there are any seats left, then we'll see."

"Thank you." She returned to Decker. "We should be fine if we wait here."

Decker nodded but said nothing.

A few passengers were stepping toward the lifeboat, but many didn't move. Mina glanced around, wishing they would hurry and load the boat, which she knew would be nowhere near full, allowing herself and Decker to board.

At that moment, as she was contemplating this, a sudden and overwhelming sensation hit her. She recognized it all too well.

Then she saw him, a tall and swarthy gentleman wearing a black tuxedo that hung on his frame. He was walking toward her at a slow pace. When their eyes met, it was like a bolt of electricity ran through her.

She shuddered and took a step back. "Decker. He's here. Amenmosep."

"Are you sure?" Decker turned and scanned the faces of the passengers milling around them.

"I'm sure."

Decker's focus narrowed to the lean figure coming their way. He glanced toward the lifeboat which so far only contained three passengers. A fourth woman was being helped aboard by a crewman, who steadied her as she stepped off the stricken liner. "This is taking too long. He'll reach us before that lifeboat ever has enough passengers aboard to be lowered. We can't stay here."

"We must." Mina's chest tightened with fear. "We might not find another lifeboat that will let you onboard. This is our best chance."

"And it will be worth nothing if that vampire reaches us," Decker said. "Under the circumstances, he won't hesitate to kill you and anyone who comes to your aid."

"That won't happen," Mina said, watching the figure draw ever closer. "There is no mention in the history books of any such altercation near any of the lifeboats."

"Which is why we're leaving, right now," Decker said, grabbing her hand and dragging her away from the vampire through the ever-expanding crowd. "Because if we stay here, those history books will change."

"Decker." Mina pulled back against him. A lump rose in her throat. "You can't do this. You will die."

"That remains to be seen." He dragged her toward the ship's Stern despite her efforts to resist. "We'll find another lifeboat after we get Amenmosep off our tail."

"We had better do it quickly, then," Mina said. She could already feel the deck tilting down as the bow dipped lower into the water. Even more disturbing, she noticed a distinct list to starboard.

"That's the plan." Decker weaved around passengers that crisscrossed in front of him, his hand still gripping Mina's.

They were running out of deck. Mina glanced over her shoulder to see Amenmosep still coming. He was walking faster now, his gaze never wavering.

"He's gaining on us," Mina said.

"I know," Decker replied.

A sharp boom echoed over the hiss of escaping steam. High above them, a flash briefly lit the deck, sending twinkling stars out in all directions. To Mina, it looked very much like a firework, but she knew it was something much more ominous. A distress rocket that would do no good because the only ship to see it, the SS Californian, would misinterpret the signal and steam on.

"This way." Decker dragged Mina sideways and raced across the deck to the ship's port side.

Mina briefly lost their pursuer but then he appeared again, rounding the corner, and drawing ever closer. Her stomach churned. If they didn't escape the vampire soon, neither of them would get off the ship alive. "We can't keep this up. He'll catch us."

"I know." Decker sounded frustrated. His free hand was tucked inside his jacket and Mina knew it was curled around the gun.

There were four lifeboats here, with a small crowd gathered around each. The boats looked nowhere near ready to be launched.

Decker must have noticed the same thing. He raced past the boats to a gap between the structures that ran down the middle of the deck and pulled Mina to the right.

Emerging back on the starboard side of the ship, Decker ignored the lifeboats to the Stern and made for the four boats at the ship's bow. The same spot where they had started this mad chase.

The first lifeboat was already gone. The davits were empty.

A second boat, still waiting to be lowered, was less than half full. Despite desperate pleas from the crewmen manning the boat, no other passengers seemed inclined to alight. It was incredible, Mina said, that with all the vessel's obvious signs of distress, passengers still believed they were safer on deck than in a lifeboat.

"There," Decker said, pointing toward the half-full boat. "That's our best chance."

Mina could sense the vampire directly behind them. She didn't need to look around to know their danger. "We have to hurry. He's going to catch us."

"Out of our way," Decker snapped at the passengers blocking his path to the boat. He pushed through them, eliciting angry glares, which he ignored.

Even as a second rocket arched into the sky and exploded above them, the passengers stubbornly refused to believe the danger they were in. No one moved to board the lifeboat.

Realizing the futility of the situation, one of the crewmen raised an arm. "All right, chaps, lower away."

"Wait," Decker shouted.

But it was too late. The crewmen were already turning the cranks that would lower the boat seventy feet to the water below. Inch by inch, the small vessel dropped slowly out of sight.

They reached the rail and came to a stop because there was nowhere else to go. Mina turned back toward the deck and soon realized their mistake.

Amenmosep was right there, pushing passengers aside as

he approached. He reached into his jacket, pulled out a pocketknife, and unfolded the blade.

Mina glanced sideways, frantically searching for an escape route. To their left was an open section cut into the rail at deck level, where the lifeboats hung when stowed. This was also how the passengers stepped off into the boats. Further back and blocking their path were the davits holding the slowly descending lifeboat. Nearby, crewmen were frantically cranking large handles to lower the boat into the water.

Passengers pressed forward to their right.

Amenmosep had them trapped.

Then she felt Decker's hand on her shoulder. He spoke quickly in her ear even as he stepped in front of her to place himself in the vampire's path. "You need to jump. It's the only way."

"No." Mina looked down over the side at the dizzying drop into the ocean. The lifeboat was six feet below the deck, drawing further away with each passing moment. "I can't."

"Yes, you can. Jump into that boat or we'll both die." He slipped the gun from his pocket and raised it, aiming at the vampire, who was almost close enough to reach out and touch them.

To her left, a woman screamed.

The surrounding passengers moved back instinctively.

"I'm not leaving you here alone," Mina said.

"I'll be right behind you. I promise. Now go before it's too late."

Mina realized there was no other choice. She hated to leave Decker on the ship but clung to his promise that he would follow behind. She stepped sideways, ducked around the davits, and stood at the edge of the deck.

A crewman rushed forward to stop her, shouting a warning. Before he could get there, Mina stepped forward off the Titanic's deck and dropped into the dark and empty air.

EIGHTY-NINE

THE DROP into the lifeboat was no more than twelve feet, but to Mina, it felt like an eternity. She briefly registered the flash of a third distress rocket that lit the ocean in a flicker of white, and then the lifeboat rushed up to meet her just as the darkness closed back in.

She braced, expecting to feel the planks of the lifeboat's hull beneath her feet, and prayed that she would not land in some awkward position, or worse, on top of another passenger.

But she quickly realized her mistake.

The Titanic was not only sinking lower in the water by her bow but also listing to starboard, which meant that instead of being directly beneath her, the lifeboat was hanging away from the side of the ship. It was only a small gap, maybe a foot or two, but it was enough.

Instead of hitting square in the center of the lifeboat's deck, she was going to miss and plunge all the way down into the unforgiving ocean below.

A swell of panic rose in Mina's throat. She tried to adjust her angle of descent, but it was impossible. A second later, the lifeboat's hull was right beside her. She threw her arms out in desperation, clutching at the frozen air for anything to halt her downward plunge.

For one horrible moment, Mina thought it was in vain, but then her arms contacted the rim of the lifeboat hard enough that she would have cried out if there had been any breath in her to do so.

And still she fell, even as her arms scraped down the side of the boat, tearing at the arms of her dress and raking her skin.

One of the passengers lunged forward and made a frantic grab to save her, swiping the air she had occupied a moment before, and missing.

At the last second, feeling her hands about to slip over the boat's rim, Mina closed her fingers and held on for dear life.

The sudden deceleration almost ripped her shoulders from their sockets. She swung sideways, slamming into the boat's outer hull hard enough that she almost lost her grip and continued her deadly tumble.

A pair of hands reached over the side and gripped one arm. Another pair of hands closed over the other. She felt herself being hauled upward and into the lifeboat before collapsing in a heap on the bottom boards between the seats.

Somewhere up above, on the Titanic's deck, came the sharp crack of a pistol.

"Decker." Mina pushed herself up, ignoring the aches and pains that seemed to come from every part of her bruised body, and looked toward the Titanic's rail above. He should have been right behind her. He had promised. But she didn't see him anywhere. Worse, the lifeboat was being lowered faster. The drop from the deck was now too dangerous to attempt. At least forty feet.

A second gunshot rang out, the sound almost lost in the racket of frantic passengers on the deck above, the rumble of escaping steam through the funnels as seawater rushed to meet the furnaces in the boiler rooms, and an unsettling groan that came from the ship's hull beside them.

Was it Decker who had fired the gun? Was that why he hadn't followed her over the side? An image of Decker fighting off Amenmosep flashed through her mind. The gold-plated bullets in Faucher's gun would do little to stop the vampire and certainly wouldn't kill him. Assuming that the thin coating of gold was not stripped away by the gun's barrel, rendering the bullets completely ineffective.

The lifeboat was almost at the ocean now. With a gentler splash than she expected, it settled into the water and bobbed on the waves near the Titanic's hull. The whole descent had taken only a couple of minutes.

She craned her neck to look back up at the Titanic's rail but still couldn't see Decker. She saw something else, though. A second lifeboat descending quickly toward the ocean, and they were drifting slowly under it, still attached to the lines that had lowered them. If something was not done, it would smash into their bow and reduce the lifeboat to kindling.

"It's going to hit us," a woman screamed, trying to scoot back out of the way, but there was nowhere to go.

Mina wondered if they would be forced to jump overboard and take their chances in the freezing water, but then a crewman in the front of the boat near the tiller stood up.

"I can't release the falls. They're jammed," he said, referring to the lines holding them in harm's way. "We have to cut the lines right now."

He produced a folding knife from his pocket and began sawing the closest line.

The lifeboat above them was coming down fast. Mina could see the faces of its occupants peering over the side in horror.

The first line gave way with a sharp snap and swung loose.

The crewman fought his way to the rear of the lifeboat, balancing against the bob and sway as he maneuvered past the frightened occupants within. He went to work on the second line, slicing it with his knife as fast as he could.

"It's too late," someone cried as the keel of the lifeboat above them loomed large in the darkness.

"We still have time," shouted the crewman, still sawing the line with his blade. "Grab the oars and push away. Quickly now."

Several passengers took up oars and leaned over the side of the boat, pushing it away from the Titanic's hull. Mina did the same, and little by little, the lifeboat edged out from under the one above.

The second fall snapped, the line coiling away into the darkness, and then they were free. The crewman grabbed the tiller and barked orders for the passengers on the ocean side of the lifeboat to start rowing. Moments later, they were moving away from the ocean liner, even as the boat that had threatened their survival settled into the water nearby.

NINETY

DECKER WATCHED Mina step into the void then turned his attention quickly back to the advancing threat. Amenmosep was almost upon them, but now the vampire stopped. His face twisted into an angry scowl as he realized Mina had slipped from his grasp.

Decker kept the gun raised, despite the pandemonium all around him. The closest passengers shrank away, desperate to escape the line of fire.

"Hey, what the hell do you think you're doing?" A crewman in a steward's uniform turned from the davits and strode toward Decker, waving his arms. "You can't wave a gun around out here. Put it away, this instant."

Amenmosep pulled his attention away from the spot where Mina had recently disappeared over the ship's side. He met Decker's gaze, then smiled and stepped toward the advancing crewman, bringing the knife up as he did so.

Decker pulled the trigger.

The bullet slammed into Amenmosep's chest.

He stumbled, tottering for a moment, and Decker thought

the vampire might keel over, but then he regained his balance and turned away from the crewman, anger blazing in his eyes.

Decker pulled the trigger again, delivering another center mass shot that was about as effective as the first.

Realizing the danger he was in, Decker turned and started back along the ship in the direction from which he'd come, drawing the vampire away from the railing. He prayed Mina had made it into the lifeboat and was even now in the water and rowing away from the stricken liner, where Amenmosep could not get to her.

He risked a glance over his shoulder and saw Amenmosep following behind him; the knife held to his side and a determined look on his face.

Decker weaved sideways past a group of male passengers standing on deck in their evening dress and calmly smoking cigars as they gazed out into the blackness beyond the ship's rail. The resignation on their faces was clear to see.

The band was still playing, although it was getting harder to hear them over the din.

Decker's mind was racing at a mile a minute. The gold-plated bullets had done nothing to slow the vampire down, and the passengers trapped on deck, most of whom would never make it into a lifeboat, amounted to nothing more than a free buffet for the creature. But he could not think of a way to stop him, and certainly couldn't kill him. The best he could hope for was to contain the monster.

The entrance to the grand staircase was up ahead. Decker hurried toward it and stepped inside. Judging by the vessel's tilt, Titanic did not have long left. If he could lead Amenmosep down into the lower levels of the ship, the vampire would end up trapped there when the liner took her final plunge. Regardless of how hard he was to kill, Amenmosep could not survive the crushing depths of the bottom of the ocean. There was one problem. Decker would end up trapped right along with him.

But it was a small price to pay.

Unlike the rest of the passengers and crew, Amenmosep could survive the freezing water until he was rescued, even if he didn't make it onto a lifeboat. Decker couldn't risk the creature reaching New York, where it would be free to take untold numbers of lives.

He raced toward the staircase. Maybe this was always what he was meant to do.

The chandelier above him, hanging from the great glass dome, was mercifully still illuminated. But as Decker reached the stairs, it flickered and went out twice before coming back on. The vessel's electrical systems were failing. Soon the ship would be plunged into darkness. There wasn't much time.

Decker stopped at the top of the stairs to catch his breath. He turned toward the doors leading back out onto the deck—the same doors he had just run through—expecting to see the vampire right behind him. But the doorway was empty.

Decker stood there for a moment, waiting for him to appear. When it became obvious it was not going to happen, he went to the doors and hurried back outside, looking both ways along the deck to locate the vampire among the terrified passengers crowding the deck.

He saw no sign of the creature anywhere.

The vampire must have given up the chase and melted into the milling throng, perhaps realizing what Decker planned to do, or maybe concluding that escaping the ship was more important than exacting revenge over Mina's escape. Either way, the result was the same.

Amenmosep was gone.

Decker cursed under his breath. There was nothing else he could do to thwart the vampire now. It was time to save himself.

NINETY-ONE

MOST OF THE lifeboats were already gone from the starboard side of the ship. Frantic passengers pushed and shoved to board one of the few remaining. Most of them were unsuccessful. The mood had shifted from one of disbelief that the Titanic would sink, to abject panic.

Decker decided to take his chances on the port side.

He stepped back inside and cut across the first-class landing past the grand staircase, soon emerging on the opposite deck. Nearby, he saw a steward handing out life vests. He veered toward the man, taking one and lifting it over his head, then buckling the straps tight around his waist.

Time was running out to find another lifeboat that would take him. He remembered what Mina had said about how the first lifeboats launched less than half full, and a few of them practically empty because no one wanted to leave the safety of the larger ship. But as the situation grew worse, that quickly changed. Decker hoped it was not too late, and set off toward the nearest boat, which was surrounded by a crowd of passengers. He edged his way around them, noting how many seats were still empty. But the crewmen in charge of the boat were already lowering it toward the ocean while another crewman stood with a pistol in his hand to ward off any attempts to jump in.

Decker turned away from the lifeboat. He would find no help here. He hurried along the deck to the next but found a similar situation. The next two lifeboats were gone, their davits hanging empty.

The deck was tilted at an alarming angle, and the vessel, which had previously listed starboard, now leaned the other way. Decker found it hard to keep his feet as he struggled toward the ship's stern. Behind him, the ocean had reached the boat deck. The forecastle was gone completely. Only the top two-thirds of the mast with the crow's nest broke the surface to show its location.

He saw only one more lifeboat still hanging in its davits and surrounded by a large group of passengers who pushed and shoved, overcome by desperation. Decker hurried to reach it, praying he could find a way on board.

At that moment, the throng on deck surged forward, as if motivated by some unspoken command. They clambered toward the boat, threatening to overwhelm it.

At his station next to the davits, an officer drew a gun from his belt and held it high in the air. He let off three quick shots skyward.

"Get back, I tell you. Get back," he screamed at the top of his lungs. "I'll shoot anyone else who tries to board this boat."

The group of wayward passengers, mostly men, shrank away. None of them, it appeared, were eager to take a bullet in their bid for safety.

Decker approached the crowd and stopped, realizing that his last chance of boarding a lifeboat was gone. He was trapped on the sinking ship along with fifteen hundred other hopeless souls. His only comfort was that Amenmosep had probably not found his way onto a lifeboat either.

He made his way back over to the starboard side and stood at the rail, peering out into the moonless night. A couple of faint white shapes bobbed on the ocean. Decker wondered if Mina was in one of those swiftly departing lifeboats. He had promised to follow behind her and failed to do so. Now he faced almost certain death when the ship took her final plunge and disappeared beneath the waves.

"Give me a hand, man," said a voice to his left. "Don't just stand there."

Decker turned to see a gentleman in a ruffled tuxedo tossing deck chairs overboard, no doubt intending to provide something for people to cling to when they found themselves in the freezing water below. He hurried toward the man and took a chair from a stack leaning against the bulkhead. He heaved it over the side and watched it fall into the darkness.

The man paused his efforts and turned him, extending a hand. "Thomas Andrews."

"John Decker."

"Pleased to meet you, Mr. Decker. Now let's get this job done and perhaps some of those who did not find a way into a lifeboat will still have a fighting chance."

"I admire your optimism in the face of defeat," Decker said, tossing another deck chair over the side.

"At this point, futile optimism is all I have left, dear boy."

Decker didn't respond. There was nothing to say. They carried on for the next fifteen minutes on the now mostly deserted deck, the majority of passengers having either climbed higher toward the stern or committed themselves reluctantly to the ocean.

Soon, when it became apparent the tilt of the deck was too great to continue, Andrews gave up his task and extended a hand to Decker. "I appreciate the help."

"It's not like I had anything better to do," Decker said solemnly.

"Quite." Andrews was silent for a moment. "Take care, old chap, and good luck." He shook Decker's hand, then turned and made his way slowly back down the sloping deck as if he were merely out for a late evening stroll, then stepped back inside, disappearing from view.

At that moment, the lights blinked twice, and then went out for good.

NINETY-TWO

MINA WATCHED the Titanic die from a quarter mile away on the cold, dark ocean. They had rowed away from the ship for what felt like an eternity before laying down their oars and drifting on the millpond calm water. Exhausted and freezing, they turned their attention back to the vessel they had so recently escaped.

At first, it sat low in the water with lights blazing and distress rockets arching into the heavens and exploding into a thousand twinkling stars like grim fireworks. But soon the bow slipped beneath the waves and the stern rose ever higher.

Mina wanted to scream. Decker had promised to follow her but had failed to do so. Now she feared he was trapped aboard the ship, having engaged in some foolhardy attempt to keep Amenmosep at bay. The likelihood of him getting into another lifeboat was remote. Their best chance had been at the beginning of the disaster when other passengers had yet to realize the peril. That opportunity had been lost before they could avail themselves of it, but Decker could still have made it if he had jumped behind her.

Mina cursed herself for allowing the situation to occur. It

had all been her fault. She should never have allowed Ignatius Faucher to kidnap and imprison her so easily. She should have anticipated Faucher and his group. Been ready for them. But she hadn't, and the end result would be Decker's death on a ship he should never have been anywhere near. She dropped her head in shame, wiping away a tear.

"It's going," someone said in a hushed voice.

Mina looked up just as the Titanic's lights flickered and went dark. The stern had lifted fully out of the water, while the bow was already lost forever beneath the waves.

She held her breath, waiting for what she knew would happen next, but when it did, she was ill-prepared, nonetheless.

A cracking sound reached the ears of those in the boat, accompanied by several muffled booms that Mina thought must be the boilers exploding. A gap appeared between the third and fourth funnels, racing down through the ship before the bow section tore away and started its long descent to the ocean floor. The stern fell back into the water, where it floated for a few moments before lifting higher than ever. It stood vertically for a few moments. Then, as if realizing there was no hope, it slipped silently from view.

The Titanic was gone.

Mina looked away, casting her eyes out over the flat and endless ocean, even as the plaintive cries of those who now found themselves in the water drifted through the steel night air.

Was Decker one of those voices crying for help in the darkness, she wondered, and slowly freezing to death, or had he still been aboard when the mighty liner made her last deadly plunge?

"We have to row back and look for survivors," someone said. A woman to Mina's right.

"Not a chance, lady," said the crewman manning the tiller.

"We go back there, and we'll be overrun by folk trying to get aboard. Then we'll all end up in the water."

Mina stood and clenched her fists. She turned to the man at the tiller with anger flashing in her eyes. "Take this boat back or I swear to God, I'll throw you overboard myself right here and now."

"And I'll help her," said another passenger, standing up.

"Me, too." This was a younger woman at the front of the boat.

"All right. Have it your way." The crewman shook his head. "Take up the oars and we will go look for survivors. But I warn you, if we end up swamped, it's on your heads."

"That's a risk I'm willing to take," Mina replied, sitting back down and grabbing an oar. She didn't know if Decker was alive or dead, or whether he was even still on the surface, but she wasn't willing to abandon him without even looking.

NINETY-THREE

THEY WENT BACK AND SEARCHED, but all they found was death. Three hours later, frozen, exhausted, and defeated, they were taken aboard the SS Carpathia, which had steamed to the area at full speed after receiving the Titanic's distress signal.

It was now seven thirty a.m.

Mina had spent the last two hours watching survivors come aboard but there had been no sign of Decker. Now she stood at the Carpathia's railing in a fugue, unable to comprehend how quickly she had lost the man who was the most like a father to her in the world. At least she had not sensed Amenmosep on board the vessel, either, although that was little comfort.

She reached into her coat pocket and withdrew an envelope with a single word written on the front.

Nancy.

It was a letter entrusted to her by Decker the previous morning. He had made her swear to deliver it in person should anything happen to him, and even though it would take more than a century to complete that promise, she had every intention of doing so. Mina drew the letter aside to reveal a second letter tucked behind it. This one had her name on it. That was the second promise that she had made to him—that she would not open this letter until all hope was gone.

The Carpathia had not given up its search for survivors, but with no lifeboats spotted for at least half an hour and no chance of finding survivors alive in the water, Mina's belief that Decker would be found alive had dwindled.

She returned Nancy's letter to her pocket and held her own letter with a heavy heart, reluctant to open it because that would mean admitting that Decker was gone for good. But in her heart, she knew the truth. He had not made it into a lifeboat and could not have survived in the water.

Turning the envelope over, Mina pried the flap gently open. Inside was a single sheet of paper folded in quarters. She opened it. The white star Line burgee adorned the top sheet as a logo, with RMS Titanic written beneath. Below that was Decker's distinctive handwriting.

Mina,

I hope that you never read this because it means I did not survive the Titanic. But if that is my fate, I want you to know how much you have meant to me and always will.

I never had a child of my own, having reconnected with Nancy at a time in our lives when we felt it was no longer an option, but if I could choose anyone to be my daughter, I could not think of a better one than you. In fact, I view both yourself and Nancy's daughter, Taylor, as my own in spirit, if not blood. I cannot express my sorrow that I will not be around to see either of you go forward with your lives, but I will watch over you from wherever I find myself on the other side. That much I can promise.

Please don't feel guilty or let the sadness you will surely feel in my passing weigh you down. There was nothing you could have done to change this outcome. This was always meant to be, just like your own journey in founding the Order of St. George and all that has occurred since. Our fates were written before we were even born and are as immutable as stone.

Go forward with your life in the best way you can, and if the opportunity arises, get to know your own daughter before it is too late. I only met her once, at Christmas, but she reminded me of you in so many ways, even though I did not know her as your daughter back then.

Farewell, and don't let grief consume you.
All my love until we meet again,
John

Mina read the letter with a lump in her throat. She didn't agree with Decker's assessment that his death was inevitable. Deep down, she knew they could have prevented it. Who was to say that the timeline they had found themselves in was unyielding? If she had not allowed Ignatius Faucher to get the better of her, neither of them would have been aboard the Titanic in the first place, thus changing their destiny. But that didn't mean the

test

timeline would have split to account for that discrepancy. For all she knew, the events that would occur in the future after the point when they traveled back in time were fluid, because events in the past had not yet played out. What happened on the Titanic merely rippled forward into the current timeline to alter the experience of those still in the future. Which meant that allowing herself to be kidnapped back in Mavendale had created this dreadful outcome and doomed Nancy never to see the man she loved again.

Mina looked down at the letter. She read it a second time, hoping Decker's words would somehow change her belief that if only she had acted differently, they could have avoided all of this. But they didn't. The weight of Mina's guilt was crushing. She folded the letter and wiped her eyes, then turned her attention back to the empty ocean.

She didn't even notice that she was no longer alone until a familiar voice spoke at her rear.

"I thought I told you not to read that unless I was dead."

Mina's heart leaped into her throat. She spun around, afraid the voice was nothing more than a phantom inside her head. But it wasn't. He was really there.

"Decker," she squealed, overcome with joy. Then she flung her arms around him and didn't let go for the longest time.

NINETY-FOUR

TWELVE HOURS LATER

DECKER AND MINA spent most of the day in the Carpathia's dining room, where many of the survivors had congregated after it became clear no one else would be rescued and all hope for those still missing had evaporated. They were given blankets and coffee, then fed a hot meal as the ship turned from its original destination of Fiume in Austria-Hungary and steamed back toward New York from which it had departed three days earlier.

Now, at seven-thirty in the evening, as the sun slipped below the horizon and wisps of fog rolled in over the still placid ocean, they walked along the Carpathia's deck.

"I thought you were gone," Mina said, choking up despite herself.

"Me too," Decker answered. "I'm still not sure how I survived, other than by blind luck."

"It must have been awful, trapped on that ship and knowing there was no way off."

"It's an experience I'll never forget. At first, my only

thought was to ensure that Amenmosep did not live. Knowing the low odds of my own survival at that point, I decided to lead him below decks and trap him there, where he would be imprisoned at the bottom of the ocean for all eternity."

Mina looked at Decker, shocked. "You would have been trapped, too."

"I know. That was the price I was willing to pay in order to save the lives of those he would have gone on to kill had he reached New York."

"So what happened?" Mina asked.

"I don't know. After you jumped into the lifeboat, I drew him away from the crowd at the rail. The gold-plated bullets did little to slow him down, so I had no choice but to distract him in order for you to escape. I fled all the way to the first-class entrance intending to lead him down the grand staircase and into the lowest levels of the ship that were still accessible. But when I turned to make sure he was still following, Amenmosep was gone. Either he anticipated my plan or decided that I wasn't worth the chase. I don't know what happened to him after that, but I do know that his ability to survive is much greater than that of a normal man. The best I could hope for was that he did not find his way aboard the rescue ship."

"He didn't," Mina said. "If he were here, I would have sensed him."

"And he would have come after you again."

"Yes." Mina nodded. "What happened next?"

"I tried to find a lifeboat that would let me aboard but failed. Then I came across someone tossing deck chairs into the ocean as rafts for passengers who ended up in the water. Although I doubted it would do any good, I joined him until it became impossible to continue. Not long after that, the lights went out, and the ship broke in half. Deciding it was my only option, I jumped before the stern made its final descent and found myself in the water surrounded by other passengers. It was so cold that I lost feeling in my extremities almost immediately. I struggled to remain conscious and would surely have died had one of Titanic's officers not pulled me onto the back of an upturned lifeboat where at least three dozen other passengers who ended up in the water had taken refuge, including that officer. I owe that man my life."

"And I owe him more thanks than I can ever fully express," said Mina.

"Agreed. But the ordeal was still not over. I spent the rest of the night on the back of that boat as it gradually sank lower into the water. Exhaustion and hypothermia overcame some of those who had climbed aboard. One by one, they collapsed and fell back into the water where we could not save them. Eventually, we came across other lifeboats with room to spare and transferred there before our own boat went under completely. Not long after that, the Carpathia found us and took us aboard. I found you on deck shortly after."

"I had given up hope." Mina stopped at the rail and turned to Decker.

"I know."

"What you said in that letter . . ."

"I meant every word. I consider you as much a daughter as if you were my own."

Mina nodded, overcome by emotion. She turned and leaned on the rail, gazing out over the ocean and the thickening fog. "I wonder how long it will take us to reach New York?"

"A couple of days, maybe," Decker replied, joining her.

"And what do we do then?"

"We find our way back to the twenty-first-century," Decker said. "Five months from now, Celine Rothman will get married on Singer Cay, then get swept up by the Bermuda Triangle and thrown forward through time."

"Which starts this whole nightmare in motion," Mina said.

Decker turned to look at her. "Yes. But it also provides an opportunity. We must get to that island and be ready to follow her into the future . . . and home."

"Do you really think that will work?"

Decker was silent for a moment, then he said: "I don't know, but there's only one way to find out."

The next John Decker Thriller
Final Destiny

New Decker Universe Novella Series - The CUSP Files
Book 1 - **Deadly Truth**

Read on for a word from the author

AN EPILOGUE OF SORTS

John decker's story is not over. Far from it. Decker will be back in Final Destiny, which will see him and Mina finally reach New York.

On another note, I want to talk a little about the historical events, locations, and people portrayed in this book. Deadly Crossing was one of the most research-heavy books I have ever written. I am now the proud owner of three non-fiction volumes on the Titanic, one of which was actually published in late 1912 after the disaster. I came across it in a Vermont antique store of all places, and of course, had to have it. I also found copies of the ship's original deck plans, which made moving the characters around Titanic much easier. In writing this book, I tried to be as accurate as possible. For example, they really did 'fumigate' third-class passengers of ocean liners such as Titanic prior to boarding. There was a real coal fire burning in the ship's bunkers, which they could not extinguish. The padded room where the Master-at-Arms held Faucher really existed and was the only place aboard Titanic where an unruly passenger could be kept under lock and key.

But this book is fiction, and as such, certain small changes were necessary for the sake of the plot, so please, if you find a discrepancy between real events or people, and those in this book—such as the order in which the lifeboats were launched, or the location of the Master-at-Arms' office, which did not exist in real life—please know it is not a mistake, but a concession.

Other details in the book might be true, but are not verified, such as Thomas Andrews—designer of Titanic and her sister ships—throwing deck chairs into the ocean as the ship sank to give passengers who found themselves in the water something to grasp. There are conflicting accounts of Andrews' last hours, but I found this one to be poetic.

The upturned lifeboat that Decker finds himself on was real. It was collapsible lifeboat B (with a wood plank floor and canvas sides). The boat ended up washed overboard before it could be launched, temporarily trapping wireless operator Harold Bride underneath. It then narrowly avoided being crushed when the forward funnel, which weighed more than fifty tonnes, toppled into the water next to it. Several dozen people, including Bride, climbed aboard and spent the rest of the night perched precariously atop the overturned boat. By morning, thirty were still alive and were able to transfer into other lifeboats before being rescued by the Carpathia.

There are so many other interesting facts about the Titanic that I learned while writing this book, most of which never made it into the novel, that I could spend another fifty pages or more on them. But I won't, because I don't wish to bore you.

Thank you for reaching the end of Deadly Crossing. I hope you had as much fun reading it as I did writing it. I have many more stories in mind for Decker and his colleagues, I promise.

Until next time

AMS

ABOUT THE AUTHOR

Anthony M. Strong is a British-born writer living and working in the United States. He is the author of the popular John Decker series of supernatural adventure thrillers.

Anthony has worked as a graphic designer, newspaper writer, artist, and actor. When he was a young boy, he dreamed of becoming an Egyptologist and spent hours reading about pyramids and tombs. Until he discovered dinosaurs and decided to be a paleontologist instead. Neither career panned out, but he was left with a fascination for monsters and archaeology that serve him well in the John Decker books.

Anthony has traveled extensively across Europe and the United States, and weaves his love of travel into his novels, setting them both close to home and in far-off places.

Anthony currently resides most of the year on Florida's Space Coast where he can watch rockets launch from his balcony, and part of the year on an island in Maine, with his wife Sonya, and two furry bosses, Izzie and Hayden.

Connect with Anthony, find out about new releases, and get free books at www.anthonymstrong.com

Printed in Dunstable, United Kingdom

71486866R00229